Praise for *Molly and the Machine*

"A delightful adventure with a nostalgic twist."
—*Kirkus Reviews*

"An absolute blast of a page-turner, jam-packed with laugh-out-loud humor, a boatload of heart, and more action than you might believe can fit into a single book. I can't wait to read more adventures from Far Flung Falls!"
—Jarrett Lerner, award-winning author of the EngiNerds and Geeger the Robot series

"*Molly and the Machine* introduces a host of eccentric characters, a 'villain' with a heartrending origin story, a madcap adventure that won't quit—and a heroine who finds more gumption, courage, and allies than she ever knew she had. Readers will be cheering her on from start to finish!"
—Margaret Peterson Haddix, *New York Times* bestselling author

Also by Erik Jon Slangerup

Molly and the Machine

MOLLY AND THE MUTANTS

ERIK JON SLANGERUP

ALADDIN
New York   London   Toronto   Sydney   New Delhi

This book is a work of fiction. Any references to historical events, real people, or real places are used fictitiously. Other names, characters, places, and events are products of the author's imagination, and any resemblance to actual events or places or persons, living or dead, is entirely coincidental.

ALADDIN
An imprint of Simon & Schuster Children's Publishing Division
1230 Avenue of the Americas, New York, New York 10020
First Aladdin hardcover edition August 2023
Text copyright © 2023 by Erik Jon Slangerup
Jacket illustration copyright © 2023 by Oriol Vidal
All rights reserved, including the right of reproduction in whole or in part in any form.
ALADDIN and related logo are registered trademarks of Simon & Schuster, Inc.
For information about special discounts for bulk purchases, please contact Simon & Schuster Special Sales at 1-866-506-1949 or business@simonandschuster.com.
The Simon & Schuster Speakers Bureau can bring authors to your live event. For more information or to book an event contact the Simon & Schuster Speakers Bureau at 1-866-248-3049 or visit our website at www.simonspeakers.com.
Jacket designed by Laura Lyn DiSiena and Ginny Kemmerer
Interior designed by Ginny Kemmerer
The text of this book was set in KazimirText.
Manufactured in the United States of America 0723 BVG
2 4 6 8 10 9 7 5 3 1
Library of Congress Cataloging-in-Publication Data
Names: Slangerup, Erik Jon, author. Title: Molly and the mutants / by Erik Jon Slangerup. Description: First Aladdin hardcover edition. | New York : Aladdin, 2023. | Series: Far Flung Falls | Summary: Fifth-grader Molly has her hands full between homework, homelife, and her best friend's schemes, but when the pets of Far Flung Falls begin to disappear, the town looks to Molly to find out who, or what, is behind the disappearances. Identifiers: LCCN 2023014070 (print) | LCCN 2023014071 (ebook) | ISBN 9781534498020 (hardcover) | ISBN 9781534498044 (ebook) Subjects: CYAC: Lost and found possessions—Fiction. | Pets—Fiction. | Family life—Fiction. | Monsters—Fiction. | Science fiction. | Mystery and detective stories. | LCGFT: Science fiction. | Detective and mystery fiction. | Novels. Classification: LCC PZ7.S628847 Mm 2023 (print) | LCC PZ7.S628847 (ebook) | DDC [Fic]—dc23
LC record available at https://lccn.loc.gov/2023014070
LC ebook record available at https://lccn.loc.gov/2023014071

CONTENTS

PART I: Downstream

Chapter 1:	Metamorphosis	3
Chapter 2:	Glimpse	13
Chapter 3:	Back Seat	25
Chapter 4:	Delta Mole	35
Chapter 5:	On the Loose	42
Chapter 6:	Huffing and Puffing	55
Chapter 7:	Pink Lightning II	64
Chapter 8:	Last Hiding Spot	70
Chapter 9:	Too-Tight Leather Pants	78
Chapter 10:	The Slew	86
Chapter 11:	*K-I-S-S-I-N-G*	95
Chapter 12:	Hunt	102
Chapter 13:	Lurker	113
Chapter 14:	A Door Opens	120
Chapter 15:	Some Assembly Required	131

PART II: Downhill

Chapter 16:	Aoife! Aoife!	142
Chapter 17:	Swear Fest	151
Chapter 18:	Doghouse	162

Chapter 19:	Search Party	168
Chapter 20:	The Boneyard	177
Chapter 21:	Collapse	188
Chapter 22:	Party Crashers	196
Chapter 23:	Big Dipper	207
Chapter 24:	Sneak	217
Chapter 25:	Popsicle Stand	223
Chapter 26:	Operation Flagpole	232
Chapter 27:	Track Thirty-Nine	242
Chapter 28:	AKA Velocipede	248
Chapter 29:	Formula X	255
Chapter 30:	The Schnoz	262
Chapter 31:	Spider Junction	273
Chapter 32:	New Crew	283
Chapter 33:	Keep Pushing	293
Chapter 34:	Booby-Trap Valley	299
Chapter 35:	Followed	313
Chapter 36:	Not the Whole Story	327
Chapter 37:	Worthy Adversary	336

PART III: Downtown

Chapter 38:	Rink-A-Rama	342
Chapter 39:	Satan's Song	350
Chapter 40:	Moonbeam	358
Chapter 41:	Secret Stash	367
Chapter 42:	Counterattack	374
Chapter 43:	Holy Fudge Nuggets	381
Chapter 44:	Call of the Camaro	390
Chapter 45:	Logan's Run	403
Chapter 46:	Chez Del Ray	416
Chapter 47:	Giddyup	420
Chapter 48:	Mesmerized	427
Chapter 49:	One Big Hole	439
Chapter 50:	Encore	449
Chapter 51:	What Actually Happened	460
Chapter 52:	One More	470

For my dad,
King of Adventures

PART I
DOWNSTREAM

CHAPTER 1
METAMORPHOSIS

From the day they were hatched, Seven, Eight, and Nine knew deep in their hindbrains how lucky they were. And not just the three of them. The luck extended to all 17,361 of their brothers and sisters too. The fact that every last one of them was still alive and wriggling right now was practically a miracle, against all odds for a school of young tadpoles.

Typically, after a mere week of life, before they'd even formed eyeballs, more than half of them would have already been someone else's lunch. But today, on the eve of their fifth week, their number hadn't dwindled by one.

This was all explained to them by their father. Perched atop the toothy ridge of a massive metal cog, he kept watch over them constantly. Just above him, the moonlight spilled in from a large circular hole in the ceiling, the single opening to a wider world beyond the steel fortress they called home.

"But who would want to eat us?" Nine asked.

The great bullfrog lifted his head to the opening above them all, the silvery light illuminating his lumpy edges. "You must understand, my children, that until you grow, anything and everything in the pond outside these walls will see you as nothing more than food... even other frogs."

This sent a ripple of shock throughout the hatchery. With every tail aflutter, the dark water churned around them.

"Papa?" Eight asked. "So... does that mean... will you eat us?"

"No! No! For croak's sake. But any frogs that aren't your father might. That's why we hatched you here. Now go and eat your algae."

At once they obeyed. Thousands of tiny mouths found a spot and began nibbling. The algae were plentiful, creeping across the steel walls that surrounded them. That's what made this the very best of hatcheries. Not the algae but the walls. They were especially helpful when everything that wasn't your father was trying to eat you.

It was a sanctuary.

Before it was a hatchery, it had been something called a robot.

Molly and the Mutants

A very large one. And that robot had died in a charred, smoldering heap. But now its body was filled with life once again—with theirs. Seven, Eight, and Nine could move about the robot's interior as far as their tails could take them. They were free to go anywhere, except for the Far End, toward the back of the chamber. The Far End was where the water buzzed and tingled for reasons no one knew, where a faint golden glow spilled out between the cracks of a large metal strongbox bolted to the back wall.

"Hey, Seven," Nine said, "whaddya think's in there?"

Seven chewed his algae, considering the question, but before he could answer.

THUMP.

"Hide, my children!" the bullfrog croaked.

The command hadn't been necessary. Instinctively, at the sound of an intruder, everyone darted to the nearest corner, behind a panel, or under a gear. More sounds followed.

THUMP. THUMP.

Footsteps. Human ones, most likely. The fortress had become an increasingly popular destination for them, usually at night. But the humans rarely ventured inside.

THUMP. THUMP. THUMP.

The tadpoles darted back into the shadows as the footsteps drew closer, then stopped. A brilliant beam of light shot through the opening, glinting off the metal surfaces around them.

"Found it!" called a voice from above. It was a boy.

The tadpoles remained hidden.

A moment later a pair of sneakers dropped through the hole and landed on the cog, just a short distance away from where the bullfrog had been. The boy crouched down, flashlight in hand. He had a light frame and perfectly feathered blond hair that looked almost silver in the pale moonlight. He stared wide-eyed into the darkened cavity.

"See anything good?" another voice called from some distance away.

"Not yet," the boy called back. "There's water inside. Looks kinda..."

"Kinda what?"

"Kinda spooky," the boy admitted.

"Bwak, bwak!" the faraway voice called. "Chicken!"

"Am not!" the boy protested. He wobbled a little on the uneven cog.

Seven, Eight, Nine, and 17,361 of their brothers and sisters watched as the bullfrog took a deep breath and let out the meanest croak he could muster.

R-r-r-r-riiiiiiiibet! the frog boomed. It reverberated off the metal walls for several seconds, filling the chamber with his unmistakable warning.

"Aaa-iiigh!" The boy's voice cracked midscream, adding a higher pitch to the echoes. He jumped, then stumbled—but didn't scramble away. This had never happened before. Instead the boy tripped and tumbled forward, moving deeper into the hatchery. He dropped his flashlight. It rolled down the slanted surface and into the water. Now in darkness, he slid down the flat side of the cog, which tilted under his weight, dipping farther into the water at the bottom.

The boy cursed.

"Ya okay in there?" a voice called.

"Scared of a li'l ol' frog?" a deeper voice added. This was followed by snickering.

"They look a lot bigger up close!" the boy said, trying to keep from slipping.

"Frogs don't count for a souvenir," the deeper voice said.

"I know!" the boy shouted, still sliding. "I know."

Seven, Eight, and Nine watched the boy raise an arm to the ceiling and try to balance himself. As he fumbled in the dark, his finger brushed a switch, activating a cluster of green lights around the strongbox at the Far End of the hatchery.

"Oh," the boy said.

Caught by surprise, he fell off the cog and into the water, scattering tadpoles everywhere. The boy froze.

"A-a-anybody there?" he called.

All 17,634 tadpoles remained silent.

Now waist-deep, he waded through, making his way closer to the greenish glow.

Some of Seven, Eight, and Nine's siblings chose this moment for a counteroffensive and swam up inside the boy's pant leg.

"Get! Outta! My! Pants!" he screamed, kicking and thrashing.

In all his movement the boy's foot got caught in a groove under the strongbox. Panicked, he tried prying the trapped shoe with the other. When he finally freed his foot, the boy heard something click, and the green lights shifted to red.

"Uh-oh," he said.

The floor below them began to vibrate. Something in the dead robot had come alive. As if by magic, the strongbox rose out of the water, opening to reveal six large canisters, three of which were filled with a sparkling yellow liquid. In the glow of the canisters' contents, the boy advanced.

What had the human done?

"I found my souvenir!" The boy whooped. "Just you wait!"

Molly and the Mutants

A strange energy emanated from the canisters.

The boy spent the next few minutes trying to pry one of them loose. Eventually he gave up, stomping his foot. Humans were so weird sometimes. The stomping caused one of the submerged cogs to turn and tip again. Snagging the boy's shoelace, the machinery began dragging him sideways, deeper into the waterlogged chamber. In a frenzy the boy pulled his foot from the shoe and scampered up over the giant gear works. As he crossed over to the upturned side of the main cog where he'd first landed, the whole thing tilted again like a seesaw, bringing the submerged end behind him back up out of the water.

C-C-C-CRACK.

Its giant teeth busted into one of the canisters, releasing the luminous substance. Slowly it seeped from the broken glass into the hatchery water.

Still shaking, empty-handed, and down a flashlight and a shoe, the boy with the feathered hair climbed out of the hole and disappeared into the night. The bullfrog hopped out after him, croaking aggressively to chase him away.

This momentarily left the tadpoles alone with the mysterious ooze. It undulated in glowing ribbons and blobs, calling to them.

Seven, Eight, and Nine wiggled their tails and approached

the substance, mesmerized by the way it sparkled—like the stars they'd seen through the opening in the roof.

Was this the Change they'd been waiting for? The portal to froghood?

It was impossible to turn around at this point. Behind them the crush from their siblings pushed the three of them into the ooze, until they were enveloped in its golden glow. Currents of energy pulsed through their tiny bodies. The tadpoles jerked and twitched... and began to transform.

"W-w-what's happening?" Eight said.

"Is it... the Change?" Nine asked.

"I think we're metamorphosing!" Eight said.

The water swirled around them, glowing ever brighter, gaining speed.

"Yessssssss," Seven moaned.

"My nubs!" Nine cried. "They're growing into legs!"

But their excitement quickly turned to dread.

"Wait!" Eight cried. "I think we need to get away!"

"Something is wrong!" Seven cried. "It all feels wrong!"

But no one could hear them over the buzzing in the water... or the thrum of tails from all the tadpoles that followed.

TWO AND A HALF MONTHS LATER

CHAPTER 2
GLIMPSE

Molly pressed her eye into the cutoff circle of pipe that served as a viewer to her land periscope. It was her latest invention, inspired by an article on nuclear submarines that Mr. Gatlin, her fifth-grade teacher, had assigned their class during the first week of school. Molly had read it and immediately thought: if the Russians could use these things to spy on Americans from underwater, why not have one of her own to peek over rooftops while she waited for the bus?

It was Thursday morning, and that's what she was doing now, waiting on the curb just outside her house. The McQuirters' was Number 42's last stop on Far Flung Falls Drive—and the entire route, for that matter.

Molly checked the Casio on her wrist. 8:28 a.m. She still had time. Number 42 usually didn't show up until at least 8:40. Her attention returned to the periscope.

The viewer hung exactly at eye level for Molly, which she recognized was a few inches higher than it would have been had she built it last year. Sometime between the fourth and fifth grade, she'd hit a long-overdue growth spurt. And she had the high-waters to prove it. Molly looked down at her socks peeking out conspicuously from the hem of her jeans. But she didn't mind. For all the changes that had happened over the summer, not being the shortest kid in her class was one she could live with.

"All right, let's have a look-see," Molly whispered.

From the viewer the periscope made a sharp turn upward and ran several feet along the side of a telephone pole, before making another right-angle turn at the top. At each joint Molly had sawed off the corners and glued a small mirror. It was just high enough to clear neighboring houses, and offered a three-hundred-sixty-degree view each morning.

She scanned the horizon, swiveling the periscope around toward Snouffer Run, the next street over. Sometimes, if she timed it right, she could catch the telltale orange roof of Number 42. But an impenetrable layer of fog had settled

Molly and the Mutants

over Far Flung Falls the last several days. It was especially thick in the mornings, clinging to the ground with a tenacity that Molly found impressive, even if it made spying difficult.

She liked how the fog softened the world's edges. It gave her street a muffled, dreamy quality, like it wasn't fully awake yet. Or maybe that was just Molly. She wiped the sleep from her eyes and continued her watch.

No sign of the bus, or much of anything besides a sea of cottony fluff. Beyond Snouffer, Molly caught the shadowy outline of the next ridge of hills. She knew that ridge well, but something about it this morning didn't add up, like it had one bump too many. Molly squinted. The moment she did, one of the hills... moved.

"Huh," she said.

Molly blinked and refocused. But the hill was gone. That couldn't be right. Maybe she was dreaming.

As she tried to make sense of it, something brushed Molly's ankle. She jumped.

"Oh! Hi, Crank." Molly let out a breath. "Whatcha doing out so early?"

"Meow," Crank answered.

Over the last few months the old tabby had become even

less of a house cat, if she ever had been one, coming and going as she pleased, and disappearing for increasingly longer stretches to who knows where.

Molly sat down on the curb and let Crank crawl up into her lap. The cat was being much more affectionate than usual. (In truth, any affection was unusual.) The bulk of her feline body felt warm on Molly's legs, and they sat together in silence for a few minutes. Then Crank started vibrating.

"Crank? Are you actually *purring* on me?"

The cat's whole body revved like a tiny engine, before she abruptly hopped off and began traipsing back toward the house.

"Okay, then. Thanks, buddy."

Just before she disappeared into the fog, Crank turned back and looked at Molly for a long moment.

"What is it, girl?" Molly cocked her head to the side. "Ya okay?"

"Meow," the cat answered again, matter-of-factly, holding Molly in her gaze. For as long as Molly had known her, it has been a mystery what went on in Crank's mind.

Then, as silently as she had arrived, she was gone.

Molly's thoughts drifted to everything the two of them had been through, especially this past summer. Sometimes the

Molly and the Mutants

memories didn't seem real, but then she'd walk around to the backyard and get an awkward greeting from the giant robot head that was now a permanent fixture on the property, right next to the old oak.

Most days she liked having it back there. It reminded her that she could do big things, like take down a towering metal giant while flying a motorcycle off a cliff. But sometimes it reminded her of her Gruncle. The image of him plummeting from the motorcycle into the robot's mouth, then vanishing down its metal throat atop a sidecar packed with dynamite. His last words to her—*Don't worry, kiddo. You got this. You always have*—echoed in her ears.

The crunch of footsteps along their gravel drive brought Molly back to the present.

It was Wally, briefly appearing out of the fog, before running off down the street like he did every morning to rendezvous with his buddy Gunther. The two had become inseparable, even when going to and from school. But rather than riding the bus, they opted to travel in the Vandervorkels' high-tech "bubble car." It was the same car they'd all ridden home in after toppling the robot and crash-landing Blue Thunder. So far that had been the only time Molly had traveled in it, but now Wally was a regular passenger.

"Hi... and bye," Wally said as he went.

"Well, nice talking to you too," Molly called back to him with an edge in her voice. Wally paused long enough to shoot her a look before disappearing into the fog, leaving Molly once again alone.

Why had she said that? It wasn't that Molly minded waiting for the bus by herself. She actually kind of enjoyed having a little time on her own every morning—especially now that she had her land periscope to keep her busy. And she didn't really want to ride to school in the bubble car with Wally and Gunther—but still, maybe it bothered her a little that she'd never been invited? They probably knew she'd just turn them down, Molly guessed.

Hearing an engine, Molly looked up. It sounded too small to be her school bus. She peered down the street to her left, squinting into the fog.

Was that a police car?

The car rolled up slowly and stopped in front of her. Its windows were already down.

Behind the wheel sat Officer Wasserbaum. Which sounded awfully close to *wash-yer-bottom*. Which is what most of the kids called him behind his back. It made Molly grateful she was

Molly and the Mutants

a McQuirter. Whatever your name was, it could always be worse.

"How's Far Flung's youngest deputy doing this morning?" Wasserbaum boomed. His voice was a little too loud for this time of day. Or maybe for any time. During the first week of school, when he'd been invited to speak at an assembly, everyone had joked that he didn't even need a microphone.

He smiled at her through the open window, then took a loud bite of an enormous apple fritter, which he also did loudly. Wasserbaum had a wide face, with eyes that were spaced far apart, which Molly thought made him look a little like a catfish. But she kept this to herself.

"Oh hi, Officer Dubya." That's what the kids called Wasserbaum to his face. "I'm okay."

"Good, good. School going all right?" A large chunk of apple fritter dangled from his mustache, then dropped.

"Going all right," she said. *Why is he asking?*

Wasserbaum shifted his eyes back and forth like someone might be listening in.

"Say," he said, his voice less booming now. "You seen anything . . . outta the ordinary lately? Any, er, *suspicious activity?*"

"Suspicious like what?"

"Well, the Ostranders seem to have, uh, *misplaced* Houdini. They moved her out to the back pen, on account of her size, an' then, *pfffffft*." Wasserbaum made a little fluttering movement with the hand holding his apple fritter, flinging crumbs everywhere.

Oh, that's why. He's on a case.

"Wait, how does a whole hog go ... um, *pfffffft*?" Molly tried to duplicate the sound.

"Peculiar, ain't it?" the officer said.

"Well, he was a truck jumper, you know," Molly said. "Maybe he's a fence jumper too?"

Wasserbaum scrunched up his face. *"That hog?"*

Molly had to admit it wasn't likely. When Houdini had first gotten his name, he'd been a much younger and nimbler creature. Now he weighed hundreds of pounds and was the most famous pig in Far Flung Falls. Or at least the one with the best story. Years ago, when a truck hauling hogs up from Akron had come passing through town, it had bumped a curb while rounding a tight corner, and Houdini had used the moment to escape. The pig had wandered through their neighborhood, snacking on what he could find, then eventually had become the Ostranders' pet. Otherwise he probably would've ended up being somebody's Christmas ham. Or bacon.

Molly and the Mutants

Molly loved bacon, but didn't like to think where it came from. She was glad Houdini had escaped that fate. Everyone said he was one lucky pig. But maybe his luck had finally run out. Maybe everyone's did eventually.

"Well," Molly said.

"Keep your eyes open," Wasserbaum said. To make his point, he pulled down one of his bottom eyelids with his finger, showing the watery pink part underneath. *Gross.* Molly looked away as Wasserbaum kept talking. "There've been a couple animals that've up and disappeared lately. Kind of a mystery."

"Oh?" Molly said. She hadn't heard this.

"That's right. There's two reports now of missing dogs over on Snouffer. And the Sorensons' goat appears to have skedaddled."

"So you think somebody's stealing them?" Molly asked.

"I don't rightly know. Haven't had much in the way of bona fide livestock thievery around these parts, not that I can recollect offhand. Thinking it's just a coincidence, or maybe some kids playing a prank. Hopefully nothing too ... sinister."

"Whaddya mean?"

"I've heard of some kids these days getting strange ideas from that heavy metal music ... like that Ozzy Osbourne fella? Or those weirdos from KISS, with all that devil makeup and tomfoolery?" Wasserbaum shook his head at the mention of them, then leaned in and lowered his voice. "You know what I heard their name stands for?"

"Stands for?" Molly repeated, now thoroughly confused.

"Knights. In. Satan's. Service," he whispered slowly, a grave expression on his face.

"Okaaay," Molly said.

"You know," Wasserbaum continued, "they're putting subliminal messages in their songs when you play their records backwards?" At this, Wasserbaum raised his eyebrows so high on his forehead, they lifted the brim of his police cap.

Molly just stared at him blankly. Subliminal messages? She had no idea what he was talking about.

"So, you think, like, *Ozzy Osbourne* came here and stole Houdini?"

"Yeah, no! But maybe . . . his minions. Doing some evil weirdo heavy metal ritual stuff with poor barnyard animals out in the woods. Can you think of anybody round here who might do anything like that?"

Molly made a quick mental inventory of her friends. She thought about Arvin, Leonard, and Margo. It was a known fact that Leonard listened to a lot of heavy metal, but there was no way he could do anything bad to poor Houdini. Besides,

Molly and the Mutants

Leonard was more of a Def Leppard fan than Ozzy.

"Nobody I know," she said.

Wasserbaum paused for a moment, reading her face before he popped the rest of the fritter into his mouth.

"All righty then, Molly. Just keep an eye out for me." His eye traveled up the length of her periscope, and he smiled. "I bet you don't miss a thing. You stay safe now." He made a wide loop where the road dead-ended just past their driveway and disappeared back into the fog.

Who would steal an old hog? The answer was likely no one. It probably had just wandered off. After all, the pig was named after a famous escape artist. Molly suspected its disappearance had more to do with a poorly mended fence than any rock 'n' roll band. Why were grown-ups always chasing the weirdest explanations when the most likely one was right in front of them?

Molly heard the rumble of the bus, then the sharp sigh of an air brake. It was getting closer but was still two stops away. Arvin, his two younger sisters, and Margo would be climbing the steps.

Another squeak. That would be Leonard's stop, just a half mile away.

The rumble got louder, and Molly shoved her Trapper

Keeper into her pack. She had been planning to finish up her math homework but would have to get to it later, sometime before third period. She took a deep breath. Her alone time was over. Not that it had been very alone, with Wasserbaum dropping by and going on about Ozzy Osbourne.

Molly first saw the faint glow of the headlights, trying to cut through the fog. Then the bright orange of Number 42 emerged. Like rectangular sunshine.

The doors swung open and she climbed in.

CHAPTER 3
BACK SEAT

"Hey, McCrusher. Whatcha know?"

"Hey, Ronda," Molly said, smiling at the nickname. It was way better than the ones she'd had in the past.

Ronda Steltzer was Number 42's new driver. She was way different from the last one, Miss Flibbert, who Molly heard had quit over the summer, saying something about it being "the single worst job of all time in the whole entire world." Miss Flibbert had been a stickler for the rules, which had made her less than popular with the passengers. Ronda, on the other hand, who was several decades younger, wore a studded leather jacket with the word *ANARCHY* stitched on the back.

So, with Ronda, pretty much everything about riding

Number 42, other than the number, had changed.

Molly climbed up the giant steps into the bus as Ronda raised up her palm. Molly caught it in a high five, then slapped it again on the way back down. It was something Ronda did with all the kids. But still, something about it made Molly feel like she was in some kind of secret club.

The immediate space around Ronda's seat held its own aroma, apart from the rest of the bus. A combination of stale cigarettes, spearmint, and the sweet chemical tang of Aqua Net.

Every day Ronda's hair was a work of art. It was shaved down to stubble on both sides of her head, in two perfect lines that curved from the tops of her temples to just behind her ears. The rest of it was teased out and piled up high on top, in a multicolored explosion that defied nature and gravity.

Her makeup was a marvel too. Alternating swaths of blue, purple, and pink eye shadow ran from the bridge of her nose over her eyelids—and kept going all the way to her ear. It looked like a tropical sunset, with a single dark stripe of eyeliner cutting across the bottom as the horizon. She was Far Flung Falls's sole punk rocker.

Molly was in awe of her, having never even tried blush herself. She wondered how early Ronda got up to make her face look like that, but was too afraid to ask.

Molly and the Mutants

Ronda turned and gave her a wink, the tropical sunset briefly expanding in colors.

"I think you're gonna like today's mixtape," Ronda said.

"Yeah?" Molly said.

"Yeah. Kicking off with Cyndi Lauper. Better grab a seat."

Molly had no idea who Cyndi Lauper was, so she just nodded.

Ronda turned back to face the wheel. As she did, her numerous earrings—which included a crucifix, a dream catcher, a spike, and an oversize safety pin—jingled like wind chimes.

The doors shut behind her, and Molly started making her way down the aisle. Beyond Ronda's seat the bus took on a different scent. A mixture of old gym socks, diesel, and grape Now and Laters.

Molly made her way down the aisle as the notes from a synthesizer flooded the space. The first week of school, Ronda had installed custom speakers at both ends of the bus. Molly could feel the thrum of the bass notes under her feet. It was almost enough to make her want to dance. But it was still a little early for that. Cyndi Lauper started singing...

And girls, they wanna have fun

Oh girls just wanna have fun...

Under the lyrics, Molly caught a few bits and pieces of conversation.

Blah, blah, blah, blah ... missing dog ... blah, blah, blah, blah ... Houdini. ... Blah, blah, blah, blah ... lost cat. ... Everyone was talking about the same thing. Throughout the neighborhood pets were disappearing. And apparently Molly was the last to know. *Maybe some things never change,* she thought.

Molly saw Arvin in the very back row, waving her over. From a distance his upper lip looked a little dirty, with the faint trace of what might be a mustache one day. He was sitting next to Leonard. Across from him sat Margo.

"C'mon, Molly," Margo called over the music, just as one of the munchkins Molly was passing said hello. Molly waved.

All the munchkins sat up front. *Munchkins* were pretty much anyone younger than the ones calling them munchkins, but usually meant the youngest of the school—the kindergartners up through the third graders. Sometimes Molly felt like she should still be sitting with them, instead of in the back with the fifth and sixth graders. And then she would remember: she was one of the older kids now. How did that happen so fast? If she thought about it too hard, it would start to feel weird, almost like she was in someone else's body. Molly pushed these thoughts aside and plopped herself down in the seat next to Margo.

Molly and the Mutants

"Hey," Molly said.

"That's some loud music," Arvin said.

"Yeah. Ain't it rad?" Margo said.

"I guess," Molly said.

"If only she played some Ozzy," Leonard said. He was wearing an Ozzy Osbourne tee that showed Ozzy looking deranged, with long fangs like a vampire. For a moment it made Molly wonder if maybe Officer Wasserbaum was onto something with his theories about rock 'n' roll. She had heard some weird rumors about Ozzy.

"Hey, Leonard, is it true he bit the head off a bat when he was onstage?" she asked, pointing to his shirt.

"Grody!" Margo said.

"I hear it was a rat," Arvin said.

At the mention of *rat* Molly caught Stevie Brunner from a few rows ahead turn to look their way down the aisle. And something else looked their way too, something with beady little pink eyes. It was Squeakers, Stevie's pet mouse, peeking out from his shirt pocket.

Why would he risk bringing Squeakers to school? Stevie had to know animals weren't allowed. Then it dawned on her: weird things were happening, and Stevie wanted to keep him safe.

Squeakers ducked back into his shirt pocket, like he knew to keep a low profile. Stevie put a finger to his lips. Molly did the same. *Your secret's safe with me, Stevie.*

"Well," Leonard said, "they don't call him the Prince of Darkness for nothing."

"Oooo, Prince of Darkness!" Margo squealed. "That's almost as scary as... *a bog monster!*" She looked over at Arvin and started giggling.

"Heard that," Arvin said. "Still not funny."

"Don't worry, Bogs, maybe they sell bat heads in the cafeteria," Margo said.

Arvin rolled his eyes. Ever since Margo had gotten back from Michigan and heard the story about Molly thinking Arvin was some kind of bog monster when she'd fallen into the robot's giant footprint, Margo had teased him about it.

Margo let out one more giggle, then got back to work with something on her lap.

"Whatcha doing?" Molly asked.

"Oh, nothin'," Margo said without looking up. Then she turned to Arvin. "Here ya go, *Ar-vie.*" She slipped him some papers, which he stuffed into his pack.

"Thanks, *Mar-gie.*

The two conspirators exchanged sly smiles.

Molly and the Mutants

Arvie? Margie? Molly's head whipped back and forth between the grinning pair. Wait a minute.... Did her friends *like* each other? When had that started? And why hadn't Margo told her? Weren't they supposed to be friends? Molly suddenly felt her ears getting hot. Having a circle of friends like this was new for Molly, so maybe this was a normal thing. But for reasons she couldn't quite explain, she somehow felt betrayed, like her circle had suddenly been ... contaminated. Without realizing it, she had been staring at Margo.

"You okay?" Margo asked.

"I'm fine," Molly muttered.

"Because you're getting splotchy—"

"I'm fine!" Molly shouted.

"Hey," Leonard broke in. "If anybody wants to do *my* homework..."

What did Molly care if Margo was doing Arvin's homework? *Wait, homework!* Shoot, that reminded her. She still had a couple of problems left herself, and no one was doing hers for her. She reached down for her backpack and—

"Whooooaaaaa!"

Number 42's tires screeched as everyone's butts slid across the vinyl seats and their bodies were slammed forward into the dark green seat backs in front of them. Since she was already bent over, the top of Molly's head smashed hard into the cushion.

"Hold on to your patooties!" Ronda yelled from up front.

The bus jittered and swerved, fighting against the inertia of a twelve-ton vehicle going slightly over the speed limit as it tried coming to a sudden stop. Stevie Brunner clutched his shirt pocket.

"Sorry, kids!" Ronda called. "Nearly hit a . . . a . . . some kinda . . . not sure what, exactly. But a big one." Ronda paused. "Did anybody by chance see a . . . Oh, never mind."

Ronda stood up and looked at everyone with wide eyes.

Molly could see that Ronda was shaken, like she'd seen a ghost or something. Ronda cut the music. No one spoke.

"Everybody okay?" she finally asked.

"You didn't hit Buster, didja?" one of the munchkins called out. "He's been mis—"

"No, no, definitely didn't hit anybody's dog."

"Was it a *hog* maybe? A really big 'un?" It was one of the Sorenson boys, who lived next door to the Ostrander farm, where Houdini had last been seen.

"Maybe it was the bog monst—" somebody started.

"Shut *up*!" Arvin said.

"You guys just sit tight for a minute," Ronda said, cutting

Molly and the Mutants

them off as she opened the bus doors and climbed down. Everyone craned their necks to watch her, pressing their faces against the windows.

Ronda walked back over to where she'd run off the road, crouched down, and touched the pavement, then quickly pulled her hand back. Molly was too far away to tell what it was. She watched Ronda rub her fingers together, then wipe her hand on her jeans. After a moment she stood back up and stared into the woods on the opposite side of the road. Then she pulled out a cigarette, lit it, and took a long drag.

Molly and the other kids watched her take a few more puffs until she flicked it to the ground and stomped it out. When she finally turned back toward the bus, Ronda had an expression on her face Molly had never seen her wear before. She looked... unsure.

Molly thought Ronda might just stand there forever, or at least until school was long over, but the bus driver got pulled from her reverie by the rumble of a car's engine that pulled up behind them.

The kids all ogled the souped-up Camaro. It was bright green with a black racing stripe and a huge chrome intake that stuck out of the hood. Molly knew the hot rod belonged to

Logan, a grouchy high schooler who sometimes hung out with Margo's older sister, Nikki.

"It's the green machine!" someone shouted.

The Camaro waited another second, then lurched out into the other lane to pass them. It was incredibly loud. But Molly kept her attention on Ronda.

"Whaddya think she saw?" Leonard asked.

"Beats me," Arvin said.

Before long Ronda was back in the driver's seat, Cyndi Lauper was back on the speakers, and they were back on the road, bumping along as if nothing had happened. But Molly knew that wasn't true. Something had happened. She just wasn't sure what.

CHAPTER 4
DELTA MOLE

Wally arrived at the fake power box and loitered for a few minutes, just as Gunther had instructed. There were only a few others in the neighborhood who knew what it really was, but they'd all agreed to keep it a secret, so it didn't get overrun by other kids. Or worse: adults.

He climbed up and sat on it, feet dangling over the weeds and clover below. Wally hadn't grown much this past summer, at least not physically. His dad said he was due for a *big spurt* any day now, and then, *Just you wait,* he'd say, *you're gonna sprout up like a weed!* Why did people always say that, *like a weed,* like it was a good thing? He looked again at the tangle of weeds below him. They didn't look very impressive.

This box sat in the no-man's-land between Old Man Murray's property and the Ostrander farm. Neither was big on landscaping, so the sprawling yards remained untouched, looking more like wild meadows.

Stealth would be extra easy to manage today, with the morning's fog being so thick. He squinted into the whitish-gray fluff, thinking he probably couldn't see more than ten feet in front of him.

Wait a minute. What if there were spies spying on him? Like the Russians? Or some evil creature from the netherworld? Or maybe somebody from school? He sat still and listened as his imagination ran wild. What if they had X-ray glasses that could see through fog? Naw, that was just plain silly. Still, he made a mental note to ask Gunther if maybe they could invent something like that.

"Hello?" Wally called into the mist. For a fleeting moment the back of his neck prickled with the feeling that someone was there, just out of view. Was Old Man Murray creeping around? Or had Molly followed him? She had sounded a little weird when he'd seen her just a few minutes ago. Like maybe she was mad? Wally racked his brain but couldn't think of anything he'd done in recent memory that could possibly cause offense.

When he was absolutely sure he was alone, Wally slipped

around to the rear of the box. The back showed even more signs of rust than the front, along with multiple scuff marks. It was brilliant camouflage for a secret passage, if you asked him. He pressed his hand onto the panel, waited for a click, then stepped back. Just like magic the box silently tilted forward on hidden hinges, revealing a metal ladder that descended into the earth. A cool rush of air flowed up from the tunnel below. Wally scuttled down, triggering the motion-sensor lights. Automatically the power box sealed shut above him.

"Another successful entry," Wally announced to the cement walls. Then he unclipped a walkie-talkie from the strap to his backpack and thumbed the red talk button. It made a loud *blip*.

"Delta Mole to Beta Mole," Wally said. "Repeat, Delta Mole to Beta Mole. I'm in. Do you read me? Over." *Blip.*

He waited. After a few seconds the walkie-talkie crackled to life.

"Greetings, Delta Mole," came the voice on the other end. "Read you loud and clear. Has your location been compromised?" *Blip.*

Wally checked again for any spies or strange creatures.

"Negative," he said after a pause. "Over." *Blip.*

"Excellent. In transit to your location. Stand by. Over." *Blip.*

"Roger that. Over." *Blip.*

Wally clipped the walkie-talkie back onto the strap of his backpack and waited on the platform. He had hitched a ride with Gunther every day since the start of school, but after nearly two months, traveling in the maglev bubble car at impossibly high speeds through a network of secret tunnels had not lost its thrill. Wally caught a light off to the right before he heard the faint hum of the approaching car. With a soft *whoosh* it pulled up just inches from where he was standing and came to a stop. The door popped open.

"Hi, Delta Mole," Gunther said. He smiled. Gunther had *not* grown like a weed yet either. Or like anything else, really. He remained as short and squat as when they'd first met... except for maybe when his hair stuck up around the cowlick on top of his head, like right now. Wally figured this gave him at least an extra two inches of height. He looked his friend over. The contrast between Gunther's jet-black hair and pale skin gave him the appearance of an old black-and-white cartoon that had jumped off the TV screen.

"Hi, Beta," Wally said, climbing into the bubble car. It bounced slightly, the magnetized sensors that lined the car's underside adjusting to his weight.

Molly and the Mutants

They had only briefly debated what their code names would be, mostly about who should be Alpha Mole. But when Wally suggested that maybe neither should be, Gunther quickly agreed. As they ran down the Greek alphabet for options, *gamma* was also dismissed. Both boys thought it sounded way too close to Grandma Mole. So they became Beta and Delta.

And that was how most things went between them. Their friendship was one of the most natural, effortless phenomena that Wally had experienced.

Things were better now with his dad and sister, but those relationships still took daily work. An occasional stray finger up his nose, for example, even if it happened way less often than before, would still bug Molly. And almost worse than that, his dad sometimes didn't notice him at all. But Gunther, on the other hand, seemed to like him just how he was without even trying. Gunther's mom, Vilomena, was over a lot, and had a calming effect on everyone. Especially their dad. He seemed a lot happier when she was around.

The car picked up speed, barreling through the secret tunnel as it levitated just a few inches above the tracks. The ride was so smooth, it was easy to forget just how fast they were going.

"Hey," Wally said.

"Hey what?" Gunther said.

"You think if your mom and my dad got married, then we'd be brothers?"

"I dunno," Gunther said. "Maybe. I'm not sure how that works."

The tunnel gently curved to the left, the bubble car tilting slightly as it took the turn without slowing. The boys held their backpacks between their feet so they wouldn't slide.

"Me either," Wally said. "But that'd be kinda cool."

"Yeah. We could all live in the same house."

"Probably yours," Wally said. "It's a lot bigger."

"True," Gunther mused. "Maybe we could get bunk beds."

"It'd be like a sleepover every night," Wally said.

Before the school year had started, Vilomena had requested a transfer for Gunther, so that the boys could go to school together. They even got put into the same class, with Mrs. Bunderloder. In truth they did just about everything together.

"So, you think they will?" Wally asked.

"Will what?" Gunther said. His eyes focused on the track ahead.

"Get married," Wally said.

"Well, they act kinda . . . you know," Gunther said. "All lovey-dovey."

Molly and the Mutants

"It's so..." Wally searched for the word.

"Gross," Gunther finished for him.

"Yeah," Wally agreed. "So gross."

Wally contemplated the future, and it sounded pretty good. Both boys sat quietly as the car slowed down.

"Here we are," Gunther said. "Ready?"

"Ready."

They climbed up a cylindrical shaft and lifted a manhole cover surrounded by a high hedge. Sounds of cars, school buses, and half the kids in Far Flung Falls could be heard all around them from their secret location. They waited for just the right moment. Then they slipped out through a narrow gap between the bushes, just a few yards from the front steps of Conklin Public School.

Beta Mole and Delta Mole blended into the crowd of bus riders, only their grins giving them away.

CHAPTER 5
ON THE LOOSE

Mr. Gatlin was rambling on and on about Greek mythology and the underworld.

It was late in the school day, and Molly was trying to pay attention, but her mind kept drifting. So many strange things had happened today. First there was that glimpse of something through her periscope. Then there was that weird conversation with Officer Wasserbaum about playing records backward and missing pets. Then Ronda almost crashed their bus! Molly stared out of the classroom's one window at the fog and wondered what was going on in their little town.

". . . And, Miss McQuirter, can you share with us what

role the hellhound Cerberus played in the Greeks' conception of the underworld, according to the text?"

It took Molly a few seconds to realize that Mr. Gatlin had asked her a question. Her book was open, but she had no idea what they'd just read. Molly looked down at her book to see an illustration of a giant, slobbering, three-headed dog.

"Ew," Molly mumbled.

"What was that, Miss McQuirter?" Mr. Gatlin asked.

"Er... umm... I think..."

Unexpectedly the school PA system crackled, saving Molly from having to answer.

"Attention, all teachers and students. May I have your attention please. We will be having an all-school assembly in... ten minutes. Please proceed to the gymnasium in an orderly fashion. Attendance is mandatory. Thank you." The speaker crackled again, indicating the announcement was over. Everyone looked up at Mr. Gatlin, while Molly breathed a sigh of relief.

"Is there a pep rally today?" somebody asked.

"Not that I know of," Mr. Gatlin said, looking just as confused.

"Did something bad happen?" asked another student.

"Are we in trouble?" Leonard asked from where he sat one row over.

"Students, you know as much as I do," Mr. Gatlin said. "Let's go find out together, shall we? We will pick back up with Cerberus tomorrow."

Molly exchanged looks with Leonard. He shrugged. Together they filed out of the trailer that was their classroom, perched precariously atop cinder blocks along with a cluster of others behind the schoolhouse. Far Flung Falls had long outgrown the space at Conklin Public, so the middle schoolers had been relegated to what their teachers called "the portables," a collection of old one-room trailers that had been dropped out back. Originally the grown-ups had said it was temporary, but the portables had been there for as long as Molly could remember.

The kids had another name for it—Trailer-Trash Academy, which the grown-ups didn't like. But no matter how many times the kids were reprimanded, the name had stuck.

A bulldozer, excavator, and steamroller were all parked behind, like they were ready to begin some kind of construction, but they hadn't budged in years. Molly had once overheard the teachers talking about a contract waiting to be signed, but wasn't sure what that meant.

"C'mon," Leonard said.

It was a short walk from Trailer-Trash Academy to the main building, where a side door deposited the fifth, sixth,

Molly and the Mutants

seventh, and eighth graders directly into the gym. Everyone streamed in together, bottlenecking at the door. Molly and Leonard squeezed through the entrance and made their way across the shiny gymnasium floor, which they quickly discovered was more than a little slippery.

"Whoa," said Leonard, his feet slipping out from under him. But Molly caught him before he fell.

"Watch your step, now. Just got polished," said the principal.

Principal Fritz, a tall, lanky man with a sharp beak of a nose stood hunched over a microphone stand in the middle of the gym. He kept one hand in the pocket of his coat and periodically flapped it like a wing, a nervous habit that gave him an even more birdlike appearance, like a giant turkey buzzard.

"Keep it moving," he said. "Nice and orderly. No falling, please." He flapped his coat a little more. Molly thought if he kept it up, he might actually take flight one day.

The kids all slipped and slid across the gym, then stomped across the old wooden pullout bleachers against the far wall. *Boom, boom, boom, boom.*

"We sound like a herd of elephants," Molly said.

"I don't think elephants are this loud," Leonard said.

The teachers at Conklin were taking their seats behind Principal Fritz on a long row of metal folding chairs, probably so they could keep a better eye on their students. Or maybe just so they could get a break from them. They all looked as eager for the school day to be over as Molly was.

Molly climbed up the bleachers, passing Wally and Gunther, who were huddled together, deep in conversation, as usual. Wally saw her and waved.

"Hey, Bro. Hey, Gun," Molly said. The two boys smiled, then quickly returned to whatever it was they were talking about. Along their row she saw a few other third graders from the Number 42 bus, including Stevie Brunner, who was discreetly stroking Squeakers, still tucked away in his shirt pocket. Squeakers looked Molly's way with his little pink eyes, then disappeared.

Molly took her seat immediately behind the most beautifully feathered flyback hair in the school, parted right down the middle in perfect symmetry. Molly caught her breath. She knew the flyback hair belonged to Finn Garrett, who had just moved to Far Flung Falls over the summer. She didn't know him very well, but for some reason she just couldn't help herself from staring at such a beautiful head of hair. It made her think about how her own hair looked, which she rarely did. As always, hers was pulled back into a single braid at the base of her neck. No muss, no fuss.

Molly and the Mutants

Just then somebody gave her braid a tug.

"Ow! Hey!" Molly whipped around.

It was Margo and Arvin, both grinning from ear to ear. They'd taken seats in the row right behind her, along with the other sixth graders.

"Hey-there-Moll-ee," Margo said in a singsong voice. "Whatcha-lookin'-at-there?" Her eyes shot over to the back of Finn's head.

"Nothing!" Molly protested, but a little too loudly. Her cheeks burned.

The feathered flyback hair started to turn around at the commotion, but stopped when Principal Fritz started talking.

"Good afternoon, students. We have recently received some reports that have raised some concern. As I'm sure you are aware, more than a few of our beloved pets have gone... *missing*."

"Yeah, they got my Snowball!" somebody shouted.

"And Rex, too!" another called.

Soon anyone and everyone with a missing pet was shouting their name.

"Students! Students, please!" the principal said. "We have a special visitor today, whom you might remember from a few weeks ago, who gave us our SAFER challenge. Do you remember what that stands for?"

"Stay... Away... From... Everything... Risky," the students droned. Molly silently mouthed the words without actually saying them. She wasn't a fan.

Leonard leaned over. "So dumb," he whispered. "That's no way to go through life. What's the point?"

"I know!" Molly whispered back.

"Very good, very good," Principal Fritz was saying. "And after Officer Wasserbaum talks to us, our lovely PTA president, Mrs. Tipper will be passing out SAFER pins to our winners. Now let's give your attention to Officer Wasserbaum."

As Wasserbaum rose from his chair, he nearly slipped on the polished floor, then caught himself. He continued in slow motion toward the microphone. Someone from the bleachers shouted a question to him.

"Is it coyotes?" the kid asked.

"My dad says it's a bobcat!" shouted another.

"Mine says it's a pack o' rabid weasels, like what happened back in '74."

Before Wasserbaum could make it to the mic, questions and theories were ringing out from every corner of the bleachers:

"I hear there's a ring of pet bandits!"

"You think maybe it's the Russians?"

Molly and the Mutants

"Or the mafia?"

Wasserbaum just stood there in silence, waiting for the crowd to settle before he spoke. He had to wait awhile, as students speculated aloud about everything from zombies, to Ozzy Osbourne, to the dreaded bog monster, which caused Arvin to lose control.

"Shut! Up!" he bellowed over everyone in the gym.

Surprised by the intensity of the outburst, everyone went silent.

"Uh, thank you, Arvin," Wasserbaum said. "Ahem. Well. Good afternoon, students. For those who might not know me, I'm Officer Wasserbaum. And I am currently leading the investigation into what's going on. So rest assured, we will get to the bottom of it! And I hope no one here is involved. But if anyone *knows* anything... anything at all related to these missing animals, please come forward and let me know. Because I will find out." At this he paused to do that weird thing he had done in front of Molly earlier, pulling the bottom lid down under one of his eyeballs and showing the pink underneath.

"Eww," somebody said.

Wasserbaum continued. "Now, as of today, we have tallied up a total of eleven missing..."

As he spoke, Molly heard a small commotion break out

in the third-grade row. It was Stevie. "Squeakers? Where's Squeakers?" he was asking, panic rising in his voice.

In answer to his question a series of screams filled the gym, each one louder than the last, indicating the path that the mouse had taken. A moment later Squeakers was scurrying across the center of the gym floor—and headed straight for the teachers.

Packed in on the bleachers like sardines, all the kids of Conklin Public School—from the kindergarteners on the first row to the eighth graders at the top—jostled and jerked into one another in a chain reaction of fumbles and bumps, which concluded in knocking Jasper, a hefty seventh grader, into the bin of dodgeballs next to his seat. On impact the balls exploded in every direction, bouncing across the polished gym floor.

Jasper was also secretly harboring his pet on his person for safekeeping. Roscoe, an eighteen-inch pet garter snake, who was coiled up in a stars-and-stripes fanny pack around Jasper's waist, took the opportunity to slip out of the small opening where Jasper had failed to zip it completely closed.

"Roscoe!" Jasper hollered as the creature slipped under the bleachers and emerged onto the gym floor. It was remarkably fast on the polished surface, and determined in its route, as it slithered to intercept Squeakers.

Molly and the Mutants

"Don't let that snake eat Squeakers!" Stevie screamed.

"Snake! Where?" others screamed.

"Don't hurt Roscoe!" Jasper screamed back.

Everyone watched in horror. Except Wasserbaum, who sprang into action.

"Stop right there!" he shouted to the animals.

The officer took two steps, and immediately tripped over the microphone cord and slid across the gymnasium floor into one of the rogue dodgeballs.

Meanwhile the mouse ran straight up the leg of the PTA president, who let out a bloodcurdling scream, dropping a handful of SAFER pins. They scattered across the hardwood floor.

The garter snake, in hot pursuit, circumvented Wasserbaum toward Mrs. Tipper, who screamed again.

"Stop! Police!" Wasserbaum shouted, raising the red rubber ball like a weapon.

"Let me help," Principal Fritz said, reaching out to Wasserbaum from behind.

Not expecting the contact, Wasserbaum jerked, elbowing the principal in his beak-like nose, then hurtling the ball in the direction of Squeakers. Mr. Gatlin leapt out of his chair to intervene—WHAP—taking the red rubber ball square in the face.

Other teachers jumped in, attempting to subdue the animals by blasting them with rubber balls. But in the heat of the moment, everyone's aim proved far from accurate, causing even more collateral damage. Mrs. Tipper tried ducking under her chair.

"GAME *ON!*" one of the eighth graders bellowed. More screams and whoops rose from the crowd, and before anyone knew what was happening, big red balls were ricocheting indiscriminately in every direction—*FOOOMP! FOOOMP! FOOOMP!*

Principal Fritz, holding his smashed nose, tried his best to regain control. He stumbled through the ruckus back toward the mic. But just inches short of it—*FOOOMP!*—he had the misfortune of taking a direct hit to the crotch from one of the rubber balls. It had been thrown by Gerald Barnhouser, the reigning dodgeball champion of Conklin Public. Gerald and his forearms—as big as Popeye's—had been held back in eighth grade twice. The principal howled, crumpling to the floor.

Molly ducked as a dodgeball flew toward her head. Arvin caught it behind her.

"Best. Assembly. Ever," he said, lobbing it back to its sender.

"Totally," Margo said.

"All we need now is some popcorn," Leonard said.

Molly and the Mutants

Molly had to admit it was quite a show. Some teachers and students tried in vain to run for cover, but no one could get very far without succumbing to the gym's slippery surface, a dodgeball, a random animal, or a combination of all three. The ensuing chaos managed to flush out several more stowaway pets; namely, two gerbils, a tarantula, a baby box turtle, and a goldfish in a little portable baggie of water. Miraculously, every furry and scaly creature survived the dodgeball melee unharmed—although the same could not be said for their human counterparts.

Molly couldn't believe what was happening. How many kids had been hiding pets in their pockets? Was everyone really that worried? And should she be too? Molly couldn't imagine sneaking Darryl or Crank into school . . . although maybe she could fit Don Carlos into her backpack. But they'd all proven pretty capable in tough situations. Molly figured they could fend for themselves. That's what McQuirters did... human or otherwise.

Seeing the loose tarantula, Mrs. Tipper grabbed ahold of Officer Wasserbaum, who had just gotten back up. He slipped again, and landed on his butt—right on the cluster of SAFER pins. He let out a wail while the PTA president tried to pluck the pins out of his trousers. Next to them Principal Fritz was still sprawled across the floor, flapping his coat uncontrollably.

Molly and Leonard had stayed in their seats, watching the scene unfold. When she looked down, she was met by two pink eyes looking back up at her. It was Squeakers, resting in her lap. She waved Stevie over and returned the mouse to its owner. Both appeared grateful.

Roscoe, on the other hand, remained at large.

"I'm thinking they should rename this place," Leonard said. "Conklin Zoo?"

Molly laughed. If the purpose of the assembly had been to reassure everyone, it hadn't exactly worked.

CHAPTER 6
HUFFING AND PUFFING

Number 42 dropped Molly off in front of her house. She was thinking the day couldn't get any stranger, until she started walking up her driveway.

"C'mon, feel that beat! And one, and two, and three, and four...." It was a very energetic voice, one she didn't recognize. "And push, and two, and three, and four."

What was going on? Molly heard the *thumpa-thumpa-thumpa* of a steady beat from inside the house before she opened the door. Her dad never played music that loud. For a moment she wondered if she was in the right place.

She still had Stevie Nicks playing in her head from the bus. Ronda had continued with her "music class" the entire ride home. Molly had started to realize that there was more to rock 'n' roll than she'd given it credit for. But what she heard now wasn't quite rock—at least not to Ronda's standard. Way too much synthesizer. Slowly, Molly entered the house and heard another voice. Definitely not her dad, but this one was familiar.

"Just a little more," said the voice.

As Molly moved closer, she heard heavy breathing. *That* was her dad.

Molly rounded the corner. And nearly puked at what she saw.

There they were, her dad and Vilomena, in the middle of the living room. Her dad was drenched in sweat, dressed in something he had definitely not picked himself. He looked so . . . colorful, and in a not-her-dad kind of way.

The two grown-ups turned toward Molly and froze in place. Like they'd been caught doing something wrong. Which, in Molly's opinion, they had. A girl should never have to see her own dad—or any grown man—in shorts that bright. . . . Or that short.

"Oh, hi Mollz," her dad said between breaths. He slumped over, bracing his hands on his knees.

Darryl, Molly's loyal canine companion, gave a few barks, as if to say, *I know, this is even more embarrassing to me.* Mondo, the armadillo they'd inherited, had already curled into a ball, trying his best to disappear.

"Hi, Molly," Vilomena said. "I was just showing your dad how to Jazzercise. He's a natural." She gave Molly's dad's biceps a squeeze. He turned even redder than before.

"Jazzercise?" was all Molly could get out.

"Yes, it's the latest thing," Vilomena said. "A splendid workout. And you can do it right at home."

Her dad shot Molly a look. *Just go with it*, said the look.

"O-kayyy," Molly said.

"How do you like his new outfit? Doesn't he look . . . marvelous?"

Marvelous wasn't the first word that came to Molly's mind. Or the second or third. She had never seen her dad in neon pink and teal—or neon pink and anything, for that matter. She had never seen her dad in a coordinated outfit. Even the sweatbands around his wrists and forehead matched. And the shorts were way, *way* too short. She couldn't remember the last time she'd seen that much of her dad's thighs, but they were so hairy, she would now never forget.

Who was this sweaty, neon-bright, color-coordinated gorilla man? And what had he done with her dad?

"Uh, I'm going to Margo's house," Molly said.

Margo wanted some help with her science project. *Some help* probably meant she wanted Molly to mostly do it for her, but at this moment Molly didn't mind. Anything was better than staying here and listening to her dad huff and puff to a Jazzercise routine with Vilomena.

"Okay, sweetie," her dad said.

"Great to see you," said Vilomena.

Molly slipped into the kitchen. Crank was nowhere to be found. Their cat had never been much into exercise, or anything that humans were up to, really. But news from the assembly of all the missing animals had Molly a little on edge.

Molly checked Crank's food bowl. It was empty, which was a good sign. Unless of course Darryl had helped himself. Which he sometimes did. She looked over at him. Darryl looked back, a quizzical expression on his face. But not a guilty one. She looked at her chameleon, Don Carlos. He looked back with one eye. The other was busy on something else. No way he'd gotten out of his cage. Finally she stared down Mondo until he partially un-balled himself, enough to return her gaze. His beady eyes said, *I wouldn't dare.*

Okay, then, Molly thought. Crank had at least eaten sometime recently. Where could she be? Maybe she was hiding out in Molly's room? Molly went to check. She hadn't cleaned it in a while, and it showed. Clothes were strewn across the floor, along with random parts to unfinished inventions, some long forgotten. A disaster by human standards, but perfect for a cat who liked to hide.

"Crank? You in here, girl?"

Silence.

Molly scanned the room once more, her eye catching the one framed photograph on her nightstand. It was of her mom and Gruncle, the same one she had discovered over the summer. It had been taken before Molly was born, and now it was her keepsake. Sometime around the end of summer, her dad had taken Molly and Wally to the old cabin so they could each collect an item to remember their Gruncle. Molly had immediately been drawn to the photograph. Wally had chosen an old pair of army-issue binoculars with a leather strap, which Molly had thought was also a good choice. Wally had said he wanted to see the world through Gruncle's eyes.

The memory reminded her of another item from her Gruncle's cabin that she had in her possession, one no one else knew about. It was a second keepsake that she had come back for later that night, alone.

Oh no, Molly thought, a terrible worry flashing in her mind. Crank loved hiding spots, and Molly had recently added a new one to her room. A secret compartment to keep the second item under wraps—at least Molly hoped that was true. But Crank was one sly cat. Had she found it? And was she stuck in there? Suffocating?

Molly quickly closed the door behind her, to make sure no one saw, then squatted down on the floor to peek under the bed. She saw an impenetrable wall of random boxes, stuffed animals, and old toys that had been crammed underneath. Or at least that's what it was supposed to look like.

Good, Molly thought, *no signs of tampering.* The hiding spot appeared secure.

She pulled a lever on the headboard. Silently the bed flipped up off the floor, lifting with it a carefully constructed façade to keep the hiding spot undetectable.

Phew! No suffocated cat under her bed.

Just her secret...

The Zap-O-Matic.

No one knew she had taken it. But she felt closer to her beloved Gruncle knowing it was right below her when she slept. It made her feel safe. Like, even if he was gone, they could still share a secret. Her own buried treasure. Molly thought her Gruncle would be impressed that she had hidden his invention with one of her own making. She ran her fingers

Molly and the Mutants

along the sides of the Zap-O-Matic's pack, making sure Crank hadn't slipped into one of the nooks or crannies along its edge. No sign of her, but Molly did feel something she hadn't noticed before.

What's this?

Along the bottom ridge of the pack, Molly's finger traced a tiny engraving: a crescent moon with three raindrops—or tears, maybe?—emanating from the center. There were some words, too. Molly looked closer.

"Protect... the... Crew," Molly read aloud. She cocked her head. "Huh."

Molly looked back to the photograph, hoping to pull an answer out of the image. Protect what crew? Had she known her Gruncle as well as she'd thought? She knew he had lived a long life before she had even been born, and she had loved hearing his stories. But maybe there were some stories he had kept to himself. Maybe this was one of them.

Molly figured her Gruncle had held more secrets than most other adults she knew. The night she'd taken the Zap-O-Matic, she hadn't even planned to go snooping around his cabin, but in her grieving she had inexplicably found herself drawn back to the place. Molly had slipped in through a cracked window, and wandered the empty rooms in the hope that being there would somehow make her miss him a little less. Before tripping over the Zap-O-Matic, she'd thumbed through more old photos, and knocked over an enormous stack of mail. Under all the **PAST DUE** notices that she'd seen before, Molly had found warnings from the IRS about unpaid taxes, and angry, hand-scrawled letters from people she'd never heard of about every kind of grievance, from stolen recipes to patent infringement. And not to mention some very official-looking papers bearing the letterhead of four different legal firms claiming to represent his ex-wives. They were all about something called "alimony," which apparently he had owed a lot of.

Oh, Gruncle. Molly could only hope that maybe he was in a happier place now, free from pesky mail or other bothers.

She rubbed the inscription one more time. Molly had no idea what "the Crew" was, but she wasn't sure who she could ask. She knew she'd be in big trouble if her dad found out she had something so dangerous in her room. But after all she'd been through in the last year—crossing chasms, dodging lasers, blowing up robots, jumping off cliffs—sleeping on top of a borrowed lightning maker didn't seem like too big a deal. She gave the strange contraption a gentle pat, careful not to accidentally flip one of the switches that powered it up. Molly pushed the lever back to its original position, lowering her bed back to floor level, which concealed the Zap-O-Matic—and the curious inscription—once again.

Molly surveyed her room, making sure she had left no clue. *I'll figure you out another day,* she thought.

She slipped past the two Jazzercisers unnoticed and made a single lap around the house, calling for Crank. She didn't want her aging cat disappearing like Houdini or any of the other neighboring pets. And Molly figured she'd probably used up most of her nine lives.

"Well, Crank, wherever you are, stay safe, and I'll be back!"

CHAPTER 7
PINK LIGHTNING II

Molly circled back to the special parking stall in the back of the carport, and there it was: Pink Lightning II, her prized possession. Seeing the revamped bike in all its glory always made her smile, even if it was hard to look at it without thinking of the last time she'd seen Pink Lightning I, mangled beyond recognition, about forty feet up a tree. It was a sacrifice that had saved her life—saved everyone's life, in fact. But thinking about it made her miss the creator. She had replayed that last day of Gruncle's life over and over in her mind, and often wondered if it had required him sacrificing himself as well. But she remembered the expression on his face before he jumped, and knew he wouldn't have had it any other way.

There had been no funeral. They had never recovered a trace of him among the wreckage.

Vilomena had been kind enough to have the Vandervorkel corporation retrieve what had remained of his massive motorcycle, Blue Thunder, and transport it to the garage at Gruncle's cabin, where it remained today, along with all his other earthly possessions. The wheels and sidecar had never been recovered, having been expelled, respectively, into a water-filled gorge and down the robot's gullet. But aside from those exceptions, the body of the monstrous motorcycle had remained fairly intact.

It was accompanied by many more mechanical wonders and oddities. Some resembled vehicles of some sort, while others were less forthcoming about what function they might perform. And Gruncle had hinted that there were even more mysteries within the cabin itself.

Molly had overheard that a few of Gruncle's many ex-wives were bickering over the property, until it had been discovered that his entire estate, if you could call it that, had been wholly bequeathed to her and her brother, Wally, upon them reaching the age of eighteen. That seemed so far into the future, she could hardly imagine it. But there was no hurry. Since he had gone, they had made one visit to the place, to make sure things had been in order. That's when they had discovered the note outlining his wishes after he was gone, along with his signature.

It was like he had known that he wouldn't be returning from the rescue.

Sighing, she pulled Pink Lightning II out of its hiding spot behind the stacks of boxes. There were fewer of them now, since her dad had been slowly cleaning out the carport. But Molly insisted that he keep some in place, to maintain a barrier between her bike and any curious eyes. She had also taken to locking it up at night. Her dad had told her that he'd never heard of anyone's bike ever getting stolen in their neighborhood, but she just couldn't bear the thought of losing it again. And now that she knew some pets were disappearing, locking things up didn't seem so strange. You couldn't be too careful, she thought. Molly pulled the key from a chain that hung around her neck, and crouched down to unlock the bike.

Shoop-click-pop. Pink Lightning II was free.

She walked it to the edge of the carport, checking all the controls. This model, courtesy of her dad and the Vandervorkel

Molly and the Mutants

corporation, had been equipped with all new features, very different from the original. Amazingly, with the last model, each one of them had proven to be nothing short of essential. (Again, Molly thought, it was like her Gruncle could see the future. What else had he seen?) Pink Lightning I had come equipped with:

A rapid-projectile basket.

A flare gun.

An axel grease dispenser.

A self-propelled engine.

Even wings.

She wondered if this new set of features would come in as handy as the last. Or did those kinds of adventures only happen once in a lifetime? Molly hoped to never again be in a situation where she was having to outmaneuver an angry robot.

Pink Lightning II held an entirely new arsenal. So far she had only activated one of its five special powers. Her bike could now emit a smoke screen, making her virtually invisible to anyone in pursuit. Unfortunately, she'd pressed the button outside the entrance to the Rink-A-Rama, the newly remodeled roller-skating rink in town. She had triggered it just as the rink was closing, which had thrown the entire crowd into a coughing fit as they were leaving. At the sight of all the smoke, the manager had panicked and called the fire department. Luckily, no one was hurt.

Cringing at the memory, Molly hopped onto the pink banana seat—a replica of the original—and navigated down the driveway and out onto the street.

As she pedaled, Molly glanced down at the button on her handlebar that had caused all the commotion. Since the *incident*, they'd installed little plastic safety covers over each one, just like the ones they use over missile launch controls. The button in question sat last in line next to the others. And each one had a little symbol inscribed on it. The smoke screen emitter was labeled with a little cartoon cloud. Next to it there were three more, like a row of hieroglyphics. A fishing hook, a disco ball, and a feather. All waiting for their moment to shine.

The fifth symbol wasn't on the handlebars. Instead it was inscribed on the end of a small lever in front of her seat. It stuck up from the top tube of the bike's frame. That last symbol was a spiral.

Unlike the original Pink Lightning's controls, these features at least gave some indication of what each button or lever held in store. Her Gruncle Clovis had adhered more to a

Molly and the Mutants

philosophy of mystery and chance. She missed him but liked the clues.

And in addition to these, Molly had made one more modification to the bike all on her own. It had come about one day when she'd been trying to shoot her slingshot while riding. Accuracy had proven difficult. So she'd fastened a long thin strand of rubber over the dip in her handlebars, with a leather pouch in the center, turning the front of her bike into a giant slingshot. This had increased her range by about double. She kept a supply of hard little green crab apples on hand in the basket as ammo.

Molly gave the strand a few test tugs. Ready for anything, she picked up speed.

CHAPTER 8
LAST HIDING SPOT

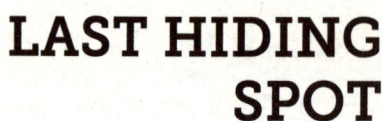

Without a sound Crank slunk out from behind the couch. It was one of the few remaining hiding spots she had left. She remembered a time when the McQuirter house had many more. Up until a couple of months ago, the whole place had been a kind of hiding spot. Every room had felt curated just for her comfort, with stacks of newspapers, piles of laundry, or random parts to discombobulated electronics that had little hope of ever being recombobulated. Ah, those were the days. It had been absolutely perfect. But that was before Stanley had started tidying up.

She had liked Stanley much better when he was more sluggish. Now he was always moving, making noise. Interrupting

Molly and the Mutants

her thoughts. Finding alone time had become nearly impossible. Crank had always enjoyed the quiet moments, observing the humans come and go, while going unnoticed herself.

She had just observed Molly leave almost as quickly as she'd entered. Crank had briefly entertained the notion of saying hello—possibly for the last time. But hadn't she done that already this morning? Yes, she decided, yes she had. Molly reminded her very much of her mother, Caroline, in how she held herself, how she moved, even how she smelled. Crank was fond of the one in the same way she'd been fond of the other. Maybe even loved them. But humans, even the not-so-irritating ones, came and went. Caroline had taught her that. And besides, what else was there to say that hadn't already been said?

Crank paused a moment to try to make sense of what the two other humans in the house were up to now. Normally humans didn't do much to hold feline interest. But they were hard to ignore. What the heck were they doing? All that stomping. And giggling. And huffing and puffing. They could be so annoying sometimes. Silently she slunk along the wall, past the terrarium that housed Don Carlos. They paused for a moment of mutual regard. Neither was big on greetings or goodbyes. Crank made her way to the flap in the back door, and slipped out onto the steps.

Ah, freedom, she thought, stretching her long, striped body out in the sun. Ugh. It wasn't nearly as nimble as it used to be, and it ached in more places than it didn't. But stiff or not, it still worked. She wasn't in any position to complain.

Crank heard the flap behind her and turned around. It was Darryl's big dumb head. He extended his snout, made a questioning *mmarrumph* sound in his throat. *You okay?*

Oh, Darryl, you big dumb dog, I'm fine.

Darryl held firm, unconvinced. He lowered his head to hers and sniffed. This was followed by a disapproving snort.

It was next to impossible to keep anything from Darryl's nose—possibly even her thoughts. Who would've guessed that in the twilight of her life a mangy mutt like Darryl would be the one to whom she felt the closest? A cat's lives could be so strange. For years Crank had been very satisfied as the sole pet in the McQuirter house. She had come with Caroline. Before that it had been just the two of them, in a small apartment off Main Street, right above DeVern's Discount Tire. This was before Stanley ever came into the picture. Then, after him, there were others. First another little girl human, then a boy human. Then Darryl. She sometimes wondered if the mother had slowly been collecting one of every species.

Even with their mother gone, the gang had kept growing.

Molly and the Mutants

There was Don Carlos, the chameleon. Sheesh, that guy was a weirdo. Then Mondo, the armadillo. Also very strange. And now this new lady was hanging around—way too much, if you asked Crank. Sometimes she even brought her boy with her. Between all the recent additions and the scarcity of hiding places, it was starting to feel a little... crowded.

Darryl continued watching her as she lost herself in the reverie. It was something she did a lot lately.

Crank was sure that dog could sense the same thing she could, that something inside her body—specifically, something in her head—wasn't quite right. Some new mass had shown up uninvited, taken root, and started to grow. One of the trillions of cat cells that all together made up who she was had decided to not follow instructions and had divided in a strange way, and that was that. One bad cell had become two, then four, then eight...

It didn't hurt. Not yet anyway. Right now it was just the dull, vague presence of something that didn't belong. The final countdown.

Sitting there on the back step, it struck her as funny that after all she'd been through, this would be the thing that took her out. This one rogue cell that had started a chain reaction. It was absurd. Having evaded a humongous metal monster.

Lasers and explosions. Cliffs and crash landings. Not to mention all the more day-to-day perils of the woods that she had navigated over the years with relative ease. The scores of racoons, opossums, skunks, badgers, and foxes with whom she'd crossed paths. Had even had a tangle with a few. She knew humans often joked that cats had nine lives. And if that were true, she had definitely gone through numbers six, seven, and eight over the course of that two-day adventure this past summer.

But humans didn't know that cats actually had much more than nine. In truth it was a number closer to ninety-nine. It was something cats didn't think about often, but Crank was starting to remember things.

Something about the tiny dark mass in her brain had pushed up against some long-forgotten memories, unlocked a door in the corner of her feline mind. A vault of experiences that stretched back in time to long before Darryl, or Caroline, or even before her memory of the cramped little cardboard box she had shared with her mother, and her litter brothers and sisters. There had been six of them in total, who one by one had been scooped up and taken away, lifted out of the box by human hands, never to be seen again.

She had been the last to be scooped. Which she hadn't minded at all. It had given her a little more one-on-one time

Molly and the Mutants

with her mom. Crank could still remember her mom lying there on her side, looking exhausted, but oh-so-warm. And all that sweet milk to herself.

But the memories stretched back even further than that now... to even before she had come into this body. Typically these were always on the outer edge of her recollection, just out of view. Until now.

A slobbery *slurp* brought her out of her thoughts. Darryl's body was too big to fit through the flap, but he had stretched his head out a little farther to give her a lick, which she normally hated but tolerated today.

She and Darryl had been through a lot together. She brushed against his snout to let him know it was okay, then made her way down the steps. Satisfied, Darryl's snout retreated into the flap door and disappeared from her view.

Crank descended into the grass, lowering her head and rolling her shoulders as she found her stride.

Ah, sweet solitude.

Crank hadn't been feeling herself lately. Or for a long time, to be honest. Even before all that nonsense with the giant robot.

The grass felt cool under her paws. She had liked it when it was longer, back when Stanley had let the mower go unrepaired. Easier to stalk prey then, to catch them by surprise. She was, and had always been, a mighty hunter.

Her flank brushed against the soft green blades. She felt alive, a charge of electricity flowing from the tops of her ears to the tip of her tail. The sensation linked her to a memory from long, long ago, transporting her to another place....

Another time...

Another life...

It was one that had been lived in a much bigger body, hundreds of pounds heavier than the one she inhabited now. But still just as stealthy. Even more so, in fact. It was a body perfectly calibrated to hunt. She felt the way the muscles along her back rippled from shoulder to hip as she navigated the steamy jungle terrain that was her home. Her massive paws pressed into the earth, leaving marks that were feared by all. Even her voice was bigger, a rich baritone that commanded respect. No human would dare pat her head, no, not if they wanted to keep their arm attached to their body. Her teeth were much more serious affairs as well, two of which curved down far past her chin, showcasing themselves even when her mouth was closed, like her own personal pair of sabers. If anyone was ever unlucky enough to see them, it was usually the last thing they saw....

Crank sniffed the air, catching a whiff of something just

Molly and the Mutants

ahead. The scent pulled her back into the present, and she ventured farther through the grass to the edge of the McQuirters' backyard. But the boundaries imposed by humans weren't recognized by her. She continued into the trees and brush, her dull orange and black stripes no longer visible from the house.

Crank didn't look back. She kept her head low, listening for the squeaks and scurries of the creatures all around her. But today she would leave the field mice and chipmunks to themselves. Even the squirrels and foxes.

For this venture, she had her sights set on something bigger.

CHAPTER 9
TOO-TIGHT LEATHER PANTS

Molly sat mesmerized by the leather-clad singer writhing around in Margo's living room. More specifically, *on the TV* in Margo's living room. From his pinched face and spastic gyrations, Molly guessed the man on-screen must be in serious pain. He was clutching a microphone, wailing in a pitch that Molly thought might shatter glass.

But maybe this was normal. What did she know? Molly rarely got to watch music videos. Her dad had finally had their TV replaced after their last one had gotten fried during the robot-induced power surge over the summer, along with most of their street. But she was pretty sure hers was the only house left on Far Flung Falls Drive that still didn't have a cable

Molly and the Mutants

box installed. That meant all they had were the same old three network channels. Plus a couple more on UHF, which came in a little snowy unless you tweaked the dial just right.

Not like here at Margo's. On top of their TV was a little box with a slider that let you choose from a whopping thirty-seven channels—including MTV.

That's what they were watching now. An entire channel dedicated to music. With music videos 24/7. Officer Wasserbaum definitely wouldn't approve. And her dad probably wouldn't either. But Molly had no idea how a goofball like that singer could get kids to steal other people's pets, or worship Satan, or do anything at all—other than laugh.

Behind Leather Pants, a horde of women in skimpy, ripped outfits and giant teased-out hairdos tried to reach for the singer from behind bars. Which made no sense, because he was sweaty and gross. The whole thing seemed kind of dumb. And Molly was pretty sure Ronda would agree. One time Ronda had told Molly that all the best rockers were women.

As for Margo's science project, it was supposed to be a model of the solar system, with painted Styrofoam balls representing the sun and all nine planets. Margo had stuck them all on little dowel rods that she'd glued to a plank of wood. But the scale was a little off. Jupiter was way too small. Saturn's pipe-cleaner rings were all bent up and twisted. And Pluto was missing in action. It had fallen off its dowel and rolled out of sight. *You can't have a solar system without Pluto,* Molly thought. Everybody knew that.

But Margo had other, more practical skills. She walked back into the room with a pair of ice cream sandwiches she'd excavated from the secret back regions of their freezer. On the TV, Leather Pants kept wailing.

Here I am!

Rock you like a hurricane!

"I think his pants might be a little too tight in the *you-know-where* department," Margo said, pointing at the screen. Molly giggled in agreement, taking one of the treats.

"Thanks," she said.

"Hey, whereja get those?" The question came from the other end of the couch. It was Margo's older sister, Nikki. She was already in high school, and had the eyeliner to prove it. Caked on thick and black, it made her look a little like an angry racoon. Everything that came out of her mouth carried the tone of a complaint.

"Oh. Last two. Sorr-eeeee," Margo said in her most not-sorry way.

"Whatever," Nikki said.

Molly and the Mutants

Mr. Too-Tight Leather Pants had finished his convulsions on TV. The scene was replaced by a young woman's smiling face. Her hair was a lot shorter than the girls' in the video, and her clothes weren't ripped.

"Hey there, rockers. I'm your veejay, Martha Quinn, and that was the Scorpions, with their latest single, topping the charts," she announced. "Now I hope you're ready to crank up the volume. Because up next we've got a caller request for KISS, with 'I Love It Loud' from their 'Creatures of the Night' album. Right after these messages."

A jingle came on for a shampoo Molly had never heard of.

"C'mon, Nik, let's get outta here. KISS blows." That was another voice. It was Nikki's boyfriend, Logan. He'd been so quiet up until now, Molly had forgotten he was there. Logan picked at the patch of acne across his chin, then stood. When Angry Racoon didn't respond, he jangled his car keys. Molly had seen Logan's green-and-black Camaro parked out front when she'd arrived. She remembered it from the bus this morning. The Green Machine.

Logan kept jingling.

"Yeah, yeah, okay," Nikki mumbled.

"Um, Nik? Aren't you, like, supposed to be watching me until Mom gets home?" Margo said.

"You can watch yourself, freezer thief," Nikki answered, then looked back at Logan. "Hey, Lo, buy me some nachos at 7-Eleven?" She managed to make that sound like a complaint too.

"Yeah, sure," Logan said.

"Don't get into any trouble," Nikki called over her shoulder.

"Oh, we will," Margo said in her best supervillain voice. "We . . . *will*." But Nikki was already out the door.

Molly had listened to the exchange without taking her eyes off the TV. The commercials had ended, and KISS was on. Molly couldn't decide if their costumes and painted faces made them look funny or scary. Maybe a little of both? The camera cut to one of the guitar players, who was waggling his tongue in kind of an I-probably-worship-Satan kind of way. She was thinking about what Wasserbaum had said. It wasn't hard to see where he got his ideas. *Creatures of the Night*. Molly wondered: Was this what one of the devil's minions looked like? With stage makeup, a ponytail, and spiked platform boots? If so, the devil was pretty ridiculous.

But what about all those missing animals?

Margo interrupted her thoughts with a sheet of binder paper that was folded into a tiny, tight rectangle. Molly instantly recognized it as the type of fold that some girls used

Molly and the Mutants

to pass notes in class. She wasn't one of them, but she knew the style.

"Oh," Margo said, "I almost forgot. Here you go."

"What's this?" Molly asked.

Margo raised her eyebrows and smirked. Molly had learned that meant she was up to no good, which was often. She was hanging out at Margo's house a lot more lately, almost every day. It had started right after Margo's family had come back from Michigan, which was also right after Molly had battled the giant robot, and the whole town had been talking about it. Since then Margo had treated her differently. She was fun to hang out with, but sometimes she did things that made Molly uncomfortable. Like now.

Molly turned the paper note over in her hand. Now it was her turn to raise her eyebrows. In a script with elaborate curlicues it read:

To: Finn
From: Molly

"You'll be happy to know he checked the yes box," Margo said.

"Wait, the yes box? Margo!" The note was still folded up tight. "What did he say yes to? What was the question?"

Margo just stared at her, waiting.

"But I didn't write this," Molly said. "This handwriting isn't even—"

On-screen KISS was shouting from onstage.

Loud, I wanna hear it loud!

Right between the eyes!

Molly felt like she was getting hit right between the eyes herself. But not in a good way. Margo might only be a year older than her, but sometimes it felt like the age gap was much wider. Finally she tugged the flap on the note, opening it up. The bottom of her stomach dropped out of her body, hit the floor, and rolled out of sight. Probably next to Styrofoam Pluto.

Inside, the note read:

Hi, Finn!

How's it going? You have rad hair.

I like you. Do you like me?

☑ *YES*

☐ *NO*

(Check which one.)

If you check the YES box, you can meet me after school today down at the Slew behind Margo's house.

Sincerely,

Molly

Molly and the Mutants

Molly reread the note several times, completely baffled. The yes box was indeed checked. But she had definitely not written the note. She looked up at Margo, slowly realizing what had happened.

"Margo! What... did... you... do?"

"Relax. I know you like him," Margo said. "I saw the way you were looking at him at the assembly."

"But—"

"You can thank me later."

Molly had no intention of doing that. *After school today?* That was now. She could feel herself getting splotchy. *Meet me down at the Slew?* This didn't sound like a fifth-grade thing, or even a sixth-grade thing—it sounded like an eighth-grade thing! Molly's heart was slamming against her chest. She was sure it was beating louder than the Green Machine.

"What about your science project?" Molly stammered, "W-what about Pluto?"

"Who needs Pluto?" Margo said. "We've got a date."

CHAPTER 10
THE SLEW

Molly and Margo tromped down the gully behind Margo's house, zigzagging down a narrow footpath that crisscrossed the slant of the earth at an angle to avoid too steep a descent. Margo led the way. They were headed to the rendezvous point.

"Have you ever kissed a boy?" Margo asked without looking back.

The question came out of nowhere, catching Molly off guard as she ducked under a fallen tree. Everything was moving too fast. She still hadn't recovered from the note.

"What? Kissed? *A boy?* No!"

"Just wondering," Margo said. "No biggie."

Molly and the Mutants

"Have you?" Molly asked.

Margot giggled.

"Well, *have* you?" Molly insisted. Sometimes it bugged her the way Margo made everything a game. She couldn't imagine that Margo had kissed a boy either. But Margo was a year older. Maybe all the sixth graders were running around kissing one another all the time, for all she knew. Molly tapped her friend on the shoulder.

"Mayyy-beee," Margo said, giggling some more.

"What? *Margo!*" Molly said. "Who? When? Where? ... Who?"

"Hold on. You sound like my mom," Margo said. "Geez."

Molly wondered what it would be like to have a mom who actually asked you questions about your life. She got quiet.

"Oh, Molly, I didn't mean—"

"S'okay," Molly said.

"Anyway, it was terrible. You don't wanna know."

This made Molly want to know even more, but she dropped it—for now.

After a few minutes they arrived at the Slew. Molly wasn't sure how it had gotten that name. But it fit. The Slew was a creek like most others, but perennially green, and for reasons no one knew, a favorite hangout spot. The rocks on either side were slick with lichen and moss. In some spots, where the rock was undercut, the water churned up clouds of a dirty, brownish foam everyone called "creek crud." It was not the kind of water you ever wanted to fall into. Unless maybe you were a slimy, disgusting frog. The Slew was home to many of them, along with all the bugs who buzzed around the surface—until they became the frogs' lunch.

Molly wondered why the bugs would hang out there in the first place if it was such a precarious spot. Maybe bugs had a death wish? Then she thought about who they'd be meeting soon, and wondered why she was there herself. Maybe she was just naturally attracted to danger.

Speaking of danger...

"Here we are. The Ghost Swing," Margo announced, stopping at a twisted-looking tree to give it a pat.

"The Ghost Swing," Molly repeated.

Although it was the stuff of legend around their neighborhood, the Ghost Swing wasn't much to look at. Molly had swung on it once, a few years ago, and had decided that was enough to test her luck. She eyed the worn, weathered plank of wood resting atop the knotted end of a rope that looked like it might disintegrate if you touched it. The rope traveled up through a whittled-out hole in the plank's center. The other end was tied to a branch that stretched out high above their heads. It was definitely not safe. But Molly had to admit that after a summer spent dodging lasers and jumping off cliffs, the old swing with its fraying rope felt like an acceptable level of danger for a school day afternoon.

Nobody knew who had tied it, or how. The tree grew sideways out over the creek, and wasn't particularly inviting for climbers. The first branch was a good thirty feet up.

"Why's it called a *Ghost Swing* anyway?" Molly asked.

"I heard on account of somebody died on it," came a voice from somewhere downstream. A boy's voice.

"Wha—?" Both girls let out a scream and turned around.

Molly let out a breath as she saw that it was just Arvin, walking up along the bank of the creek. Right below him, just along an undercut in the rock, a wobbling tower of fresh creek crud looked like it was trying to reach up and pull him in. But Arvin sliced through it, sending little foamy globs sailing across the surface. He was carrying a net in one hand and a little mesh cage in the other. Finn Garrett—with his perfectly feathered flyback hair—was following right behind him. But he wasn't so mindful about where he stepped, and was doing as much slipping as he was walking. Maybe it was the hair, but Molly thought he seemed out of place among all the muck and goo. Out of place, but still pretty cute.

"Yep," Arvin continued. "True story. Some kid snuck down here all by himself one night, around midnight, swung all the way out, far as the swing could carry him... and slipped. Dropped headfirst right onto that rock o'er yonder, busted his skull wide open like a watermelon. Brains washed all the way down the Slew, to Bottom Basin."

"Grody!" Margo squealed.

"Careful you don't fall in," Molly said to them both—but mostly to Finn.

"Planning on catching some fish?" Margo asked, nodding at the net.

"Naw," Arvin said. "Just need some bug samples for my science project."

"Well, you've come to the right place," Margo said.

"How's yours coming along?"

"Not bad."

Molly pictured the sad solar system back at the house and wasn't sure she agreed, but if Margo wasn't worried, why should she be?

Their eyes all followed the flow of the Slew as it wound its way toward Bottom Basin, the lowest natural point in all of Far Flung Falls, where several creeks converged.

"You think his brains are still there now?" Finn asked. It

was the first time he had opened his mouth, and Molly realized she had actually never heard him talk before.

"Still where?" Arvin asked.

"At Bottom Basin?" Finn said.

"Naw," Arvin said. "Walleyes probably ate 'em all up."

"I don't think walleyes eat brains," Molly said.

"Unless they're zombie walleyes," Arvin said. "Gaaaaaaaaaahhhhh."

"I wouldn't be surprised if there were zombie fish in the Slew," Margo said. "I mean, just look at it."

Again they studied the dark green shimmer of the creek's surface. But its secrets remained intact. Slowly their attention shifted.

"Who's first?" Margo said, grabbing the swing's seat.

"You kidding?" Arvin said. "That thing could never hold me."

"Oh, if you're scared..." Margo let her voice trail off.

"Who said I was scared?" Arvin said. "I just... whadda I get if I do it?"

Margo whispered something into Arvin's ear, then giggled.

Molly's eyes narrowed. What was she up to now?

Arvin blushed.

"Okay, I'll go," he said. He smiled a big goofy smile at Margo, grabbing the rope.

Arvin got into position on the wooden board and pushed off.

"Wahooooooo!" Arvin yelled. The rope made a strained creak as it carried Arvin out into the air above the trickling petri dish below. Molly held her breath, thinking the worn-out rope would snap at any moment. But it didn't. In seconds the Ghost Swing returned its occupant to his original position, where he touched back down on the ledge.

"Easy-peazy, lemon-squeezy," he said.

Arvin had never really been much into adventures—unless they were in a video game, of which he was the neighborhood expert. But that was before this past summer, when he'd had to escape the clutches of the giant robot who had invaded their neighborhood. Molly remembered when she and Arvin had crossed Crook's Chasm—and nearly died in the process. Compared to that, swinging over the Slew seemed, well, pretty *easy-peazy*.

Molly didn't notice Finn standing next to her.

"Oh. Hi," she said.

"Whaddya think Margo told him?" Finn asked.

"I dunno," Molly said.

"You got a little dirt or something," Finn said. To indicate, he pointed to the corner of his own mouth. "Right there."

Molly and the Mutants

"Oh," Molly said. She tried to wipe it, but the wrong side.

"Uh, other corner," he said.

Molly wiped her mouth with the back of her hand, smearing chocolate from the ice cream sandwich. "Oh," she said. "It's not dirt. It's chocolate."

How did she still always manage to do that? Molly felt her chest and neck getting hot. She was probably getting splotchy again. Which would be the third time today. But Finn just smiled.

"Oh, cool," he said. "I like chocolate too."

Every hair on his head was perfectly in place.

"Okay, your turn, Finn," Arvin said, interrupting the moment.

Finn shrugged his shoulders, then trudged over to the ledge and got in position. He hesitated a moment, then pushed off and swung high over the creek. Molly prayed that the swing held.

Finn let out a small whoop, but it was cut short when the rope started to unravel and he dropped by half a foot. He made it to the far side just in time to grab the root of a tree—right as the entire rope came falling down, along with the Ghost Swing, into the Slew. *Sploop.*

Molly couldn't believe it. Even though the Ghost Swing had

been threatening to fall apart at any moment for as long as she could remember, its demise had still been unexpected. For Molly, the Ghost Swing had represented a kind of perpetually looming danger—but one that never actually arrived. And now that the swing had met its end, it felt like an era was ending with it.

They watched the shredded bits of rope flow down the creek until they disappeared into its green depths. Slowly Finn crawled down from the opposite bank, caught his breath, and then hopped over a few stones that poked out of the Slew, to rejoin the others.

"You okay?" Molly asked.

"Yeah, I think," Finn said, looking himself over.

"Okay, we did it," Arvin said.

"The rules were, if the boys took a turn on the swing . . . ," Margo started.

"The girls had to do their homework for a month," Arvin finished.

"What? No way!" Molly said. "I didn't agree to any—"

"Orrrrrrr give the boys . . . a kiss," Margo said. Molly's eyes flashed to her friend. She was making that face again.

CHAPTER 11
K-I-S-S-I-N-G

"Margo, you just made that up," Molly said.

Arvin grinned again. "No, it's true, those have been Ghost Swing rules for years," he said. "You can ask my sisters."

"Who conveniently aren't here," Molly said. But she had little doubt Arvin's sisters had kissed somebody. Probably every boy on their street.

"Well, no way am I doing anyone's homework," Molly said. She crossed her arms to let everyone know this was non-negotiable.

"Okay, it's settled, then," Arvin said, looking at Margo.

Without another word, Margo walked over and kissed Arvin.

On. The. Lips.

Molly and Finn stared, wide-eyed, like they were watching a car crash.

After a few painstakingly long moments, Margo and Arvin finally pulled away from each other, and both sucked in a big breath. *Wait,* Molly thought, *when you kiss somebody, do you have to hold your breath?* How long were you supposed to go? Maybe this would be harder than she thought. Molly started to worry even more.

Margo started giggling. Arvin laughed too. They didn't seem nervous or anything. Had they kissed before? Something smelled fishy about this whole thing. And it wasn't just the Slew. This felt like a setup. But who was in on it? Definitely Margo. Possibly Arvin. Maybe everyone? Molly wasn't sure. Arvin wasn't exactly very sneaky. She looked over at Finn.

Finn looked back at Molly with an expression akin to terror. He smiled awkwardly. Beads of sweat broke out across his forehead. So, he had been set up too. For some reason, that made it feel not as bad. She wasn't about to get shown up.

"Okay," Molly said, "let's get this over wi—"

Molly and the Mutants

"Okay, okay," Finn blurted, a little too fast, and a little too loudly. "Uh, if you're..."

Molly gulped and nodded.

Finn started to lean in.

She noticed his perfect hair again, the way it caught the little spots of sunlight that broke through the trees above them. Everything slowed. The insects started buzzing more loudly. Molly got ready to hold her breath. Then a thought popped into her head.

"Hold on," Molly said. "Lips only." She thought of the guy on MTV waggling his tongue. "Because anything more than that is just... gross."

"Yeah, no. Totally. I'd never. Yeah, totally gross. Just lips."

Their faces were closer. Molly could smell the Hubba Bubba on his breath. Maybe raspberry? Or watermelon? Molly wasn't sure, but it made her feel like she was in a candy store. Her head began tilting to one side. She noticed the sunlight dancing on his hair again, making it glow, just as she started to close her eyes and...

THWACK!

Something wet and slimy smacked against her cheek, and hard.

Molly's first thought was that when she'd closed her eyes, she must have missed his mouth. This was quickly followed by a second thought: that Finn hadn't listened to her "lips only" rule they had just talked about.

But something didn't feel right. Too cold to be his tongue.

Was Finn playing some kind of joke? Or had Margo planned it this way all along? Well, whatever it was, it wasn't funny.

Molly waited one more sec for the cold, wet, slimy thing to get off her cheek. When it didn't, she opened her eyes.

It wasn't Finn. And she hadn't missed at all.

Finn had pulled away. He was staring at her with a look of confused horror. Oh no, what had happened? What had she done wrong?

"Finn?" Molly whispered. "What is it?"

Molly looked down to the cause of the wet, sticky sensation on her cheek. Her eyes widened. It was long, pinkish, and shiny, like someone had stretched the biggest wad of Hubba Bubba in history. She followed the pink strand to its point of origin, which was the open mouth of the biggest bullfrog Molly had ever seen. And she had seen more than a few in her life. Bullfrogs were commonplace here, and some of them could weigh up to a pound. But this one was in another category altogether. It was bigger than Crank, covered in hideous lumps and bumps, sitting atop an exposed tree root. It must've weighed more than twenty pounds.

Everyone's eyes followed hers, until all four kids were staring at the creature. The creature stared back, casually blinking its big yellow eyes.

Molly felt a tug on her cheek. The frog was making a weird gulping sound. In a sickening realization Molly understood that the frog had caught her, like a fly. And it was trying to reel her in—for food. So gross. Molly wasn't about to be some freak frog's lunch.

"Finn!" Molly screamed. "Get! It! Off! Me!"

But Finn was paralyzed.

"I got this!" Arvin called, leaping into action.

He crouched down, grabbed hold of a fist-size rock, and chucked it as hard as he could. The rock flew, and found its target—whack! It hit the root directly under the frog, knocking the creature from its perch. Instantly the tongue released its sticky hold on Molly's cheek with a drawn-out *mwwwah*.

And that, Molly would later realize, was her first kiss. Not with Finn—which she hadn't been sure about in the first place—but with a giant, disgusting, slimy frog. She hadn't been too sure she even wanted a kiss, but she was definitely sure she hadn't wanted this.

"Blech!" Molly said, wiping the sticky mucus off her cheek and flicking it into the dirt.

"Sorry," Finn mumbled. He was looking down.

"S'okay," Molly said. "Not your fault." She shot an accusing look at Margo. "None of this woulda happened if—"

Just then something rustled in the bushes, cutting her off. Everyone froze.

Brrrreeeeeeeeeeep!

Shrieking like a banshee—or at least the amphibian version of one—the bloated bullfrog flew out from the bushes, right over Molly's head, and into the creek with a cannonball of a splash. It turned around to face them, and stared them down with its protruding eyes. The frog made a deep croaking sound as it began to inflate its throat like a mottled balloon, making the animal appear even bigger than it already was. The throat was much paler than the rest of its body, which was a dark olive green.

"Watch out," Margo called.

"Yeah, it might try to lick one of us again," said Arvin.

"Don't worry, I'm watching," said Molly.

"Me too," Finn offered softly.

But instead of launching another attack, the frog suddenly

lost interest, or maybe just gave up. It turned and hopped away, making a loud splash with each landing as it retreated downstream.

"What. Was. That?" Margo said.

"*That*," Arvin said as he picked up his net, "is going to be my science project. C'mon."

CHAPTER 12
HUNT

Just as they started to give chase, there was a rustle up the hill behind them. Molly, Margo, Arvin, and Finn all spun around. They were on high alert for another frog.

Instead they found Leonard.

"Hey, guys," Leonard said, bouncing down the trail to meet them. "You'll never guess what I saw on the way here—"

"You saw it too?" Arvin said.

"I ran into Nikki and Logan at 7-Eleven," Leonard continued. "He spilled nacho cheese all over her shirt, and she was so steamed, it was hilarious. Anyway, they said you guys were—"

The four of them stared at him without a word.

"Wait, what?" Leonard said, finally noticing their expressions.

Molly and the Mutants

"Leonard," Arvin said. "Forget the nacho story. We're going... froggin.'"

"Okaaaay," Leonard said. "What's the rush?"

"You shoulda seen its tongue shoot out and hit Mol—" Finn started.

"Finn!" Molly blurted, cutting him off. She didn't want him spilling the beans that anything close to a kiss had just happened. "We just saw a really big frog, okay?"

"Really big," Finn repeated.

"Yeah, super big." Margo said.

"Basically Frogzilla," Arvin said.

"Frog... zilla?" Leonard asked, excitement washing across his face.

"Frogzilla," Arvin said again, holding up his fishing net. "I'm not even sure if this'll be enough to hold him."

"I'm in," Leonard said. "Totally."

They started down the trail, careful not to step too close to the Slew.

"Wait, guys, why are we even doing this?" Molly said.

"Are you kidding me?" Arvin said. "Capturing the world's largest frog of all time? That's got to be worth an A in science."

The thought of Arvin getting an A without putting in any of the work really rubbed Molly the wrong way. But after the shock of getting slimed by that monster-size frog, part of her wanted to see it again, just to make sure it was real, that she hadn't imagined the whole thing. And a part of her wanted it captured, possibly put into frog jail for assaulting her cheek. It seemed only fair.

Together the five of them hurried along down the bank, keeping their eyes peeled for any amphibious activity.

As they walked, Arvin recapped the details of the encounter to Leonard—careful not to mention anything about kissing, which Molly appreciated. The mere thought of people talking about it made her feel embarrassed. Plus, ever since the day she had rescued Leonard from his cell inside the giant robot, he'd always looked at her, well, differently. Molly liked Leonard, but she wasn't sure she *like*-liked him, at least not in that way. Heck, she wasn't sure she liked anyone in that way. But like-like or not, she didn't want to hurt anyone's feelings. Especially Leonard's.

"No way it was that big," Leonard was saying, reaching into the back pocket of his jeans. "But if it is, I'll be ready."

He produced a small slingshot and gave it a few test pulls.

"Me too," Molly said, padding the slingshot in her own back pocket. Until now she'd forgotten it was there. Between the

Molly and the Mutants

two weapons and the fishing net, their crew seemed ready for anything.

"We all saw it, Leonard," Arvin said. "I'm telling you, it was bigger than Mr. Hornberger's head." Mr. Hornberger taught sixth-grade English and was known for his oversize noggin. Kids joked that if it ever rolled off his shoulders, it would flatten the entire class.

"You think maybe it was something else, like a box turtle or something?" Finn asked.

"Box turtles don't have tongues like that," Molly said.

"Maybe it's a mutant turtle?" Leonard said.

"Mutant turtle?" Margo said. "That's ridiculous."

"Yeah," Molly said, leveling her gaze at Margo, "there's been a lot of *ridiculous* today."

Margo looked down.

Molly wasn't finished talking to her friend about what had happened—from the forged note to those obviously made-up rules by the Ghost Swing. But she needed some time to think about it. And besides, they had a frog to catch first.

"My dad says the Russians are dumping radioactive waste into our drinking water," Leonard said, "to turn us all into commies, or cannibals, or commie cannibals or something."

"Way out here in Far Flung Falls?"

"Um, stranger things have happened." Molly looked at Arvin.

"True," Arvin said.

"I think it was a bullfrog," Molly said. "Probably made right here in America."

They rounded a bend in the creek, where the water dropped incrementally in a stair-step series of small waterfalls. The descent slowed their progress a little, but the hunters carried on.

"One by one our hearty band of travelers entered the abyss...," Leonard said, narrating their actions like they were in a comic book. Molly laughed.

"Shut up," Margo said.

"... uncertain of what perils lay ahead ...," Leonard continued.

Now everyone laughed.

"Shhh. Seriously, quiet, guys," Margo whispered. "Listen."

The group stopped where they stood. Over the constant trickle of water, they heard a splash. Then another. After that there was a rustling in the bushes.

"Hey," Arvin whispered, "I think that's our frog."

"Or box turtle," Leonard said.

Molly and the Mutants

"It's *not* a box turtle!" Margo shouted.

"The mutant creature readied itself for another attack"—Leonard was narrating again—"coiling its tentacles and licking its razor-sharp teeth..."

At that, Molly raised her slingshot.

"Whatever it is, don't hurt it," Arvin said. "That's my science project you're talking about."

Molly thought she might let one pebble fly, though, just to even the score.

They crept on a little farther, taking care that each of their steps found sure footing. As they made their way down, the tree cover thickened, blocking out all but a few thin rays of sunlight. Tiny glowing bright spots amidst a blanket of shade. It made frog-spotting much harder. Molly could feel the air get cooler by a few degrees on her arms and legs. She gave her slingshot a few more tentative pulls.

Two giant birch trees on opposite sides of the creek had fallen into each other, crisscrossing over the water. Their bone-white trunks created a giant X that stood out in stark contrast from all the green and brown hues behind it.

"X marks the spot," Leonard said. "This must be the place."

"The place for what?" Margo said. "Creeps me out."

"Just needs a skull above it," Arvin said.

"I've got a bad feeling about this," Finn said.

Molly was just about to point out that those were famous last words when...

Thwit-thwit-thwit! All at once they were bombarded by multiple tongues from all directions. One hit Margo in the shin, causing her to let out an ear-piercing scream. Another landed on Finn's elbow, which he tried to swat away. A third tongue shot out from behind them, and stuck to Arvin's backside.

"My butt! It got my butt!" Arvin spun in a circle, trying to slap it off.

"Fire!" Molly yelled. She pulled back and let her pebble fly. It hit the tongue that was stuck to Arvin's bottom. The sticky tissue promptly recoiled into the tall grass. Leonard drew his slingshot and joined the fray, rapidly reloading and firing anywhere he saw movement. His aim wasn't quite as true as Molly's, but he wasn't a bad shot.

"Take that, you ugly buggers!" Leonard said.

"Just don't scare them too bad. I need one," Arvin said.

"For science, right?" Molly said.

"Naw, for a grade!"

Molly rolled her eyes. Arvin would never not be Arvin.

The volley between slingshots and projectile tongues

Molly and the Mutants

continued back and forth as the would-be frog hunters made their way deeper into the gorge. But the creek got much wider here, and the bank dwindled, funneling them into a corner where the side of the ravine became very steep. There was nowhere to go, Molly thought, unless they wanted to brave the mucky water....

"No thanks," Finn said, somehow reading her mind. "I didn't bring a swimsuit."

"But we're sitting ducks here!" Molly said.

Until now the frogs had mostly remained hidden, taking shots from behind the cover of grass. But more and more of the oversize creatures were venturing into the open, showing Molly and her friends that they were vastly outnumbered.

"Evasive action!" Arvin called, jumping onto a rock. There was a cluster of boulders poking out of the Slew, like stepping stones, just a few feet away. Most of them barely cleared the creek's surface, except for a broad, moss-covered boulder in the center of the line. Arvin nearly lost his balance on that one but quickly recovered, net in one hand and cage in the other. After a couple more leaps he was on the other side.

"Hurry up!" he called.

"This better not get my sneakers dirty," Margo said.

"They're brand new." She looked down to admire her bright white Reebok high-tops.

"Then don't fall in!" Arvin said. "C'mon!"

The rest of them stumbled their way across. The rocks were all different shapes and sizes, some more slippery than others. But each one was encircled by the same dirty, brownish foam.

"That's some gnarly creek crud," Leonard said.

"Yeah," Molly said. "Careful."

"It's okay," Leonard said. "My shoes aren't new."

"Mine either," Molly said. They smiled.

"Whoa!" Margo said, taking another step.

"Watch out," Arvin called. "That big one's really slippery."

"And wobbly," Finn added.

"Now you tell me!" Margo said.

The frog assault had subsided, and they walked along the opposite bank in relative peace for a few minutes, with Arvin bringing up the rear, fishing net at the ready.

"Gotcha!" he said.

They turned. Arvin had actually caught one of the giant frogs and was hefting it in his net.

"Ugh! He's heavy!" he said.

"He's gross!" Margo countered.

Molly and the Mutants

"Aw, I think he's kinda cute," Leonard said.

The frog fought against the netting for a moment to right itself, then settled. Maybe it didn't mind being captured, or had resigned itself to its fate.

Molly stared at the creature. It looked familiar, something about the splotchy pattern of yellows, greens, and browns. She knew what it felt like to get splotchy, which was what happened to the skin around her chest and neck whenever she got nervous, embarrassed, or mad. She wondered how this frog must be feeling right now. Was it nervous? Or in shock? Was it embarrassed it had gotten itself stuck in a net with a human holding the handle? Something about it being in the net didn't look right to her. Maybe it was the scale. The frog was just so massive-looking, filling up a net that could typically hold several fish at once.

"Maybe we should let him go," she said.

"Are you kidding?" Arvin said. "I worked hard to get this guy."

"*We* worked hard," Margo said. She was still brushing the slime off her shin.

"Okay, we all did," Arvin admitted, carefully transferring his captive from net to cage.

Margo smiled. *A win.*

Molly looked at the frog again. It fidgeted a little, then blinked. The creature looked so awkward there, but maybe it wasn't the cage. It looked like maybe it wasn't comfortable in its own body. Like it didn't belong in this creek, or these hills. Or maybe even in this world. Molly could relate to that feeling, of not feeling at home in her body, or in the world. Maybe everyone felt like a freak on the inside?

And that's when she realized, this was the one. The same frog that had wound up being her first kiss. She could feel it. *Hey there, fellow freak*, she thought. *I forgive you. I guess.*

"I wonder what it's thinking," Leonard wondered aloud.

"It doesn't look... mad," Margo said.

"That's coz he knows I'm gonna make him famous," Arvin declared.

R-r-r-r-ribbit, it croaked in a deep froggy voice.

CHAPTER 13
LURKER

P rize in hand, they began trekking back up the bank of the Slew. In all the excitement of the chase, Molly hadn't realized just how far down they'd traveled. The sun had dipped a little lower in the sky, drawing out more shadows.

Arvin was walking with his chest out, the triumphant hunter.

"Man, those frogs can kiss my butt," he said.

"Actually, I think they already did," Leonard said.

Margo and Molly both doubled over and snorted in perfect sync.

"Yeah, at least one did," Margo said.

"Shut up," Arvin said.

"Okay, frog butt," Margo said. The girls giggled a little more.

"At least I didn't get a frog tongue to the face—" Arvin started.

"How about a fist to the face?" Molly said.

"Okay, okay, just kidding. Sheesh," Arvin said.

"Wha—" Leonard started to ask.

"Never mind," Margo said, cutting him off.

They made it back to the stepping stones.

"That's funny," Leonard said, staring at the rocks that poked up from the creek's slimy surface.

"Whaddya see?" Molly asked.

"It's not what I *see*." Leonard brushed away the hair that had flopped over his eyes. "It's what I *don't*."

They all stopped to see what Leonard was talking about.

The biggest rock, the wobbly one that had been covered in moss, was gone. Now there was just an eight-foot gap between the smaller stones, with nothing but the putrid green of the Slew flowing downstream between them.

They all looked at the open space in the middle, dumbfounded. Leonard scratched his head.

"There's no way a creek as lazy as the Slew could move that boulder in the time we were gone," Finn said. "Unless there was some tidal wave we missed?"

Molly and the Mutants

He leaned back against a rock tucked into the brush line.

As he did, the rock moved away, receding farther into the brush. Molly watched in shock. No one else caught it.

Finn stumbled. He let out a long high-pitched scream that rivaled Margo's from earlier.

"What?" Margo asked. "What is it?"

"Th-th-the... rock!" Finn stammered.

"We know, it's missing," Arvin said.

"Guys!" Molly said. "Not *that* rock. *Another* rock. But not a rock.... I think there's something *else* down here."

Just then Arvin's frog croaked from inside its cage. Its cry was answered by another from somewhere nearby, then another. In moments there was a deafening chorus of bullfrogs. The ribbits rose and fell in waves all around them, like the kids were in the center of an arena.

"How many of them can there be?" Margo asked.

"I don't wanna find out," Arvin said. "We need to get outta here."

Cage in hand, he made a mad dash across the stepping stones and leapt with all he could muster across the open spot. Molly was right behind him, barely clearing the divide. She was followed by Finn, then Leonard, who fell a foot short and landed in the green goop of the Slew.

"Really?" Leonard said to no one in particular, scrambling out of the creek with one sneaker soaked.

That left Margo on the far bank... by herself.

"C'mon, Margo!" Molly called. "You got this!"

But Margo stood frozen, paralyzed by the frog-fueled cacophony all around her.

Just then, rising above the din, came something even louder. Something between a croak and a growl, from directly behind her. It was a deep sound, making the earth vibrate under their feet, like the bass from Logan's Camaro.

YUUUUURRRP.

The army of frogs fell silent. An eerie quiet held them all captive for a second, before Margo finally took that as her cue to run for her life. She sprinted the short distance to the first stone, flew over it to the second and third, and then hurled herself through the air and—

Splaaaaap!

Even faster than Margo, something shot out from the bushes behind her, in the exact spot where Finn had tried to lean moments before. A thick strand of shimmering muscle caught the bottom of Margo's left Reebok. She dropped face-down into the Slew.

Molly and the Mutants

"Uuuuuunnh—" Margo cried, before going under.

It was another frog tongue, only much bigger. This one was as thick as Margo's leg.

"Help!" Margo gurgled, coming up for air. "Help me!"

The monstrous tongue began reeling her in, flexing its muscly mass as it dragged her back through the slime of the Slew.

"Margo!" Molly screamed. "Grab a rock!" She was still more than a little peeved at her friend for the antics she'd pulled today—but didn't want her to get eaten.

In desperation Margo threw her arms around one of the stepping stones, interrupting the beast's progress. But that wasn't going to last for long. Pulled by unnatural force, the stone Margo was hugging started dislodging itself from the bed of the stream.

Molly reloaded her slingshot and fired off a few rounds into the slimy strand of flesh. They hit, but to no effect. The tongue was too powerful.

Arvin jumped back over the gap and landed with a splash just short of the stone Margo was hanging on to. Thrashing through the knee-deep water, he reached for her shoe, but it was so slick from its submersion in the creek, it was hard for him to keep a firm grip. Fumbling wildly, he finally grabbed hold of the Velcro flap at the top of the Reebok, and ripped it loose, then went for the shoelace below.

By this point the end of the tongue had completely enveloped the bottom half of Margo's shoe in its sticky grip. It pulsed and tightened, lurching her out of the creek and farther toward the bushes—where who knows what was waiting. Arvin stayed with her, yanking harder on the soaked laces.

"Stupid double knot," he grunted.

"Hurry!" Molly screamed. She and Leonard fired off several more shots at the unseen creature. One after another their munitions flew into its shadowy lair, but to no avail. In fact they seemed to have the opposite effect. The tongue appeared to pull even harder.

Finally Arvin managed to loosen the knot on Margo's laces, and she kicked it off with her free foot. Immediately the shoe vanished into the bushes, which rustled and shook.

YUUUUURRRP.

"My shoe!" Margo said.

"You're gonna lose more than that if we don't go!" Arvin said, grabbing her hand. The two splashed through pond scum to the other side.

"Ew. Ew. Ew. Ew," Margo said with every step. She was

Molly and the Mutants

minus one Reebok, and coated in a green film from head to toe. Arvin matched her from the waist down.

"Sorry about your sneaker," Finn said. "Happened to me once too." Then he lowered his voice, casting a wary look at their surroundings. "I think maybe these woods like to collect 'em."

Margo grumbled a little more as the five of them doubled back up the trail to higher ground, stealing glances over their shoulders and hoping whatever they heard wasn't following them.

Molly listened to the rhythmic *squish-squash* of Margo's and Arvin's scum-soaked footsteps behind her. She was grateful everyone was alive, of course. But at the same time, all the way in the back of her mind, behind all those blaring fear receptors that kept her moving, there was a quieter section that was busy doing something else. It was where her sense of fairness remained ever on the lookout . . . and it was there that Molly couldn't help thinking that maybe the two kissing conspirators might've gotten what they deserved.

But she decided to keep this thought to herself. They'd already been through a lot. Molly checked behind her again and caught the yellow-eyed stare of Arvin's captive.

Whatever that fat frog was thinking from inside its cage, it kept silent too.

CHAPTER 14
A DOOR OPENS

Molly was exhausted, both physically and emotionally. The full-scale frog assault had been a little more than she'd bargained for that afternoon. Not to mention the first-kiss catastrophe. How mortifying! What had Margo been thinking? Molly had wanted to talk about it. But by the time they'd gotten back to Margo's place, it hadn't felt like the right time. So Molly hadn't even bothered to stick around. Instead she had headed straight home.

After carefully parking Pink Lightning in its secret spot at the back of the carport, Molly circled around to the backyard and headed to the picnic table under the oak . . . and right beside the giant robot head that was now a permanent

Molly and the Mutants

resident. Molly wasn't sure why, but hanging out back here with this big hunk of metal always had a calming effect on her nerves. And she needed a serious dose of calming right now. She gave a few friendly taps to a rivet along the head's jawline.

The robot head always powered down when no one was around, but never actually slept. After a few moments she heard it hum to life. Her arrival had triggered its motion sensors. Molly watched its big circular eyes flicker on.

She was still shaken by getting slimed on the face by a giant frog, not to mention the encounter with whatever that other thing in the bushes was. Maybe they had imagined something. Maybe all the crud floating down the Slew had infected their brains with something that made them hallucinate? There was no way a frog could grow even bigger than the one Arvin had captured, was there?

As questions swirled in Molly's mind, Darryl sauntered out across the lawn to join her.

"Hey there, boy."

Darryl plopped down by her feet.

Molly remembered a time, not too long ago, when she would fiddle around out here for hours with just her pets and her thoughts to keep her company. That was before she'd started hanging out with Margo all the time, before she had toppled an impossibly large robot, and before her backyard had become the landing site for that impossibly large robot's noggin. It was before a lot of things had changed, maybe everything. Molly remembered she used to get so irritated when her little brother interrupted her—but now she barely saw him. And after a day like today, she kind of missed those times... even the interruptions.

Back then she would wander out to this table, and before long Crank would appear out of nowhere. Which reminded her, she hadn't seen the old tabby since this morning.

Molly looked down at Darryl. "Hey, boy, you seen your favorite cat?"

Darryl looked back at her blankly. She gave him a scratch. "Where's Crank?" she asked.

At the sound of her name, Darryl gave out three decisive barks, then stared at her intently.

"What is it, boy? Have you seen her?" Molly asked. "Where's she run off to?"

Darryl jumped up, took a few steps toward the woods behind them, and held his nose high, pointing. He let out a small whine.

Had Crank gone on one of her epic walkabouts again? In

Molly and the Mutants

the last year Molly had had to track her down twice, canvassing Far Flung Falls Drive with her brother until the cat had turned up, once as far away as Margo's house.

The memory of Margo made her mind jump back to their harrowing adventure just an hour ago in the Slew, and a terrible thought crept into her mind. She looked at Darryl, who was still facing the woods. The thought swelled into a worry:

Those frogs could easily make a meal out of a cat the size of Crank. *Oh no.*

"Crank? Are you out there?" Molly cupped her hands to her mouth as she called into the woods. "Come home!"

She waited for an answer.

"GOOD. MORNING."

The last word was punctuated by a low crackle, like the feedback you got if you stood too close to a microphone.

"Oh, hi there, robot. Haven't heard from you in a while."

"SORRY."

"Oh, it wasn't a complaint. Just..." Molly's voice trailed off. She wasn't sure what to say. Was she really talking to a robot? Or, more accurately, a robot head? And who was she truly talking to anyway? Was there something in there, something alive running through all those circuits and wires? Or was it the same as trying to have a conversation with a toaster?

Well, Molly thought, whatever the robot head was or wasn't, it might make a good listener.

"Hey, robot?"

"YES."

"Ya got a minute?"

"I. HAVE. MANY. MINUTES."

"Good."

Molly began unloading all her feelings onto her metallic friend.

"The thing about Margo is, most of the time she's a great friend. I really like hanging out with her. But then she'll do something I don't like, or that bugs me, and I wonder, is she really a friend?"

The robot gave no reply, just a low electrical hum. But that was okay. The buzzing was enough to let Molly know it was there, and listening. She moved on from her mixed feelings about Margo to the episode down by the Slew.

"I mean, Finn's got nice hair. Really nice hair. But still. I didn't really want to kiss anybody in the first place, furthest thing from my mind, actually. I just felt pressured all of a sudden, and ya know what? I mean, I think maybe Finn did too. He seemed kinda nervous. So I dunno. In a way I guess it's

Molly and the Mutants

okay that the whole thing got interrupted by a giant, disgusting frog."

Molly paused, took a breath, then said, "I just feel like I blinked and everything is different. I'm happy for my dad, but does Vilomena have to be here all the time? Same with Gunther. It's fine, I guess. It's just... different, ya know."

"I. KNOW. LIFE. CHANGES. FAST. LOOK. AT. ME."

"Let's just keep this between us, okay?"

"OF. COURSE."

"Maybe just one more thing..."

Then Molly told the robot something else. It was something she hadn't even realized herself until she said it out loud: that in the middle of all these changes and worries and strange happenings, there was a great big hole in her life where her Gruncle had been, and she worried that no matter how many new people might try to make themselves a part of her life, none of them would ever be able to make that hole feel any less empty.

While she confided these final contents of her heart, they came with a tear. Then two. And Molly started feeling a little better. It felt safe talking to the robot, like she was depositing all her worries into a big robot-head-shaped vault for safekeeping.

When she was finally done talking, Molly sniffed, stepped back, and looked at her mechanical confidant for a moment. It gave no reply, just a low electrical hum. But that was okay. Sometimes she forgot how giant it was, or how strange. Funny how things become less strange after you get used to them, no matter how unusual they are. So much had changed in her life since this enormous piece of machinery had made a home in her backyard. Maybe she had changed too. It was hard to tell.

Maybe after losing Gruncle—and her mom—she was just worried about losing anyone else in her life.

"Crank, where are you?" she whispered.

"SORRY," the robot said again.

"Thanks, robot. It's not your fault."

"SAW. CAT. LEAVE," it said.

"What?" Molly spun around. "You saw? How? When?"

"SHOW. YOU."

"But . . . I thought . . . Okay."

Molly had never considered that the robot head could actually help. But it still housed quite a bit of computing power in there. She heard a quick series of pops, followed by a short hissing sound. The door between the robot's two giant circular eyes pushed outward by a few inches, then swung straight down on invisible hinges. From the interior of the door, steps unfolded into place, turning it into a ladder.

Molly just stood there and stared. She hadn't stepped foot inside the robot since they had exited through that very same door, back when the robot was still intact. Before it had briefly gone berserk and tried to destroy them all. In fact, no one had been back inside the control room since any of that. Gunther had come by a few times to take a look, had fidgeted with a few of the exposed circuit boards where the exterior panels had been ripped away. But he had mostly left the head alone. It just didn't seem to want to open for anyone. Until now.

Before she moved, Molly looked around, suddenly worried that someone might see her. But who cared if anyone did? It was her own backyard, after all. And even though it had gone unspoken, it was understood that it was her robot head, too. She could do what she wanted.

Molly walked over to the ladder and climbed up.

Inside, the command center looked eerily similar to what she remembered from her last visit, when she'd discovered it through a secret hatch along with Wally, Arvin, and Leonard. But now it felt different, standing there alone. Wrapped around the edge of the room, a control panel held countless dials, levers, and lights. But the once-pristine walls above and below were now decorated with long streaks of black. The scorch marks emanated from every vent. They were reminders of the explosion that had separated the robot's head from its body, which remained miles away at the bottom of a marshy gorge.

Molly shuddered at the memory. If not for Gruncle, she and her friends could have wound up there too. She checked the room for any sign of activity. Random panel doors had blown off their hinges, with jumbles of tubes and wires spilling out onto the floor. Some stray cables hung from tears in the ceiling. A large, complicated-looking gyroscope dominated the middle of the room. The leather harness inside it, now empty of an operator, hung in the center.

As soon as she stepped foot on the floor, more lights flickered on. They blinked from the far side of the room.

"OVER. HERE." It was the same tinny robotic voice as before. But inside, it sounded softer.

Molly walked over to a small television screen that started to glow as she drew close. At first it was only static, but gradually the picture came into view.

"What is this?" Molly said.

The view it displayed came from a good fifteen or twenty feet off the ground. Maybe from a camera on top of the robot's head? The image was a bit grainy, but after identifying a stack

Molly and the Mutants

of wooden pallets in the corner of the screen, she could make out that it was a section of their backyard.

Molly watched for a moment, but nothing happened. She thought the image might be frozen, but then, from the side of the frame, she saw Crank slink into view. The cat paused center frame, looking up at the camera—directly at Molly—then nodded. It was like the cat knew. *But this isn't live*, Molly thought. *It has to be a recording.* The cat crept off-screen. A second later the camera angle changed, and Molly watched Crank continue down the trail, out toward the woods, until she vanished behind a clump of trees.

"Where did you run off to, girl?"

Molly knew that Crank was tough, but even she would be no match for whatever had been lurking in the bushes this afternoon. It had nearly gotten Margo—or maybe all of them, if they hadn't hustled out of there when they had. Molly looked around at the other controls.

"Robot, when was this?"

"TWO. FIFTY. EIGHT. P.M."

"Okay." Molly looked at her watch. It was 5:04. "Have you seen her since?"

"NO."

Molly imagined Crank somewhere deep in the woods, stuck up a tree, surrounded by mean, hungry monsters with long sticky tongues.

I've got to save her, Molly thought.

"Thank you, robot," she said.

"WEL. COME."

"Keep me posted on anything new."

"YOU. BET."

She poked her head back out of the opening, and saw someone waiting on her.

"Darryl!" Molly shouted. "Think it's time for another rescue?"

Darryl wagged his tail in a resounding yes.

CHAPTER 15
SOME ASSEMBLY REQUIRED

Molly clambered back down the ladder from the robot head and ran into the house.

"Dad!" she shouted. "Dad? Dad, where are—"

"Hey there, Mollz," her dad said without looking up. "Over here." He was hunched over the kitchen table, peering into the wiry insides of a mostly disassembled VCR, like a surgeon might examine the guts of a patient during an operation. He was wearing a strap around his forehead, with a little light affixed to the middle, adding to the whole look. "Perfect timing. Can you hand me the medium Phillips?"

Molly reached into her dad's open toolbox without looking. Over the years, she had pilfered enough of his tools to know each one by feel alone. Her fingers glided over the various handles, until they slid across the textured grip of the screwdriver she was looking for.

"Here ya go," Molly said.

"Thanks, superstar."

With one hand her dad was holding up a plastic cartridge, connected by a bunch of tiny wires. *The patient's heart*, Molly thought. It didn't look too dissimilar to where she'd just been, only it was much smaller. And no signs of explosions. She recognized the JVC logo on the side of the VCR. Not quite as fancy as Vandervorkel Robotics.

Her dad finally looked up, blinding her with his headlamp.

"Oh, sorry!" He flipped the light up. "Hey, ya wanna hang around and help me out? I could use a little assist—"

"Dad, I'd like to, but..." Molly hesitated. Not too long ago she would have loved more than anything else to spend time at the kitchen table with her dad, like when she was little. But between a missing Crank and something lurking in the woods, she was just too worried to think about anything else. She realized her dad was still talking.

"... doing a little freelance work for the Oberdinks. I think they're kinda hard on things, ya know? But I'll give it a try." Then he leaned over to her, cupping his hand conspiratorially.

Molly and the Mutants

"Don't tell anybody, but I'm pretty sure the *J* in *JVC* stands for *junk*." He chuckled under his breath.

Molly had heard this joke before. Every time he worked on a JVC, which was often. They had a JVC too. Probably because they were way cheaper than a Sony. Theirs was tucked away in their TV stand. But her dad always said one day they'd buy Sony-brand everything.

"Dad, I can't help. Crank's missing!"

"Honey, you sure?" He looked up at her. "You know how Crank is. She kinda likes to keep to herself sometimes. Most times, actually."

"Nobody's seen her for hours, Dad. The robot head just showed me some footage, and—"

"What?" Molly's dad dropped the Phillips. "The robot head? Since when is—"

"Since today, I guess. It invited me inside, so I took a look."

"Okaaay." Her dad paused. "It did, huh?" He looked toward the back door, like maybe he was waiting for the robot to speak up from the backyard and corroborate this.

"Dad?" Molly said.

"Well, maybe we should make some flyers, post 'em around the neighborhood. You know, like people do when their cat goes missing. Somebody's bound to spot her, right?"

"No, Dad. I'm pretty sure she wandered off into the woods. I don't think flyers are gonna help when she's out there." She pointed out back with her thumb.

"Hmmm," he said.

"Plus, Dad? I think there's ... something else out there."

"Something else? Like what? Did Gunther make another giant robot? If he let another one of those loose in the hills, I will be having a talk with his mother!"

"No, no, Dad, not a robot. Something *else* else."

"Like what?"

"Well, Arvin caught a really big bullfrog out by the Slew this afternoon."

"Oh. Yeah, they can get hefty, those guys. Up to a pound sometimes." He was back at work. "But I'm pretty sure Crank can take care of herself. Especially around some frogs. Bullfrogs have been known to eat small mice, maybe, even other frogs if they're hungry enough, but a cat as big as Crank? I mean, she's gotta be pushing, what, twenty pounds, right?"

It was true. Crank was very large for a house cat, if you could even call her that. Years ago, when she was more orange than gray, neighbors sometimes mistook her for a red fox or some other critter when she came slinking through the backyard on one of her hunts.

Molly and the Mutants

Molly thought about the other creature in the bushes, the one they didn't really get a good look at but that might be much bigger. Then her mind flashed back to the look on Ronda's face this morning after she'd nearly crashed their bus. And before that she was sure she'd caught sight of something in her periscope—it was like the ridge had somehow moved. How did she share this with her dad without it all sounding... crazy?

"I think there was something else too, something even bigger."

"Hmm. Like how big? Bigger than Darryl?"

Molly remembered the giant frog tongue shooting out from the shadows and making Margo fall into the creek.

"Bigger."

"Bigger than... *me*?" Her dad tapped his fingers against his chest.

Molly nodded. Her dad raised an eyebrow. "Bigger than me," he repeated, the incredulity clear in his tone. Her dad was six-foot-four, at least two hundred fifty pounds, maybe more. "You sure? That'd be like a frog-a-saurus, ha! You guys didn't build a time machine, didja?"

Her dad's joke made her wonder. Could she be wrong? Could they have all imagined something? There were lots of shadows around that section of the Slew. And they hadn't actually seen where or what the tongue had come from. Maybe it hadn't even been a tongue. Maybe it had been a stray branch, or a falling vine? All of a sudden Molly felt less than certain.

"I'm not sure what it was, Dad," Molly said. "All I am sure about is that I'm worried about Crank. And nobody's seen her in a while."

Molly's dad slipped a finger into the open cavity of the VCR, fished around, then finally retrieved a stray wire and reconnected it with all the others. "There we go. Back where you belong."

Just then Molly remembered something else.

"Hey, Dad, have you heard Houdini's gone missing too?"

"Yeah?" her dad said.

"Yeah. And maybe a few other animals."

"Huh. It's a little early for coyotes. People might just be getting careless, sweetie."

Molly thought back to what Officer Wasserbaum had said. She still couldn't imagine there could be some secret cult of devil worshippers in their neighborhood, skulking around at night, sacrificing their neighbors' pets to Ozzy Osborne, or KISS....

Molly pictured Leonard and Arvin pledging allegiance to

Molly and the Mutants

the Prince of Darkness, and swallowed at the thought.

Her dad sat and thought a minute. He popped the cartridge back into place and set both hands on the table, showing Molly he was giving her his full attention.

"Tell ya what, Mollz. There's not much sun left today, but if Crank doesn't turn up tonight, why dontcha get a few of your friends together after school tomorrow. You can circle around the bike trails, make sure she didn't get lost out there."

"Okay," Molly said.

"And stay in a group, to keep safe from the frog monsters." He bugged out his eyes and stuck out his tongue, in what Molly figured was his best frog impression. She smiled.

"Ribbit, ribbit," he croaked.

Molly started laughing just as Wally popped his head through the doorway.

"Frog monsters? Cool," he said. "Can Gunther and I come too?"

Molly and her dad spun around.

"Um, sure," Molly said.

"Where'd you come from?" their Dad asked.

"Just got home," Wally said. "From Gunther's house. Is dinner ready?"

"Oh yeah, dinner . . . Haven't got to that yet, buddy." Their dad looked down at the VCR parts that still needed to be put back together. "I'll letcha know."

"Okay," Wally said. And his head disappeared.

"That brother of yours," Molly's dad said, shaking his head. "He just pops outta nowhere!" He furrowed his brow. "Wait, what was I saying?"

"Keep safe from the frog monsters," Molly recited.

"Right, right," he said. "And keep an eye on Wallz for me."

"Okay, Dad."

"In the meantime," her dad said, "I'll make some calls to the neighbors—since we actually have a working telephone!" He was still very proud that he'd been paying the phone bill. Molly hadn't seen a disconnection notice or a past due letter in months.

"If anyone has spotted our wanderer, you'll be the first to know. I'll keep watch here."

Having a plan made Molly feel better. They both sat in silence for a moment.

"Okay, then," he said.

"Okay, then," she said.

"Hey, Dad?" she said.

"Yeah, sweetheart?"

Molly and the Mutants

"How old were you the first time you ... kissed a girl ... on the lips?"

At the mention of kissing, her dad's hands twitched, knocking the VCR. It bumped a pile of tiny nuts and bolts off the table and sent them skittering across the linoleum floor. He laid his palms on the table and took a breath.

"On the lips, huh?" her dad said, meeting her eye. "I see you saved the scariest part for last."

Part II

DOWNHILL

CHAPTER 16
AOIFE! AOIFE!

Crank continued on her quest. This was starting to feel fun.

She had spent the night safe and dry, nestled in the crook of a towering black walnut tree. The sheer size of it had made her feel like a kitten again. But her joints reminded her that that had been a long, long time ago.

Crank licked her lips. Breakfast had been a simple but joyful affair. A small field mouse had suffered the misfortune of traveling onto her path. It had practically knocked on her front door and served itself up. She had made quick work of it, never one to play with her food. Unlike some other cats she'd observed in her life. That was just cruel and unnecessary. But

Molly and the Mutants

she wasn't apologetic about her hunger or her habits. The littler things were eaten by the bigger things. And the bigger things were eaten by even bigger things yet. And on and on it went. That was just how the world had always worked. It was true in this life, and every life before it.

Crank washed her breakfast down with several draws of fresh morning dew, which had conveniently collected in the cupped curves of several nearby leaves while she had slept. Things were going her way.

Satisfied, she descended into the first of many ravines. The temperature dropped by a degree or two, but she kept moving so she wouldn't feel the chill of it.

Silently, expertly, Crank made her way back up the other side of the dip and continued her journey. Here and there golden beams of sunlight punched through the layers of leaves above her. She made a game of batting the bright little pillars with her paw and watching the motes inside them swirl.

After an hour or two, or three (she wasn't really keeping track), the terrain went from up-and-down to just down. And farther down still. Here, at these lower depths, it was harder to keep her paws dry. The soft squish underfoot brought back another memory from her youth....

Crank had been the youngest and smallest in her litter

before Caroline's then-teenage hands had reached in and lifted her out from the box that up until then had been her world. That had been nearly fifteen years ago, which she had to admit was a good stretch for an ol' tabby cat like herself.

For the first few years it had been mostly just the two of them. And when Stanley had come into their lives, Crank had known it wouldn't be forever. She knew Caroline wasn't really made for long-term relationships. Crank may have been the only one who wasn't surprised when Molly's mom left in that Wizard Wheels van a couple of years ago. But the cat could forgive Caroline for that, since Caroline had been the one who'd brought Molly into Crank's life.

And also, because Crank was leaving now in the same way. Slipping off without a word of explanation. Forgiveness always came a little more easily when you were guilty of the same sin yourself. She hoped Molly would understand.

The cat stopped on a slanted log to stretch and think, to ponder her next move.

Since the day Molly was born, she had been Crank's favorite human. Crank could picture her now, just as clearly as if Molly were standing in front of her. Crank made an inventory of every detail she knew about the girl's face. The smattering of freckles, the wide brow, the bright, curious eyes ... As she did, Crank felt a deep throb pulse at the back of her brain, expanding until it enveloped her entire head. The sensation didn't quite qualify as pain, not exactly. But it was enough to command her full attention.

Her body went still there on the felled tree. But at the same time, inexplicably, she felt herself traveling an impossible distance. The picture she was holding in her mind's eye pressed into itself again and again, then stretched out beyond the horizon.

Crank felt herself transported to another land....

Another life...

Another... *Molly?*

...

"Aoife! Aoife!"

Crank found herself perched on the edge of a large, damp stone, overlooking a brook. Crystal-clear water rushed under her nose, its icy spray tickling her whiskers.

"Ja! Sealgair bhig! G'un deònaicheadh na diathan deagh fhortun dhut!"

Crank turned her head in the direction of the strange guttural sounds.

Standing just a few feet away, a girl was speaking to her. At least that's what she appeared to be doing. Crank couldn't understand any of it. The girl had Molly's face—same freckles, same friendly expression, same sparkle to her eyes—only, she wasn't Molly. No, this one spoke from a place deeper in her throat than the Molly she knew. And she smelled more like... the earth. Crank sniffed the air. Peat and moss, with some notes of campfire smoke... oh, and ripe onion. She crinkled her nose.

Who was this imposter?

She had Molly's red hair, but it was all woven together in the most elaborate of braids, like a pile of coiled rope. And a bright blue stripe of paint ran from the girl's bottom lip to the underside of her chin. She wore a coarse-looking tunic with a shiny brooch fastened just below the left shoulder. Like the girl's hair, the ornament was made of an intricate knot that turned back in on itself in a continuous loop. Something about the way it caught the light felt almost familiar....

As Crank tried to make sense of what she was seeing, the girl's mouth split into a broad grin, making tiny cracks in the paint below it.

"Aoife!" the girl repeated.

Who was this Aoife? Or what? To her cat ears it sounded like "eee-faah." It wasn't a sound she could recall hearing any of the humans around her make... at least not in a long, long time. The girl reached into a woven basket and threw something her way.

Molly and the Mutants

With a loud squish it landed at her paws, and flopped frantically on the rock. Crank jumped backward.

It was a silvery fish—a live one.

"Ithe!" the girl said, laughing.

Crank pounced and tried to hold the wiggling fish in place. It was incredibly slippery, but she managed.

"Tha, Aoifa, ithe!" the girl insisted.

Crank took a bite, and the wiggling stopped. Oh, this was heavenly. Invigorated, she took another bite, and another. After the cat got her fill, she looked back up and realized with a newfound clarity that she had indeed been here before, that she knew this place, this brook, this girl. And deep in her bones, Crank knew that she loved the girl, and that this girl loved her back. Over and over they had looked out for each other. And she knew that this girl with plaited hair and a painted chin wasn't Molly... but also, that she was. That she and Molly had known each other for much longer—generations longer, in fact—than the story of any single life could contain.

And as this truth washed over her, Crank knew she didn't ever want to leave this rock. She wanted to stay here forever, over this brook, dining on fish, listening to the sweet, throaty sounds of this girl who looked just like Molly. Crank wanted to stay in this moment.

But a breath later it dawned on her that this moment had already long passed, that it belonged to another life, one that had already been lived. And gradually the babbling brook grew more muffled, and the girl who looked like Molly began to fade, and the scene before her stretched away until it was gone from view.....

. . .

Crank was back on the fallen log again.

A faint scuffle below her had pulled her out of the memory and back to the present, back to her body. Her claws had sunk even deeper into the old log's bark. Gradually the pressure that had gripped her skull ebbed away, and Crank craned her head a little to the left to catch a better view of what was happening below. A scritch-scratch. The snap of a twig. She spotted a pair of redheaded skinks, both looking very furtive. Instinctively the lizards froze in place. They hadn't seen the cat directly above them but probably sensed danger. An alarm in the back of their tiny reptilian brains was ringing. No doubt they would be tasty, but Crank was already satiated. She let the lizards carry on, unaware of just how lucky they were.

Maybe the same was true for her, Crank mused. Maybe she was much luckier than she realized. She climbed down, the memory of the girl who had been the spitting image of Molly still clinging to her like a warm blanket. It felt good, but at the

Molly and the Mutants

same time it made her feel a little torn. At the outset of this quest, Crank had felt so certain. But now, still weaving her way through the foliage, she questioned her resolve. Maybe this wasn't the time for a final hunt, or a final anything. Maybe it wasn't time to say goodbye to the human she felt bound to across time and across lives. Maybe it never would be.

Crank searched her surroundings for a sign, for some confirmation she was on the right path, that her dear Molly would be okay without her. That she'd understand. But the forest gave no clue. Instead the only answer came from within—in the form of a familiar dull throb at the back of her skull. *Ah yes,* she thought, *that's it right there. Some choices are made for you.* So Crank carried on. Soundlessly she passed a family of shrews. She passed a lone garter snake, a pair of voles, and a small party of robins....

For a veteran hunter like herself, the entire forest was one big snack bar if you knew where to look.

But somehow the sweet taste of that silvery river fish still lingered in her mouth and kept her content. So she ignored them all, however loud, or clumsy, or easy they might have been to claim. Besides, something else had grabbed the attention of her nose. It was just a whiff. But the more Crank's head cleared from the fog of the memory, the harder it was to ignore. There, rising up within the menagerie of scents from every little thing that scurried across the forest floor, there was a distinct undercurrent. Something wondrous and new. Something dangerous. The smell was faint but persistent. Rich and murky. It called to her from somewhere deeper in the woods.

Whatever this scent belonged to, Crank was certain it promised to be much more than a snack. She ventured farther downhill, the echoes of "Aoife! Aoife!" growing softer with each step.

CHAPTER 17
SWEAR FEST

Another school day had dragged on. When the last bell had rung, Molly had been the first out the door. At least it was Friday.

Sitting in the back row of the Number 42 bus, Molly pressed her head against the cool of the window as the vehicle's ancient engine cranked back up to life. The glass was smeared with greasy buildup from a million handprints, distorting her view. It made the teachers directing traffic outside look more like human-shaped blurs than people. They'd be making sure everyone had found where they needed to go, especially the younger ones. Another bell rang, and the last of the munchkins filed in, taking their seats up front. A minute later the decrepit bus lurched into motion.

Molly checked her Casio watch. Right on time. She'd be home in thirty-nine minutes, give or take a few seconds. The last stop on the route.

It was midafternoon, so the fog had thinned a little. But not entirely. Overhead the sun wasn't much more than a milky glow behind a curtain of gray.

"TGIF," a voice next to her said.

Molly turned from the window to see Margo. Lost in her own thoughts, Molly hadn't even noticed that her friend had sat down next to her.

"Yeah," Molly said, making an effort to smile.

As Number 42 pulled out onto the street—and more important, out of earshot of any other grown-ups—the speakers Ronda had installed crackled to life with the first song on her playlist. Ronda was starting with a softer tune than usual, which matched Molly's mood perfectly. How did she always know?

Gentle guitar licks filled the bus. Then a voice that Molly couldn't quite place until the song reached the chorus...

We're back on the train, yeah...

Oh, back on the chain gang...

Molly and the Mutants

Back on the chain gang. That sounded about right to Molly. It was the Pretenders, one of Ronda's go-to bands. At the beginning of the year, Ronda had revealed to Molly that their lead singer, Chrissie Hynde, was an Ohio girl, born in Akron. Until then Molly had had no idea rock stars could come from Ohio. But they had to come from somewhere, right?

Ronda had even met Chrissie one time, at a concert up in Cleveland. Even though the connection to Molly was once-removed, it almost made her feel like she knew the singer too.

What was the word for this song? Melancholy. That was it. Different from sadness. Just right for a bus ride back home on a dreary day, when your cat was missing.

They passed the Far Flung Falls cemetery, which butted up to the edge of the road. Some of the headstones were so close, Molly bet she could reach out and touch them if her window were down. She counted row after row of grave markers, of all shapes and sizes, gradually disappearing into the gloom. Many of them were more than a hundred years old, Molly remembered from a field trip. Residents who had died before the turn of the century, long before she was born. Most of these older ones were leaning at odd angles or starting to crumble.

One gravestone pointed upward at the corners, like cat

ears. It made her think of Crank again. Maybe she was out there somewhere, wandering around? Molly watched a little more closely, trying to discern any movement in the fog. There were plenty of crosses and spires. But some of the headstones had more unique shapes. There were statues of angels and animals. And others were just geometric shapes. One in the distance looked like a big half circle, only a little lumpier. It almost resembled a...

The gravestone... bounced.

Molly's eyes nearly popped out of her head and hit the window. Gravestones weren't supposed to bounce like that. They weren't supposed to bounce at all. She tried to find it again, but the bus was moving at such a fast clip now, it was hard to tell. Molly looked around to see if anyone else had noticed. Everyone was too busy talking. Margo was the first to catch her expression.

"Molly?" Margo asked. "You all right? Hey, about yesterday... I didn't mean for—"

"Did you see that?" Molly blurted.

"Oh?" Margo looked relieved. "See what?"

Molly searched again, but the headstone was gone.

"Wait. It was just...," Molly said. "Never mind."

Molly and the Mutants

They passed the end of the cemetery, and Ronda's playlist had moved on from the Pretenders to the Eurythmics. Annie Lennox was crooning.

Sweet dreams are made of this...

Who am I to disagree?...

It was a catchy tune.

Maybe Molly had just dreamed that she saw something in the cemetery?

"You're worried about Crank, huh?" Margo said, knitting her eyebrows in an unusual show of concern. "Don't worry, we'll find her."

Molly had mentioned the rescue plan to her earlier that day, and Margo had quickly gotten the whole gang excited about it. Maybe she had been motivated by guilt from the previous day, but Molly didn't mind. Leonard, Arvin, and Finn had all agreed to help. Wally and Gunther were going to join too.

"Thanks," Molly finally said. "Hey, you doing okay? I mean, after yesterday and all?"

"Yeah, I guess," Margo said. "Just mad I fell in, is all. Totally shoulda made that jump. And those Reeboks were brand-new. What am I gonna do with one shoe!"

"Bummer," Molly said.

"Yeah," Margo said, before lowering her voice. "Hey, whaddya think it was that took it?"

"I dunno," Molly whispered back. "But I have a feeling we're gonna find out."

Across the aisle Arvin was doing an impression of Officer Wasserbaum from yesterday's assembly, and everyone was cracking up.

Molly laughed too. It was hard not to. Arvin had it down. He even pulled his eyelid down in that weird way. She felt her mood lighten just a little. She nodded her head along to the song, let the steady beat of the synthesizer pull her out of the melancholy she'd been feeling. She felt grateful to have Ronda for a bus driver.

Molly wondered what Ronda must have been like when she was a fifth grader, what she would've thought about the assembly with Officer Wasserbaum and President Tipper and their SAFER pins. Ronda probably would've just snuck out the back of the gym or something. Molly bet she'd already been smoking cigarettes by then. Sometimes Molly wished she could be more like Ronda, and not care what other people thought about her. She had heard rumors that Ronda had gone off to college for a year, dropped out, then hitchhiked across the country with an all-girl punk band. Had maybe even gotten arrested once. It sounded too crazy to be true. But maybe not.

A worry crept into Molly's mind. There was no way Ronda could be mixed up with those missing animals, could she? Could girl-band punk rockers be in cahoots with the devil too? Molly saw the back of Ronda's head up at the front of the bus. Her teased-out hair was extra tall today.

Naw, Molly thought. *Ronda was just Ronda.* As if in response to this thought, the next song blasted its way through the speakers and into the bus. It was loud, and fast, and not parent-approved. Joan Jett and the Blackhearts.

Idontgiveadamnaboutmybadreputation

She spit out the lyrics so fast that it took the bus a moment to register what they'd heard. The next time Joan Jett said the d-word, everyone spontaneously broke into a howling "Ooo-oooooooo," like when somebody got called to the principal's office.

As soon as Ronda realized what was happening, she solved the problem by honking the horn every time the cuss word came up, to cover the sound.

I don't give a—BEEEEEP—about my bad reputation...

As a form of impromptu censorship, it left something to be desired. All the kids could still hear the word. Instead it felt like Ronda had joined the band, with the bus as her instrument.

Beep-beep-beep. Everyone was having a great time, laughing and singing along—even the cuss word.

Ronda tried a new approach. When the d-word came up, she turned the volume down. But in the vacuum, all you could hear was the kids singing along.

Even the munchkins were swearing now. It became a total swear fest. They were cheering Ronda... and Joan Jett... and swearing.

"Ronda is the raddest!"

"Yeah, she don't care about nuthin'!"

"Um, I don't think we should cuss," Finn whispered from the back row. "We might get in troub—"

"Whaddya mean, Finn?" Arvin asked. "*Damn* is a totally okay word. It's in the Bible. Just like *Jesus*. And *hell*."

"Arvin!" Margo squealed.

"Trust me, it's true. I should know," Arvin said. "I've spent, like, a zillion hours in Bible study. They're *all* in there."

"Well, I know they're in the Bi—" Finn said.

"The *real* bad words are the ones that *aren't* in the Bible," Arvin explained. He lowered his voice. "Like the s-word... and the f-word."

"Like... *f-fart?*" Finn asked.

Molly and the Mutants

"Ha! You said *fart!*" a munchkin screamed from a few rows ahead of them.

"Um, worse than *fart*," Arvin said.

"Worse!" Finn's voice cracked, incredulous at the assertion.

In fairness, Finn was a Mormon. Which meant he'd probably spent even more time in Bible study than Arvin. Mormons were always at church. And Molly had heard that they weren't allowed to do anything, even the grown-up ones. They couldn't swear, or see R-rated movies, or wear tank tops in the summer, or even drink Coca-Cola. There were only two Mormon families that Molly knew in Far Flung Falls, but they were both really large. Finn had something like ten brothers and sisters.

"Fart! Fart! Fart! Fart!" The munchkins were chanting it now, whipping themselves into a joyous fart-filled frenzy. Kids were falling out of their seats.

"Okay, I get it!" Finn said.

"I'm just saying...," Arvin said.

Molly was only half listening to the debate. Or the chanting of FART-FART-FART-FART. It all fell away to background noise. Instead all she could hear was the song. It was like Joan Jett and the Blackhearts were talking just to her, delivering a truth directly to her soul. She looked up and caught Ronda's eye in the giant rearview mirror tilted over her head. Was that a smile? She smiled back.

And in that exchange, in the middle of all that chaos, Molly felt for a moment like it was just the three of them on that bus: her, Ronda, and Joan Jett—each with their own reputation. Molly thought about her own, and realized it was the reputation of someone who, even against steep odds, came to the rescue. With each drumbeat she felt her confidence grow. Molly was going to find Crank—no matter what was out there lurking in the woods.

The song was fading, and Molly noticed that the chanting had changed. Now it was being directed a Carter Wilkerson, a shy third grader sitting a few rows ahead. Somebody had figured out that *Carter* rhymes with *farter*.

"Carter is a farter! Carter is a farter!"

More were joining in. Carter slumped deeper into his seat.

The chanting triggered a memory in Molly. A kind of pain she wasn't about to let anyone else feel, not while she was around. She jumped up.

"Hey! Knock it off!" she yelled from the back. Her voice came out much louder than she'd expected.

Immediately the chanting stopped and the bus grew quiet. Through the speakers Stevie Nicks sang.

Molly and the Mutants

Stand back, stand back...

Carter un-slumped just enough to look back at her over the seat. His expression was something between gratitude and surprise.

Molly was surprised too.

CHAPTER 18
DOGHOUSE

"Hey, what's that?" Arvin asked.

Molly caught the unmistakable alternating red and blue flash of a police car up ahead. She craned her neck to see what was happening. They were on the last stretch of Far Flung Falls Drive, with just three stops to go.

"Hey, Arvin," Leonard said. "I think it's parked right outside of your house!"

It was.

Ronda cut the music as they approached the scene. There were only six kids left on the bus, and they were all pressing their faces up against the windows to see what was happening. Molly saw Arvin's mom talking to Officer Wasserbaum. He had a furrowed brow, and a notepad in his hand, where he was writing things down.

Number 42 stopped behind the squad car, and Ronda opened the door.

"Officer Wasserbaum," Ronda said. "Everything okay?"

"Hello, Ronda," Wasserbaum said. Not unfriendly, but not friendly either. "Still collecting some information. Looks like we've had some hooliganism here."

"Hmm. I didn't think we had any hooligans here in the fine city of Far Flung Falls," Ronda said.

"Oh, you'd be surprised," Wasserbaum said.

Arvin and his two sisters exited the bus and looked at their mom. Margo was right behind them.

"Whatever it was," Arvin said, "wasn't me."

"Me neither," the sisters said in unison.

"Oh, I know, babies, I know. Happened while you were all at school. Wait, you *were* at school, right?" Arvin's mom paused to eye her children carefully. "Okay, then. Well, it was the strangest thing! Someone... or something... wrecked our doghouse! Busted up some of the fence too."

"Hooligans...," Wasserbaum mumbled.

"But! Is Fifi—?" Arvin couldn't finish.

"Oh, Fifi's just fine," his mom said. "She came tearing in

through the doggie door like her butt was on fire. Something spooked her for sure. When I came out, the doghouse was smashed to pieces."

Wasserbaum scribbled a little more in his notebook.

Just then Fifi came up to the officer and sniffed around his leg. Massive and muscular, with a wide square jaw, the dog looked like anything but a *Fifi*. It was hard to imagine her getting spooked by anything, except maybe a *Tyrannosaurus rex*.

Molly and Leonard were still on the bus. They opened their windows.

"Crazy," Leonard called down from above.

"But glad Fifi's okay," Molly called from the next window over.

"Me too," Arvin said. "She never stays in that doghouse anyway.... That's why I put my science project in there...."

Arvin stopped talking. His demeanor suddenly changed, all the blood draining from his face. "Wait! My science project!"

"Arvin, what are you talking ab—" Leonard tried to ask.

But he was already running around the house to their backyard. Now it was like *his* butt was on fire. Wasserbaum looked up from his notes.

"Hey! Don't disturb my crime scene!" he called, but Arvin

Molly and the Mutants

was already out of sight. A moment later Molly heard him yelling, "Nooooo! No! No! No!"

Arvin came back around to the front of the house, shoulders slumped. He was holding a mangled wire cage. It was empty.

"What's wrong?" Margo asked.

"He's go-o-o-o-o-one," Arvin moaned.

"Who's gone?" his mom asked.

"Mr. Froggerton. My amazing best-ever science project," he said. "You said I couldn't keep him inside...."

"Oh, *that*! So you turned our doghouse into a *frog*house...," his mom said. She let out a long sigh.

"I figured he'd be safe in there...."

"Hmmm. Another missing animal," Wasserbaum muttered.

"*Mr. Froggerton?*" Leonard asked.

Arvin looked up at Molly.

"Sorry about your frog," she said, trying to keep her voice calm and measured in front of the adults. But Molly's mind was racing. If frogs weren't even safe on their street, then what about Crank? The missing pets and giant frogs had to be connected—but how? Molly turned to Leonard.

"We need to get to the bottom of this," Leonard whispered, reading her mind.

"Yeah," Arvin agreed.

"Okay," Molly whispered. "Meet at my house in an hour?"

Leonard nodded. Arvin looked up at her.

"Definitely," he said.

"Okay," Margo said.

Number 42 pulled away. Molly and Leonard, the only two passengers left, rode in thoughtful silence until he got off at the next stop.

"Later," he said.

"Later, Leonard."

Molly was the last one. She always enjoyed this final stretch of the bus ride to her stop, with just her, Ronda, and whatever tunes she decided to play. Molly came up and sat in the front-row seat.

Ronda looked over her shoulder. Her earrings jingled.

"Hey, Crusher," Ronda said. "Strange times..."

Another track from the Pretenders came on. Chrissie Hynde was singing:

I went back to Ohio...

But my city was gone...

"See?" Ronda said. "Remember what I told ya?" She pointed to the speakers overhead. "Ohio girl."

"Yeah, I remember. Pretty cool."

"Yeah," Ronda said. "Ohio girls. By the way, good job back there today."

"What'd I do?"

"You shut down that 'Carter farter' nonsense."

"Oh, *that*."

"Yeah, that." Ronda looked up and caught her eye in the big rearview mirror. "It's what leaders do."

CHAPTER 19
SEARCH PARTY

"**R**eady?" Molly asked.

Everyone around her nodded. They were all gathered in a circle on their bikes. Arvin, Margo, Leonard, and Finn. Molly looked at their faces, Ronda's words on the bus still echoing in her head. Was this what leaders did too? Bring your friends along on a quest in the woods to find a missing cat... and maybe solve a mystery?

Darryl popped his head into the circle and barked.

"Sorry, Darryl, boy." Molly gave the dog's head a good scratch. "Too many pets already missing. I'd love your help, but can't risk it."

Molly and the Mutants

Darryl gave a single bark of protest, then slowly retreated back to the house.

Under their feet a busy mole had left a trail of raised earth that wound its way between their bicycles and across Molly's backyard toward the woods. For a moment Molly wished cats were as easy to track as moles.

"What if we run into . . . you know what?" Leonard asked. His eyes darted from side to side, as if the *you-know-what* might hear him and attack.

"Yeah," Margo said. "I can't lose another shoe. My mom'll kill me . . . twice."

"You still look pretty alive to me," Arvin said.

"We're gonna keep to the trails," Molly said. "And we'll stay together. So we'll be fine. And if anything comes up . . . I've got this."

Molly turned at the waist to reveal the strange contraption strapped to her back.

"What is *that*?" Leonard asked.

"Oh no. That thing almost killed me . . . twice," Arvin said, recognizing it immediately.

It was her Gruncle's Zap-O-Matic. Sneaking it out of the house undetected had required speed, precision timing, and patience, waiting for her dad to use the bathroom so she could hustle it out the door and deposit it outside. (Gruncle's design had made it too cumbersome to simply slip out the window without causing a ruckus.) Molly flipped a switch, and the machine hummed to life. She reached back over her shoulder to unholster the elongated barrel. It looked like some prop for a sci-fi movie.

"How'd you get that?" Arvin said. "Did you inherit it? . . . Or steal it?"

"Well . . . ," Molly said. "Maybe a little of both."

She related the "keepsake" trip she'd taken to her Gruncle's cabin with her dad and brother, how she had left a window cracked before they'd locked up, then gone back for the Zap-O-Matic on her own.

"So you definitely took more than one keepsake," Margo said.

"Yeah, plus, that thing should count for, like, three!" Finn said.

"That's cool. I feel a little safer if you're packing a froggy fryer, just in case we run into any trouble," Leonard said.

"I'm not *frying* anything today. Got it on half power. See?"

"Aye, aye, captain. Set phasers to stun," Arvin said, quoting a line from *Star Trek*.

"Also . . . I brought this too," Leonard said. "Just in case."

Molly and the Mutants

Leonard slipped his left hand into the metal wrist rocket dangling from his handlebars. As he gripped it, the camo brace hugged his skinny forearm. This was a much more serious weapon than the simple wooden slingshot he'd had in his pocket yesterday. With his other arm he reached into the backpack behind him and retrieved a small round object. It was dark brown, marked with a light brown circle—like an eye.

"Buckeyes," he said, patting his pack full of the hard inedible nuts.

Leonard notched the buckeye, stretched out his arm, and drew back the band until it nearly touched his eye. "The dummy o'er yonder, in the schnoz," he called, indicating the old Evil Wizard target from last summer. *Fwing.* Molly and the others watched as the projectile nut shot across the backyard and smashed into the plastic mannequin's face. *Wham.* The Evil Wizard tumbled over. Molly couldn't help but smile.

"Diiii-rect hit," Arvin said. "Rad."

"All we're missing now is a grenade launcher," Finn said.

"Let's go find Crank!" Margo said.

"Hey, I thought Gunther and Wally were joining us," Leonard said.

Molly hadn't seen them since school, and daylight was burning.

"They told me they were coming," Margo said.

"Probably forgot."

"I saw their bikes in the driveway," Leonard said. "Which means—"

"They're racing around underground somewhere," Arvin said. "Like a couple of moles."

"Well," Molly announced. "We need to get going. If they want to help, they can catch up."

And just like that, the five of them were off. Molly was happy Leonard had showed up. Otherwise this rescue mission would probably feel like another awkward double date Margo had schemed up. And after that kissing debacle with the bullfrog, Molly was ready to put all that business on permanent hold. Molly thought Finn was nice, or at least he had nice-looking hair. But that was about it.

Molly took the lead around the outer edge of the yard, all the way to the back, where a small path met up with one of the larger, well-worn trails. It was the very same route she'd taken on her quest to save Wally just a few months ago. That had started as a solo trip, unless you counted her animal companions, which at the time might've counted for her closest friends. But now she felt a little more connected to some of the humans in her life. And it wasn't a bad feeling. Nothing against dogs, or chameleons, or armadillos, but hanging around other people had its advantages.

The trail curved to the right and descended. They all picked up speed.

"Keep your eyes peeled," Molly called over her shoulder.

The group pedaled onward, hill after hill, scanning the woods for anything out of the ordinary. Mostly they were quiet, but occasionally one of them would call out for Crank.

"Wait, I see something," Finn said.

They all braked and looked in the same direction as Finn.

"What is it?" Molly said. "Is it Crank?"

"It's something... weird," Finn said, pointing to the right.

They turned off trail and headed down a bumpy slope in the terrain, weaving in and out of a cluster of trees that curled in strange directions, like you were looking at them through a fun-house mirror. The ground held more moisture here from the previous night's rain, so their tires sunk a little deeper into the damp ground, leaving clear lines that connected them back to the trail uphill. Like mole tracks in reverse. Molly breathed in through her nose. She liked the rich, peaty smell of the wet earth when she traveled deeper into the woods. The crisp aroma of younger plants mixed with the sweet decay of older ones. It felt like a spot Crank would like too.

There was something bright ahead. Could it be?

"Craaa-ank!" she called. "Is that you? It's me, Molly."

"Crank!" the others called.

Arvin was in the lead and stopped right in front of the thing, blocking everyone else's view. Molly heard him say, "Oh."

"Is it Crank?"

"Well, only if she magically transformed into a fungus."

Molly pulled up beside Arvin to see for herself. It was a big cluster of shelf mushrooms. There were layers upon layers of them, in thick ruffly ribbons, piling themselves up around the bottom of a giant walnut tree. One of the ribbons curled up to almost resemble a cat's tail. The brightness of their color, a deep yellowish orange that gradually faded to white around the edges, struck a hard contrast to all the dark greens, browns, and grays of the landscape around them.

"My dad calls those chicken mushrooms," Leonard said.

"*Chicken* mushrooms? As in 'bawk, bawk'?" Margo asked.

"They look more like clouds than chickens," Finn said.

"They look grody," Margo said, crinkling her nose.

"M'mm, m'mm," Arvin said, leaning in like he was about to take a bite.

"Arvin, don't!" Margo said. "Seriously."

Molly and the Mutants

"I ain't chicken of no mushroom," Arvin teased, his mouth just inches away from the fungal growth.

"You should be," Leonard said. "One bite will probably turn you into a frog."

"Or worse," said Finn.

"Like a bog monster," Margo said.

"Okay, okay—" Arvin said. He pulled away.

Molly slumped on her banana seat. She looked back up and scanned the area, hoping for a sign, anything that might give a clue that Crank had been here. Just then she started to notice other patches of mushrooms farther down the slope. Clusters of little cream-colored caps. The ground got progressively wetter as they descended, with water pooling in this dip of earth before the roots could absorb all the moisture.

"Wait, I see something else, down by those rocks," Finn said, pulling her from her thoughts. He pushed off and weaved through more trees as he tore farther down the hill. The mud splattered up behind him in a spectacular arc, like the dorsal fin of some mammoth subterranean creature trailing right behind him. It made for quite a sight. Leonard noticed it too.

"Hey, Finn's got a fin," he said.

"He probably just sees more mushrooms," Arvin said.

Finn stopped. The imaginary mud monster behind him immediately vanished.

"Hey, come look at this!" Finn said.

Molly and the others took off after him, kicking up their own sprays of mud. They all stopped and stared at what was definitely not mushrooms. Or a cat.

It was a pile of bones.

CHAPTER 20
THE BONEYARD

"It's a... a skeleton!" Margo screamed.

Margo started hyperventilating, her rapid breaths the only sound anyone heard for a few moments, highlighting just how remote a spot they'd already traveled to in the woods.

"Don't worry, Margo, it wasn't a person. Look." Arvin pointed to the skull, which had an elongated snout. "This didn't belong to a human. At least not one that any of us would recognize."

They all stared at the pile. It was like the bones had been dumped out of a bag.

"Arvin's right," Finn said, poking the pile with his finger. "Look, it's a hoof."

All at once it occurred to Molly what—or who—they were looking at.

"Houdini," she said.

"Who's... *dini*?" Finn asked. He was the only one from their gang who didn't live on the same street of the semi-famous pig.

"Not 'who's dini,'" Molly said. "*Houdini.* You know, like the legendary escape artist? That's what the Ostranders' named him. He was their prize pig."

"The truck jumper?" Arvin said. "Yeah, I heard about him."

"I heard he could escape anything," Margo said.

"Well, everything except . . . whatever did this." Leonard sounded like something was caught in his throat. Molly looked his way. Was that a tear?

"Maybe he died of natural causes," Finn said.

"If you died of natural causes, do you think we'd find your bones all stacked in a pile like this out in the woods?" Margo asked.

"Then who would've done such a thing?" Leonard asked, his voice still a little strained.

"Um, somebody hungry? Duh," Arvin said.

Molly liked this theory a lot better than some sacrifice by devil worshipers.

Molly and the Mutants

"I mean, no disrespect to Houdini," Arvin said, "but bacon is delicious."

"True," everyone agreed. Except Leonard, who held silent.

"But still," he finally said, "shouldn't we at least pay our respects or something?"

Leonard's reaction to the animal's remains surprised Molly. She had never seen this side of her friend, who was always cracking jokes. Molly knew Leonard lived next door to the Ostranders. Maybe they were closer than she'd realized.

"Pay respects for a hog?" Margo asked.

"Yeah, a hog that was alive," Leonard said. "And now . . . isn't."

"Plus, it wasn't just any hog. It was Houdini," Molly added, putting her hand on Leonard's shoulder. "He belonged to the Ostranders. And he was our neighbor."

"Houdini was a pretty amazing hog, I guess," Arvin said. "Yeah, okay, we should. Um . . ."

Everyone got quiet, not sure what to say next.

Molly wasn't too sure what *paying your respects* even meant, to be honest. She'd never been to a funeral. Her Cramp Cletus had died before she was born. And since they'd never recovered a body for her Gruncle, they hadn't held any kind of service for him. But she had heard that the city had recently installed a plaque somewhere over Far Flung Falls to commemorate his "selfless act of heroism." Her mind jumped to what those final moments for him had been like. Then she wondered what it had been like for Houdini. Had he been afraid? Poor little piggy. Had all his artistry at escaping ultimately been for naught? She looked at the dead hog's pile of bones, laid here in this moldering hallow, and understood that no matter how tricky any of them were in life, there was one escape that no one could master.

Then Molly felt the air change.

Leonard was the first to start nodding his head, then slapping his thigh. His eyes were closed, like he was trying to channel a beat out of the ether. The others watched, unsure.

Finn tried to ask him a question. "Leonard, wha—"

"Shhh," everyone else said.

"Bada-bum-bum-bum ... ba-dundun-dada-dum," Leonard sounded.

The wind stirred a little, swaying the trees overhead. Leonard threw his shoulders into it, his bony little body rocking back and forth. Molly was hoping she wasn't witnessing the start of some satanic ritual.

Molly and the Mutants

"Bada-bum-bum-bum," Leonard continued, "ba-dund-un-dada-dum…"

One by one, recognizing the tune, the others joined in. Molly was last, relieved to be wrong about her suspicions.

"Bada-bum-bum-bum… ba-dundun-dada-dum."

With everyone in sync, Leonard took a step forward and broke into the most tender, heartfelt rendition of "Another One Bites the Dust," Queen's famous rock 'n' roll ode to death. And in yet another surprise move for the day, Molly thought, Leonard could carry a tune. There in the middle of the forest, between the mushrooms and the moss, he channeled Freddie Mercury, Queen's lead singer, belting out the lyrics with such power and feeling that Molly couldn't help but have her spirits lifted.

Everyone else continued with the backup beat as Leonard hit the refrain:

And another one gone, and another one gone
Another one bites the dust!

Molly admired the shape of Houdini's bones at her feet as Leonard carried on. She imagined putting them all back together, like a puzzle, or like one of the electronics her dad repaired on the kitchen table, reconstructing them like one of the skeletons at a museum her class had visited in Cincinnati one time. The biggest skeleton she remembered was an eight-point buck. The rest had been smaller critters. But Houdini had been so huge. Molly figured that, fully assembled, this would be even bigger.

She admired how clean and white the bones looked. Then something occurred to her. Something that didn't seem right. Clean and white?

"Hey, guys?" she asked, interrupting the last notes of the song. "Oh, sorry, Leonard."

"That's okay. I think I was running outta lyrics. At least ones I remember."

"That was really nice," Margo said.

"Yeah, totally rad," Arvin said.

"Totally," Finn said.

"Yeah, well, I was just thinking what I'd like somebody to sing if they ever came across my bones out in the woods one day. It was either that or maybe 'Highway to Hell.'"

"That's a heavy thought, man," Arvin said. "But AC/DC's a solid choice."

"Wait, guys. When exactly did Houdini go missing?" Molly asked, interrupting them and trying to get them back on track.

"Well, according to Wasserbaum," Leonard said, "last time anybody saw him was Wednesday."

Molly and the Mutants

"Yeah. So. You think three days is enough time for a whole hog to decompose down to the bones like this?"

"Hard to say. Houdini was huuuuuge," Arvin said.

"Turkey vultures mighta coulda helped some?" Finn said.

"Yeah, but still," Margo said. "How'd they get so clean so fast?"

"Unless something helped get 'em this way," Leonard said.

"Exactly," Molly said.

Margo shivered. "Did it just get colder?"

"You guys think whatever tried to grab Margo down by the Slew coulda done this?" Arvin asked.

"Let's have a look around," Molly said. "See if we can find any more clues."

"You guys go ahead," Leonard said. "But I think somebody needs to let the Ostranders know what we found. I'll go."

"Good idea, Leonard," Molly said. She looked down at the bones again. Molly wasn't sure how exactly, but she knew this had to be connected to whatever it was they'd run into yesterday. Before those frogs had come along, she'd never come across anything like this. But something still didn't make sense.

"Yeah, man, don't worry. There's still plenty of us to look for Crank," Arvin said.

"Okay," Leonard said. "I'll catch up with you guys later. Oh wait. Here." He slipped off the backpack full of buckeyes and handed it and the high-caliber wrist rocket to Arvin.

"Thanks, man," Arvin said.

"No prob. Just in case," he said.

He flipped his bike around, but then didn't move. Molly heard him let out a soft sniffle.

"You okay, Leonard?" Molly asked.

Leonard turned around, meeting Molly's gaze. He looked like maybe he'd gotten something in his eye again.

"Yeah, I'm okay. I just . . ." Leonard wiped his nose on his forearm. "Houdini was a good pig, is all. Good luck."

"Thanks," Molly said.

Leonard nodded, sniffled once more, then pedaled back up the hill. Molly watched him until he was out of sight.

The remaining four hopped back onto their bikes and rode a little farther off trail, deeper into the woods, until a large cluster of fallen trees blocked their way. They dismounted and climbed over the jumble of logs to continue their search. Molly leaned Pink Lightning up against the tangled mass of roots from an upended sycamore, hoping and praying they didn't find anything that resembled cat bones. She wasn't sure what she would do.

"Guys, I found another pile!" It was Arvin.

Molly and the Mutants

Molly's heart fell into her stomach. She was still several feet away, but they looked like...

"No, no, no, nooooooo!" Molly cried.

How could she have let this happen? Molly could already feel the tears welling up in her eyes. She walked her bike closer to the pile, a flood of memories passing through her.

"Uh, Molly, that's not a cat skeleton." It was Finn.

"You sure?" Molly asked.

"It's an opossum, see? You can tell by the mouth here. Just look at the teeth," Finn said. "I haven't met Crank, but I'm pretty sure she didn't have fangs like this."

Molly stared at the long, pointed upper teeth. She let out a long breath.

"Finn, you're right! I'm sooo happy you're right," Molly said. She paused to exhale relief. It almost came out as a laugh. "I don't think I've ever been so happy to see a dead opossum. Okay, that sounded weird, but..."

"I get it," Finn said. "It's okay. We'll find her."

Molly moved past the opossum's remains, and the others followed suit. They wandered around a bit, discovering more piles of bones.

"It's like a graveyard down here," Arvin said.

"Yeah, a creepy one," Finn said.

"Aren't all graveyards creepy?" Margo asked.

Molly surveyed their surroundings, her eyebrows knitted together in thought.

"Okay, whatcha thinking?" Margo asked.

"I'm just wondering," Molly said, "Whaddya think did all this?"

"You thinking those oversize frogs we ran into yesterday gobbled up Houdini?" Arvin asked. "And every other critter in sight?"

"I dunno," Molly said. "Thing is, as big as those frogs were, still no way one of 'em could take down a three-hundred-pound hog."

"That's it!" Finn said. "Not *one* of 'em. *All* of 'em. Maybe they swarmed him in a group. You know, like piranhas!"

"Not a bad theory, Finn," Arvin said.

"Yeah," Molly added. "I'm just not sure frogs work like that.... How did they carry him this far into the woods?"

"You got a better theory?" Arvin asked.

"Maybe . . . ," Molly started. She thought back again to the weird glimpses of movement she'd caught recently all around the neighborhood. "I mean, until yesterday none of us had ever seen a frog that big."

"Yeah," Margo said. "Biggest *I'd* ever seen."

Molly and the Mutants

"Exactly," Molly said. "Biggest *we'd all seen.*"

"So?" Margo said, eyebrows raised.

"So," Molly continued, "that doesn't mean they didn't already exist before we saw them, right?" Molly said.

"O-kaaay." Arvin nodded when he said it, like he was beginning to follow.

"So," Molly said, pausing to look around. "Who's to say—"

She let the question hang in the air, incomplete, until Arvin finished it. "That there aren't even bigger frogs out there right now."

"Yeah," Molly said. "We just haven't seen 'em yet."

"Uh, if that's true, I'm not sure I want to," Finn said.

No sooner had Finn spoken than they heard a sound. It was a deep, guttural croak, quickly followed by another.

"G-guys?" Margo said, a slight tremble in her voice. "Maybe we should p-pause this conversation and get outta here, ya think?"

CHAPTER 21
COLLAPSE

Wally and Gunther rocketed through the earth at maximum speed, hovering just inches above the magnetized tracks in the Vandervorkels' bubble car. But as fast as they flew, nothing would change the fact that they were more than an hour late to rendezvous with the older kids. And they only had themselves to blame.

"We'll never catch up to them now," Wally grumbled.

"Don't worry, we'll find them," Gunther said. "I'm sure of it."

"Uh, do you know how big the forest is?"

"Relax," Gunther assured him. "They're on bikes, right? So, they'll be sticking to the trails. Shouldn't be too hard." He paused to check the controls. "Just a few more minutes before we get to your street. Hold on."

The tunnel began gradually veering to the right. Normally Gunther would take the turns a little more gently, but since they were running behind, he kept the car at full throttle. Wally started to lean sideways. He gripped the side handle against the door to keep from getting pulled over from the centrifugal force.

The two boys were flattered that they'd been invited to the search party with the older kids. Wally didn't quite share his sister's concern about Crank's whereabouts, but hated the idea of letting Molly down. Things had seemed a little off between them lately, and he wasn't sure why. He'd made a concerted effort to be less annoying—including almost never picking his nose anymore, at least not around her. In fact he wasn't around her much at all. *Wait*, he thought, *is that it?* Did his sister miss him? No, that couldn't be it. Wally thought back to all the times she'd shooed him away. Sometimes big sisters were an unsolvable mystery.

Finding a missing cat seemed a lot less difficult. Wally still wasn't sure how he and Gunther had lost track of time. They had been chatting on their walkie-talkies, each positioned on opposite sides of the Vandervorkels' private garden, to spy on their parents, who'd been sitting on a bench next to a fountain. The trickling water had made it almost impossible to eavesdrop on what they were saying. Wally wondered: Had that been on purpose?

At the time, Wally had been so sure they hadn't been seen, but then Vilomena had looked right where Gunther was hiding and said, "Aren't you boys supposed to be helping find Crank?" Then his dad had looked right at the hedge Wally was crouched behind and said, "Yeah, Wallz, better hop to it while there's still light."

They'd known the whole time. But how?

The curve in the tunnel was starting to straighten out. Wally let go of the grip. He always marveled that even at breakneck speeds, the maglev track was a smooth ride. At the precise moment he was thinking this, for the first time they hit a bump. The bubble car bounced slightly. The two boys looked at each other.

"Hmm," Gunther murmured. "That was odd."

"Yeah," Wally agreed. "That never hap—"

BANG.

Something hit the top of the bubble car. Something heavy. The tunnel's lights grew dim as dust and small pebbles

Molly and the Mutants

showered from overhead. It was raining debris, hitting the top of the bubble car in a steady patter.

"What's happening?" Wally asked.

"I dunno," Gunther said, eyes locked ahead. "The tunnel walls are lined with reinforced concrete all the way around. They shouldn't—"

Another bang. This time the bubble car was hit even harder. The seats wobbled back and forth under the protective dome.

"It's dropping rocks!" Wally cried.

"Remain calm," Gunther said, in a voice that didn't sound very calm at all. "The windows are made of a crack-resistant polymer. It can withstand hundreds of pounds of pressure per square—"

"Watch out!" Wally screamed, pointing down the track.

They had just rounded the last stretch of the turn, and now the tunnel was a straight shot ahead for as far as they could see. But something was wrong. A short distance ahead the ceiling was completely caving in. Big jagged chunks of concrete and rocks came crashing down from above, burying the tracks under a mountain of rubble that would be impossible to pass. But the car hadn't slowed. And now the boys were seconds away from a collision.

"Hold on!" Gunther said, reaching for a lever to activate

the emergency brake. Wally felt the safety straps cut into his shoulders as the magnetized vehicle came to an abrupt halt, just inches away from the wreckage. The boys stared at the wall in front of them.

"Must be... an earthquake," Gunther said.

"*Earthquake?*" Wally snorted. "We're in *Ohio*! Ohio doesn't have earthquakes!"

A few of the larger rocks shifted, and the ceiling caved in a little more. Dirt and rubble poured from above, completely filling the space ahead of them.

Gunther punched a button, sending the car in reverse before it stopped again.

A moment later a boulder that had been hanging precariously dislodged and came crashing into the tunnel, right where they had just been. It rolled twice before slamming into the side of the circular wall. A shaft of sunlight poked through the hole it had left.

"Okay." Gunther turned to Wally. "Well, if it wasn't an earthquake... then what was it?"

The tunnel started shaking, kicking up clouds of dust, which was followed by a deep, rumbling groan.

GWAAAAAAAAAAARRRRR...

"Um," Gunther said. "I think we need to—"

Molly and the Mutants

"Evacuate!" Wally finished.

Gunther punched the exit button, and the bubble car's glass doors slid open. Both boys started coughing as soon as they breathed in the dust-filled air.

"Well, there's no way we're getting through that." Gunther gestured at the wall of rocks in front of them before turning around. "But the coast looks clear behind us. I think we just passed station seventeen."

"Which one's that?" Wally asked.

"Oh, you'll recognize it when you see it," Gunther said.

"What about our bikes?" Wally said. "They're still at my house, remember?"

"I think I've got something better." Gunther said. He raced around to the back of the bubble car and popped the trunk.

"It's got a trunk?" Wally said.

"We'll use these," Gunther said, lifting up something Wally didn't recognize. "Much faster than bikes."

"What ... are they?" Wally asked, marveling at what he saw.

"Our mode of transportation for the day."

Another groan shook the tunnel all around them, raining more debris onto their heads.

GWAAAAAAAAAAARRRRR...

"C'mon!" Gunther said.

They scooped up the strange contraptions and doubled back up the tracks on foot until they reached the station platform with a ladder. As soon as Gunther popped the hatch, Wally knew exactly where they were. It was the artificial tree stump they'd discovered when they'd crashed Blue Thunder. A flood of memories from that day washed over Wally as he stepped out into the meadow.

They looked behind them for whatever could have caused the cave-in. There it was, in the field, an enormous indentation in the middle of an otherwise flat patch of land. But no sign of what might have caused it. What was heavy enough to crush that much earth? And break through reinforced concrete?

Wally eyeballed his friend. "Gunther?"

"Yeah?"

"Have you checked on your robot recently?" Wally asked.

"Impossible!" Gunther shot back.

"How do you know?"

"I just do."

"Okay, okay," Wally said. "Any other ideas?"

The two boys, still covered in dust, stared at each other.

"Allllll right," Gunther finally said, letting out a sigh. "Let's check. It's the direction we need to go anyway."

The matter was settled. They would catch up with Molly

and the others soon enough, but first they had to make sure no headless, armless, two-hundred-ton robots had wandered out of the gorge under Far Flung Falls.

Wally looked at the contraptions they'd carried with them out of the tunnel. Whatever they were, they didn't look very fast. Maybe Gunther had gotten hit in the head by a stray rock and wasn't thinking straight.

"Okay, I give up," Wally said. "How do you ride these things?"

"You don't ride them," Gunther said, grinning. "You wear them."

CHAPTER 22
PARTY CRASHERS

The chorus was getting louder.

Rrrrrribbit-rrrrrribbit-rrrrrribbit-rrrrrribbit...

"Oh no, not this crowd again," Arvin said.

The four of them tightened their circle, looking out in all directions. More croaks started sounding off from just up the opposite hill.

Molly scanned the slope ahead of them. It was covered in thick vine and underbrush, too hard to make out what might be in there.

But they didn't have to wait long to find out. Just then one of the oversize frogs hopped into view. It was about the same size as the one Arvin had hoped would earn him an A in science class, before it had mysteriously disappeared. The frog sat there center stage, regarding them with its bulbous yellow eyes.

Rrrrrribbit, it said.

"How many giant frogs can there be?" Margo asked to no one in particular.

A second later more frogs popped up beside the first one, creating a line.

"Sorry I asked."

The frogs began croaking together, syncing up their rhythm. They were still several yards away and didn't look very menacing.

"Finn, you better not be right about your piranha theory," Arvin said.

"I don't think their tongues can reach us from there," Finn said.

This was true, Molly thought. And if they needed a quick getaway, their bikes weren't far behind them.

"They're kinda cute," Molly said. "Almost."

"Emphasis on the *almost*," Margo said.

"Yeah, in their own maybe-we'll-suck-all-the-meat-off-your-bones kind of way," Arvin said.

The chorus grew louder, more insistent, picking up the pace.

The frogs' yellow throats pulsated in unison, like they were all following the direction of the same conductor. Suddenly the strange music was interrupted by a desperate *Eeeeeeeeep* as the first frog snapped backward and out of sight, even more quickly than it had appeared. This was followed by the abrupt exit of two more in the same fashion, their cries cut short as they vanished back into the brush. Then a lower, deeper croak, like the one they'd heard after Margo had fallen into the Slew.

Yuuuuuurrrrrp. The sound echoed through the trees.

"I've got a bad feeling about this," Finn said.

Molly remembered what had happened the last time Finn had said that. What if he was right about them?

The remaining frogs continued in their frantic croaking, nervously pivoting left and right to see what was happening, until they were joined by a frog that was twenty times bigger than the largest of them. It landed with a wet thud on a large rock in the middle of the crowd.

"What. In. The—" Arvin said.

The monster was easily as big as a bear. On all fours it sat about four feet high and six feet across, and looked like it weighed upward of five hundred pounds. Molly watched its long webbed toes grip the top of the boulder it had landed on, the bulbous tips curling around the upper edge, claiming the space as its own. The muscles in its massive hind legs rippled. Its yellow eyes were the size of basketballs. As it opened its mouth, the face of one of the smaller frogs that had just been snatched was visible at the back of its throat, calling helplessly before it disappeared into the muscly folds of the monster frog's mouth. A final *Eeeeeeeeee*—then the giant frog made a forceful swallow, and it was gone.

"Wait... you mean it eats its own kin?" Arvin whispered.

It was more of a statement than a question. They left it unanswered, but its truth lingered in the air a moment, its inference sinking in for the four of them. *If this new, even bigger frog was so indiscriminate as to devour its own kind, what would stop it from trying to make one of them a snack?*

Nobody moved. The grizzly-size frog was still some distance away. They looked at one another, wondering what to do next. Molly had faced down an even bigger foe than this, but something about this creature—the way it eyed her, the way it twitched—chilled her to the bone more than any robot could ever do.

Another monster frog leapt into view, just as massive, but this one sported a long dorsal fin that tapered all the way down its back to a nubby tail, like it had never fully converted from a tadpole. The hulking creature leaned forward and wagged its tail in the air, like a dog ready to play. But the gesture was far from friendly.

Then from high above a third massive frog appeared. How many of them could there be? As this one sailed through the air, Molly's eye caught thin membranes connecting the monster's forelegs to its hindlegs. *Great, now they have wings*, she thought. This flying beast landed a little closer than the first two.

With each arrival the smaller frogs cast off in every direction, desperately trying to escape the fate of their recently eaten cousins. Pandemonium ensued. Dozens of smaller frogs flew into the air. Some of them crashed into each other midjump; others landed on top of one another. Bumping, slipping, sliding, croaking. The three larger frogs took advantage of the chaos, shooting their monstrous tongues into the center of the action to grab the less fortunate.

The monster frogs croaked loudly, like they were burping after a feast.

Yuuuuuurrrrrp. Yuuuuuurrrrrp.

"It's like fish in a barrel," Arvin said.

"Um, are we in the barrel too?" Margo asked.

The three monster frogs paused, as if they were considering Margo's question.

"Maybe they had their fill," Molly said, taking a step back.

Molly and the Mutants

"Orrrr . . . they're thinking about their next course," Finn said.

Arvin and Margo followed Molly's lead, slowly at first. Then they broke into a full-fledged run up the hill, back to their bikes. The frogs remained still, watching them with expressionless stares.

Yuuuuuurrrrrp.

"Where's Finn?" Molly asked.

As they made their way back to their bikes, she looked left and right. Margo and Arvin were just ahead of her. But Finn was nowhere to be found. *Finn?* Molly felt a sinking in the pit of her stomach.

Molly was moving a little more slowly than her friends, the bulk from her pack slowing her just a little. *Her pack!* That's right. She was prepared for just this instance. Molly spun around and drew the gun, then reached under her arm and flipped the switch. She felt the Zap-O-Matic thrum to life, sending tingles up her spine all the way to her neck.

Another giant frog had appeared, making four. This one looked even bigger than the others, if that was even possible. And instead of two eyes protruding atop its head, it had three. Oh crap. They were being invaded by mutant frogs. Three Eyes, Shark Fin, Bat Wing, and Muscles. This was way worse than anything she had imagined. Certainly worse than a bunch of kids who listened to heavy metal records backward. Now Molly and her friends knew who was truly responsible for turning people's pets into piles of bones. But what they didn't know was, how many more of these things were there?

On top of her fear Molly felt a growing sense of guilt for having brought her friends into the middle of such danger. What had she been thinking? If anything happened to them, she'd be responsible....

"Finn?" she called. "Where are you?"

Yuuuuuurrrrrp.

Molly tried not to imagine the worst. But that's exactly what she did. The image was stuck in her mind: Finn's face, with his perfectly feathered flyback hair, disappearing down the gullet of one of those prehistoric-looking creatures. While she tried to shake the image, Muscles took a long-toed step forward in her direction. Shark Fin the same. The four of them started sounding off. A monstrous quartet.

Yuuuuuurrrrrp-yuuuuurrrrrp-yuuuuurrrrrp-yuuuuuurrrrrp.

"You . . . just . . . hold it right there," Molly said, more to herself than to the monsters advancing toward her. Her grip tightened on the Zap-O-Matic. She raised the drum-shaped nozzle. A few more hops forward.

Molly took a breath and squeezed the trigger, releasing a bright, hot arc of electricity that burst from her Gruncle's contraption and touched down on the ground just in front of Three Eyes to her left. An explosion of dirt and sparks illuminated its motley green hide. The frogs all retreated a few paces, their shiny, mucous-coated bodies shimmering in the eerie light.

But to Molly's astonishment they didn't run.

The Zap-O-Matic was harder to aim than she had imagined. She tried to pull the barrel higher, to increase the length of the arc—and just maybe give these ghastly-looking frogs the shock of their lives. But the lightning current continued to flow from gun to ground, drawing Molly's aim to the right. As it did, the electricity blasted through the earth, leaving a scorched, smoking trail.

Molly hadn't intended to, but she was drawing a line in the dirt. A *do-not-cross*.

She took another step backward, and her calf bumped something. It startled her and she released the trigger, bringing the outpouring of electricity to a halt. Without it the shaded grove felt much darker. Molly shot a look down to whatever had hit her leg, fearing it was another frog. Luckily, instead it was the giant hollowed-out log they'd all jumped over to get down here. Carefully she lifted one leg over the fallen tree, then returned her focus to the four monster frogs downhill.

They had stopped, looking like they were deciding what to do next.

Molly crouched down behind the log for cover. The blackened line in the earth still smoldered between her and the monster frogs. A thin curtain of smoke had drifted up from the spot, giving the creatures an even more menacing look, like demons from the underworld. An acrid smell from the Zap-O-Matic lingered in the air. Maybe that was enough to keep them at bay?

It wasn't.

One by one the giant green demons crossed the line, lumbering their way toward her and her friends.

"C'mon, Molly, we gotta go," Arvin said.

"Not without Finn," Molly said.

"But what if—" Margo didn't finish the thought.

"Right here," said the log. The tiniest squeak of a voice.

Molly jumped.

Molly and the Mutants

"Finn!" She slid over to peek into one of the holes and found a bright blue eye staring back. He was inside the log. Their faces were as close as when they'd almost kissed yesterday. Now that seemed like forever ago.

"How did you—" Molly asked.

"I hid! Whaddya think I did?" Finn said. His voice went up an octave.

"Okay, okay," Molly said. "Let's just—"

Before she could finish the thought, the monster quartet resumed their croaking. Then a giant tongue smashed through the decaying wood, missing her head by inches. Molly spun around. Arvin and Margo were charging uphill to their bikes.

Molly started running too, screaming at Finn to do the same.

He didn't answer. Instead all she heard was a terrible crunching sound behind her that shook the earth and showered splintered wood all around her. Three Eyes had landed on the hollow log, smashing it to bits.

Finn!

"Nooooo!" Molly screamed. But there was no time. She sprinted the last few steps, pounced onto her banana seat, and stomped hard on the pedals. Then—*Whoomph!* Before she could gain any traction, the earth shook again, and Molly felt herself moving, but in the wrong direction. She was going straight up.

Bat Wing had overshot by several yards, sailing over Molly's head and landing right in front of her, on the other end of the upturned sycamore. The monster's weight turned the tree into a giant seesaw. In a flurry of physics too fast for Molly to process, the tangle of roots where she'd parked Pink Lightning hooked under her frame and launched her—bike and all—high into the air.

CHAPTER 23
BIG DIPPER

Molly somersaulted, clutching her handlebars in a white-knuckle grip as the ground dropped below and the world spun all around her. Midspin her eyes caught the row of buttons across the center bar. Just as she completed a three-hundred-sixty-degree turn and began to fall back to earth, she punched the one inscribed with a feather.

Please let this work, Molly prayed.

Pfffffft! Below her feet and all around her, balloons popped out from secret compartments in her frame, inflating at impossible speed. She hit the ground with the lightest touch and bounced three times before the balloons detached. *As soft as a feather*, Molly thought. Incredible.

Now, instead of bringing up the rear, she was in the lead of their gang again. Molly called behind her, "C'mon, everybody!"

"Right behind you," Margo said.

"Right behind her," Arvin said.

"I don't wanna die!" Margo screamed.

"Nobody's gonna die!" Molly screamed back. Then she remembered Finn. *Please don't let him be squashed. Or eaten. Or both.* She heard more thumping and croaking behind them.

"Anybody seen Finn?" Molly called. "Fiiiinn?"

"Right here," Finn said, pulling up beside her. He was panting hard.

"Wha—?" Molly turned and nearly fell off her bike. When she saw Finn's face, her eyes began to well. Molly was still feeling dizzy from her acrobatics, and now everything felt even more topsy-turvy. "How? But I thought you... What happened?"

"That frog... the one with three eyes? It crashed down on my hiding spot and—boom! Sent my end of the tree flying! I thought I was dead for sure."

"Me too," said Arvin, right behind them. "You shoulda seen him, Molly! It was like he was in a... *a log rocket*!"

"Yeah, *log rocket*," Finn repeated. "Landed right next to my bike, ha!"

Finn kept laughing uncontrollably. Molly thought maybe he

was in shock. Maybe they all were. She couldn't believe Finn's luck. If that log hadn't been so soft from decay, it would've broken every bone in his body—and she would've been to blame.

"Finn! See that trail ahead? Hang a hard right. I've got an idea."

"Okay," he said.

"Wait. We're taking BMX Alley?" Arvin said.

"Yeah," Molly answered.

"Rad," Arvin said.

"Not *rad*," Margo said. "*Bad!* If the frogs don't kill us, those jumps will."

"I'm so sorry I got you guys into this," Molly said, "but I think this might be our best way out."

BMX Alley wasn't a course for beginners. It was usually the domain for older kids, boys mostly. High schoolers and dropouts. As evidence there were countless piles of crushed soda cans, gum wrappers, beef jerky, cigarette butts, pouches of chaw. Molly had been here before, but always on the periphery, spying on the older kids as they performed various levels of death-defying tricks on their dirt bikes. She had never been this far in, having felt like maybe she didn't belong. There wasn't a specific age requirement to be here. It just felt like a space she wasn't ready to inhabit.

But here she was, being thrown into it by some crazy circumstance outside of her control. It felt kind of like how the rest of her life was going at the moment. Like there was some force pushing her to grow up quicker than she wanted to—even if she would never admit that to anyone. She definitely wasn't going to now.

"Let's go," she said.

They careened down the first hill, with Finn quickly pulling to the lead. Molly had never seen him—or anyone—pedal so fast. It was like his legs were possessed, pumping the crank at crazy speeds. The last few minutes had really spooked him.

"Careful, Finn! Some of these—"

"Whoa!" Finn called out. He was airborne, having launched off the first of several jumps that made up the course. Maybe this could give them the lead they needed over their pursuers? Molly hadn't heard any telltale thumps or croaks for a few moments. Maybe the mutant frogs had given up.

Molly stole a quick glance over her shoulder. Okay, no giant killer frog, at least none in sight. Maybe she and her friends had lost the beasts.

Then the kids heard it in the distance. A deep, bellowing croak. It sounded angry. A moment later Molly heard another that sounded even closer. Did these creatures ever quit?

Molly and the Mutants

"Let's keep bookin'," Arvin said.

"Yeah, no way I'm slowing down," Margo said.

Still running on adrenaline and terror, the four of them launched themselves down a rickety wooden ramp, and somehow managed to keep going. It wasn't pretty. After what felt like a never-ending succession of impossible jumps, bumps, dips, and berms—along with an equal number of spills, screams, and near collisions—they arrived at the edge of the Big Dipper . . . and abruptly came to a halt. They were bruised and shaken, but all still alive, and wondering if they could press their luck any further. This was considered the grand finale to the course, and all but impossible for everyone but the most practiced daredevils. Which they were not.

"You gotta be kidding," Margo said.

Before them lay an enormous U-shaped dip that looked to have been scooped out of the earth by the hand of a giant. Over the years a mixture of erosion and bike traffic had carved dozens of grooves that ran down one side and back up the other, ensuring a quick wipeout if you veered off course. Every week there was at least one new story of somebody trying to cross the Big Dipper and ending up with stitches, or a broken bone, or worse. Some kids called it the Big Ripper.

The heavy, wet thumping sounds behind them were getting louder.

"Guys," Molly said, "If we can make it across, I don't think they can follow."

"If," Arvin said.

"Yeah, I don't think I can do it," Finn said.

"I *know* I can't," Margo said, leaning over her handlebars. "I mean, that's gotta be twenty feet straight down."

Arvin inched his front wheel to the edge of the Big Dipper to get a better look.

"Maybe twenty-five," he said.

"Margo, I've watched guys do this, like, a hundred times," Molly said. "You just pick a groove, keep your front wheel straight, and go. You let gravity pull you down, and inertia take you back up the other side. It's simple physics."

While she explained, Molly motioned with her hands, drawing a big letter *U* in the air, hoping that would help convince them.

It didn't. But something else did. A massive tongue shot out from behind them, barely missed Arvin, and landed in the pile of trash to his left. The impact scattered cans in all directions—at least the ones the tongue didn't stick to—before the tongue retracted with its catch.

Molly and the Mutants

Molly had the strange thought that between the cigarette butts, candy wrappers, and soda cans, the frog had, in one fell swoop, just picked up about every bad habit humans had created. If it wasn't already a mutant, it definitely would be now.

Arvin inhaled and dropped down the U. Instead of crashing he zoomed right back up the opposite wall until he popped up onto the far ledge. It took about two seconds. Arvin looked back at his companions, the expression on his face showing that no one was more surprised than he was. He let out a long whistle and grinned.

"That was easy," Arvin said. "C'mon, guys!"

It looked anything but easy. But now wasn't the time to debate.

"Grab a groove and bust a move," Molly said. It was something she had heard the older kids say before they dropped down the side.

All in a row the remaining three pushed their front wheels over the edge of the Big Dipper, hovered for a moment, and then plummeted straight down.

Well, two of them did. As Molly and Finn raced down, across, and back up the far side of the U, Margo sat behind, frozen in place. Why was she always last?

"I can't do it, I said!" She was starting to cry.

"You can, Margo!" Molly yelled back. "You *have* to! Go!"

They all watched and waited from the other side. The only sound was Margo sucking in gulps of air, in and out, in and out. Until another sound joined her.

Yuuuuurrrrrp.

Directly behind her, several yards up the course they'd just raced through, one of the mammoth frogs came into view, landing with a hard thud. It was Shark Fin. The monster caught sight of Margo and wagged its tail in excitement. Then it leapt into the air again, impossibly high, and landed nearly on top of her.

The impact from the hundreds of pounds of amphibious mass bounced Margo's powder-blue Huffy a full six inches off the ground. In silence she dropped into the U as the frog's tongue shot out over the divide and caught only the empty forest air where Margo's head had just been. The tongue retracted back into the monster's mouth. But before it could try again, Margo was already barreling up the other side of the dip. She stuck the landing with the smoothness of a pro, rejoining her wide-eyed friends.

Margo's bottom lip trembled.

"Just breathe, Margo," Molly said. "You made it. You're okay."

"You are the raddest," Arvin said. "Will you be my girlfriend?"

Molly and the Mutants

"Huh?" Margo turned to Arvin. "I thought I already was."

Hearing this exchange made Molly nearly gag. But she was still feeling too guilty for endangering everyone to make any complaints, so she kept it to herself. Even if her friends got on her nerves sometimes, they were still her friends. And they had shown up for her. That was what mattered most.

From the opposite side of the Big Dipper, Shark Fin puffed up its throat, then let out a long, unhappy croak. A moment later Muscles appeared beside it and joined in. The two mutants and four kids stared at one another from across the divide. Then Muscles went quiet. It opened its mouth incredibly wide... and held it, perfectly still.

"What's it doing?" Finn asked.

"No idea. Maybe showing off its tonsils?" Arvin said.

The frog remained still, mouth agape.

"Wait, I think it's blowing a bubble?" Margo said.

The fleshy interior of the creature's mouth pulsated, then pushed outward. In the center of its throat, what at first looked like a small balloon began to expand. Unlike the frog's green exterior, this was a pale pink, riddled with a network of dark veins.

"That's one sick frog," Arvin said.

The beast continued until its stomach was completely

inside out, the contents spilling to the ground along with thick globs of ooze. A random assortment of bones clattered over the edge of the Big Dipper, to collect on the hard-packed dirt below.

As she witnessed the scene, Molly felt her heart drop from her chest and into the ditch with the bones. *Please, oh please, oh please, don't let those belong to Crank,* she silently pleaded. But now it made sense to Molly why Houdini's remains were so clean. They'd been bathed in a pool of stomach acid that digested everything down to the bones, and then had been barfed up. It was...

"Grody to the max," Margo said.

Three Eyes and Bat Wing had crept up behind the other two frogs. It looked like they were about to do the same thing.

"Let's go," Molly said. "Before those things figure out how to cross the dipper."

CHAPTER 24
SNEAK

"And there we go," Stanley said, plugging in the VCR and seeing the digital readout flicker to life. Another thing fixed. He stood up and stretched, his hands nearly touching the ceiling of their cramped kitchen. Stanley went to the fridge and grabbed a carton of milk, then looked both ways before chugging straight from the carton. Something about it, the way the fold of the cardboard rested on his bottom lip, made it taste better. Maybe it was that he was breaking a rule.

Stanley had been a rule follower most of his life. Unlike his soon-to-be ex, Caroline. He had finally started the process with an attorney in town to get an official divorce, but the paperwork seemed to be taking forever. And Caroline wasn't exactly helping to move things along. He could remember a time when he had loved her, but that felt like another life.

He didn't even feel mad about it anymore.

He was pretty sure she'd never met a rule she hadn't broken, or at least tried to. That wasn't the case for ol' Stan. Except for his illicit milk-drinking-out-of-the-carton habit. Not even Vilomena knew about that. But he wouldn't mind telling her. Part of him wanted to tell her every single thing that popped into his head. Like he could share every part of who he was, milk-sneaking and all, and she would understand.

The VCR made a few more promising noises, *whirr-ka-thunk-ka-thunk*, then kicked out the videocassette it had been holding on to when it had died. Stanley looked at it and nodded to himself. In that moment he was feeling like there was nothing he couldn't fix. Even the trajectory of his own broken life. With Vilomena, there was nothing he couldn't do.

He's even conquered Jazzercise.

Stanley caught a flash of green light from the back kitchen window. For a moment it illuminated the whole kitchen, then was gone. He froze, milk carton still in hand.

"SECRET. SAFE. WITH. ME."

Stanley surprised himself with a long belly laugh. How

was he supposed to respond to a robot who had caught him? As he considered this, the same door that had opened for Molly began to move, pushing outward, then unfolding into a set of steps. Through the opening, Stanley saw the interior of the robot light up—like an idea had just popped into its head.

Was he hallucinating? Stanley checked the date on the milk carton. As he did, another pulse of green light flashed his way, then another, bidding him over. He opened the screen door to get a better look.

"Hello?" he said, wiping the milk off his mustache with the back of his arm. "Uh, everything okay?"

The giant robot head was quiet. But its two circular eyes flashed green again, like traffic lights giving him the go ahead. Stanley had always been a little curious, ever since it had landed in his backyard. He walked outside toward the robot head.

Why not? Stanley said to himself. He climbed the ladder and entered.

Once inside he made a quick assessment of the damage, letting out a long, low whistle. There were scorch marks everywhere, most likely from the explosion that had launched the robot's head from its body.

But it wasn't all ruined. Stanley saw potential. He always did.

As if sensing his thoughts, a compartment opened right below the control panel, and a shelf slid forward, covered with a perfectly arrayed bright and shiny set of new tools. (If it was one thing that Stanley had a hard time saying no to, it was a perfectly arrayed bright and shiny set of new tools.)

"REPAIR. ME?" the robot asked.

"Sure," Stanley said. "Sure thing."

The truth was, Stanley was far from sure. As confident as he had just been feeling in the wake of fixing a particularly tricky VCR, he'd never worked on anything remotely this big, or this complex, or this damaged. But the kids were out. And Vilomena wouldn't be over until later. What else did he have to do for the next few hours?

"Where do I even start?" he asked aloud.

In response another panel opened.

"IN. HERE," said the robot.

Stanley set down the milk carton and got to work.

After a couple of hours of tinkering here, tightening there, Stanley was starting to get a better picture of exactly how the robot worked. Circuit boards that had looked foreign now felt more intuitive. He jumped around from console to console, crawling around on all fours to pop off panels and reconnect wires. With every touch the robot seemed to be coming back to life. In its stilted voice it offered bits of direction, interspersed with a few words of encouragement.

"OH. THAT. FEELS. MUCH. BETTER. THROUGHOUT. MY. MAINFRAME. THANK. YOU. MISTER. MCQUIRTER."

"Please," he said, "call me Stan."

"THANK. YOU. STAN."

"So, now that we're not strangers, what should I call you?"

"I. AM. AFRAID. I. DO. NOT. HAVE. A. NAME. OF. MY. OWN. OTHER. THAN. 10101010101111110000110010100000010011001 0100010."

"Binary doesn't quite roll off the tongue."

"YOU. ARE. TELLING. ME."

Stanley laughed.

"AND. THAT. WAS. ONLY. HALF. OF. IT."

Stanley laughed again. "You're killing me!"

"OH. NO." The robot emitted a very worried-sounding beep.

"No, no, yeah, it's just an expression. I ... I didn't know you were programmed to ... be so funny."

"ME. EITHER."

"So, how about we shorten your name to... *Number One*? I mean, if we have to choose between the two numbers, it's way better than *Zero*."

"I. AM. NUMBER. ONE?"

"Yeah, you're Number One!"

"I. AM. NUMBER. ONE."

More lights blinked on all around him, digital readouts flickered back to life, and the entire command center thrummed under his feet.

Stanley couldn't decide who felt more energized, the robot or himself.

CHAPTER 25
POPSICLE STAND

This was no longer just a search-and-rescue mission. It was a search-and-survive. Molly might have set out to simply bring Crank back home safely, but now she needed to do the same for her friends. The pressure weighed on her. Before they could do anything else, Molly knew they had to put some distance between themselves and those monsters.

But this far out, beyond any marked path, it was easier said than done.

Even though Molly's legs were aching, she kept on pedaling. So did everyone else. The four of them carried on without speaking, with only the sound of their breathing to counter the silence. Since they'd crossed the Big Dipper, the trail had grown more erratic, with twists and turns, ups and downs, and multiple dead ends. Thick underbrush covered a lot of the way, making it hard to know which direction to go. Not even the high schoolers ventured this deep.

The sun was starting to sit a little lower in the sky. Molly checked her watch. 4:39 p.m. It had only been an hour. But it seemed like they'd been traveling for weeks.

"Hope Leonard made it to the Ostranders all right," Arvin said.

"It was a straight shot back," Molly said. She figured they had drawn all the frogs their way, leaving Leonard to get back without much trouble.

The trees above them grew thicker. The forest seemed a lot older here.

"Everybody doing okay?" Arvin finally asked.

"If by *okay* you mean not eaten by some kinda . . . *frog-a-saurus*, then yeah, I guess I'm okay." Margo was still pretty shaken up from her narrow escape through the Big Dipper. "What even were those things?"

"You mean the ones that came in *large*?" Arvin said. "Or *extra, extra, extra large*?"

"The *extra, extra, extra*."

Molly and the Mutants

"I dunno, guys," Arvin said. "I've been riding these trails since I was old enough to pedal a bike, and I've never seen anything like that."

"I've heard some crazy stories," Margo said. "But figured they were just that... ya know, stories."

"You mean like the legend of the frog men... or the bog monster?" Finn asked.

"Those are just campfire stories," Molly said. "No way are they real."

"Well, the frog monsters had to come from somewhere," Margo said.

"We are *not* talking about the bog monster," Arvin said.

Arvin and Molly exchanged looks. Suddenly they both started laughing.

"Seriously? How can you be laughing right now?" Margo asked. "Those things—"

"Gotta be far behind us by now," Arvin said. "We've been pedaling our butts off."

The trail dipped again. They all took advantage, giving their legs a brief respite as they coasted downhill.

"Trust me, we're saaaaaaaaaafe..."

Arvin's bike slipped right out from under him, skittering across the ground.

"Ahhhhhh!" he said.

A second later the rest of them were slipping and sliding too. They all came to a stop at the bottom of the hill, crashing together in one tangled pile of bodies and bikes.

"Oof! That's the hardest dirt," Margo said.

"What in the world..." As Molly spoke the words, she could see white puffs of smoke forming with each breath. She put a hand to the ground to lift herself up, then jerked it away. The ground was solid ice.

"Uh, g-guys?," Finn asked, his voice a little shaky as he eyed the frozen landscape. "How far did we go?"

"Feels like Alaska," Arvin said.

"How would you know?" Margo said. "You've never been outta Ohio."

Arvin shrugged.

"Maybe Cleveland?" Finn asked.

"Since when did it start freezing in October?" Molly asked.

Molly could see the same white puffs of air around her friends' mouths as they spoke. She shivered. The temperature was noticeably colder by several degrees, the chill seeping through her clothes and settling into her bones. But winter was still months away. It didn't make sense. They

Molly and the Mutants

slowly got to their feet, taking care not to slip and fall.

"Maybe we somehow got transported back to the Ice Age," Arvin said. "When prehistoric frog monsters ruled the earth."

"Well, it wasn't iced over just a few feet that away." Molly pointed a thumb behind her. "There's gotta be some other explanation."

"This is usually how those campfire stories start, just sayin'," Arvin said.

Psssshhhhhhhhht.

"Wh-what was that?" Finn asked, his voice even shakier.

"Sounds like it came from over there," Margo said, pointing up the hill in front of them.

"Let's find out," Molly said.

They trekked upward, the air getting colder with each step.

"You feel that?" Arvin said.

"Yeah," Margo said.

"We must be getting close," Molly said.

"To what?" Arvin said. "The a-bomb-able snowman?"

"It's *abominable*," Molly corrected him. "And no, I don't think so—"

She stopped as they crested the hill. Just on the other side, surrounded by a thick white crust of ice, sat a long metal capsule. The sides were fluted with rows and rows of metal tubes. It looked like something between a missile, a coffin, and a pipe organ.

"Whoa," everyone said. In unison, four white puffs of breath punctuated their awe.

Psssshhhhhhhhht. The capsule sighed again, releasing a thick cloud of vapor into the air.

"Look over there, behind it." Finn pointed. "I think maybe it crashed."

A long concave groove trailed the capsule at one end. And at the other the earth was heaped up into a pile, like the capsule had plowed into it.

"Not as smooth a landing as a log rocket," Arvin said. Finn smiled at him.

Molly was standing over it now.

"Be careful," Finn said.

She looked down at the surface, following the seams of what appeared to be a hatch. A recessed glass window sat tucked in the middle—but was frosted over. Molly crept around to the other side. There a small rectangular opening revealed something that looked like a control panel.

Below the blinking lights she could make out a few letters, but the entire side was badly scraped.

Molly and the Mutants

"It says something here," Molly read aloud. "C-R-Y-O-G-E-N."

Then, underneath that, she found a word she knew.

VANDERVORK...

"It's a Vandervorkel!" she exclaimed.

"No. Way," Arvin said.

"Way," Molly said.

"Way what?" Finn asked.

No one answered. Instead they all stared at the panel. One of the buttons was blinking red. Molly pressed it.

The capsule hissed again, much louder than before, emitting even more vapor. Then the hatch popped open and slid down. White fumes poured from inside like a dry ice machine. Everyone stood frozen—now more by caution than the cold. Molly leaned forward, trying to peer into the thick white clouds.

Among all the mechanical clicks and beeps there was a long muffled groan. But it sounded human.

"Gunther?" Molly called into the fumes. "Gunther, is that you?"

"Who...the...h-h-heck...is...Gunther?" the fumes sputtered back.

That voice. Molly knew it. But it couldn't be. She had seen him dive headlong down the robot's throat, then watched the robot explode. No one could have survived that. Not even...

"Gruncle?" Molly said. Slowly, shakily, the outline of a familiar form rose from the icy mist. Molly suddenly felt light-headed. "But I thought... I thought you were dead."

"W-w-wait a sec," the voice answered. "Y-y-ya mean I'm *not*?"

"What... in... the—" Arvin said.

The vapor dissipated, revealing the craggy, frost-covered face of none other than Molly's Great-Uncle Clovis. He was ashen and shivering, but appeared to be alive. Fighting shock, Molly's brain raced to make sense of what exactly she was seeing. Could it be an imposter? Molly searched the man's face for some detail that would give it away. But it was him, down to the curlicue tips of his handlebar mustache, perfectly encased in a delicate sheen of ice crystals. Even in the dimming light he glittered like something otherworldly. Maybe it was a ghost, Molly wondered. Or some Vandervorkel hologram? She tried in vain to reach out and touch his face, to see if he was really there, but her arms wouldn't budge. Then her vision began to narrow. A moment later—*psssh*—the ice crystals on his mustache shattered into a spray of white dust as her Gruncle attempted to smile.

Molly and the Mutants

That tiny explosion was the last thing Molly saw before the world started spinning. Then it all turned sideways. From far away she heard Margo scream her name just as everything went black.

CHAPTER 26
OPERATION FLAGPOLE

Molly came to, her surroundings atop the frozen hill slowly returning to focus. She saw Arvin, Margo, and Finn staring back at her, bewildered expressions on their faces. Then—

"Hey, there she is!"

It was her Gruncle. "Barely caught ya before ya hit the ground."

Molly blinked hard several times. He was holding her. Had she fainted? His hands felt cold... but *real*.

That meant he wasn't a ghost.

Reflexively Molly's arms snapped around her Gruncle like a bear trap had been sprung. Her eyes burned, and tears streamed down her face. She pressed her nose into his shirt and breathed him in. Sure enough, it was Gruncle. A combination of peanuts, whisky, and hair tonic—with a trace of BO. It was faint, but that was probably because he hadn't fully thawed. She clutched him tighter, worried that if she let go, he might disappear again.

A few minutes passed in silence, broken only by the occasional sniffle.

"W-w-watch it there, kiddo," Clovis said after a while. "You might just break your ol' freeze-dried Gruncle in two, heh!"

"Too bad," she said. Cheek to chin, Molly's face was slick from a steady flow of tears and snot. But her heart was bursting with happiness.

Clovis reached into his back pocket and produced a white hanky, which was as stiff as a board from the cold. He let out a laugh, which turned into a coughing fit, which ended in a shiver. Molly eventually loosened her grip to get a better look at him. She still had so many questions, but none of them mattered as much as the fact that her Gruncle was here. Alive.

Free from the bear hug, Clovis stretched as far as his limbs could extend, even standing on his tiptoes. As he did so, every single bone in his body popped. It sounded like the man was breaking to pieces, yet somehow he remained intact. The kids watched and listened in awe. He ended the performance by interlocking his fingers and cracking his knuckles.

"There, that's better. *Brrrrrrrr!* What happened? And why is it so c-c-cold?" Then he slapped his forehead, like his memory was suddenly coming back to him. "Hold on—Molly! You're safe!" He looked around. "You're all safe. Did we get him? Did it work? How about Wally. Is he okay?"

"Yes, the robot won't be hurting anyone, Grunk," Molly assured him, "and we're all safe, Wally too. Well, at least from the robot." Molly really hoped her brother wasn't out in the woods somewhere looking for them right now. "Um, what's the last thing you remember?"

Gruncle recounted his freefall journey down the robot's throat, the beautiful room of electric chaos, then everything going bright white.

"I figured that was the end—and to be honest, I was okay with it, under the circumstances. Not that I was looking to check out early." Gruncle paused. "Can't believe I'm still here... and frankly, I'm confused as to how."

Molly didn't have an answer, only guesses. But she explained that after he had disappeared, there'd been a fiery explosion, with pieces flying off the robot in every direction— even its head. Then the rest of the robot had toppled into the gorge below the falls, where it still was today. And that this had all happened several months ago.

"Pieces were flying off, you say?" he asked.

"Yeah."

"Hmph." Gruncle mused, looking back at the frozen capsule. "Well, I'm guessing this traveling Popsicle stand here musta been one of 'em."

They were interrupted by a deep, long rumbling sound.

"They found us!" Finn shouted.

In seconds Arvin had loaded the borrowed wrist rocket with a buckeye. Molly had unholstered her weapon too.

"*Who* found us?" Gruncle asked.

Another monstrous roar filled the air, louder than the last.

"They're getting close! I can hear 'em," Margo said.

"Oh, *that*! Sorry for the scare." Gruncle patted his stomach. "That was my ol' tummy-tum. Just realized I'm starving. Anybody got a fluffernutter on 'em?"

"This should warm you up." Arvin reached into his back pocket and tossed Gruncle his last strip of spicy jerky.

"Thank you, friend. Uh, what's got you kids so jumpy?"

There was another rumble.

"T'weren't me that time!" Gruncle said with a mouthful of jerky, raising both his hands in a show of innocence.

There was a shuffle, then a squeak. It was the monstrous frogs. They were trying to make their way up the hill—but luckily were slipping on the icy surface.

Spotting them, Clovis let out a long, low whistle. "Holy horny toads! Them's the biggest hoppers I've ever laid eyes on."

They started croaking again. Then one of their tongues shot out and hit Arvin in the back. Luckily, he was still wearing Leonard's pack full of buckeyes. As soon as the tongue started yanking, Arvin wriggled free of the straps. Buckeyes spilled everywhere as the pack got pulled into the frog's hungry mouth.

"Gaahhh! My ammo!" Arvin cried. "You'll pay for that!" Quickly, he scooped up a handful of the fallen nuts and shoved them in his pockets before taking cover behind the capsule.

"That's gonna be one sick frog," Margo said. "Buckeyes are poisonous."

"Let's hope," Finn said.

More tongues shot in their general direction, but missed.

"Where are your manners!" Gruncle said. "Guess I'm not the only one who's hungry."

He raised an angry fist in the air. Not a moment later a tongue stuck to it, enveloping his hand in the sticky ball of mucus.

Molly and the Mutants

"Hey! Whaaaa—"

Without thinking, Molly aimed the Zap-O-Matic at the quivering tongue that was dragging her Gruncle across the ground and squeezed the trigger. She was only a few feet away, and the lightning found its mark. The tongue shook back and forth, then finally released its prey, retracting back into one of the giant frogs' mouths. It was Shark Fin. The monster croaked, a single plume of smoke escaping its green-and-yellow lips.

"That's a nasty habit there, fella. I should know," Clovis said. Then he turned to Molly. "Hoo! I feel tingly all over." His hair was sticking straight up from the voltage. Even the whiskers of his mustache were standing at attention. "Yessir. Got some pep in my step."

Gruncle jumped into the air and clicked his heels together, popping more joints.

Molly fired again. But the Zap-O-Matic spurted a few sparks before completely sputtering out.

"Oh no, it's outta juice!" she cried.

Molly gave it one more try, but all the barrel could muster was a flicker, giving the effect of a strobe light. As she watched the frogs down the hill, their syncopated movements in the flashing light reminded Molly of what the skaters looked like at the roller rink when the strobes were turned on. A frog disco.

But even though the Zap-O-Matic wasn't firing, it seemed to be having some effect. The four frogs just sat there, staring at the barrel of Gruncle's contraption, their yellow, glassy eyes mirroring the light show. She noticed their jaws all go slack. Arvin launched another buckeye at the closest one, which hit its right forearm before bouncing off. The frog didn't even flinch.

"I think they're hypnotized," Arvin said.

"Great. What do we do now?" Margo said. "Besides wait for the battery to die ... and then become frog food."

"Who's that one?" Gruncle whispered to Molly.

"My friend Margo," Molly whispered back.

"Quite the optimist."

"She's had a rough coupla days."

"Figured as much," Gruncle said. "But she has a point. We need a plan."

Molly racked her brain. Behind her the capsule rattled again, then made a loud *clunk*. A blast of icy vapor hissed out from the rows of pipes below. *The pipes. That's it.*

"I got it!" she said. "Arvin! Remember last winter when you dared all the munchkins at Conklin to lick the flagpole?"

Confused at the memory, Arvin followed Molly's gaze to the frosty core rods that lined the underside of the capsule.

Molly and the Mutants

They looked remarkably similar to flagpoles in the winter.

Arvin understood.

"Geeeenius," he said.

"Quick, everybody!" Molly called. "Climb around to the other side of this capsule!"

They all hustled, but Margo lost her footing on a patch of ice, her feet swinging out from under her. She began sliding down the hill... directly toward the frogs.

"No-no-no-no-no-no," she cried.

But the frogs, still mesmerized by the flashing light of the Zap-O-Matic, didn't appear to notice, even when she bumped right into Bat Wing. But as the battery continued to drain, the flashes became more irregular, and the mutant beasts appeared to rouse from their stupor. Bat Wing shuddered, then dropped his gaze.

"Quick, Margo!" Arvin yelled. "Get back up here!"

She scrambled back up the hill and joined the others just as the frogs resumed their pursuit. But their mucous-slick skin repeatedly slipped on the ice, then froze in place, buying Molly's group some time.

"Okay, everybody, push down on this side," Arvin instructed. "We want the core rods on the bottom to face the frogs."

Molly guessed that the capsule must weigh hundreds of

pounds, but its crash landing had bored a perfect cylindrical groove into the earth, which was now frozen solid into a slippery sheet of ice. With the five of them, it rolled pretty easily.

As the cryogenic chamber turned, it sounded like nails scraping a chalkboard, which grabbed the frogs' attention.

"Incoming!" Gruncle shouted. Everyone ducked.

All at once the four frogs fired their projectile tongues at the noise, and the tongues slammed against the core rods. Immediately their sticky ends froze to the hyper-cold surface.

"Not so tough now, are ya?" Margo said.

"Yes! Operation Flagpole successful!" Arvin declared.

The capsule rattled and shook. It made a short high-pitched whir, then stopped humming altogether. Green letters flickered across the digital display:

CORE BREACH DETECTED / POWER 3% / INITIATE THAW MODE

"What does that mean?"

"It means we gotta get outta here, is what," Gruncle said. "Before that Frigidaire rocket calls it quits."

The frogs all made a kind of half-croaking, half-gagging noise as they tried to retract their tongues. Seizing the opportunity, the humans made a beeline for their bicycles.

"Grunk?" Molly asked. "Do you think you can ride with me?"

Molly and the Mutants

Clovis arched his back and cracked his knuckles. "Sure thing, kiddo! I tell ya, after my deep-freeze nap, then a little *electrotherapy*, I feel like a whole new man. Tip-top. Ne'r been better!"

"Great... c'mon."

They hustled past the tongue-trapped frogs and mounted their bikes. At Molly's direction Clovis hopped onto the restored Pink Lightning, his boots finding footholds on its rear-wheel pegs.

"Hey," he said, "this looks a little different. Did you—"

"No time to explain, Gruncle," Molly said. "I'll tell ya later."

They hurried farther down the trail, the rattling of the capsule growing fainter in the distance.

Earlier in the day Molly's only worry had been finding Crank. Now it was finding her before something found them.

CHAPTER 27
TRACK THIRTY-NINE

"How long you think that'll hold 'em?" Finn said, looking back over his shoulder.

"Long enough for us to get far, far away, I hope," Molly said.

Eventually they made it out of the woods and into a field. The sun dipped down over the horizon, painting the sky with bright strokes of pink. It was beautiful.

Molly stopped to get her bearings.

Off in the distance and to the north, she caught sight of the round, lumpy peak of Ole Stoney, one of the larger hills in Far Flung Falls, large enough to get its own name at least. (Some even referred to it as Mount Stoney, but it was on the smaller side for a mountain.) What couldn't be contested, though, was that it was the largest single exposed chunk of Black Hand Sandstone in the state of Ohio, not to mention the most interesting. From various angles its rough, dark gray surface bore an uncanny resemblance to a man's head popping out of the ground. Not a handsome head by any measure, but nonetheless human-looking. Because of the way the sandstone had formed over the millennia, Ole Stoney sported several prominent features, including a considerable brow that overhung on the eastern-facing slope, giving its face a look of permanent disapproval. On the northern and southern sides of the hill sat two massive hollowed-out protrusions suggestive of ears. Their interiors were homes to great colonies of bats. But the most famous feature was a long narrow ridge that jutted out eastward below the brow, at just the right angle to simulate a nose. This was affectionately referred to as the Schnoz.

"Okay, guys," Molly said. "All we need to do is circle around the far side of Ole Stoney, then cut back through where the trails meet up on the high ground to the west."

It would make for a longer, harder, more circuitous route home, but it seemed safer. The frogs seemed to prefer the lower, wetter ground. And there was no way they were chancing another encounter if they doubled back from here. Everyone in the party agreed. They charged ahead.

"How's the ride, Grunk?"

"Peachy! I like whatcha've done with her," he said, patting the extendable banana seat. "This was a nice addition."

"The Vandervorkels got the idea from Blue Thunder."

"Well, then I guess I won't raise a fuss about *patent infringement*, heh!"

Molly still couldn't believe her Gruncle was here, talking to her. She couldn't wait to tell Wally, or her dad, or . . . She thought of her mom. *I guess I should tell her, too.* She was excited to share the news with everyone. Gruncle gave one of her shoulders a little squeeze, as if he were reading her mind. Molly reached back and gave his hand a pat. His body temperature seemed to have warmed a little. She took a deep breath, inhaling her Gruncle's familiar scent.

Their trail merged with a gravel path that veered off to the left. It was home to an old train track, long abandoned by the railroads.

"Hang a left, guys! We can follow these tracks around the mountain," Molly said.

In the few feet between the rails, the combination of ballast and earth had leveled out perfectly with the old railroad ties. It made for a surprisingly smooth bike path.

Molly and the Mutants

"Ah, track thirty-nine!" Gruncle exclaimed. "Come to think of it, Molly, there might be a shortcut."

"Oh? How's that, Grunk?" Molly asked.

"Yeah," Arvin added. "We can't go through solid stone."

"I'll take any shortcut," Margo said. "My legs are pooped."

"Me too," Finn said.

In response Clovis just mumbled "Thirty-nine" a few times, then started humming a tune. Molly thought, for as good as her Gruncle looked on the surface, maybe his innermost brain cells hadn't fully thawed yet. Like a TV dinner that was still cold and hard in the center. Maybe he just needed a little more time. His humming turned to singing, softly at first but gradually becoming more enthused. He held the last note of each verse like he was calling to a friend.

Nothing ever seemed so fiiiiiine...

As ridin' along track thirty-nine

They hurried along inside the dilapidated tracks, toward Ole Stoney.

Molly could hear the squeaks of Arvin's old Huffy just ahead of her, a steady rhythm that fell in line with her Gruncle's song....

What's mine is yours and yours is miiiiine...

On a long-forgotten railway line

But then she heard the rhythm of another squeak entirely, this one on a lower pitch, coming from down the track. Molly stole a glance over her shoulder. Her friends did the same.

"I think somebody's tailing us," Margo whispered.

"Or some*thing*," Finn said.

"Whatever it is, as long as it doesn't wanna eat me, I'm good," Arvin said.

Molly looked again. Was that a train? There was no way this weed-covered track could still be in use.

But there in the waning light, something was creeping up on them at a steady pace, along the track. Not a train, but something like it. A large table on wheels, with something smaller hitched to the back. There was a single figure standing on top, the silhouette of shoulders rising and falling in the same rhythm as the squeaking. Then the figure went still and the whole thing came to a halt just a few yards in front of them. Suddenly Molly recognized the shape of the silhouette's hair. She and her friends skidded to a stop in the dirt.

No way, she thought.

A voice from the silhouette, a few octaves higher than her Gruncle's, joined the tune.

Molly and the Mutants

May the ol' wind blow and the new moon shiiiiine...

As we make our way 'long thirty-nine

"Well, hullo there, Ronda," Gruncle said.

CHAPTER 28
AKA VELOCIPEDE

"Clovis? That you?" the Ronda-shaped silhouette said. "I thought you were... well, dead."

"Heh, me too!"

"Done in by a big ol' killer robot, was what I heard." Ronda stopped pumping the handcar.

"Well, maybe *done in* a little... but not all the way," Gruncle said. He hopped off the back of Molly's bike, stretching out his arms and wiggling his fingers to show he was still intact.

"Well. That's good."

"Yeah, ain't it?" Gruncle said. "Darndest thing."

"R-r-r-onda?" Molly stammered, too shocked to manage anything else. Could this day get any stranger? What was her

Molly and the Mutants

bus driver doing way out here? But as confused as she was, Molly found herself suddenly smiling. For some reason, the unexpected sight of her punk rock hero—casually talking to her definitely-not-dead Gruncle—gave Molly a tiny tinge of hope. There on the abandoned tracks, after being dealt one blow after another, it felt almost like the world might be tipping in their favor just a little. Like maybe things would be okay after all.

"Hey there, McCrusher," Ronda said, smiling back.

"Ronda, what are you doing out here?" Arvin asked.

Ronda paused a moment, considering the question. Her eyes passed over each of them in silence, assessing the situation.

"What am *I* doing out here? Just making some deliveries," she finally said. "School buses aren't the only thing I drive, ya know, not with what they pay me." To emphasize her point Ronda turned her head and spat. As she did, Molly heard her earrings jingle. Ronda returned her attention to Clovis. She hopped off the platform and took a step toward Gruncle.

"Gotta make a living someway somehow," she said.

Gruncle raised his eyebrows and smiled.

"Gotta make a living somehow someway," he slowly repeated, reversing the order of the last two words.

Molly wasn't sure what, but just then something passed between the two adults. They gave each other a little nod, extending their hands.

Molly watched them shake, but it wasn't a normal shake, like most grown-ups did. They kept their thumbs pointing up, and interlocked their little fingers, so their thumbs and pinkies both stuck out. Molly had so many questions, but they'd have to wait.

In the distance a *yuuuurrrp* cut the greeting ritual short.

"That's a new sound for these parts," Ronda said.

"Uh, we best be on our way," Gruncle said.

Another deep guttural croak echoed in the distance—only not as distant as before.

Ronda's brow furrowed. "Hmm. Might you be requiring some assistance this evening on your journey?" she asked, climbing back onto the platform.

"Yes please!" Margo said.

"We would be much obliged," Gruncle said.

"All aboard, then," Ronda said.

Gruncle was the first to mount the handcar. Molly, Margo, Arvin, and Finn loaded their bikes next to some cargo on the small trailer hitched behind, then joined Gruncle and Ronda on the platform up front. And without another pause Ronda resumed her pumping of the crank.

Molly checked behind her to make sure their bikes were secure. That's when she noticed exactly what Ronda was transporting. Four open crates with neat rows of ceramic jugs inside. The stems of the jugs, with their little loop handles and cork stoppers, poked out of the top of the crates. Molly immediately recognized the containers. She'd seen them before at her Gruncle's cabin.

Under normal circumstances, Molly wasn't sure if a bunch of kids hitching a ride with all that moonshine was a good idea, but these were definitely not normal circumstances. And she appreciated the lift. Her legs felt all wobbly from the miles they'd covered, up and down hills. Still, it didn't seem right for Ronda to be doing all the work.

"Can I help?" Molly asked.

"Sure thing, McCrusher," Ronda said.

"I can too," Finn said.

"Well, all right then," Ronda said, stepping aside and smiling. "Be my guest."

Molly and Finn stood on opposite sides of the pump, taking turns pushing down on the handle. She exchanged glances with Finn. Amazingly, his hair still looked great. After a few moments they found their rhythm, and they were cruising. Something about the repetition in the movement made it feel almost normal, which was funny, because absolutely nothing was normal about running for your lives from ravenous mutant frogs aboard a... who knows what.

"Hey, whaddya call this thing?" Molly asked.

"Some call it a handcar... aka a *velocipede*.... That's the term I prefer. This one here is double-geared. Watch." Ronda reached over and pulled a lever. *Thoomp.* Molly felt something heavy shift under her feet. Suddenly the handle became slightly more resistant, but now each push propelled them much faster.

"Double time!" Gruncle shouted. "Ha!"

"Ve-loc-i-pede." Molly repeated the word. "I like it."

In hushed tones Gruncle caught Ronda up on their situation. The tracks rumbled underneath them as they rolled along the rails.

Kachunka-chunka-chunka-chunka-chunka-chunka-chunka...

It was a soothing sound, steady and sure, every pump putting more distance between themselves and danger. The velocipede rounded a bend, and they were flanked on both sides by thick patches of wildflowers. The blur of pink and

Molly and the Mutants

purple blossoms gave Molly a feeling that everything would be fine. How could something bad happen in such a beautiful setting like this? Molly inhaled, taking in the sweet scent that filled the air.

Still, in the back of her mind she couldn't shake the worry that those monsters might catch up to them. But the presence of her Gruncle and Ronda gave her a little more confidence in their odds. These were grown-ups, after all, and they'd know what to do—they would deliver them to safety, then maybe call some other grown-ups... the park ranger, or the police, or the army. Molly wasn't sure. But whatever the grown-ups did, it had to take care of things. And that would get them one step closer to finding Crank.

Molly had learned that you couldn't always count on grown-ups to do the right thing. Not every single time. But she wasn't ready to give up on them completely. These were two of the best she'd known. Molly craned her neck over to the side while she pumped, watching to make sure they weren't being followed. Behind them, nothing but old track and wildflowers.

"See anything?" Finn asked.

In the dusk it was hard to make out what was happening too far down the track.

But then an unmistakable croak, followed by a few more.

Soon, in the distance, giant shadows were hopping along the tracks, coming in their direction.

"There," Ronda said, pointing.

"C'mon," Arvin said to Margo.

The two jumped up to help with the pumping, doubling up on each handle.

"What if we don't make it?" Margo said.

"Oh, we'll make it," Arvin said.

"Well," Clovis said, rubbing his chin, "looks like if we wanna stay outta one belly... we're gonna hafta go into another."

"You sure?" Ronda said. She raised an eyebrow.

Clovis nodded.

"To the Schnoz," she said.

The croaking continued in the distance at regular intervals, spurring them on.

Molly looked up at the darkening sky, hoping her brother had stayed clear of the woods tonight.

CHAPTER 29
FORMULA X

Wally lowered his army-issue binoculars. They were a keepsake from his Gruncle's cabin. It felt fitting to be using them on the cliff's edge, scanning the countryside for any sign of his sister and her friends. After they had barely escaped getting buried alive in the tunnel, he and Gunther had been happy to move to higher ground. And maybe they could get a better view of what was happening from up here.

Bringing the binoculars had been Gunther's idea, which Wally thought was genius. They could use all the help they could get finding Crank. There was a lot of ground to cover, and Wally really wanted to come through for his sister. Even if he had never felt much of a connection to their old tabby himself, he knew Molly had. And he felt like he owed her one. After all, she had saved them all from getting incinerated over the summer by a rogue robot.

The two boys were standing just a few feet from the spot where Blue Thunder had jumped off—with both of them on it. Sometimes Wally still couldn't believe he had done that. It had only been a few months, but to Wally it felt like a lifetime ago. He raised his binoculars again, but this time tilted them down. Nearly a hundred feet below, the fallen robot lay sprawled out in the water-filled gorge. Partly submerged, arms detached, and riddled with scorches and holes, its metal body looked like it had been through a war.

Which, in a way, it had. They all had.

"I can't believe we made it all the way up here in no time," Wally said.

"I know," Gunther said. "They're pretty fast." He shot a glance at his newest inventions, which they'd taken off and left on the bank of the creek, just a little upstream of the waterfall. The boys were still getting the hang of them and weren't sure it would be safe to wear them this close to the cliff's edge. Together they scoured the horizon.

"Any sign of them?" Wally called out. "Or Crank?"

"I don't see anybody," Gunther called, his hand shielding

his eyes from the late-afternoon sun. "But don't worry. We'll find them."

This entire spot was a kind of memorial now. Wally took a few steps to his left and brushed his fingers across the newly installed plaque, feeling the raised letters along the top:

CLOVIS OBADIAH STOKES

"Is that for your Gruncle?" Gunther asked.

"Yeah," Wally said. He read the writing out loud. "In honor of a hometown hero of Far Flung Falls, this plaque commemorates the sacrifice of Clovis Obadiah Stokes, a beloved and respected member of our community. On May 28, 1983, when the time came, he leapt into action."

Wally still remembered watching his fearless Gruncle springboard off the bottom of the airborne motorcycle, far out past the cliff's edge, where he had been dangling from a thread, and dive headfirst into the jaws of the robot, which now lay in a heap.

"That's really cool," Gunther said, gliding his fingers across the plaque.

"It is, isn't it?" Wally said. He had never thought of his Gruncle as a "beloved and respected member" of the community, but Gruncle was very beloved by Wally.

"He deserved it," Gunther said. "I only knew him for . . .

well, for a few minutes really. But he was one of the bravest, kindest... and funniest men I ever met. I'll never forget him."

"Me either."

The creek water spilled over the cliff's edge in a steady stream. For a minute or two it was the only sound as the boys scanned the massive gorge and sprawling woods below.

"Wally?" Gunther said.

"Yeah?"

"About your Gruncle. I wish I—"

"I know," Wally said. "It's okay." He gave his friend a smile that said, *I don't blame you.* "You wanna know something funny? Whenever I come out to the woods, I feel like... he's still here. Isn't that weird? I mean, I know what I saw that day. So many 'splosions."

"So many," Gunther agreed.

Wally eyed the robot's body again. That's when he noticed the small circular hole directly in the center.

"Hey, Gunther. Was that hole always there? The one that looks like... like a belly button?"

Gunther followed Wally's gaze. His eyes widened.

"No," he said. "That was a safety feature, an escape hatch. But..."

Gunther didn't finish. They sat together in silence. The

sun sank lower on the sky, dipping into the trees to the west. Warm, golden light danced across the water's surface.

"Wally?" Gunther piped up again. "That feeling that you mentioned, that your Gruncle... is still here?"

"Yeah?" Wally said.

"Well, I think you might be onto something," Gunther said.

"Yeah?"

"Yeah."

Wally lowered his binoculars and let them rest on his chest. A leather strap held them in place around his neck. He rubbed his eyes. They'd been looking for a while.

The sun slid past the trees. Gold flecks from its rays that had played along the water's surface disappeared. Wally kept his gaze fixed on the circular hole in the robot's center.

"That's funny," Wally said.

"What?" Gunther asked.

"You see how the sunlight isn't reflected on the water anymore?"

"Yeah," Gunther said.

"Except for there. Look." He pointed again to the small circular hole. A soft golden glow emanated from within.

Gunther's eyes widened even more this time.

"Oh no," he said.

"What?"

"Oh no, no, no," Gunther repeated. "The canisters. The ones that held... Formula X. They must've... Wally, I think there's been a breach."

"Wait," Wally said. "Whaddya mean, a breach? What's *Formula X*?"

"It's what my dad called it," Gunther explained. "One of the experimental compounds he created... a way to kind of supercharge heavy machinery. I might've *borrowed* it to power the robot."

"You mean *stole*," Wally clarified.

In response Gunther made a kind of humming noise, and Wally couldn't tell if it was an admission or not.

"So, the thing is, Formula X is a teensy-weensy bit, uh, radioactive."

"A teensy-weensy bit," Wally repeated.

"Yeah," Gunther said. "So now I've got a theory about what happened when we were in the tunnel. And what might be happening out here. And it's not good. C'mon, we better go and find the others."

"Which way?"

Gunther looked at the belly button again. "Good question," he said. He held up his thumb in the air and turned around, like he was trying to line something up. "Do you remember which direction the robot was facing before it fell?"

"Yeah, back at the cliff, a little to the left." Wally gestured with his hand.

"Okay, let's go that way," Gunther said. "Hopefully we can catch up with the others... before anything else does."

The two hurried back to their contraptions and suited up.

"Anything else like what?" Wally asked.

Gunther didn't answer.

CHAPTER 30
THE SCHNOZ

"Uh, guys? I dunno if we can outrun them on this," Finn said, eyes fixed on their giant green pursuers.

"We're pumping as hard as we can!" Molly said.

"Yeah, let us know if you have any other ideas," Arvin said.

"I don't!" Finn said.

"Okay, then!"

The rattling of the velocipede's wheels continued along the track, now at a higher tempo:

Kachunka-chunka-chunka-chunka-chunka-chunka-chunka...

"Mr. Clovis?" Margo asked.

"Call me *Gruncle*!"

"Okay, Gruncle? What's the Schnoz?"

Molly and the Mutants

"It's our best chance," he said. "You'll see."

Molly knew what the Schnoz was but had no idea how a giant nose-shaped rock sticking out of the side of a hill in the middle of nowhere could possibly help them escape. But she had faith in her Gruncle. He hadn't failed her before—well, not when it really counted, at least.

Ole Stoney came closer into view, and from the angle of their approach, the hill bore an uncanny resemblance to the upturned face of a grumpy old man, as if he were looking toward the sky, and found it lacking. Or had just got a whiff of something unpleasant. One of the face's most prominent features was the Schnoz, a sharp, angular nose that jutted out in their direction. The underside of the formation was marked by a pair of side-by-side indentations. The nostrils.

As the group approached, they passed by an immense boulder with an overhang at the top, disturbing a colony of bats that had been loitering there. The bats reacted to the passing handcar as if someone had thrown a grenade. Immediately a hundred pairs of tiny leathery wings went flapping in every direction.

Margo noticed first and screamed. Arvin and Finn turned their heads and screamed even more loudly.

"Rad," said Molly, unfazed. She didn't mind bats.

"Totally," Ronda agreed.

They were literally going to pass right under Ole Stoney's nose, looping around the bend of the mountain, with the mutant frogs not far behind.

"They're gaining on us!" Margo said.

"Not if I can help it," Arvin said.

Arvin had taken up point on the back of the trailer, unloading his remaining supply of buckeyes from his pockets. He was a good shot, but the impact only gave his targets the briefest pause.

"You weren't lying," Ronda said. "Those are the biggest frogs I've ever seen. You sure they're even frogs?"

In response the closest one shot out his projectile tongue, came up just a few feet short of them, nabbed one of the bats right out of the air, and pulled it back into its mouth.

"Well then, I guess they are," said Ronda, answering her own question.

The other frogs seemed to notice the new quarry. They all slowed a bit to snack on the bats darting overhead. They were good shots. Or maybe there were so many bats, it was hard to miss, like fish in a barrel. Either way, Molly was grateful for the distraction.

Molly and the Mutants

They kept pumping the velocipede. Molly could feel her arms burning. She saw the tracks fork up ahead.

"Shortcut?" Gruncle said.

"Definitely," Ronda replied.

Gruncle nodded and turned to Molly.

"Molly, we got no time to stop, but we need to hit that switch marker. See it?" He pointed to a small metal stand. It was up ahead on their right, with a short arm that stuck out to one side. "You got any sugg—"

"Arvin!" Molly said, before her Gruncle could finish.

"On it," Arvin said, turning around and aiming Leonard's wrist rocket at the marker. He notched a buckeye and let it fly. It was a miss, smashing against the center stand without moving the lever.

"Again!" Finn said.

"I know," Arvin grunted.

He took a breath, retrieved another buckeye, then turned it over to get it perfectly positioned. They were about to pass the marker. Quickly he pulled back and let it rip. *WHAM*. The buckeye smashed into the arm, flipping it a full one hundred eighty degrees. There was a loud THUNK as the rail markers shifted to the left, adjusting their route to the turnout. The tracks locked in place without a moment to spare. At the junction the velocipede veered to the left, along with everybody on it.

Molly did a quick head count and thought maybe with the six of them they stood a little better chance at making it through. Even if they hadn't located Crank, Molly was happy to have added the two grown-ups to their party. Especially her Gruncle.

They barreled down the rails, straight for the Schnoz.

But before they arrived at the mountainside, they had something else to contend with. Up ahead an enormous tree had fallen over the tracks.

"We're blocked!" Finn shouted.

"Oh crap," Molly said.

"We need to brake," Arvin said.

Behind them their pursuers were croaking again. Apparently, with the frogs' bellies empty, the bats had just been an appetizer—which still left the kids and grown-ups for the main course.

"Can't," Ronda said. "But don't worry. That tree's just a diversion."

"*Diversion?*" Finn squeaked. "We'll crash for sure."

"Arvin, you got one more shot in ya?" Gruncle said.

Molly and the Mutants

"Definitely," he said.

"See that ol' boot setting atop that post o'er yonder?" Gruncle said.

"I do."

"Knock it off."

"But I didn't do anything."

"Hah! No, my boy." Gruncle grinned. "I mean... Knock. It. Off!"

"Oh! Yeah. Okay." Arvin fished in his pocket. "I got one left!"

They raced toward the tree. Finn closed his eyes. Margo turned her head. Molly bit her lip. And Arvin fired off his last buckeye, easily knocking the boot from its post. It fell, but not all the way to the ground. Instead it hung halfway between the top and the bottom of the post, suspended. A second later a series of pops erupted from all around, with sprays of leaves and dirt flying into the air. A rope sprang up from one end of the fallen tree, drew itself tight, and—*SNAP!*—hoisted the tree right off the ground, like they were being admitted into a parking garage. Two seconds after they'd passed underneath, the tree crashed back down onto the tracks with a thunderous *BOOM*.

"Nice shot," said Margo.

"Dead eye," said Molly.

Moments later they watched Three Eyes hop right over it. Shark Fin followed.

"A more effective deterrent with wheeled pursuers," Ronda said.

"You ain't lying," Arvin said.

"Good thing we got one trick left," Gruncle said. "Ronda, should we ... crank 'er up?"

"Crank who up?" Finn asked.

"You got it," Ronda said. "All right, kids, you've been doing a fine job. Now just leggo the pump and stand back a sec."

"Are you crazy?" Margo said. "They're practically on us!"

"Trust me."

They relented, and Ronda reached over and lifted a hidden compartment at the handcar's the base. She reached down and paused.

"Everybody find something to grab ahold of, and quick," Gruncle said.

"Wait, this thing had a motor?" Finn asked, rubbing his arms. "The whole time?"

Everyone braced themselves, reaching for one of the low iron railings that lined the car's edges. Ronda grabbed a cord and pulled. Nothing. She sighed, then pulled again. On the third yank something finally caught and made a gurgling sound, and the cart lurched forward. Thick black clouds of smoke belched from under their feet, enveloping them in darkness.

Molly and the Mutants

The kids all started coughing.

Yuuuuurrrrrp. Yuuuuurrrrrp.

The croaks were louder, which meant the frogs were closer.

From its hidden compartment the small compact engine sparked to life, kicking out a little more smoke. And just like that they were off, the sudden acceleration pressing everyone back.

All the passengers tightened their grips on the railing. Except Finn. He hadn't grabbed anything nearly as secure. Instead he stumbled backward onto the cargo trailer, searching for anything to hold. Finally, he gripped one of the ceramic jugs, hooking his finger through the loop on the handle. It wasn't much, but it was better than nothing.

"Whooaaa," said Finn.

"Careful there," said Ronda.

"Yes!" said Arvin.

"Now you're talking!" said Margo.

"Why didn't you do that before?" asked Molly.

"You'll see," said Ronda.

They charged along toward the face of Ole Stoney. The tracks appeared to dead-end right under the Schnoz. Or into its left nostril, to be more exact.

But the nostril in question was boarded up with a

mishmash of old wooden boards, and it looked like things had been that way for a long time. Across one of the boards red letters spelled out **NO TRESPASSING**.

"Um, Gruncle?" Molly asked.

"Just another diversion. Don't you mind."

Molly spun her head around to see all four frogs now clearly in view, and they were gaining ground.

A second later their handcar must've triggered a lever on the tracks. Because as soon as they passed the spot, the barricade swung open like two hinged doors. Tripping the lever had caused the velocipede to bounce—and for the trailer hitched behind it to bounce even more. Everyone held on in place, gripping the rail, one another, or the pump handle itself.

"Whoaaaa!" Finn said again, bouncing several inches off the platform's base. The motion traveled up his body and into his arm, cracking it like a whip ... and flinging the ceramic jug high into the air. The jug spun as it flew, and landed upside down in the crook of a branch overhead. Molly's hunch about the jug's contents was confirmed when she caught a distinct **XXX** on its side—the mark for moonshine. As it lodged, the force of the impact unstopped the cork from its spout.

Watching helplessly, Ronda let out a tiny groan, followed by a word that probably shouldn't be said around children.

Molly and the Mutants

"My recipe," she sighed.

"Sorry," Finn whispered.

"That was a good batch."

Blub-blub-blub-blub-blub. Behind them the upside-down jug began emptying its contents directly onto the tracks below, a steady stream of clear liquid, just as the first frog passed underneath. It was Muscles. The burly beast paused, turning its head. Just behind its protruding eyes, Ronda's recipe splashed onto the creature's head and trickled down its body and legs.

"What's it doing?" Ronda asked.

"Taking a shower?" Finn said.

"Getting drunk?" Margo said.

"Don't look like it's drinking." Gruncle said.

"Might be," Arvin said. "Frogs actually drink through patches in their skin."

"How do you know?" Molly asked.

"School. Duh," said Arvin.

Muscles was several yards behind them. It appeared the jug was now empty. The frog hopped, but went sideways, crashing into the tree beside it, then scrambled with its brawny hind legs to get itself upright again.

Maybe it was drunk. Had Finn accidentally saved them?

"Way to use the ol' noggin there, Finn," Gruncle said.

"And my recipe," Ronda said.

"Sorry," Finn said again.

Everything around them shifted to dark as the mountain swallowed them up. The scene they'd been watching was now framed by a rectangular rock entrance, getting smaller and smaller by the second.

They were inside the Schnoz, heading deeper into the solid rock of Ole Stoney. Molly had never known about a secret tunnel, which made sense. Wasn't that the point of secret tunnels, for people not to know about them? She wondered how many other things these woods kept secret... woods she'd thought she knew, but now wasn't so sure.

The entrance was growing smaller behind them, and the boards swung back on their hinges, closing off the dangers outside, as well as any remaining light.

With the mutant frogs on the other side of that barricade, Molly thought she should feel safer now. Then how come she didn't?

CHAPTER 31
SPIDER JUNCTION

Inside the mountain it was several degrees colder. As the handcar pushed them deeper into the tunnel, farther and farther from the entrance, the darkness become almost impenetrable.

"I can't see a darn thing," said Arvin.

"I'm scared," said Margo.

"Hold up just a sec," Ronda said. "I've got a light somewh—"

"I got it," Finn said, flicking on a small flashlight and shining it in everyone's faces, promptly blinding them.

"Hey, not in the eyes, Finn," Arvin said.

"Oh, sorry." Finn pointed it down.

"That's good. Keep it right there," Ronda said. As their eyes adjusted, she made her way to the front of the velocipede, knelt down, and reached around the front of the platform.

While Ronda searched for something, the motor slowed from a low roar to a putter. It sputtered a few more times before giving out completely. They rolled in the darkness for a while longer before creeping to a stop. The tunnel was eerily quiet, save for a faint breeze that whistled through the passage.

"Sounds like ol' Schnoz's got hisself a nose whistler, heh!" Gruncle said.

"I've had those before," Finn said.

"Guess that makes us the booger," Arvin said.

Some giggles echoed in the dark.

Click.

"There we go," Ronda said.

A soft amber light emanated from a headlamp fastened to the front of the car, illuminating the tracks before them down a tunnel that looked like it never ended.

"I think we're back to elbow grease," Gruncle said.

"Whose turn at bat?" Ronda asked.

"I got it," Arvin said.

"Me too," Margo chimed in.

They were soon back in action, pumping the handle up

and down, making steady progress into the dark depths of the tunnel, the headlamp giving them a view of just a few feet ahead.

"Gruncle, what's this tunnel for?" Molly finally asked.

"Yeah, and how did you know about it?" Margo looked at Ronda.

"I heard this railroad was abandoned, like, forever ago," Arvin said.

"It was," Ronda said. "Well, not *forever*. But officially it stopped being used nearly thirty years ago. At least by trains."

"It's true," Gruncle said. "But *we* didn't stop, did we, Ronda? No we didn't, no ma'am!"

"What your Gruncle Clovis here is saying is that this particular offshoot that runs through Far Flung Falls, *track thirty-nine*, was once connected to the great Buckeye Line, which still runs today, all the way up through the state capital, and on and on to Bowling Green way up north—"

"I thought Bowling Green was down in Kentucky?" Margo said.

"There's another one in Ohio," Ronda said.

"Yeah, the better one," Gruncle said, smiling.

"Oh," Margo said.

"And back in 1954," Gruncle continued, "when I was a

younger man, the railroad muckety-mucks just abandoned these tracks to... the *wilds*."

"If by *wilds* you mean us," Ronda said.

"That's right," Gruncle said. "We'd been using it too, on the sly, if you will, to transport various, uh, *essential sundries and such* to our friends and neighbors since the 1920s, when things started getting squeezed."

"The twenties?" Margo said. "Wait, how old are you guys?"

"We're talking about *families*, my dear," Gruncle said. "On Molly's mama's side the Jorgensens have been bootlegging for generations."

"The Steltzers, too," Ronda said, naming her own family. "Since the days of Prohibition."

"We studied that in history," Finn said. "So, are you guys, like... *criminals*?"

"No," Molly said, "not my Gruncle." She wasn't sure if that was entirely true, but bristled at the accusation.

"Well, I like to think of it more like ... *entrepreneurs*," Gruncle said.

"Yeah, we're a couple of entrepreneurs!" Ronda said.

The two grown-ups started laughing, until Arvin interrupted.

Molly and the Mutants

"You're talking about moonshine," Arvin said. "I know what that is."

"Oh, do ya now?" Ronda said, giving him a look. "Not too familiar, I hope."

"Oh, no ma'am!" Arvin said. "I've never actually tried it or anything."

"Good," Ronda said.

"But what I don't get is, why sneak around at night on this abandoned track?" Arvin asked. "Hasn't Prohibition been over for like a million years?"

"Try fifty," Molly corrected.

"That's true," Gruncle said, "the Prohibition Era ended back in '33, I believe."

"But out here in Far Flung Falls, it's still a business, and highly competitive," Ronda said.

"And the family recipes that've been passed down for generations are closely guarded secrets. Priceless!" Gruncle said. "If we stick to the way we've been doing it, we steer clear of any nosy neighbors, or prying eyes."

"Or the government," Ronda said. "Don't forget about them!"

"Ah yes, how could I? Those fellas are no fun at all! But to answer your question as to why we still do it this way," Gruncle said, "it's tradition."

"And community," Ronda added.

"Yes, and . . . this spectacular view!" Gruncle said. At that the two moonshiners broke into laughter again. Gruncle's laugh turned into a cough.

Years ago, Molly had taken a whiff of one of the uncorked jugs at her Gruncle's cabin, and nearly burned her nose off. Her eyes had watered forever. Since then, she couldn't understand why anyone would want anything to do with something as pain-inducing as moonshine. But she loved her Gruncle. And she couldn't argue with things like *tradition* or *community*. Grown-ups just didn't make sense sometimes.

Ronda's and Gruncle's laughs echoed down the tunnel, which gradually widened into a high-ceilinged cave, with hundreds of stalactites hanging from above, each one tapering down to a very fine point—that was aiming right at them. From the view below, the stalactites looked less than welcoming. But Gruncle and Ronda appeared unconcerned, so Molly relaxed a little. The floor of the cave was a kind of mirror image, with equally pointy stalagmites of every size rising up from the ground. Some actually met in the middle to form columns. To Molly the space felt sacred somehow, like an ancient cathedral.

Molly and the Mutants

The track continued straight ahead. No longer hemmed in by tight walls on either side, for the first time in a while, Molly breathed a little easier. Maybe they were safe here in this subterranean sanctuary.

When they reached the cave's center, the rail crossed over a wide raised wooden platform that stood flush with the railway ties, so it didn't interrupt the track. The floor was circular, made from thick wooden planks, and framed with iron. At its center, under the tracks, the blackened image of an enormous spider was burned into the wood, its eight spindly legs splayed out evenly in every direction, like the spokes of a wheel.

"Welcome to . . . *Spider Junction!*" Gruncle announced with a dramatic flair, extending his arms wide.

"How come they call it Spi . . . *oh*," Finn said, figuring out the answer before he could finish the question. As they made their way onto the rounded platform, they found themselves in the middle of an eight-way intersection. They stopped in the circle's center.

"Eight legs. Eight directions. All set to the points of the compass. See?" Gruncle pointed around to each tunnel. There were letters marking the top of every one. The handcar had come through the one labeled **E**, for *east*. Molly followed the line of the tracks to the opposite wall, labeled with a **W**, for *west*. Perpendicular to those, another track ran between tunnels labeled **N** and **S** for *north* and *south*. And in between, Molly found four more, marked **NE**, **NW**, **SE**, and **SW**.

"That's right. Take you in just about any direction you wanna go," Ronda said, following Molly's stare.

"Of course, a couple of 'em lead straight to nowhere," Gruncle said.

"That's true . . . but *nowhere* might be exactly where some people wanna go sometimes," Ronda said.

"You're right about that," Gruncle said.

"Whenever I'm here," Ronda said, "I like to think that each entrance takes me to a different possible future."

"Where'zat one go?" Arvin asked, pointing to the one marked **W**, opposite the way they'd come. After the **W**, someone had scratched some more letters into the cave wall, so it read **WRONG WAY**.

Ronda and Gruncle exchanged looks.

"Nowhere we need to go tonight," Gruncle said. "We've seen enough danger."

When he said it, Molly noticed her Gruncle's face darken for a moment, before he turned away.

"There was . . . a sinkhole," Ronda said, "many years ago. Before you guys were born. Just outside the face of the mountain. It got wider and deeper in just a matter of days. Some people called it the Bottomless Pit. It swallowed up everything. The land, tracks... even a few people." At the mention of people, her face tightened.

The Bottomless Pit, Molly recalled. Why did that sound so familiar? Then she remembered the story about Gruncle's long-lost brother, her Gramp Cletus, how he'd been so curious, then disappeared. She'd always figured that was just a story, but maybe it was true.

"Well, I'd like the tunnel that takes us all home safe and sound, please," Margo said.

"Me too," Arvin said. "How do you turn this thing?" He gave the velocipede a few taps.

Ronda strode over to a giant lever, nearly as tall as she was, and gave it a hard yank, locking the platform in place. As she started to explain the mechanics of the junction, how it had been in operation for nearly sixty years, Molly only half listened. She kept peering around the stalagmites, scanning all the other tunnel entrances, thinking about all the different possible futures that lay ahead, and which one they'd choose.

Only now, for some strange reason, she wasn't in quite such a hurry. At least for the moment. Maybe it was being surrounded by so many solid rock formations that had stood there for eons. The cave felt like a fortress, removed from the rest of the world outside. A world where cats go missing, and giant frogs try to eat you and all your friends, and everything moves a little too fast. She felt like she could stay here for a long time, maybe forever.

"Before we go, lemme show y'all something," Gruncle said.

"You sure?" Ronda said to him in a voice that said she wasn't.

"Well, they're *here*, ain't they?"

CHAPTER 32
NEW CREW

"Okay, then," Ronda finally said. "Let's go."

She lifted the headlamp off the front post of the velocipede and swung it to her right. Everyone hopped off the platform and followed. As they walked, Molly craned her neck upward to see just how high the ceiling went, but it was a little too dark to tell for sure. Up against the far wall, next to the tunnel labeled **N**, lay a long wooden table and chairs. In place of legs the table was held in place by four perfectly placed stalagmites that poked up through its corners.

It looked as if the tabletop had fallen from the ceiling, quadruple-impaling itself to the spot. But that wasn't even the most interesting thing about it. Molly's eye zoomed in on something sticking straight up from the table's center, a collection of rather large and scary-looking bowie knives, their points all deeply embedded into the wood like they'd dropped from above and murdered the table even further after its initial fall.

Ronda lit a few more lanterns on the table. With the additional light Molly got a better sense of the scale of the place. The stalagmites nearest them cast long shadows across the cave floor. And the ceiling seemed to go up forever, stretching farther than the lamps could reach.

"What's this?" Finn asked. He had wandered over to the far wall, drawn to the engravings that covered it. Scores of names and dates, all scratched in different hands, going back for decades. Above them all a large symbol was etched into the stone. Molly immediately recognized it as the same one she'd found on the Zap-O-Matic. Three drops emanating from a crescent moon.

"This is where the Crew used to have our meetings," Gruncle said.

"The Crew?" Margo asked.

"The Moonlight Crew," Ronda said.

"Who are all these people?" Arvin asked.

"Everybody who's ever been here," Gruncle said.

Molly and the Mutants

One of the names off to the side caught Molly's eye. *Caroline "Li'l C" Stokes*. It was her mom. Molly ran her fingers over the roughly etched letters.

Of course my mom was part of this, Molly thought. She and Gruncle had been as thick as thieves. Molly pictured her mom running around at night, pumping handcars by the light of the moon. How many things didn't she know about her mom? Or about any adult? Did they all carry secrets like this in their hearts? Was every grown-up a member of some secret club? Then she spied more names. *Cletus Zebadiah Stokes*. Her long-gone gramps. And just below that his brother, *Clovis Obadiah Stokes*. Also known as Gruncle. Someone she had thought was gone, but now wasn't. The list continued. . . .

Jefferson H. Murray Jr.

"Wait, Old Man Murray?" Molly asked. "He's a member?"

"One of the originals," Gruncle said.

"Murray's a *junior*? Isn't he, like, a hundred?" Arvin asked.

"Well, heh, maybe close. He doesn't get out much, 'tis true," Gruncle said. "But still very helpful to the cause."

Dorothy "Big Dot" Bigelow

Leroy "Lightning" DuGraw

Abigail Casternally

Deloss G.

Molly read off the names to herself. There must have been dozens of them, many belonging to people she didn't know. Then she found another familiar one: *Ronda Steltzer*. She looked over at her bus driver, whom she'd always suspected but now knew was much more than a bus driver.

"And now it's time to add yours," Ronda said. "Grab a knife."

Molly was relieved the knives were for etching into the rock, and not something more sinister. Each of the four of them pried a blade out of the table and picked a spot on the wall. Molly placed her palm against it, the stone cool to her touch. She felt her heart slowly unclench in her chest. Something about this spot gave her the feeling like she belonged. Like home.

"Ouch," Finn said, the tiniest droplet of blood blooming in the center of his thumb.

"Oh geez," Arvin said.

"Yessir, they're sharp," Gruncle said. "No need to test 'em. Nobody go losing a finger, now."

It took a few minutes, but with a little pressure and persistence, the ancient black sandstone of the cave eventually gave in to the steely will of their knives. Completing the *M* and onto the *O* of her name, Molly soon discovered that straight lines were a lot easier to make in the rock than curvy ones. But

Molly and the Mutants

she found the simultaneous scritch-scratch of the four blades working all at once to be comforting. So she took her time. When they were done, the Moonlight Crew boasted four new members:

Molly Jean McQuirter

Margaret "Margo" Keen

Finn D. Garrett

Arvin Shadrach Simmons

Besides their names, they'd all written the date: *October 7, 1983.* Finn's was accented with a few fresh smears of blood from his thumb. And Arvin had carved one extra detail. Below his name the arcade champion had added his trademark three initials—in large capital letters.

"Arvin!" Margo blurted, the first to notice.

"Eh... had to," Arvin said. He gave a shrug.

Everyone laughed.

But under the jokes and the laughter, and Finn's still-bleeding thumb, to Molly there was something about the act of adding their names to this roster deep in the earth that gave an air of ceremony to the moment, a feeling that made her feel connected to everyone around her.

"We were here," Arvin whispered, picking up on the feeling. "We can always say that."

"Well, now it's official... even sealed in blood, heh!" Gruncle laughed. But then his expression turned serious. "Just one thing, though."

"You can't tell anyone about it," Ronda said.

"That's right," Gruncle said. "It's top secret."

"Why's that?" Finn asked.

"Tradition," Ronda said.

"And it's more fun," Gruncle said.

"Well, my mom and dad are gonna need some explanation for why I'm out so late," Finn said.

"Yeah, whadda I tell my folks?" Margo asked.

Molly was wondering the same thing. It was well past dark. She checked her Casio. 7:46 p.m. Her dad would probably be starting to worry right about now... if he wasn't too busy playing kissy-face with Vilomena.

"Excellent point," Gruncle said. "Ronda, how about we fire up the shortwave?"

"You mean you got electricity in here?" Arvin asked.

"When the generator's running we do," Clovis said. "I'll go give it a crank, see if we can't give our squawk box some juice."

"Deal," Ronda said. "I'll run point on the horn."

Without pause Ronda and Clovis marched over to the nearest stalagmite. In its shadow there was a small desk that Molly

Molly and the Mutants

hadn't noticed. On top sat a metal box and a microphone, and beside it was a rusty old portable generator. Gruncle got to work. He fiddled with the choke, yanked the cord, then finally began beating the ancient engine with a large monkey wrench. Eventually, the combination of tactics brought the generator back to life.

In contrast, Ronda simply flipped a few switches and turned the dial. The box spit static.

"Pretty sure that's a CB radio," Arvin said.

"A cee-bee-what?" Molly asked.

"You know, like truckers use?" Arvin said. "My uncle's got one."

Molly saw a couple of wires travel out from the back of the box and along the cave floor until they disappeared down one of the tunnels.

"We've got an antenna rigged up the side of a pine tree, right outside the southwest pass," Gruncle said with pride. "Gives us a thirty-mile radius of two-way communication."

"Breaker, breaker, three-nine. This is Jangles on the horn," Ronda said into the mic. "Calling all Moonlighters with a ten-seventeen. Repeat, ten-seventeen. Any good buddies on the waves tonight?"

"Who's Jangles?" Molly asked.

"Must be her handle," Arvin said.

An old, raspy voice broke over the speaker. "I read ya, Jangles."

"Mur-dog? That you?"

"Sure as Shinola. What's your ten-twenty?"

"Calling in from the Spider."

"Oh, are ya, now? Everything hunky-dory?"

"Yep. Just need a cover story to a few parents regarding their kiddos."

"Wait," Molly said, "who's Mur-dog?"

"Sounds like Old Man Murray to me," Marvin said.

"Bingo," Gruncle said.

After getting briefed on the situation, Mur-dog offered to make a call to each of the kids' parents to tell them the kids were helping him with a little project of his—which wasn't entirely a lie, Molly supposed. He would just tell the parents how helpful their kids were, and that they could expect them home soon. Molly, Arvin, Margo, and Finn all took turns giving him their home phone numbers, and that was that.

Molly could see some benefits to being a Moonlighter.

"Okay, then. We best get on our way," Gruncle said. "But first, how about a few vittles to tide us over?"

Molly and the Mutants

"Roger that."

Ronda reached above the CB, where the end of a rope dangled. Its other end trailed upward and disappeared into the darkness overhead. Without looking she pulled.

"Incoming," she said.

A split second later something heavy plopped onto the table with a thud. It was a gunnysack that must have been suspended high above their heads. The sack was packed full, spilling its contents on impact.

It was a mother lode of Twinkies.

The kids all stared, incredulous. Molly looked at her Gruncle.

"What can I say? They last forever," Gruncle explained. "Pretty sure these 'uns here are from '78." He picked one up and sniffed the cellophane wrapper like he was a connoisseur of fine pastries. "Ahhh, 'twas a very good year."

Molly didn't care how old the Twinkies were. In the time it had taken for the sack to fall, she had realized that she was starving. And, even if they weren't fresh, they were still Twinkies.

"Water's over here," Gruncle announced. He gestured to a wide, natural stone basin that was raised several inches off the cave floor. It was collecting water one drop at a time from a spindly stalactite that hung just above it. Tin cups fanned out along the basin's edge.

"Just dip and sip. Best you'll ever have to wet yer whistler," Gruncle said. "Mother nature's own, filtered through a hundred feet of Ole Stoney, just for us."

The Moonlighters all dipped, sipped, and gorged on Twinkies. As she munched, Molly felt the rush of sugar re-energize her arms and legs. She looked up again at the symbol on the wall, above all the names.

"What do the three drops stand for?" she asked.

"Oh, those." Gruncle mused. "That's our crew's motto . . . blood, sweat, and . . ."

"Tears?" she asked.

"Naw! We're way too high-spirited a bunch for any cryin' or moanin'. . . . It's blood, sweat, and . . . *cheers*!"

Ronda raised her cup. "Cheers to the Crew!" she said.

"To the Crew!" Everyone repeated through mouthfuls. Some raised their cups. Others raised half-eaten Twinkies.

But the celebration was cut short by another sound. A deep, guttural croak echoed from the direction of the tunnel they'd entered through. And it sounded perturbed.

CHAPTER 33
KEEP PUSHING

Margo dropped her Twinkie onto the table.

"The frogs!" she said. "They found us!"

Yuuurrrp. Yuuurrrp.

The croaks grew louder, echoing throughout the cave. Finn stuffed the rest of his Twinkie into his mouth. Arvin grabbed one of the bowie knives, ready to fight.

"But how'd they—" Finn asked, mouth still full of Twinkie.

"Doesn't matter!" Molly said. "Let's get out of here." They sprang from the table and sprinted back to where they'd parked the velocipede.

"Ronda," Gruncle said, "I'm leaning toward the southwest pass."

"Booby-Trap Valley?" Ronda said.

"Yeah, I think we might need a few." Gruncle paused to listen for more croaks. "Maybe all of 'em."

Without another word Ronda ran to the giant lever and flipped it back to its original position. With a loud pop the circular platform under the handcar unlocked. The rest of them gathered around it, each grabbing one of the handles bolted to the platform's edge. They threw all their weight against it and pushed. The circle didn't budge.

"It's not moving!" Arvin said.

"It can stick just a little," Gruncle said, "from time to time."

"Too ... heavy ...," Finn grunted.

"Keep pushing," Molly said.

"I *am!*" Margo snapped. "Not my fault this wheel's as old as dirt!"

After several long moments the platform squeaked and finally began rotating counterclockwise, aiming the velocipede toward the southwest pass. But in the tunnel behind them, something large moved in the shadows, just out of view. Molly looked over her shoulder just in time to catch a set of long green webbed toes taking a step into the junction. It was joined by another set. This was followed by the thing's massive head, all gaping mouth and bulbous yellow eyes. The mutant

Molly and the Mutants

frog bobbed and jittered awkwardly as it squeezed its bulging frame through the last stretch of tunnel and out into the open. It was Muscles, leading the way. Luckily, its bulk had made it unable to hop in the cramped tunnel, which had slowed the beast down considerably.

"Keep pushing!" Ronda said. "Put your shoulders to it."

The kids all leaned their bodies against their handles, but their eyes were glued to the advancing monster. Inch by painful inch, the center track—with the velocipede on it—spun around on the old wooden disc, like a giant record player in slow motion, only backward.

Finally free of the confines of the tunnel, the frog gathered its powerful hind legs and launched itself into the air. But something about the jump wasn't right. The creature shot sideways and crashed into a nearby stalagmite. The wet, squishy sound of the impact bounced off the cave walls, causing a small tremor that Molly could feel up through her feet. She looked overhead at the stalactites hanging down from above. The thought of one of them falling onto them filled her with dread.

"Almost there," Ronda called.

"Keep! Pushing!" Molly screamed.

They watched the monster hopping sideways, crash-landing each time with a wet, heavy thump. It was bumping into everything around it, but still gradually getting closer.

"I think that frog's still drunker than a skunk," Gruncle said.

Another *yuuurrrp* joined the commotion. This one was slightly higher-pitched than the other. It appeared that at least one other frog had followed—Shark Fin—who decidedly *wasn't* as drunk as a skunk. It gave its nubby tail a little wag.

"Oh crap," Molly said. "C'mon, guys!"

They grunted and groaned one last time, straining with all their might until the junction had turned a full forty-five degrees and lined up with the southwest pass. Ronda pulled the lever one last time to lock it into position.

The four kids piled on top of the handcar and crouched down, just as Muscles reached for them with its tongue. But since the creature had veered off the tracks, it no longer had a clear shot, and its tongue hit another stalagmite. The cave rumbled again, shaking debris from the cave's ceiling. Dust rained down onto their heads.

"We gotta go!" Finn said.

"Shhhhhhh," Arvin said.

Slowly, quietly they began pumping the velocipede. Molly and Finn on one side, and Margo and Arvin on the other.

Molly and the Mutants

Gruncle and Ronda both pushed from behind. The handcar and trailer rolled off Spider Junction's platform toward their escape.

"Slow and steady," Ronda said.

"Okay, okay," Molly said.

The croaks got louder as the frogs closed in. Molly peeked in between the stalagmites as they inched toward the southwest exit. Here and there she caught a slick flash of green, or a darting shadow. One sailed high near the ceiling before landing. Bat Wings.

"I think all four of them are in here," Molly whispered.

"Almost there," Margo said.

"Once we're in the tunnel, they can't move as fast if they don't have room to hop," Ronda said.

The two adults jumped aboard. They passed through a little open space of track, just before entering the safety of the tunnel.

A tongue shot out in their direction and hit the wall, shaking the cave. Some of the stalactites overhead wobbled precariously. To their left, another frog stepped into view. It was Three Eyes, just a few feet away.

Margo screamed, emptying every molecule of air from her

lungs like she was staring in a horror movie. High-pitched, intense, and volume set to max, the scream reverberated through every square inch of Spider Junction, its rocky surfaces carrying the sound better than a symphony hall. Bewildered by the noise, the monsters all froze in place.

Then things started to fall.

From just above Three Eyes, a long pointed stalactite dropped like a spike and pierced the webbed tissue between the second and third toe of the frog's right hind foot—and buried itself into the craggy cave floor. The colossal creature was literally pinned to the spot. Caught by surprise, it let out a deep, gurgling complaint, which was quickly lost amidst the echoes of Margo's shriek. The monster tried in vain to retract its foot, but it was stuck.

"Nice scream," Arvin said.

"Thanks. I try," Margo said.

The newest members of the Moonlight Crew pushed their party into the cramped darkness of the southwest pass, hoping no one would follow. Just as the trailer cleared the entrance, another stalactite dropped, shattering where they had just been.

They had picked a future. Molly hoped it was a good one.

CHAPTER 34
BOOBY-TRAP VALLEY

Once again they found their rhythm on the hand pump and picked up speed. It was no comparison to the engine Ronda had cranked up earlier, but they had already spent that. And with every pump they increased the distance between themselves and the mutant frogs. Molly just hoped this time they could keep it that way.

"Any company behind us?" Gruncle asked.

The little rectangle of light from the cave continued to shrink as they pushed deeper into the southwest tunnel.

"I'll keep lookout," Molly said, stepping to the back of the trailer, where they had kept their bikes, next to the jugs of moonshine. She tallied up the jugs, wondering where they were supposed to go. She couldn't imagine why anyone, grown-up or not, would want to drink something like that.

Molly's dad mostly drank RC Cola—and sometimes milk from the carton when he thought no one was looking. She had spied him doing it once or twice but had never said anything. When Molly thought of her dad, she felt a sharp pang of guilt that Old Man Murray—or "Mur-dog"—had fibbed a little on her behalf. But it was only a small one, and they'd be home soon—or at least she hoped they would.

Something darkened the rectangle far behind them, something that moved.

"Finn, can I see your flashlight?" Molly asked.

"Sure," he said, pulling it out and flicking it on. Just like before, he waved it in everyone's face.

"Not in the eyes," Arvin hissed. "Geez."

"Oops. Sorry," Finn said.

"No biggie. Thanks, Finn," Molly said, grabbing it. When she did, her hand brushed his. It was warm and clammy. She looked at him.

"Dark spaces make me nervous," he whispered.

"Oh, sorry," Molly whispered back. "Why didn't you say anything?"

Molly and the Mutants

"I dunno," Finn said. "Maybe because giant frogs make me even more nervous!"

"Yeah, me too," Molly said.

"What? I didn't think you were scared of anything," Finn said. "The girl who took down a giant—"

"Are you kidding?" Molly blurted. "Those frogs terrify me."

Finn smiled. "Don't worry, your secret's safe with me."

"Yours too," she said.

They each let out a short, nervous laugh. And for the first time Molly realized that under that perfectly feathered flyback hair, Finn was just a kid dealing with his own struggles like everyone else in the world. Perfect hair didn't fix any of that.

Molly shone the beam behind them, but it wasn't very powerful and didn't travel far enough to illuminate anything. At least not any mutant frogs. Maybe that was a good sign. Just then they hit a bump in the rails, or something hit them. Molly wasn't sure, but everything bounced. The jugs, the bikes, and Molly. She fumbled the flashlight, nearly losing it.

"Oh!" she gasped.

When she firmed up her grip, Molly used the frame of Pink Lightning for balance, leaning as far out as she could, then peered at the tracks behind them one more time.

Three yellow eyes stared back at her.

The creature sure had gained a lot of ground! Maybe Three Eyes had less trouble navigating its way through the close confines of the tunnel than its more muscle-bound friend. That, and it wasn't drunk. As the light shone in its face, the frog shot out its tongue and enveloped the entire flashlight—along with a couple of Molly's fingers.

"Aagh!" Molly gasped, losing her grip as she pulled her hand free.

Without hesitation the frog yanked the flashlight into its mouth, and disappeared back into darkness.

Molly shook the slime from her hand. She was grossed out but grateful her hand was still attached to her arm.

They were in danger. Barely able to see behind them, Molly felt around for something else that might help defend them against another attack. Then she remembered that Pink Lightning still had a few tricks up its sleeve—even if she wasn't riding it. Molly turned her wheel and hit the switch marked with a disco ball. *Click.* Dual lights in her handlebars lit up the frogs in their wake, then began strobing rapidly, turning the tunnel into a kind of nightmare disco hall.

Behind her the movements of their monstrous pursuers took on the air of an old-time movie, their desperate, herky-jerky motions captured in the repeated flashes from the strobes. But then the frogs appeared to relax a little. Their glassy-eyed expressions were hard to read, but they seemed less tense, less focused. And they stopped shooting out their tongues altogether. They were still following them, but now kept the pace of the handcar.

"I think you've got 'em hypnotized," Gruncle said.

"Yeah, just like when the Zap-O-Matic was about outta juice," Finn said.

"We should take 'em to the Rink-A-Rama," Margo said. "That place is strobe light city."

"Yeah," Finn said. "If we could fit 'em through the door."

"The door! That's it!" Molly said.

"What's it? What'd I say?" asked Finn.

"Ronda," Molly said, "does this exit have a gate with rafters up top like the one we came in?

"They all do, why?" Ronda said.

"Just an idea," Molly said. "How far from the exit?"

"About a minute or so?" said Ronda.

"Okay, can you do a quick stop when we pass under the gate?" Molly said. "And maybe spare one more jug? I've got a plan."

"This is becoming the most expensive run I've ever made," Ronda said.

They slowed down and briefly came to a stop under wooden boards that framed the exit. Molly stood on Arvin's shoulders to wedge a jug into the rafters above them, then loosened the stopper. After a second it popped onto the ground, followed by a steady trickle.

"That's what I call testing your hypotenuse," Arvin said.

"You mean your hypothesis," Molly said. "But yes."

"Whatever you call it, let's hope you're right," Gruncle said.

A moment later the first frog, Three Eyes, passed under the stream of booze. It paused briefly, then continued, drawn by the strobe. The others followed right behind it, Shark Fin, then Bat Wing, each taking a turn under the steady drip-drip-drip. Last in line was Muscles, still demonstrably under the influence from the last jug.

"Drink up, boys," Ronda said. "This round's on me."

The handcar rolled out from the confines of the tunnel and back into the open air. Here, on the southwest side of Ole Stoney, the track was flanked on the left by thick vegetation, but to the right the earth fell away in a fairly steep slope and curved out at the bottom into a field of patchy grass. The drop reminded Molly of the Big Dipper they'd all crossed a couple of hours ago. But now the woods were much darker, and the fog had rolled back in, giving everything an eerie feel.

Molly and the Mutants

Molly shivered. She looked farther, trying to make out what lay beyond the field, but saw only a wide swath of darkness, like everything had been sucked into... a hole.

"The Bottomless Pit," Gruncle whispered, following Molly's gaze. He pressed his hand onto her back.

"Good thing we didn't take that track," Arvin said.

Everyone nodded.

"Anybody got a knife?" Ronda looked at Arvin.

"How'd you know?" He pulled one of the bowie knives from the table at Spider Junction out from his belt, where he's stashed it. "Anyway, I was just borrowing it...."

He passed the knife to Ronda.

"I see everything," she said, testing the blade's edge against her thumb—but unlike Finn, she didn't cut herself.

"Wait, whaddya gonna do?" Molly asked. "We can't just..."

She was more than a little scared of these overgrown frogs, for sure. She definitely didn't want to get eaten, but she didn't exactly like the idea of Ronda stabbing them all to death while they were mesmerized from Pink Lightning's strobe light. Were those the only two choices? Kill or be killed?

Molly felt conflicted. She thought about cops and bootleggers. Mice and snakes. Humans and mutant frogs. Did everything in life come down to a fight for survival? Either us or them?

"Don't worry, I won't be dissecting any frogs today. You'll see," Ronda said, reading her thoughts. She held her hand out to Molly. "Hold tight, and keep me steady."

As they passed a stump by the edge of the track, Ronda held on to Molly's arm, then leaned way out over to the side of the platform, blade extended. Assuming the pose of a stuntwoman, Ronda sliced through a taut line of rope invisible to everyone else. Molly only knew what Ronda had done by the sound. The two ends popped apart with a sharp twang that lingered in everyone's ears. A perfect F-sharp. In rapid succession more noises followed. The severed line unleashed a thick, low branch from a young beech tree that had been bent back and tied to keep clear of the tracks. The freed bough whacked Three Eyes and Shark Fin across the sides of their big round bodies, sending them both rolling pell-mell down the hill and into the field far below.

"A twofer!" Ronda whooped.

"But aren't they just gonna climb back u—" Finn started to say.

"Only if they can make it through that field," Gruncle said. "Also known as . . . Booby-Trap Valley!" A sly grin crept across his face.

Just as Finn had worried, the two tossed frogs righted

themselves, returned their attention to Pink Lightning's flashing lights uphill, and once again began to follow. But no sooner had they taken their first steps when a loud snap echoed through the night air—and the earth below one of the creatures disappeared into a wide hole. The mutant frog thrashed to get out of the netting that had snagged it, but every effort only tightened the trap's grip. In short order the giant frog grew still, resigning itself to capture.

A moment later another snap, and the other frog met the same fate, just a few yards to the left of its friend.

"How many of those traps you got set out there?" Arvin asked.

"More than enough, believe me," Ronda said.

"Wrapped up like a coupla Christmas presents! Ha!" Gruncle said. "Just need some bright red bows on top."

"Hold up. We still got two left," Molly said.

Bat Wing and Muscles were close behind them, still enthralled with the strobe.

"Hope that thing's got fresh batteries," Finn said.

"Me too," Molly said.

"Whadda we do now with these two?" Arvin asked.

Molly knew the answer. It was the same tug in her heart that she always felt at moments like this. She pulled Pink

Lightning from the other bikes and jumped on.

"Wish me luck," she said. Molly launched herself off the trailer's platform and tore down the hill. It was a bumpy ride, but before long she was zooming across the field.

Muscles immediately turned to follow her.

"Where are the other traps?" she yelled over her shoulder.

"Just stay on the grassy parts!" Gruncle yelled back.

Molly looked down at the white mist of fog swirling around Pink Lightning's tires, obscuring her view of the ground. She slowed a little.

"Uh, how can I tell?"

"Good question. . . . Just go fast," Gruncle said.

Molly peeked at the bike's rearview mirror and saw two giant yellow eyeballs staring back at her. Muscles was hot on her heels. With her strobe lights aimed away from the frogs, their effect was quickly diminishing.

Molly was fast, but there was no way she was going to be able to outrun this spring-legged beast. She spun her bike toward the lone tree in the field, nearly thirty yards away, and took a deep breath. Would it be able to reach? Molly hoped so. She flipped the safety cover and punched the button on her handlebars marked with a fishing hook. *Fwiiiiing!* Out shot a tiny three-pronged grappling hook trailed by an ultrathin

Molly and the Mutants

steel cable. The hook flew toward the solitary tree, looped over a branch, and anchored deep in the bark with a reassuring *thunk*.

"Here goes nothing," Molly whispered.

She pulled one of the levers on her frame, activating the spindle to reel in the line. With a *whirrrr* it snapped taught, then nearly jerked Pink Lightning out from under her. The cable dragged Molly across the foggy field at breakneck speed—on a collision course for the tree. Molly held tight, listening to the string of booby traps her bike triggered as she crossed. Each snapped right behind her, a fraction of a second too late.

"That's it! Go, Molly, go!" Gruncle called.

Intrigued by the rapid motion coupled with the high-pitch whine of the reeling cable, Muscles gave chase to intercept. Molly was live bait.

The frog's entire body rippled as it crouched, then launched itself in her direction, closing the distance between them by half. No sooner had it landed than it jumped again. Molly flew over another booby trap, made a quick calculation, and shoved the lever back, detaching the cable and bringing her bike to a stop.

"Molly!" Finn screamed.

All alone in the foggy field, Molly braced herself. With

uncanny speed the hulking frog sailed through the air, limbs spread wide, mouth beginning to open in anticipation of a long-awaited catch. But Molly's gambit paid off. Unable to course correct midhop, the giant frog missed its target, landing right in front of her instead—and dead center on one of the field's many hidden traps. Just inches away, the heavy creature disappeared with a crash into a false floor and netting.

The impact made Molly's bike bounce two inches off the ground.

"Hook, line, and sinker!" Ronda shouted.

Molly, perched on the edge of the hole, watched the frog thrash against the netting as the trap cinched tight over its head. After several kicks it seemed to acknowledge that it had been bested, letting out a sullen croak of defeat. Molly exhaled.

"Three down, one to go," she whispered to herself.

She was closer to the massive sinkhole now, and could almost make out the edge of it through the fog. Something about this strange opening in the earth—and the stories behind it—called to her. But there was no time. Her friends were counting on her. Molly spun her bike around to aim the hypnotic light at their final threat.

And just as she did, the strobes fizzled.

"Crap."

Molly and the Mutants

Bat Wing had kept its position on the tracks above, and seemed to snap out of whatever trance it had been in. In front of it everyone was pumping the handcar as hard as they could, reaching maximum velocity. Bat Wing leapt into the air, attempting to pounce on its prey. Everyone screamed. But with its webbed wings—and perhaps its depth perception slightly diminished from the moonshine shower—the mutant frog sailed high over the heads of everyone in the handcar, overshooting its mark and landing hard on the rails in front of them. It immediately started pivoting for another attack. Maybe this was their chance.

"Cha-a-a-arge!" Gruncle hollered.

"Ramming speed!" Arvin shouted.

The handcar slammed into the side of the immense frog with an audible squish.

Everyone screamed again.

Yuuuurrrrp, said the frog nonchalantly, holding its position. It was simply too big and too heavy to budge. Desperate to dislodge the monster, Arvin pushed down one final time on the pump's handle, pressing the nose of the handcar into the frog's slimy green flank.

Sssssssssssst...

Even from several yards away, Molly could hear a sizzle

as the red-hot headlamp made direct contact with the monster's hide. At this the frog changed its tune, letting out an anguished, high-pitched croak as one of its back legs jerked and it half leapt, half stumbled out of the way and tumbled down the slope, onto the field below and—*ker-snap*—into the nearest trap.

"And then there were none," Gruncle said.

"That was awesome," Margo said.

From the middle of the field, Molly slowly weaved her way back to her friends, careful not to fall into one of the traps herself.

CHAPTER 35
FOLLOWED

Ronda now stood alone on the handcar, just as she had when they'd first encountered her, only maybe a couple of jugs short. The kids had pulled down their bicycles from the trailer, but at Gruncle's suggestion Molly had left the depleted Zap-O-Matic on board with Ronda for safekeeping. Molly figured it would've been hard to sneak it back into the house anyway. Besides, who needed a memento when she had her Gruncle back?

"Remember," Ronda said. "You never saw me." She paused after that, taking a moment to give each of them a hard look in the eye. She looked at Molly last, and nodded. They all took turns giving Ronda the secret handshake they'd learned.

Molly looked around. She liked knowing that they were all in on something secret.

"Thank you," Molly said.

"No worries, McCrusher," Ronda said. "Nice work back there."

"Yes indeedy!" Gruncle chimed in. "Not sure where those critters came from, but glad to have 'em confined to quarters."

"Say, where *do* ya think they came from?" Ronda asked.

The group pondered the question until Molly broke the silence.

"Well," she said, not sure if it was even worth mentioning, "before we came across the frogs, Officer Wasserbaum told me he thought all the missing pets had something to do with, uh, kids listening to heavy metal.... You don't think that coulda unleashed some . . . evil force or something out here in the woods, do you?"

"You mean, like, those creatures were summoned from the underworld by some rock 'n' roll songs?" Ronda asked.

"I dunno. He said maybe if you play the records backwards?" Molly offered. Her mind flashed back to the guy in leather pants on Margo's TV, then to Leonard's Ozzy T-shirt. It all seemed kind of silly, but there had to be some explanation....

Her Gruncle began laughing so hard, Molly thought he might collapse. The laugh turned into a coughing fit but kept on going. Clovis hunched forward, slapping his knee several times. Ronda started laughing too, and pretty soon everyone had joined in, including Molly.

"Hooo!" Gruncle wheezed. "That sounds just like Officer Wasserbaum."

"You tell him to stick to parking tickets," Ronda said.

The laughing made Molly feel a lot better.

"The funny thing is," her Gruncle said, finally catching his breath, "some adult folk have been trying to pin the blame for just about everything from bad weather to bad manners on the next generation's choice of music or fashion or whatever since before I was a kid... and that was some time ago. But I've never heard a tune that could turn a frog into a monster—or make a person do anything they weren't willing to do in the first place."

"True," Ronda said. "Well, I need to get going. But I'm sure we'll get to the bottom of it."

She turned a crank on the platform's mounting, reversing the primary gear, then began pumping the handcar up and down. It started traveling in the opposite direction. Part of Molly didn't want Ronda to go.

"Back to Spider Junction?" Molly asked.

"Not quite," Ronda said, already putting distance between them. "There's a split in the tracks we passed just a li'l ways behind us. If I take that, I should be back on my original route before too long."

"Hairpin's Pass?" Gruncle asked.

"Yup," Ronda said. "Easy-peazy."

"Lemon-squeezy," Gruncle said, then called out again. "Keep your eyes peeled."

"And your lips sealed," Ronda hollered back.

Molly was wondering just how many little rhymes and sayings these Moonlighters had among themselves when she heard Ronda begin to sing again. Her raspy voice carried through the night air.

The moon may wax, and the moon may wane
Then the moon will do it all over again
When the night is dark and it's far from day
Just look for a moonbeam to guide your way

In moments she had disappeared into the fog. But they could still hear her voice.

The moon may wax, and the moon may wane
But the light o' the moon will ease your pain
When the night is dark and it's far from day
Just look for a moonbeam to guide your way

"Well, well, well," Gruncle said, turning to the kids. "Our newest members of the Crew. How about we get on our way?"

Molly and the Mutants

"What about the frogs?" Finn said.

"Yeah, what if they get out?" Margo asked.

"Don't you fret about them at all. The more they fight those nets, the tighter the traps get. You leave those buggers to me."

"You're not gonna hurt 'em, though, are you?" Molly asked.

"Wouldn't dream of it, no! Although I do love me a plate of fresh fried frog legs from time to time, I've got a feeling these would be a little tough for my taste." Gruncle paused to think. "I'll place an anonymous call to the park rangers in the morning."

Satisfied, Molly mounted her bike, patting the back of her banana seat for Gruncle to climb aboard. Ronda was long out of earshot now, but as they started the ride home, he picked up the same tune that she had been singing....

When the hour is late and the going is rough

The light from a sliver may just be enough

As they rode over the first hill, the familiar sound of his voice had a soothing effect on Molly's nerves, especially after such a harrowing night. In time Molly could swear she heard an accompanying beat to Gruncle's tune.... Was she starting to hear things? It was a distinctive, rhythmic thump to every other word, like a foot stomp, or...

A hop.

Thump... thump... thump...

The beat was getting louder. Molly's blood ran cold. She weaved her bike sideways to steal a glance behind her. Could those monsters have already escaped? And would she and her friends ever be able to shake them?

"What is it, Molly?" Finn asked.

"You hear that?" Molly asked.

They all braked to listen. And there it was.

Thump... thump...

"Oh no," Margo said.

Molly strained to see behind her, but it was well past dark by now, and Booby-Trap Valley had receded into the fog. Then she caught some movement. Whatever it was, there were at least two of them. And they were big.

"They found us," Finn said, voice cracking.

"Go, go, go!" Molly said.

As they started pedaling, the thumping behind closed in. Between thumps Molly heard something else: a squeak. It didn't sound very frog-like, but these were no ordinary frogs. Maybe their joints squeaked when they were in a hurry—or when they were mad. Or both.

Gruncle had taken to sitting backward on the back of her banana seat, so he could keep watch.

"Well, I don't think we can outpace 'em—" he said.

Molly and the Mutants

"Don't say that."

"But I don't think we'll have to. Whatever they are, they ain't amphibious."

Then Molly heard another sound. It was her name. The jumping things behind them were calling her name.

"Maaawwwwllll-eeeeeee!"

"Wait up!"

It was Wally! And Gunther! Only, they were both a couple of feet taller, and moving incredibly fast, like they had giant springs under their feet.

Because they did.

As the two got closer, Molly got a clearer view. Both boys were wearing what looked like some kind of complicated leg braces, with thick straps that held them in place from ankle to thigh. The braces were jointed at the knee, so they could bend. And under their feet the braces extended for nearly a yard, like they were walking on stilts, only each one was wound in a tight metal coil.

"And I thought *I* had some spring in my step," said Gruncle. "Heh!"

In a few seconds the two boys, who were all but inseparable, were bouncing all around them, firing off questions faster than anyone could answer.

"Where *were* you guys?"

"And how'd you get all the way out here?"

"Did you find Crank yet?"

Gunther and Wally quickly recounted that they had already been running late for the rendezvous, but then had a close call in the tunnel, making it impossible for them to catch up, so they had decided to go off on their own. Since then they'd been looking for the older kids—and Crank—everywhere. Molly was just grateful they hadn't run into the monsters.

"So whaddya think of Gunther's latest invention?" Wally said as he bounced. "They're called *spring feet!*"

Then for the first time, there in the dusk, he noticed Gruncle—and immediately stumbled on his landing, falling headlong into the dirt.

"C'mere, kiddo!" Gruncle called. "We thought you an' your jumping-bean buddy there were a pair of giant killer frog-a-sauruses!"

Wally didn't appear to be listening. He just stared googly eyed at his great-uncle like he was seeing a ghost. Molly could appreciate this reaction, since she had done the same thing only a few hours earlier. She told her brother about the frozen capsule.

"Just as I suspected!" Gunther said. "We came straight

Molly and the Mutants

from the battle site, and Wally noticed the escape hatch was open. Honestly, after all the destruction, I'd forgotten about it. But yeah, the robot was equipped with a getaway pod. And it did have an emergency cryogenic feature. At least that's what one of my displays monitored before it . . . well, anyway, I'm not sure how it launched on its own. It wasn't programmed for automatic response."

"I'm guessing twern't programmed to shoot death rays outta its eyes neither," Gruncle said.

"Uh, that's true." Gunther looked down. "Sorry, sir."

"Water under the bridge, my boy. Or *over the falls*, I should say, heh!" Clovis paused a moment, then spoke a little more softly. "It was a truly marvelous contraption, I tell ya. Had that been my final moment—which at the time I truly believed it was—well, I could not have asked for a more spectacular send-off. And from what I can see here, it looks like it brought about some good."

He looked at the two boys and smiled.

Gunther appeared to stand even taller in his spring feet, like a weight had been lifted from his shoulders. He made a little bounce.

"Yeah," he said, looking over at Wally.

"You know they made a plaque for you and everything? Right by the cliff where we jumped. It says you were a *beloved and respected member of our community . . ."* Wally paused a moment to remember the rest of the words. "And *performed an act of heroism.*"

"Beloved and respected?" Gruncle repeated the words. His face beamed with pride. "Ya don't say?"

"Yeah . . . it was really cool," Wally said. "But I'm glad you didn't get all 'sploded up, Grunk. I like you better alive."

"Me too, Wally, me too," Gruncle said, blinking back a tear.

"Wally, listen," Molly said. "Did you run into . . . *anything unusual* in the woods?"

"I was about to ask you the same thing," Gunther murmured.

"You mean like a hideout for lost cats?" Wally said. "No, but we've been looking everywhere!" He tapped his binoculars. "I'm sure we'll—"

"No, Wally, there's . . . something else . . ."

Molly explained their encounter with the giant frogs, how she and her friends had nearly became their lunch, and what they'd done with the cryo-chamber to stall the monsters, then the booby traps to keep them secure. While she explained, she almost spilled the beans about Ronda, the velocipede, and Spider Junction, but stopped herself. Wally might be family, but as a member of the Moonlight Crew, Molly was bound to keep her word.

Molly and the Mutants

Gunther was listening intently to Molly's account of their run-in with the mutant creatures.

"This is what I was afraid of," Gunther said. "How giant were they?"

"Huge!" Arvin said, stretching his arms as wide as they'd go.

"It's true," Molly confirmed. "Big enough to swallow you whole."

"I see," Gunther said. "Any sign of more?"

"No. I think we got 'em all," Molly said.

"Let's hope so," Gunther said quietly.

"Now we just gotta get back home," Margo said. "But we're, like, on the farthest edge of the woods."

"And I am *exhaustified*," Arvin said.

"Exhausted," Molly corrected him.

"That too."

"Molly," Gunther said, "I . . . I think I might know where these mutants came from."

"W-w-what?" Molly said. Her jaw nearly dropped to her chest. She couldn't understand how Gunther could possibly have the answers. But then it made sense. "Wait, don't tell me you've got a secret laboratory where you conduct weird experiments on poor frogs."

"I bet it's for a science project, isn't it?" Arvin asked. "I knew it!"

"No! No, no... Okay, this might sound weird," Gunther said, "but I think they could have come from... my robot."

"Like, your old blown-up robot had mutant frog babies at the bottom of the gorge?" Margo asked.

"Well, kinda, yeah," Gunther continued. "See, there's this special top secret formula inside of it—Formula X—which should've been totally secured... but I think maybe it could've been tampered with, because when Wally and I were just out there, we noticed something glow—"

"Um, excuse me?" Finn interrupted. "Can we focus on getting home first?"

"Oh, yeah, sure," Gunther said. "Like I said, it's just a theory. Probably better to get home first."

Wally quickly shifted his attention to a compass he had pulled from his pocket, laying it over a small folded map. He looked up at the trail, then traced his finger along the map, getting his bearings.

"Even with Old Man Murray's cover, my mom's still probably gonna kill me," Margo said.

"At least you didn't lose a shoe this time," Finn said. His eyes darted from Molly to the others, then to the darkening shadows that surrounded them.

"Yeah, no way we're making it back anytime soon," Arvin said.

Molly and the Mutants

"Depends on your mode of transportation," Gunther said, folding the map back up.

"Well, we don't all have fancy frog legs like you two," Margo said.

"Oh, I'm not talking about these," he said, giving the spring feet a little bounce. "Follow me."

"You can trust him on this," Wally said.

In less than five minutes they'd arrived at a large moss-covered boulder at the bottom of a hill. Gunther gave it three taps.

The boulder opened up along an invisible seam like an Easter egg. Only instead of a prize inside, there was a stairway that led straight down into the earth.

"Gun! My man!" Arvin said. "How many of these you got?"

"Enough," he said.

"What the heck?" Finn said.

"No way I'm going down there," Margo said.

"Trust me, you'll love it," Arvin said.

Before long they had all crammed into another one of the Vandervorkels' maglev bubble cars and were racing along the subterranean track, far away from anything that was trying to eat them. It was a little snug with all seven of them, but they fit. And the cushioned seats felt amazing on their tired butts. There was even a rack on the back to hold their bikes. Sometimes it seemed like the Vandervorkels thought of everything.

The first-time riders were especially impressed.

"Smooth ride," Margo said.

"Yeah," Finn agreed. "Feels like we're floating."

"Actually, we are," Wally said.

"I'll say," Gruncle said, closing his eyes.

"I can't wait to show everyone you're alive!" Molly said.

"Oh, yeah," Gruncle said, one eye popping back open. "About that..."

"About what?" Molly asked.

Her Gruncle paused a moment and rubbed his chin.

"So," he said, "everyone thinks I got myself blown to bits with the robot?"

"Yeah," Molly said.

"Let's just keep it that way for a spell," Gruncle said. "Wouldn't want to rob the town of their memory of *a beloved and respected member of the community who performed an act of heroism* . . . at least not just yet." Then his face took on a sober expression. "Can I count on you all to keep me a secret?"

"Sure thing, Gruncle," Molly said. The night had been chock-full of secrets. What was one more?

CHAPTER 36
NOT THE WHOLE STORY

Gunther popped open the hatch to the secret entrance on Far Flung Falls Drive, just a few houses down from Molly and Wally's house. The street was quiet and dark, and appeared to be free of giant killer mutant frogs.

Everyone breathed a sigh of relief. They'd finally made it back.

It was just the six of them now. They'd dropped Gruncle off at an earlier stop near his cabin. He'd thanked them all again for finding him, reminded them one more time to not say a word, and promised Molly he'd see them again soon.

Although her Gruncle hadn't fully explained, Molly had a fairly solid hunch as to why he wanted to keep his survival a secret. She remembered all those stacks of bad-news mail she had spied at his cabin... back taxes, legal squabbles, old debts, angry ex-wives. If anybody was ever in need of a do-over button in life, it was probably Clovis. Besides, who wouldn't want to be remembered as *a beloved and respected member of the community who performed an act of heroism*? After all he'd done for them, didn't he deserve that... along with a clean slate?

Whatever his reasons might be, Molly was just happy her Gruncle was alive. On top of that, she had returned with everyone else in one piece. Given the circumstances, it was almost too good to be true, and made Molly feel like anything was possible. Hopefully, Old Man Murray's cover story would be enough to keep them out of trouble. She climbed up the ladder.

"Keep quiet," Wally said. "Nobody knows about thi—"

"Evening," came a voice from behind them. It was Old Man Murray, leaning on the split-rail fence just a few feet from the fake power box.

All six of them jumped.

"How did you know about—" Wally asked.

"Oh, I know lotsa things," he said, smiling. "Speaking of, thanks for your *assistance* tonight.

"What assis—" Wally started to ask, having no clue about the CB conversation earlier.

Molly and the Mutants

"Ahh, don't mention it!" Molly blurted, cutting him off.

"Anytime," Arvin chimed in.

"You may want to all head over to the McQuirters'. Finn, Arvin, and Margo, that includes you too. I hear there might be something for all of you." He patted his tummy and winked, indicating that the *something* was food. "Don't worry, it's cleared with all your parents."

"What about mine?" Gunther asked.

"And who might you be, son?"

"Gunther Vandervorkel."

"Oh, I've heard about you. I believe your mama is keeping Molly's dad company. Does she know you're out and about?"

"Uh... probably not. I kinda sneak out a lot."

"Me too," Wally said.

"Mm-hmm, right. I see. . . . Well, I'm sure they'll be happy to see you both. How about I give one more call to tell them you're on your way—and let them know you're all together?"

"Thank you," everyone said.

They all took turns shaking Murray's hand. Wally and Gunther gave regular handshakes, but the newest members of the Moonlight Crew were sure to interlock their pinkies and extend their thumbs in the Moonlighter's secret sign. Then Murray was walking back to his home.

They all headed out for the last house on the street. Even from a distance Molly could see that the porch light was on, and the sight of it made her smile.

Darryl started barking before they even made it to the front door. He dashed across the yard to greet them, his snout intrigued by all the smells they had brought home from their adventure.

Molly's dad was standing on the front porch, alongside Vilomena. They were waving and smiling, looking not very mad at all. *Whew*.

"There they are!" Stan said. "That was so nice of you all to help our neighbor out."

"Uh... no problem," Molly said.

"Sorry it's so late," Margo said.

"Me too," Wally said.

"Yeah, sorry, Mom," Gunther said.

"No worries," Vilomena said. "Happy to see everyone together."

"Um, hi, Mr. McQuirter, Miss Vandervorkel," Arvin said.

"Please, call me Stanley."

"Yes, and you can call me Vilomena."

"Okay, Mr. Stanley, Ms. Vilomena," Arvin said.

Margo and Finn just waved, not sure what to say.

Molly and the Mutants

"Wait, where's Leonard? I thought he was joining you," Molly's dad said.

"Right here, Mr. McQ," Leonard said, popping out from behind them.

"Oh, hey, Leonard!" Molly said, relieved to see him, too.

"Well, I'm just glad you guys are all back," her dad said. "If Mr. Murray hadn't called when he did, we might've had to send a search party for the search party!" He laughed at his own joke while the kids smiled awkwardly.

That's right, Molly thought. They had started as a search party. With all they had gone through over the last few hours, she'd almost forgotten the reason for their little trip in the first place. And they'd come up empty-handed.

"Well, any sign of Crank?" Vilomena asked.

Nobody said a thing. Molly lowered her head.

"It's okay. You gave it a good effort," Stan said. "Why doesn't everyone come on in and relax. It's Friday, and pizza's already here. I bet you guys are hungry."

"You guessed right," Arvin said.

"Margo," Stan said, "why don't you call your folks, let them know you'll be home after you eat. And, Arvin and Finn, you can use the phone after Margo."

They inhaled the pizza. Besides the secret stash of

Twinkies back at Spider Junction, Molly had never tasted anything so good. After all that running, she was starving.

"Did you tell the Ostranders?" Molly asked Leonard.

"Yeah, I did," he said.

"Tell the Ostranders what?" her dad asked, a long string of cheese still connecting his mouth to a slice.

Molly described the scene of the bone pile, how some of the bones had clearly belonged to an adult pig, which they were pretty sure had been Houdini. Then she described the gigantic frogs. She was still a little surprised that her dad wasn't more upset. But ever since he'd been seeing Vilomena, she couldn't remember him getting mad once. He was almost always smiling. Was that what falling in love did to grown-ups? Maybe it was a good thing.

"So how big we talking this time?" Stan finally asked.

Molly stretched out her arms as wide as they could go, but that didn't quite cover it. So she asked Arvin, whose arms were a little longer, to do the same.

"Even bigger than that," she said. "We all saw."

Arvin, Margo, and Finn nodded their heads to confirm.

"It's true, we did," Margo said.

Her dad raised his eyebrows and looked over at Vilomena, who pursed her lips thoughtfully.

Molly and the Mutants

"That would be quite a frog specimen indeed," he said.

"Dad, I'm serious. But then we—" Molly paused. She wanted to tell them everything, but they'd made an oath to not talk about Spider Junction or the Moonlight Crew to anyone who wasn't a member. And she couldn't tell them about Gruncle, either. The secrets burned inside her.

"Well?" her dad pressed. "But then we what?"

Feeling suddenly overwhelmed by everything she was holding inside, Molly started to cry. They still hadn't found Crank. And for all she knew, there might be even more monsters lurking out there. Molly couldn't stop thinking about all those piles of bones.

"Hey there, Mollz. I know. I know. It's tough," her dad said. He wrapped her up in a big bear hug as she sniffled.

"Maybe I'll take you up on your offer with the flyers," Molly said. "I guess they couldn't hurt."

"Okay, yeah, great, okay," her dad said. "Tell you what, first thing tomorrow I'll run down to Carmine's Express Printing and print, like, a hundred flyers."

"Maybe more?" Molly said.

"Yeah, right, more. We'll print up two hundred. You and your friends could put 'em up everywhere. If anyone has seen Crank, we'll find her."

"Thanks," Molly said, wiping her eyes.

"And I'm betting their office is probably closed right now, but I'll give the park rangers a call and tell them to stay on the lookout for any... oversize wildlife."

Molly could tell by her dad's tone that he thought they were exaggerating, but she still appreciated the gestures. If she hadn't seen it with her own eyes, she might not have believed it either. But something about Vilomena's expression gave Molly the impression that she wasn't so incredulous.

"I could call the police station, too," her dad offered, "give Officer Wasserbaum a heads-up—"

Molly noticed a look pass between the woman and her son.

"I think the park rangers will be enough," Gunther blurted.

"Gunther," his mother said in very calm voice, "we might also want to make sure the robot remains are... completely secure."

Gunther nodded. So did Wally. At that moment Finn began violently choking on his pizza. A giant partially chewed wad of cheese shot out of his mouth, and Darryl caught it midair, like he'd been waiting—which he probably had.

"Ya okay there, buddy?" Stan asked.

"Sorry... wrong pipe," Finn croaked.

Molly and the Mutants

"Oh, and I almost forgot!" Stan added. "Molly, wait till you see what I did with Number One out back!"

"Who's Number One?"

"Oh, that's the robot's name now. More of a nickname, actually. Long story. Lots of ones and zeros... Anyhoo, I fixed him. He's quite a talker. Maybe he can help us. Wait till you see."

They all piled out the back door, slices still in hand, and were met with the friendly, familiar glow of two bright green eyes.

"WELL. HELLO. THERE. MOLLY," the robot intoned, only much more smoothly than it had ever spoken before. "SO. NICE. TO. SEE. YOU. AND. YOUR. FRIENDS. I. AM. NUMBER. ONE."

CHAPTER 37
WORTHY ADVERSARY

Crank awoke at the first sign of daylight and stretched. It had been another night spent in the wild, and she felt invigorated. *Forward*, she thought, pushing herself deeper into the woods—and further along her quest.

After an hour or two—it was really hard to keep track—Crank found herself perched atop a ledge that appeared to be secure. But wasn't.

The rotted wood underfoot gave way, and for the first time since she had embarked on her quest, the mighty huntress slipped. In one point two seconds she dropped from the height of a rooftop, righted herself midair, and landed on her feet. (This was a cat, after all. Would you have expected anything

Molly and the Mutants

less?) A thick spongy layer of moss by the water's edge cushioned the impact, making her arrival nearly silent. Nearly. The swiftness with which her movement both started and ended did not go unnoticed, and the air around her went quiet.

Crank held as still and inscrutable as the Sphinx. *Play it cool*, she told herself. But she couldn't contain the excitement bubbling up inside her body. A single whisker twitched. Then another. This was definitely the place. A front-row seat to destiny befitting her station. All she had to do now was wait.

But not for long. Before her, something rose out of the slime and muck to greet her, filling her view. Something shiny and glistening, like a present. Something very big.

No, not something. Some*things*.

The eyes of the somethings blinked open. All six of them. *Welcome*, the somethings' eyes said. *So good of you to... drop in.*

Oh, so the somethings had a sense of humor. *We'll see how long that lasts*, she thought.

Crank focused on the pair of eyes belonging to the something in the middle. The eyes were completely at ease, as unafraid as her own. These were eyes that knew the game she was playing, and played it well. Eyes that didn't miss a thing.

At last, a worthy adversary. Oh yes. From deep in her chest an involuntary thrum began percolating its way up her throat.

What was this? Was she actually purring? How embarrassing for a warrior cat. But she simply couldn't help herself. This was what she had been searching for. Something both ancient and new. Familiar and strange.

Crank blinked. Incarnations this magnificent were merely fossils, weren't they? And yet, here was one before her.

The thing's gargantuan presence, now so close, made the tiny dark mass in her head throb almost pleasurably, pressing up against the back of her brain and releasing a flood of memories. All at once, every life she had lived, every moment, rushed into her head, playing before her eyes like scenes from a thousand different movies. Battles with monsters of every size and shape from past eras.

She had been here before. In this very situation, paws clutching the moist earth below. She breathed in. *Time to fight.* The atmosphere had been thicker then, the concoction of another age, a little more oxygen, a little less nitrogen, perhaps. The foliage had been different too, when the world had been an endless forest of ferns.

But the twin scents of fear and hunger were timeless, electrifying the air. A tingle moved through her body, dropping every clue as to what she needed to do. And in that necessity of action came a clarity so thrilling, so sweet.

Molly and the Mutants

Bring it, Crank thought.

As you wish, came the reply.

One of the somethings' countenance, mottled and green, split sideways into a gaping maw. The opening made a deep, rumbling croak that shook the earth below her, and brought her tail to stand as tall as a banner for war. Was this the gate to the next life? The path to what lay ahead? Crank arched her back to give her best bristle, making herself as formidable as possible. She flattened her ears.

Hisssssssssssss, she announced, fangs drawn. *I'm ready.*

And without further ado, the spring she'd held in the center of her being—so tightly coiled for so long—finally released.

Claws out, the cat lunged forward.

Part III
DOWNTOWN

CHAPTER 38
RINK-A-RAMA

Molly looked down at the empty basket on her bike as she turned the corner. She was all out of flyers. After posting them all over her neighborhood, Molly had decided that wasn't enough. What if Crank had wandered into town?

So Margo, Arvin, Leonard, and Finn had all agreed to help her stick them on every streetlight pole, in every shop window, and at every gas station in Far Flung Falls, which had taken a good chunk of their Saturday afternoon, and crept into the early evening. They had divvied up downtown into five sections, agreeing to meet at the Rink-A-Rama as soon as they were through.

Molly was the first to arrive. She made a soft brake, sliding

Molly and the Mutants

Pink Lightning's front tire into an empty slot at the far end of the bike rack, which already held a couple dozen bicycles, maybe more. She figured this spot on the end cut the chances by 50 percent of her pride and joy getting scuffed by someone less careful than she was.

Seeing the bottom of her basket reminded Molly what she had found in it that morning when she'd first gone out to her bike. A note that could only have been from her Gruncle. It had read:

> Hey, Kiddo,
>
> Sorry, no sign of your kitty cat yet.
> Still on the case.
> But don't worry, our four hopping hungry friends have been neutralized.
> They won't be causing any more trouble, rest assured.
> And there don't appear to be any more of their proportions.
> But this fact might raise a bigger concern.
> Fill you in soon!
> Until then, your discretion regarding my aliveness is much appreciated.
> Blood, sweat, and cheers!
>
> Yours truly,
> —GC

Molly pulled the note out from her pocket and read it again. His cryptic message left her with many more questions than answers. What did he mean by "neutralized"? She couldn't imagine her Gruncle actually killing the beasts, even if they were dangerous. And what on earth could be a "bigger concern" than those giant killer frogs?

She sat on her bike and wondered. It was the first time in two days that she'd had a moment to herself to think. What had happened to those frogs they'd supposedly captured? And what was her Gruncle up to?

Lost in her thoughts, she didn't notice Leonard pulling up beside her.

"Good spot," Leonard said, pointing to the far end where Molly had parked. "Some kids around here can get sloppy." He slammed his own bike into the rack with significantly less grace than Molly had. "Like me."

"Oh, hi, Leonard," Molly said.

"I got one left," he said, holding up his last flyer. "How about here at the Rink-A-Rama?"

"Good idea," said Molly. "I'm all out. Thanks."

Leonard ran over to the building, fumbled with a roll of masking tape, then stuck the flyer to the wall beside the doors.

Molly and the Mutants

Under a grainy black-and-white copy of the last photo they had taken of Crank, the text read:

LOST TABBY CAT

ANSWERS TO THE NAME "CRANK"

Large, old, and orange-ish/gray-ish with black stripes

Wearing fuchsia collar with tags

Be careful! Not very friendly to strangers

Might bite, or scratch, or run away

REWARD IF FOUND

Molly's phone number was printed at the bottom. Her dad had reminded her that the phone line was not dead. He was still so proud to have paid the phone bill on time for a few months in a row now.

Finn showed up a moment later. The three of them waited a few minutes until Arvin and Margo arrived.

Meeting at the skating rink had been Margo's idea. She had said they deserved a little fun after all they'd been through—especially after capturing those four creatures who had been gobbling up all the animals around town. Molly couldn't find a reason to disagree. And after all, it was the weekend.

Molly had been to the rink a few times before, but during

the daytime, and now sundown was only an hour away. It wasn't a rule, but on Friday and Saturday nights the crowd tended to be a little older. There were usually some fifth graders like her, Finn, and Leonard. But lots more sixth and seventh graders. Even a few eighth graders. Sometimes Molly saw some of them hanging in the alley between the Rink-A-Rama and DeVern's Discount Tire next door, usually up to no good.

Molly looked up at the sign. Taking up a fair chunk of the last block on State Street, the Rink-A-Rama was one of the oldest buildings in Far Flung Falls. City hall sat a few blocks in the other direction, at the corner of Main. And just like on her street, things gradually got less fancy toward the end of the road. Over the last few hours, she and her friends had canvassed the whole downtown area, posting flyers at the barber shop, a Texaco station, a Shop 'n Save, Chez Del Ray, the Far Flung Falls First Credit Union, an insurance agency, the sheriff's office, Saint Barnaby's First Presbyterian Church, three pawn shops, and every telephone pole and lamppost in between.

The Rink-A-Rama was the last stop. After that there was only a small patch of broken-up asphalt, then an old empty lot that was intermittently marked by the remains of a chain-link fence. Beyond that, civilization gave way to the surrounding

Molly and the Mutants

woods, which were already attempting to reclaim a portion of the space, some brambles and bushes creeping in through the cracks.

Molly and most of her friends had only known the building as a skating rink, but it had been many other things before that. Its previous lives included a warehouse for farming equipment, an assembly hall, and a factory that made baseball gloves. Molly had even heard that, many years ago, it was something called a *speakeasy*, which she understood to be a kind of secret club where grown-ups went to eat dinner and dance on the table or something silly.

As old as it was, it was hard to believe the building was still standing, but, made from poured concrete, it might just be the sturdiest building in town.

"C'mon, you guys ready?" Margo said.

Molly really liked having Leonard around. Without him, it felt like it might be a double date, which made her anxious. But Leonard made it feel like just a big group.

They walked in the front door and were immediately met by the vocals of Journey's lead singer, pumping through the speakers at full volume.

Don't stop... believin'...

Hold on to that feee-lay-eee-ayyn'...

Margo grabbed Molly's arm like it was a microphone and started lip-syncing the song as if she were onstage. It made Molly smile. She wasn't going to stop believing. Crank had to turn up somewhere. Or at least give them some sign where she was. She was too crafty to let one of those monster-size frogs make her their lunch. And with all the flyers they'd put up around town, somebody was bound to know something.

The five of them made their way to the counter to trade in their sneakers for skates. Molly watched the disco ball spinning from the middle of the ceiling. She could feel the vibration of the bass coming up through the floor to her feet, relaxing her. She liked this place.

Molly felt extra connected to her fellow flyer-passer-outers. They could get on her nerves a little from time to time, but they had really been there for her over the last couple of days, especially while Crank was still missing. They'd run around through every corner of the woods, dodging giant killer frogs. And now they were bound by secrets and a solemn oath. They weren't just friends; they were members of the Moonlight Crew.

Well, all except one. Molly felt a stab of guilt that Leonard hadn't had the chance to be initiated... yet. But she was planning to fix that.

Molly and the Mutants

In the meantime they deserved a night of fun.

"Heya, Teach!" Leonard said to the man behind the shoe counter.

"Hiya, kids."

"Mr. Gatlin?" Molly asked. "What are you doing here at the Rink-A-Rama?"

"Just a part-time job I do on the weekends. You know, to make ends meet." Mr. Gatlin kept talking as he collected their shoes. "Unfortunately, ol' President Reagan's *trickle-down economics* haven't quite trickled down to most of us teachers yet. So I moonlight a little."

He gave Molly a wink as he said it, taking her sneakers.

"What's your size?"

CHAPTER 39
SATAN'S SONG

Margo's idea for some fun was a good one, but Molly felt guilt creep in as the night went on. Skating under a disco ball to the tunes of Styx while Crank might still be out there didn't feel right. But after everything they'd already done—and nearly dying along the way—Molly didn't feel like she could ask her friends to do one more thing. And even if she did, what more could they do? Yesterday they had scoured the forest, and today they'd covered the town in flyers. Maybe Margo was right: time to have a little well-earned fun... if Finn would stop falling down.

"Whoa!" Finn exclaimed for about the eleventh time, not that she was counting.

It was his first time on skates, and it showed. As skilled

as he'd been on a bike, Finn's abilities definitely didn't carry over to the skating rink. After his third fall Molly had offered to help him out with his balance until he got the hang of it, not realizing until after she'd offered that this would necessitate some hand-holding. After two laps Molly tried to free her hand, but Finn had it in an iron grip.

The Styx song faded as the DJ's voice crackled over the speakers.

"Listen up, skaters! This next one is... *couple's only!*"

The reaction to this news was predictably mixed, with equal parts squeals and groans. The soft tinkling of a piano signified a gooey love song. More squeals and groans from the skaters.

"I'm out," Leonard said, making an immediate hard left off the floor and toward the bank of video games flashing against the far wall.

"Me too—" Arvin attempted.

"Nope," Margo said. "You're with me."

"Um, I think I'll just join Leo—" Finn said.

"You're good right here with Molly," Margo said.

Molly wouldn't have minded a little break herself. She could see the soft pretzels and pizza slices turning in heated carousels over the countertop, and felt her stomach growl.

But the music was too loud for anyone to hear.

"Margo, my ankles are sore," Arvin said. "I need a break."

"Fine," Margo said.

"Um, me too. Yeah, really sore ankles," Finn said.

"That's cool," Molly said, happy to finally get her hand back. Both their hands had been so wet and clammy, it had been getting hard to hold on. She wiped her palm on her jeans, then shook it, trying to get it to feel normal again. Finn and Arvin hurried ahead of them.

"*Boys . . . ,*" Margo said.

"Yeah," Molly said. "*Boys.*" Although, she wasn't really sure what Margo's point was.

The two of them skated along together side by side, enjoying a little extra room on the floor since the "couple's only" announcement had scared off so many skaters.

"Pizza?" Molly said.

"Definitely," Margo said.

They rolled off the skate floor and crossed the carpeted area between the video games and the entrance, making their way to the counter.

The music changed again. The heavy guitar chords ushered in KISS's "Lick It Up." Excitement rippled through the rink. Very few of them were allowed to listen to KISS at home, ever since so many of their parents had started raising a fuss about devil worshipers. Molly's dad had laughed at this assertion, like Ronda and Gruncle had, but still. Apparently, the DJ at the Rink-A-Rama hadn't gotten the memo. Or more likely, he didn't care.

Lick it up, lick it up, ahh-ahh-yeah!

A group of eighth graders sitting at a table against the wall paused from devouring their pizza for a head-banging interlude, rocking to the beat. They gave their best impressions of Gene Simmons, waggling their tongues and holding up the sign of the horns with their hands, otherwise known as the rock 'n' roll salute. Molly caught the DJ saluting back.

Leonard and Finn broke out into air guitar, while Arvin went after the high score on *Centipede*, just before a pixelated spider snuck onto the screen and dashed his hopes.

"Gah!" Arvin said, stepping aside. "Player two is up."

The contraband lyrics kept wailing out over the speakers.

Lick it up, lick it up, ahh-ahh-yeah!

Molly and Margo rolled up to the counter, but suddenly felt the floor move under their feet. Several skaters fell over at the same time. What was happening? Had the DJ turned up the volume?

A second before Leonard took position in front of the

Centipede controls, there was a deafening boom as the metal doors at the entrance flew off their hinges, clattered across the floor, and landed with a boom. Moments later a gargantuan tongue, as thick as a tree trunk, barreled through the hall like a battering ram, smashing against the *Centipede* game on the opposite wall and enveloping the top of it in a slimy ball of mucus. The impact knocked the game so hard, the change panel popped off, spilling a small mountain of quarters onto the floor.

The tongue flexed, sending ripples down the length of it, then pulled back its catch, dragging the arcade game across the floor on its side with a screech until it got stuck in the doorway.

Bang, bang, bang. Molly thought the repeated impact might smash the whole console, or the doorway, or both. But the concrete walls of the Rink-A-Rama held firm.

With a long wet *sluuuurp*, the tongue finally released its prey, leaving the video game lying sideways in front of the door.

Molly stood motionless. Only a moment earlier and she and Margo would have been right in the tongue's way. Arvin, too.

The music had stopped. Molly looked over and spotted the DJ tiptoeing up a circular staircase behind his booth and disappearing into the ceiling. An eerie quiet settled over the rink, except for the sound effects coming from *Centipede*, a

Molly and the Mutants

sad *bweep-bweep-bweep*, signifying *Game Over*, which seemed a little unnecessary at this point.

"That... was... gonna... be... my... high score," Arvin said, still dazed at having barely missed getting taken. "What is th—"

Molly looked over his way. She watched it slowly dawn on him what had just happened, as he wiped the splatters of amphibious mucus from the front of his shirt.

Leonard and Finn, standing just to the other side of him, had been slimed as well.

"Ewww," they said in unison.

Before anyone else could react, the monstrous tongue was back. This time it fell short of the opposite wall, holding position in the center of the rink. Stunned, the skaters all watched in terror as hundreds of sparkling lights from the disco ball danced across the slimy, muscular mass. Finally it retreated back through the battered entry.

All at once dozens of kids started screaming. Already clumsy on their skates, they moved in every direction, crashing into one another and falling into heaps all over the rink's floor. It was pure chaos. The echoes of "Lick It Up" lingered in Molly's ears. She looked to where the older kids had been head banging and eating pizza. Now they were cowering under the table.

Molly didn't know what to think. Maybe *KISS* really did stand for "Knights in Satan's Service." Who knew? Maybe playing this song had called up some demon from the depths of hell, just like Officer Wasserbaum had warned, and now it was too late....

But Molly knew that tongue. Only this one was bigger. Much, *much* bigger.

The only music now was the screaming. Above the din, Molly heard the voice of a single adult. It was Mr. Gatlin, by the shoe rental. He was motioning with both arms.

"This way! Hurry! Behind the counter! Before it comes back!"

Roughly half the group skated in his direction, passed through the **EMPLOYEES ONLY** gate, and crouched down. The other half moved to the other end of the rink, up against a half wall that separated the skating floor from the carpeted area. The protection wasn't as good as the counter, but it was better than nothing. And nobody wanted to cross the firing zone in the middle.

The kids near Mr. Gatlin huddled down on the greasy tile floor, bombarding the lone adult with a million frantic questions:

"What *was* that, Mr. Gatlin?"

"Is it a demon from you know where?"

"Is this because the DJ played KISS?"

"My mom says their name stands for 'Knights in Satan's Service'!"

Molly and the Mutants

"Does not!"

"Does so!"

"Are we all gonna die?"

"No, no, kids, the music didn't cause any of this, I promise. And you are most definitely not gonna die. This counter here is as sturdy as they come, see?" He gave it a couple of raps with his knuckles. "Now lemme do a little investigation... you know, employ the scientific method, just like we do in class. What we first need is a little more data. And I'll be right back."

His words calmed the huddled mass by just a few notches, or at least quieted them down. He crawled on his hands and knees through the kitchen door behind them and disappeared.

"I think it was a frog," Molly said. She exchanged looks with Margo, Arvin, Leonard, and Finn, who all nodded in agreement.

"Definitely," Margo said.

"A frog?" one of the older kids said. "No way they can get that big."

"Yes way," Arvin countered.

"Believe her," Leonard said.

"We've seen... *things*," Finn said.

"Yeah, very scary things," Margo said.

"But looks like we haven't seen it all yet," Molly said.

CHAPTER 40
MOONBEAM

As instructed, the kids all huddled together behind the counter and waited. Minutes passed.

"Okay, now what?" someone finally asked.

Molly looked left and right and realized that all eyes were on her. Who did everybody think she was? What did they expect her to do? Maybe it was true that she had taken down a giant killer robot over the summer, but did that make her an expert on giant killer frogs?

"Not sure yet. Lemme see what's happening," Molly said.

Quietly, on hand and knees, she followed where Mr. Gatlin had gone, around the length of the counter and back into the small kitchen. As she did, Molly felt the weight of everyone's stare, and their expectations. Maybe once you became a hero, that's just what you were forever. In the kitchen Molly saw two older teens who worked there crouched up against the wall. Their eyes were wide with fear. One of them had a giant Adam's apple that bobbed up and down as he tried to stifle a cry, or a scream, or both. Molly looked at them and put a finger to her lips. They nodded.

Molly glanced around. She'd never been in the Rink-A-Rama's kitchen before. It was fancier than she'd expected, with marbled tile walls and wood paneling. The ceiling was higher here than out in the rink. And Molly noticed a long narrow row of windows running along the top of the wall. The leaden glass looked mottled and old, each pane set with intricate designs. These were surely a holdover from one of the building's many past lives, Molly thought. They reminded her a little of the stained glass she had seen in church once, only less angular and more swirly-looking. The row of panes bowed outward, forming a curved, concave shape inside.

With the overhead fluorescents turned off, the windows had caught Molly's eye because of the way they seemed illuminated on their own. Diffused by the fog that had once again enveloped Far Flung Falls, the moonlight still managed to bathe the room in a soft, milky glow. But maybe that glow was from something else, too. Something greenish, and moving, and much closer than the moon....

Mr. Gatlin cracked open the door to peek outside. Molly could see his back rising up and down as the science teacher tried to steady his breaths. Then he opened the door a little wider, stepped outside, and disappeared.

That's when she heard the sound, loud and clear. A deep, rumbling growl. No, not just one, Molly thought. A chorus of growls. Two, maybe three of them. The growls were incredibly loud, vibrating the floors and walls even more than the Rink-A-Rama's sound system had before. They continued in a pattern, rising and falling.

Gwaaaarrrrp... Gwaaaarrrrp... Gwaaaarrrrp...

It was unmistakable. They were croaking. Molly had been right. Frogs.

And Mr. Gatlin was out there. She had to warn him.

Slowly Molly took a step closer to the door. The croaks were deafening. She poked her head out the doorway, and shot a look down the alley. At first it appeared empty. Then she spotted Mr. Gatlin creeping along the side of the wall, trying not to draw any attention. Something was casting a green glow on the opposite wall. Molly waited, not sure what to do.

Molly and the Mutants

Part of her wanted to run back into the Rink-A-Rama kitchen and hide under the counter. But another part of her had to see for herself what was out there, what was happening. And her friends were counting on her to find out.

Mr. Gatlin fumbled for his car keys, then turned back toward the door. As soon as he noticed Molly watching him, he jumped. She motioned for him to come back, but the long creased expression on his face seemed to say *Sorry*. That's when Molly realized, he wasn't going for help. He was just . . . going. Mr. Gatlin was abandoning all of them to whatever was out there. A couple of hours earlier, when he had said "moonlighting," she had thought maybe . . . well, none of that mattered now.

Molly tried to call out, to tell him to stop, but the word got caught in her throat, and couldn't find its way out. She balled her fists and watched helplessly in silence as he started the Oldsmobile and slowly made his way down the alley. At the end the brake lights flashed red as the car stopped. Molly thought maybe he was reconsidering. But then Gatlin pulled the old sedan out to the right and . . .

What followed next was an awful crunching sound, punctuated by the brief, sad, single-note cry of a car horn, then silence. To Molly's astonishment, the car was gone.

The entire vehicle had vanished under an avalanche of slimy green tissue of such scale that it took Molly a beat to even register what she had witnessed. In horror her eyes tried to follow the contours of an endless green mass. She made out what looked like long slender toes, bulbous on the ends, connected to each other by a thick, shiny web.

It was a frog's foot, only hundreds of times bigger than anything she had ever seen.

The foot lifted back up, revealing a flattened heap of metal. There was no sign of Mr. Gatlin among the crumpled folds of what had been his car. One of the wheels rolled in her direction, then fell over.

Molly realized she was hyperventilating.

Think, Molly, think! What could she do? Definitely not go in the direction that Mr. Gatlin had gone.

The frog shifted its footing, bringing more of its gargantuan body into Molly's view. It was sidestepping in a strange, clumsy way, crushing the concrete and asphalt under its weight. A wall of glistening green flesh began blocking the potential exit from the alleyway, until a massive yellow eye appeared from around the corner, nearly level with the height of the Rink-A-Rama. The bulbous eyeball, as wide as a water well, scanned the alley until it rested on Molly. As soon as it did, the creature's entire body rippled in what looked like excitement. It continued to shuffle and slide into view, until part of the mouth was visible. Its jaws began to open, revealing an impossibly cavernous space within, big enough for a truck to drive through. The croak that followed shook her to her bones.

Then came the smell. Even worse than Darryl's farts. The stench wafted over her, filling her nostrils. It was bitter, rancid, full of decay. Molly's eyes watered. She gagged.

At that moment the dense fog that had been lingering for days on end finally dissipated, revealing the monster—or at least the part of it she could see—in all is grotesque glory. Like a creature from some age long past, but twisted somehow, misshapen. Molly gulped. Proportionally something about it didn't look quite right, beyond its towering size.

This wasn't like the creatures that had chased them just yesterday—creatures that now seemed almost small by comparison. This was something in a category all its own. From her view in the alleyway, Molly couldn't even tell where the thing ended. It seemed to bulge in all the wrong places, occupying the entire street. And its movements seemed labored, unnatural. Molly had so many questions. How could something possibly grow that big? Where had such a thing come from? What was it doing here in Far Flung Falls? And just how many of them were there? But something told her she couldn't afford to wait to find out.

Molly regained her senses and jumped back into the kitchen. She was about to slam the door shut behind her when the whole thing was enveloped by the end of a humongous sticky tongue and ripped from its hinges. Molly fell backward, slipping on the greasy kitchen floor. She eyed the room for something that might help, anything that could be used as a weapon. . . .

Pizza dough sat on the countertop, a few ladles for red sauce that had hastily been dropped when the Rink-A-Rama staff had run for cover. The marinara had splattered everywhere, making the counter look like a gruesome murder scene. *Hopefully,* Molly thought, *that wouldn't prove to be true tonight.*

But the light in the room looked different than before she had stepped outside. With the fog lifted, it seemed much brighter. Maybe it was because the door was now gone. Or maybe it was just the unhindered moonlight. Molly looked around for the source. That's when she noticed a silvery beam shining from the beveled glass high above her head. The light from the bowed windowpanes gathered into a single shimmering ray, aiming at a mirrored tile on the opposite wall, and ricocheting back to the far end of the counter.

Molly and the Mutants

In the half-light of early evening, the luminous shaft pierced through the darkened room.

A moonbeam.

In her head Molly heard Ronda singing:

The moon may wax, and the moon may wane

Then the moon will do it all over again

When the night is dark and it's far from daaay

Just look for a moonbeam to guide your waaay

Could it be a sign? Molly's heart filled with hope. Softly humming the tune to herself, she circled around to the other side of the counter, seeing where the beam ended.

The glowing crescent landed exactly on a thin metal seam running up and down between two large wooden panels. A moon shape. What could this mean?

The inlaid metal seam looked textured somehow. She looked closer, squinting to see, and saw that engraved in the metal were the tiniest letters. So microscopic, they would have been invisible without the light of the full moon glinting right off them. A little arrow pointed to the top of the seam, and underneath, three letters, vertically stacked:

P

R

Y

Taking it as direction, Molly ran her finger up the cold metal to the top, where it almost met the countertop. She felt a thin gap there, and worked her fingernail into it until, *clink*, the metal strip popped out at a sharp angle.

Molly stopped and stared. A lever? She pulled on it. At first it didn't budge. But Molly persisted until it made a loud *shu-u-u-u-unk*. This was followed by more pops and clicks, and Molly felt things moving under her feet. Then the entire countertop lifted several inches off the floor.

"What are you doing?" the teenager with the Adam's apple asked.

"I don't know, exactly," Molly said. "But I'm trying to . . . do something."

"Um, okay . . ." The owner of the Adam's apple didn't sound very sure.

Molly pushed up against the countertop, trying to raise it even higher. Maybe there was something underneath that could help? Something from the Moonlight Crew? Maybe it was something from her Gruncle? But it seemed stuck. Molly needed some additional muscle, and the two older kids frozen against the wall didn't seem very likely to help.

She ran back into the main room for backup.

CHAPTER 41
SECRET STASH

"Arvin! Margo! Leonard! Finn!" Molly called to her friends. They were all still cowering behind the shoe counter. "I need your help."

"With what?" Leonard asked.

"With trying to get outta here alive, is what," Molly said.

"I'm in for staying alive," Margo said, standing up.

"Yeah, me too," Arvin said.

Molly was heartened by their answer. Together maybe they could figure something out.

"Hey," Finn said, pointing to the only telephone on the premises, sitting on the far end of the counter. "Maybe we could call for help? If we could just get ov—"

Just then a monstrous frog tongue shot through the open doorway. But this one looked different from the first. It was shorter, hanging suspended in the center of the hall. And the end of it was rounder, and pockmarked all over, like a wet, cratered moon.

"Ya missed," said Leonard. "Now it's my turn." He pulled out his slingshot and took aim.

The cratered-looking part started pulsating, like it was about to burst. Leonard fired his pebble and hit the glistening mass dead center. On impact all the craters twitched, puckering and then expanding. From each of them, in a blur of motion, a long thin ribbon of flesh shout out in every direction.

Molly gasped. It was a tongue ... with tongues.

"Look out!" Arvin yelled.

The volley of smaller tongues claimed anything and everything in the Rink-A-Rama that wasn't hiding or nailed down. A rapid succession of wet, sticky thuds resonated throughout the hall. They snatched up a discarded roller skate and a half-eaten pizza box. One ripped the disco ball from the ceiling. Another popped half of the balloons tied to the helium stand. They claimed an empty can of RC Cola, the ball cap off one of

Molly and the Mutants

the kid's heads ... and the Rink-A-Rama's one and only telephone. Ripped right off the counter, cord and all.

"There goes calling for help ...," Finn said.

One more mini-tongue snatched the slingshot out of Leonard's hand.

"Aaigh! Hey—" Leonard shouted.

The tongues retracted with everything they'd collected. Then the entire mass disappeared back out the door.

"C'mon, now's our chance," Molly said.

"Quick, before it comes back," Margo said.

"It's gonna pay for my slingshot," Leonard said, wiping the mucus from his hand on his jeans. "Not. Cool."

Together the five of them hustled back into the kitchen, leaving all the other kids to sit tight until they put a plan together. After they passed through the doorway, Arvin was the first to notice the countertop.

"Uh, you picked a weird time to remodel," he said.

"Just help me lift this up," Molly said.

Finally it budged, turning a full ninety degrees up on its end with a squeak.

They looked down.

"No way," Finn said. "Stairs."

"Great," Margo said. "Another secret set of steps leading to who-knows-where."

"Ya gotta admit, the last one lead to something pretty cool," Arvin said.

"True."

"Guys, look at this." Finn pointed to a message inscribed on the underside of the countertop above:

The moon may wax, and the moon may wane

Then the moon will do it all over again

When the night is dark and it's far from day

Just look for a moonbeam to guide your way

"It's Ronda's song!" Arvin said. "Maybe it's an escape tunnel. Look!"

"What song?" Leonard asked. No one answered.

Was this another secret hideout for the Moonlight Crew? Molly wondered.

As if in response to her thought, a row of crescent-shaped lights flickered on along the walls of the stairwell, showing a carpeted hallway at the bottom.

"Nice going, Molly," Finn said.

"C'mon," Molly said. "This could be our way out."

"I hope so," Margo said. "Because the front door and the back door aren't looking too good at the moment."

Molly and the Mutants

Gwaaaarrp, gwaaaarrp...

More bellows from whatever awaited them outside.

One by one the five of them crept down the steps and along a narrow hall. At the end of it they came to a door labeled **MEMBERS ONLY**. The newest members of the Moonlight Crew all exchanged looks. But when they opened it, Molly's heart sank. Nothing but an empty cellar. It was a dead end. Why would someone go through all the trouble to create a secret passage that lead to ... nowhere?

The kids all wandered into the room, hoping maybe they had missed something. Molly dropped her head. That's when she noticed the faded rug on the floor, with a distinct pattern of a crescent moon and three drops emanating to the right.

"Blood, sweat ... and cheers ...," she whispered.

"Whadja say?" Arvin asked.

Molly walked over and stood on the first drop. *Click.*

"Finn, come stand on the second drop!"

When he did, another *click*.

Margo stepped on the third.

As soon as she did, the entire wall to their right began to spin around, revealing the other side, which was lined floor to ceiling with built-in shelves. They stared at row upon row of the same type of jugs that Ronda had been delivering on the handcar. But these had clearly not moved in a long time. Molly approached the secret stash. Every jug was coated with a thick layer of dust. Molly brushed her hand over a few of the jugs in search of some clue. Each label was the same:

LEROY'S LIQUID LIGHTNING

Finn was peeking over her shoulder. "Who's Leroy?" he asked.

"Beats me," Arvin said. "But I'm guessing he likes moonshine."

"Or *liked*," Molly said. "No telling how old these are."

"But how'd they end up under the Rink-A-Rama?" Margo asked.

"It wasn't always the Rink-A-Rama," Molly said.

"Well, if it's not an exit, I don't know how it's gonna help us," Margo said.

Just then they heard another round of screams from the terrified kids up above, followed by a burst of pops. Without seeing it, Molly knew what had happened . . . and a plan hatched in her mind.

"Did you guys hear that?" Molly asked, the start of a smile curling around the corners of her mouth. "Balloons! That's it!"

"What?" Margo asked. "Molly, have you lost your—"

Molly and the Mutants

"Don't worry, I'll explain everything," Molly said. "But first we're going to need everyone's help."

"Help for what?" Leonard asked.

"Whatever's out there, it's time we threw 'em a party... compliments of Leroy."

Molly turned around and ran.

CHAPTER 42

COUNTERATTACK

After a little coaxing. Molly and the other members of the Moonlight Crew got all the other kids in the Rink-A-Rama to form an assembly line. There were nearly sixty of them in total. The line wound around the kitchen, down the stairs, and into the cellar, before looping back up. Between the balloons and the moonshine, the operation had gone remarkably fast.

Molly's plan was coming together. Hopefully, it wouldn't fail.

At her direction the kids had all quietly switched back from roller skates to their everyday shoes, so they could travel up and down the secret stairway without crashing. After they'd

Molly and the Mutants

completed the initial task, everyone was holding two loaded weapons, carefully cradling a full, wobbly balloon in each hand so as not to drop them. A few older kids were muttering under their breath.

"Are you sure this'll work?" one of them asked.

"No, but we've seen it work once before," Molly said. "So I think it's our best bet."

"And if you got a better idea," Margo said, "be my guest."

There was more muttering, followed by a heated discussion on the physiology of frogs and how they absorbed liquid through their skin. Molly had never seen so many kids give such rapt attention to an improv science lesson. But the giant attacking tongues of death seemed to have piqued everyone's interest about the finer points of amphibious life.

While the kids made their preparations to fight back, the tongue attacks seemed to fall into a kind of pattern, with breaks in between. Probably to allow time for the frogs to try to digest whatever random objects they had collected. Molly wasn't sure if giant frogs ever experienced indigestion, but she couldn't imagine that random roller skates, plastic chairs, and ceiling tiles could be very appetizing, or sit well in the stomach—even for a ravenous prehistoric-looking monster.

During the breaks in action, the kids made their way in small groups across the skating hall, hustling to the back corner that housed the abandoned DJ booth, where Molly had spied the previous occupant make his escape up a small circular stairway that rose to the catwalk. From there Molly hoped that somehow they could reach the roof.

Molly popped open the hatch, and was nearly clobbered by the DJ, who had been hiding up there since the assault had begun.

"Sorry, I thought you were... uh, something else."

"Did you get a look at what's attacking us?" Molly asked.

The DJ nodded.

"How many of them are there?"

"Uh... that depends on how you count..."

The roof wasn't much more than a thin layer of tar, topped with gravel and surrounded by a low wall. It wasn't the best fortress for defending against a monster attack but could've been worse. One by one the kids made their way to the front-facing side of the building.

"Margo, you got my eyes?" Molly asked.

"Aye, aye, captain."

Molly had given her a special assignment earlier, while everyone else had been filling up their balloons, since Molly

Molly and the Mutants

had known that Margo already had a couple of ingredients on her: a compact and gum. All Molly had needed was a paper towel roll from the restroom and another compact. Just stick the mirrors from each compact to the ends of the roll with bubble gum, and you had a periscope.

Molly looked back to the crowd of scared faces behind her. They all looked just like she felt. But there was something else in their expressions that made Molly even more afraid: they were looking up to her to fix this, to save them. They were counting on her. And more than anything else, she didn't want to let them down. Molly opened her mouth.

"Don't worry," she said. "I don't think they know we're up here."

"Yet," one of the scared kids added.

"Yet," Molly agreed. She looked through her makeshift periscope. And nearly gasped. It took Molly several long seconds to make sense of what she was seeing. But now she understood what the DJ had been saying about "depends on how you count." In addition to a few extra legs, the beast had three heads.

That explained the three different kinds of tongues attacking them. It wasn't three different mutant frogs. It was three mutant frogs rolled into one. *Frogzilla.*

"Guys, I have good news...and bad news...and then some more good news."

"What's the good news."

"There's only one creature out there trying to eat us."

"Okay...What's the bad news?"

"It's a three-headed mutant frog monster with more eyes and legs than I can count."

"That sounds pretty bad," one of the kids said.

"You said there was more good news?" another kid asked.

"It's gonna be hard to miss," Molly whispered. "That thing's bigger than a combine."

Everyone's eyes widened at the thought.

"Ready?" Molly asked.

Everyone nodded. They cocked their arms back, prepared to throw.

"Fire!"

In unison they all lobbed the first volley of fifty-eight birthday balloons high over their heads. The balloons undulated in the air, each one loaded with the ancient stash of Leroy's Liquid Lightning. Red, yellow, green, and blue, the balloons were illuminated by the moon, which had crept a little higher in the sky. A shimmering, wobbling, 180-proof rainbow, tinted

Molly and the Mutants

by the eerie green glow of the unnatural monster lurking just past the wall as the makeshift bombs dropped to meet their target.

They waited a second, then heard the percussion of fifty-eight pops and splashes, followed by a series of long belch-like croaks that shook the building.

GWAAAAAARRRRRP...

"Cheers, you monster," Molly whispered.

Molly lifted up her periscope again to check the position, and saw colorful shreds of burst balloons scattered across the top of the beast. She gave Leonard a thumbs-up.

"Direct hit!" Molly said. "Ready next round."

Molly then signaled to the group that their target had shifted a little to the left.

Suddenly the periscope was ripped from her hands. A tongue had shot upward and snatched her view, along with whatever hope of surprise she'd had for the remainder of their little operation.

"Fire!" Molly screamed, no longer concerned with stealth.

They let their second round of balloons fly, fifty-eight more colorful latex-and-whiskey grenades. They listened to more pops and splashes, followed by more croaks.

The last croak was long and deep, like a yawn. The street below got quiet.

Molly stole a glance over the wall to see that Frogzilla had turned away from them, edging toward the town's center. She saw the remains of several popped balloons on the asphalt around the monster, soaking the street in booze. Molly made a guess that nearly half of their second round had missed their mark. Would that be enough alcohol to lull such a large beast to sleep? Molly tried to calculate the dose relative to the creature's body mass, but it was impossible to tell. They'd have to wait and see.

Curious, her accomplices began poking their heads over the wall to watch things unfold. After a minute the creature slowed even further, then stumbled over its own feet. The monster swayed sideways, then crashed headlong into the building on the opposite side of the street, shattering windows and reducing the brick wall to a crumbled ruin. Finally it fell to the ground, closed its eyes, and drifted off into a drunken stupor.

Her plan had worked.

"Now's our chance," she whispered. "Let's go."

CHAPTER 43
HOLY FUDGE NUGGETS

Quietly the kids all peeked out from the Rink-A-Rama's smashed main entrance. At a ground-level view the creature looked even bigger than it had from the roof. Bigger, and more deadly.

"Okay, who's going first?" Margo asked.

"Not me," everyone said at once.

"Okay, I'll go," Molly said, her voice sounding a little unsure.

"Go, McCrusher!" somebody called from the back, before everyone shushed him. But it was just the boost of confidence she needed. If everyone else believed in her, why shouldn't she believe in herself?

Molly crept outside, watching the multi-headed,

multi-legged hulking green mass taking up most of the street in front of her. She watched its back rise and fall in a slow, regular rhythm. Each of its three throats inflated and deflated in sync with the rest of its gargantuan body. Molly sighed in relief. She was familiar with this kind of deep breathing from having seen her dear Gruncle in the same state. The creature was passed out cold. Leroy's Liquid Lightning had done the trick.

Molly inched across the street. Just then one of Frogzilla's colossal hind legs gave an involuntary kick, barely missing the bicycle rack, which was completely full. Was the creature dreaming? If it was, Molly hoped it was a peaceful dream, one that didn't cause any more sudden movements. Without a sound Molly hopped onto Pink Lightning and cruised back over in front of the entrance. She gestured for the others to follow.

In the distance a police siren blared, its familiar *whooo-ooooo-whoooo-oooo* carrying across the night air. The monster stirred. Its center mouth let out a long, low *gwaaaaarrrp*. But all of its eyes remained closed. At least for the moment.

Molly beckoned the others to hurry. She had a feeling they didn't have much time. As more kids retrieved their bikes, a few were louder than others, adding a jangle or clang to the

Molly and the Mutants

otherwise quiet escape. But Molly could tell the siren was getting closer. It must've been the smashed storefronts, she thought. Probably triggered a silent alarm or something. Or maybe somebody had heard the commotion and called it in? Either way they had to move, unless they wanted to wind up frog food.

"Hurry up," Molly whispered.

The last of the bikers passed by the monster. Most of them headed straight down Main Street, the quickest path back to their homes. But some turned onto side roads. Margo, Arvin, Leonard, and Finn held back, just a block away, waiting for her. With everyone clear of the monster, Molly put a foot to her pedal, just as the red-and-blue lights came into view, and Officer Wasserbaum came peeling around the corner, lighting her up in high beams. Frozen, all she could do was put her finger to her lips to make a shush sign.

It didn't work.

The police car stopped just a few feet in front of her. She winced at the piercing crackle of static, then an amplified voice calling out to her over the PA.

"Molly McQuirter! What in the Sam Hill are you doing in the middle of the ever-lovin' street? You could get run over!"

Her index finger remained pressed to her lips. Then she

rotated it ninety degrees to her left, pointing to the reason for her position, just as all three pairs of its eyes began fluttering back into consciousness. The monster made a deep rumbling growl.

GWAAAAARRRRRP...

Wasserbaum jumped out of the car.

"Holy f-f-f-f-fudge nuggets!" he screamed.

At that moment the fog dissipated, allowing the creature to reveal its true form. In the center of the glowing mass, two giant yellow eyes sprang open, then two more on the right, and another two on the left. The six black-and-yellow orbs blinked a few times, taking a moment to focus, while Molly's eyes did the same.

Then the head on the creature's left side opened its mouth.

"Molly McQuirter," Wasserbaum said without taking his eyes off the three-headed beast, "this is most assuredly *not* the way to earn yourself a SAFER pin...."

"Go, go, go!" Molly cried. "Run! Before it—"

But Wasserbaum stood his ground. He drew his Taser gun and stammered, "F-f-freeze!"

The prehensile tongue moved incredibly fast. *This must be the wrecking ball,* Molly thought, watching the lumpy round mass on the end of it fly sideways in a sweeping arc. SMASH! It

Molly and the Mutants

landed squarely on the hood of the police cruiser, completely caving it in. On impact the windshield shattered, spraying bits of glass in every direction. Its work complete, the wrecking ball pulled back into the monster's mouth. The *whoooo-oooo* of the siren made one final whimper before falling silent.

Molly was already pedaling for all she was worth, while Wasserbaum took up shelter inside a phone booth. It wasn't a very good hiding spot, since it was mostly glass—and very see-through. Also, as soon as he closed the door behind him, the entire booth lit up from within. All he was missing was a target painted on his chest. Molly didn't have time to help him reconsider his position. All she could do at that moment was go as fast as she could. Her friends were just ahead of her.

"Go!" Molly said. Her friends didn't hesitate. In seconds they were racing at top speed, in a loose V formation, with Molly at the lead.

The frog let out an angry croak behind them.

"I don't wanna die, I don't wanna die, I don't wanna die...," Leonard repeated.

"Just keep pedaling," Arvin said.

The monster took a step forward in their direction. Then another. It was quickly gaining on them. Molly looked behind her, then ahead for someplace, any place, they could go. That's when she heard the sound she feared most. Something big, wet, and slimy coming her way impossibly fast. For a split second Molly thought about all the other kids whom she'd helped escape from the Rink-A-Rama, most of them probably halfway home by now. If the five of them didn't make it through the night, at least others would....

"Molly!" Finn screamed, voice cracking. "Watch out!"

His words slammed her back into the present. Molly didn't look back. She didn't even take time to think. She just reacted, reaching down for the lever in front of her seat—the one inscribed with a spiral. She yanked the arm up hard and fast, activating a mechanism inside the bike's frame that released two pressurized jump sticks below her forks. The jump sticks punched into the blacktop below with a force that launched Molly and Pink Lightning up into the air. As she and the bike cartwheeled three hundred sixty degrees above the street, everything slowed down. For a split second, as she was upside down and facing backward, Molly caught sight of the giant tongue slamming into the asphalt below her—exactly in the spot where she'd just been. She came landing back down on the street just as the tongue was retracting into the monster's maw. Empty.

"Molly!" Margo screamed.

Molly and the Mutants

"That was incredible," Finn said.

"That was way too close." Arvin said.

"I know!" Molly said. "Hang left!"

"I think I'm gonna need a bigger slingshot," Leonard said.

They all turned the corner onto State Street, pedaling with all their might under a colorful display of banners that crisscrossed overhead. Every lamppost on the street had been decorated in anticipation of Far Flung Fall's Annual Fritter Fest, just a week away. They rode past Saint Barnaby's First Presbyterian Church, just as Reverend Evans was locking up from Bible study.

"Oh, hi there, kids! Hello, Molly!" he said as he waved. "Getting late—"

A second later the gargantuan three-headed beast leapt behind them, filling the entire street with its unholy green glow.

The reverend gasped, his face turning as white as his collar.

"Have... you... been... playing... *KISS*?" he asked.

"Go back inside!" Margo said.

Leonard gave him the rocker's salute.

Molly didn't have time to talk to the reverend. She was thinking about her friends. She couldn't keep leading the giant frog their way. What could she do? Another one of the bike's gadgets sprang to mind, and this seemed like the perfect moment to use it. She hit the button on her handlebars marked with a puffy cloud symbol, and heard a long hiss. Thick black smoke billowed from a small metal tube that ran along the bottom of her frame. The ensuing cloud was impenetrable, and quickly created a wall of invisibility separating them from their pursuer.

"Find a spot to hide," Molly called.

The smoke screen ran out just as they all took refuge down a dark, narrow alley that cut between Zigler's Shoe Repair and a laundromat. Both shops were closed.

Enveloped in the darkness, the monster quickly got itself tangled in all the festival decorations that had been so carefully hung throughout the street. Keeping absolutely still, Molly and her friends watched in silence as the gargantuan creature filled their view. A slimy, glowing, endless wall of green. With heavy footsteps it lumbered by them without taking notice. The creature was draped in dozens of Fritter Fest banners, dragging more of them in its wake. It reminded Molly of the cars she'd seen hastily decorated outside city hall when someone got married. The last of the streamers slid across the street in front of them in long jerky movements until they

Molly and the Mutants

disappeared from view. Slowly the glow from the creature faded, leaving them in darkness.

"Worst parade float ever...," Arvin whispered.

"Definitely the worst," Leonard agreed.

"Rad move, though," Margo said to Molly. "Thank you."

"Yeah," Finn added. "Is there anything that bike can't do?"

Molly was about to answer when a voice behind them made everyone jump.

"What are you losers up to?" It was Margo's sister, Nikki. And she sounded as grumpy as usual.

CHAPTER 44
CALL OF THE CAMARO

When Molly and her friends had turned into this alley to hide, no one had noticed Logan's shiny green Camaro. It was parked at the very end, beside a dumpster. With the lights out and the engine off, the Green Machine was easy to miss in the shadows. Nikki had poked her head out the back window, the expression on her face something between confused and irritated by the fact that she and Logan suddenly had company.

"Hey, Sis! What are *you* doing here?" she asked Margo. "Seriously, you *better* not tell Mom that you saw—"

"All I saw was you parked next to a smelly garbage bin," Margo said. "Gross."

Molly and the Mutants

"C'mon, Nikki, let's get outta here," Logan interrupted. "This spot's getting... crowded."

"No wait, Sis. It's not safe—" Margo said.

"Yeah, whatever," Nikki said, dipping her head back into the Camaro and disappearing.

Molly, Arvin, and Finn took turns trying to explain the situation, but neither of the older kids was listening. How could they not have noticed the prehistoric-looking monster that had just passed right in front of them? Molly couldn't believe it. They'd probably been too busy doing whatever it was high schoolers do in the back of parked cars... in dark, abandoned alleys. Molly gagged a little at the thought.

Logan flicked on the headlights and turned the ignition, bringing his prized hot rod to life. He started revving the engine. *Too bright,* Molly thought, *and too loud.* The rhythmic rapid-fire knocking from just under the hood upped the tempo. Then the exhaust backfired a few times.

As if to answer the rumble of the engine, there was an equally rumbly croak from around the corner. Then another, but this one sounded closer. Molly and her friends braced themselves for the worst as an eerie light began spilling into the alley from just behind the corner of the laundromat.

"Logan!" Margo screamed. "Turn off the car!"

But it was too late. The next instant a giant green glowing foot planted itself in front of them. Then one of the monster's three faces came into view.

Finn, Leonard, and Arvin ducked behind the dumpster.

On the other side of the alley, Molly and Margo tried to press themselves against the wall, the downspout in front of them not providing much cover.

Vroom, vroom. Logan revved the engine even louder. Then the speakers came on. AC/DC wailed.

I'm on the highway to hell...

Finally, looking up from the dash, Logan saw the monster.

"What in th—"

He screamed. Nikki screamed. They both screamed. Louder than the engine. Louder than the frog. Even louder than AC/DC.

One of the mouths started to open.

"Nikki!" Margo cried.

The Camaro's tires squealed on the blacktop, sending twin plumes of smoke billowing up the wall behind the cornered car. Logan shifted and tore out of the alley just as the wrecking-ball tongue came slamming down where the car had been, leaving a large crater in the blacktop.

Molly and the Mutants

The Camaro spun wildly, fishtailing to the left and knocking over a trash can before the car's rubber caught the road again. As soon as it did, the Green Machine lurched forward, then rocketed down the street, with Frogzilla immediately giving chase.

"Nikki...," Margo whispered behind them, the worry heavy in her voice. Molly understood that even if Margo's sister wasn't the nicest person in the world, that didn't change the fact that they were still sisters. And nice or not, sisters looked out for their own.

After a moment both car and creature were out of view. The scent of burnt rubber hung heavily in the air. They stepped farther out of the alley and waited. Molly could still hear the Camaro's engine trailing off somewhere in the distance, now at least several blocks away. In the dim light of the alley, she strained to catch Margo's eye, and thought she caught the first trace of a tear starting to well. Her own eyes were burning too, maybe from the acrid smoke. But probably not.

"Don't worry, Margo," Arvin said. "I don't think there's a faster car in the state."

"Yeah," Leonard said. "No way it'll catch 'em."

Molly wasn't so sure about that, but she kept her doubts to herself. The problem seemed too massive for any of them to fix. The five of them stood there in silence for several moments, the gravity of their situation weighing them down. No one seemed sure what to say or do next.

"We need reinforcements," Molly finally announced.

"But from where?" Finn asked.

"Good question," Molly said. She scanned the street until she found what she was looking for. Just across the town square, past the gazebo, in a side lot next to the Texaco station...

"There," she said, pointing to a parked eighteen-wheeler.

"What?" Leonard said. "No way we could outrun Frogzilla in that thing. I bet it barely gets up to fifty. We'd get crushed for sure."

"Yeah," Margo agreed. "Plus, don't ya think we're a little young to drive?"

"But not to operate the CB in that rig," Arvin said, clueing in to Molly's plan. "Genius."

"You guys stay here," Molly said to Leonard, Finn, and Margo. Then she turned to Arvin. "You said your uncle was a trucker, right? So... you think you can help me get in touch with... *our friends*?"

"Totally." Arvin smiled.

Without wasting another second, the two Moonlighters hotfooted it across Main Street and diagonally through the town square. When they reached the gazebo in the center, a thunderous croak in the not-too-far-away distance stopped them in their tracks, and they crouched down behind the structure, peeking through its latticework to spot any signs of danger. A block away they caught a glimpse of the Camaro tearing through an intersection, the multi-legged mutant trailing closely behind. The mammoth creature dwarfed its intended prey, moving with an awkward, loping gait, but it was just so big, it was still somehow able to keep pace with the souped-up car. Molly and Arvin stared at the chase once again, the whole scene briefly illuminated under the light of the streetlamp on the corner before they were out of sight.

Molly and Arvin sprinted the rest of the way until they arrived at the driver's side of the cab. Arvin jumped up onto the first of two steps and reached up to check the door handle.

"Locked," he announced.

"Okay," Molly said. "Hold on."

"To the door?"

"No ... just ... hold ... on."

She started working her way around the rig, patting the underside of the truck with her hand like she was searching for something.

"What're ya doing—"

"It's gotta be here somewhere..." She felt into the dark cavity of the front wheel well, her arm disappearing all the way to her shoulder. When she pulled it away, her palm was blackened with soot. Then she did the same with the rear wheel.

"Molly, there's no way—"

"Here we go," she said, producing a spare set of keys and jingling them in front of Arvin. Like a jewel from some lost treasure, the keys glinted in the moonlight. "You were saying?"

"I was saying c'mon.... No telling when that thing'll be back."

Molly could tell he was trying to sound exasperated, but knew he had to be impressed.

"Nice work," he admitted, a smile taking over his face. She smiled back.

They unlocked the cab's door and climbed inside. Molly slid over a pile of greasy hamburger wrappers to the passenger side so Arvin could sit behind the wheel. Immediately the would-be carjackers were overpowered by the stench, a toxic combination of old beef jerky, chewing tobacco, and industrial-strength farts. The floorboards were covered in Styrofoam cups overflowing with chaw-darkened spit.

"Phew!" Arvin gasped. "You had to pick the grossest, smelliest, dirtiest truck on the block?"

"It was the *only* truck on the block," Molly protested.

Molly and the Mutants

"Still. Crack a window. Before we both puke."

"Right," she said.

As they cranked down the windows to breathe, Molly looked over at Arvin at the opposite end of the bench... and suddenly got a weird sensation. Was this déjà vu? She knew she'd never sat in a puke-inducing cab with him before, but something about this moment felt intensely familiar. Ever since she'd come across Arvin at the bottom of a giant muddy footprint, they'd been working side by side to solve problems together—crossing ravines, tracking robots, dodging frogs. Arvin was always there.

"Hey, Arvin?" Molly said.

"Yeah?"

"I just... Thanks for always being somebody I can count on," Molly said. "I haven't had a lot of those."

"Wha—? Oh." Arvin was caught by surprise. His face twisted into an awkward smile. "Sure. Uh, you too. You're pretty amazing, you know... when you're not dragging me somewhere totally disgusting."

"Whatever." Molly socked him in the shoulder, but not too hard.

"Owww!" Arvin said. "Kidding!... Seriously, though, I'm sorry for all those times I teased you. I—"

"S'okay," Molly said.

"Cool."

"Cool."

Arvin extended a hand to shake. When Molly took it, she noticed his pinky and thumb were extended. *That's right,* Molly thought, they were official Moonlighters now.

Molly got oriented to the inside of the cab. The dashboard was covered in stickers, some of which were so obscene that Molly had to look away. What kind of degenerate drove this truck? But the CB looked similar to the one inside Spider Junction. *Okay,* she thought, they could do this. Her plan might just work.

"Ready to save the town again?" Molly asked.

"Yes," Arvin said.

"Okay, you turn on the engine so I can call for help." She tossed him the keys and grabbed the speaker to the CB. The speaker cord dragged across the floorboard, knocking over one of the cups. Arvin scooched forward on the seat to reach the ignition.

Just as the semi's diesel engine thundered to life, the Camaro returned, streaking in front of them at full speed. A moment later the entire windshield was filled with green as the monstrous frog continued its pursuit. Panicked, Arvin fumbled with the dashboard and accidentally turned on the truck's high beams, illuminating the creature's flank and causing the pupil in one of its many eyes to contract. It stopped to consider them.

Gwaaaarrrp, the monster said, with a slight inflection—almost like it was asking a question. A few more of its bulbous eyes rolled their way.

"Arvin!" Molly hissed.

"I know!" Arvin hissed back.

He was fumbling with the dashboard again while Molly sat frozen in place. It occurred to her that this would be a terrible place to die, among all the chaw spit, reeking odor, and dirty decals. After what felt like an eternity, Arvin finally managed to cut the lights. Back under the cover of darkness, they watched the monster gradually lose interest, returning its attention to the Camaro.

"Um, let's try the *interior* dash lights," Molly said. "So we can see what we're doing ... and not get eaten."

With Frogzilla out of sight, Arvin quickly found the right switch, lighting up the controls of the CB. The truck idled in the parking lot as Molly flipped on the radio and began tuning the dial. She pressed the button on the speaker.

"Uh, breaker, breaker, three-nine. Anybody out there tonight? Hello?"

Molly lifted her thumb off the button and waited. She was answered only by static. And maybe the squeal of the Camaro's tires in the distance. She knew they didn't have forever.

"Hello? Anybody?" Molly tried again.

"Hey," Arvin said. "Didn't Ronda have it, like, set to a special channel or something?"

"That's right!" Molly said. "Wait, what was it?"

"Thinking," Arvin said. He closed his eyes and let out a great sigh, like it was taking all of his concentration to retrieve the memory. "I remember... it was the same number as something else...."

"Okay," Molly said. "That's something."

"The railway line," he said.

"Thirty-nine!" they both shouted at the same time.

There were only forty channels on the entire band. Molly moved the dial down to nearly the end and tried again.

"Hello? Any Moonlighters out there tonight? I've got a ten-seventeen. It's... an emergency."

"Ten-four. Who's asking?" came a gruff voice. But a familiar one.

Molly paused a moment. "It's... McCrusher," she said. For the first time the nickname felt like something that fit.

"Well, howdy-do there, McCrusher! And welcome to the

Molly and the Mutants

Crew," came the voice. "This here's Mur-dog. What's your ten-twenty?"

Molly felt a wave of relief wash over her body as she heard Murray's voice. Immediately she explained their predicament, from the assault on the Rink-A-Rama, down to their breaking into the world's smelliest rig.

"Oh, that must be Dirty Dan's truck," Murray said. "Sorry about that."

Molly explained more, and together they hatched something close to a plan, occasionally stopping to hear a beeping and clicking sound. She hadn't remembered hearing this before when they'd tuned in from Spider Junction. Maybe it was just how Dirty Dan's CB sounded.

Molly depressed the speaker button.

"Arvin, you hear that?" she asked.

"Hear what?" Arvin was only half listening, keeping his attention on the scene unfolding in front of him. He was gripping the steering wheel so tight, his knuckles were white.

"Like a beeping sound?" Molly asked.

"Maybe," Arvin paused. "But as long as they send some help, I don't care what sounds that thing makes."

"Right," Molly said.

Molly wondered if maybe somebody was listening in. Like

maybe Officer Wasserbaum . . . if he hadn't gotten himself eaten. She didn't want to be the one to blow the Moonlight Crew's code of secrecy. But more important things were at stake right now.

"Just stick to the plan," Murray said. "And don't get ate by no frog-a-saurus. Reinforcements are on the way."

"Thank you," Molly said. "Ur, I mean ten-four."

"TEN. FOUR." Came another voice over the airwaves. It definitely wasn't Murray.

"Mur-dog, was that you? Is anybody else there?"

No answer, but it didn't matter. It was time to get back to their friends.

CHAPTER 45
LOGAN'S RUN

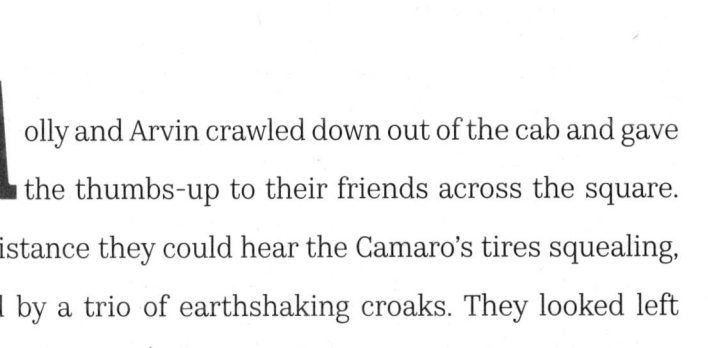

Molly and Arvin crawled down out of the cab and gave the thumbs-up to their friends across the square. In the distance they could hear the Camaro's tires squealing, followed by a trio of earthshaking croaks. They looked left and right, following the trail of shattered windows and overturned cars where the monster had muscled its way through the streets of downtown Far Flung Falls. Runaway Fritter Fest banners, along with Molly's flyers for **LOST TABBY CAT** fluttered through the air and littered the street.

The entire right half of the marquee in front of Saint Barnaby's was gone, a jagged edge marking where the beast had ripped it apart. Now instead of the message...

O BABYLON, REPENT, AND THY DEAR ONES SHALL RETURN TO THEE

... only two words remained along the left-hand side:

O

DEAR

"Looks like World War III," Arvin said. "Think it's safe to cross?"

"Coast looks clear to me," Molly said.

The two hurried back across the destruction and debris to rejoin their friends, who were still cowering in the alley. But halfway through the square, they were nearly run over by the Camaro—then, moments later, by the monster itself. Molly and Arvin stood frozen on the town square's curb as the amphibious mass lumbered just a few feet in front of their faces. Maybe Logan was trying to tire the monster out?

"We can't just wait here for something else to happen!" Margo said.

"You're right. More people are gonna get hurt," Molly said, her mind flashing to the moment before Mr. Gatlin disappeared. "Or worse..."

"But what can we do?" Finn asked.

"I've got a plan," Molly said. "Help is on the way. We just

need to get Logan to lure the monster back to the Rink-A-Rama... and from there back to the woods where it belongs."

"But how do we let Logan and Nikki know?" Margo asked. "They've been going in circles. If we make him stop, that thing's gonna catch up with them. Eventually he's gonna run outta road or gas or something."

Molly looked up and down the flag-festooned street, and found her answer.

"Old Glory," she said.

"Old Glory?" everyone else asked. They looked at her like she'd lost her mind.

"Yeah, Old Glory," Molly repeated, pointing down the street. Every shop had the Stars and Stripes hanging by their entrance. "We're gonna use flags. Just like they do in the races... to show Logan where to go."

The five of them split up, spreading out in different directions on their bikes. Each of them pulled the nearest American flag from its mounting and carried it to a different spot on the route to the Rink-A-Rama.

Molly took up the first position on the corner of State and Main where Logan needed to turn.

She waited, until a new series of crashes, screams, revs, and croaks let her know they were getting closer.

Two blocks away the Camaro flew out from behind the church, spun in their direction, then roared their way. A moment later the gargantuan frog followed behind it. A trio of monstrous tongues shot in all directions, busting windows, flattening street signs, and leaving several parked cars completely flattened. They had been playing cat and mouse (or car and monster) for what felt like forever.

Molly waved her flag, desperately gesturing for Logan to turn.

He did.

From there Logan followed the directions of Arvin and Leonard to the Rink-A-Rama, where Margo and Finn signaled for him to stop.

The Camaro screeched to a halt in front of the last two flag wavers, just a few yards before the street ended and the woods began. Behind them, Molly, Arvin, and Leonard rode to catch up until they were all together. Molly thought maybe this would work to lure the thing back to where it had come from. At least before the entire town had disintegrated.

She looked over at Logan, and almost didn't recognize him. For as long as she'd known him, he'd had a permanent scowl plastered onto his face. But right now he was actually smiling. And not just a half smile but an ear-to-ear grin.

Molly and the Mutants

"That. Was. So. Rad." he said, nearly breathless. "Did you see how we took that last corner? That thing will never catch us—"

"Hey, Logan?" Molly asked.

"Yeah?"

"Help is coming. In the meantime, you think you can get it to go back into the woods over there?"

"Sure thing. Frogzilla's getting tuckered out."

A deep *gwaaaarrrp* warned them that the mutant frog was getting closer. Then it appeared, still staggering a little as it doggedly trailed the hot rod. It looked tired. All six of its eyes rolled in different directions. The glow-in-the-dark creature was still apparently feeling the effects of Leroy's Liquid Lightning. Maybe enough of the balloons had hit their target. Molly shuddered to think what they might have been up against if the giant had been fully sober. Then, for a brief moment, Molly's terror was replaced with another feeling. Was it sympathy for the mutant beast?

It looked so out of place, pausing there at the intersection, too big for the space it was inhabiting. It looked lost. Like it had taken a wrong turn from some other dimension where it should actually exist, and somehow had wound up here in a kind of cosmic accident. In Far Flung Falls. A million miles from home.

In a weird way Molly could relate. Sometimes she felt like a giant three-headed, six-legged mutant frog herself, something outside of the natural world, apart from everyone else, standing at the corner of Third and Main, unsure where to go. Who really belonged anywhere at all?

Logan revved the Camaro's engine, a deep guttural sound, like something alive. Its shiny green hood vibrated.

In response all three heads of the monster croaked back. Logan revved again, and the exchange continued, back and forth. It was a conversation.

"Hey, I didn't know the Green Machine could speak mutant," Logan called from the driver's window. "Suh-weet."

"It does kinda look like a frog," Arvin admitted. "With wheels."

Logan kept it in park, but stepped on the gas, revving the engine louder and louder. The three monstrous heads picked up the pace of their rumbling chorus, sending ripples through the earth that Molly could feel through the soles of her sneakers. The Camaro had the frog entranced.

"We just need to keep it here until reinforcements arrive," Molly called.

"Hope they got some bazookas or something," Logan called back.

Molly and the Mutants

"Maybe you could just tell it to go back into the woods?" Margo said.

"Yeah, do it," Nikki said.

"You got it, babe. Gonna let *Frogasaurus rex* here know who's boss."

He revved one more time, deep and loud, shaking the hood of the car. The tailpipe backfired once, then coughed up a black cloud of smoke. *Thwang.* The engine made a kicking sound, like it was throwing a piston. It sputtered a few times and fell silent.

The Camaro had stalled out.

With the spell broken, six yellow eyes seemed to regain their focus. They stared at the lifeless car in front of them, waiting. Then ever so slowly the center head hunched down and forward, inching closer to the Camaro. It glowed a little brighter and its jaws began to open. But this time there was no croaking to be heard. The conversation appeared to be over.

"Quick, do something!" Nikki screamed.

"I'm trying...," Logan said. "It's not..."

"Nikki," Margo screamed. "Get ou—"

From behind them the gigantic tongue shot forward like a battering ram and engulfed the Camaro's entire back fender in a wet, sticky mass. The impact shoved the car forward by several feet, screeching the tires across the blacktop in a desperate squeal, like prey succumbing to predator.

Logan's face fell. The euphoric smile that had been there during the chase was instantly replaced by a look of sheer terror.

"But—" he said.

"Nooooo," Nikki cried.

And with unnatural speed the Green Machine—along with its helpless driver and passenger—got yanked backward, lifting completely off the ground before disappearing into the gaping maw of the beast. All of Molly's insides melted. She was still trying to register what she had just seen, but it couldn't be true. How could it swallow something as big as a whole entire car?

"Noooo!" Margo screamed. "You can't eat my sister!"

"Do something!" Finn shouted to no one in particular. "Anything."

Arvin looked around and reached down by one of the walls that had fallen victim to the massive frog's clumsy tour around town. He threw a brick. It was a good toss, sailing through the air and hitting its mark—one of the frog's many eyes. The giant monster blinked and shuddered, taking a half step backward. Leonard and the others joined in, chucking bricks at the beast.

Molly and the Mutants

Some hit their mark, whereas others fell a little short.

"That's it! Make it give them back!" Margo yelled.

The frog remained still. Its heads took turns squinting, like it had indigestion. Then it made a loud rumble. The noise grew in pitch and volume. Something between a belch and a small earthquake.

Molly spun around on Pink Lightning, reached into the basket, and pulled out a stone.

The center head opened its mouth impossibly wide. The inner lining was rippling in greenish-yellow waves of frog flesh. Then it looked like it was blowing a balloon. The rumble got even louder and the balloon grew, shiny and slick with mucus. Oh no. Molly realized the mutant was doing the same thing she'd seen one of the other, smaller frogs do back in the woods. Full from feeding, and having digested everything it could, it was turning its stomach inside out to make room for more.

As the wet folds of skin expanded, giving way to the deeper recesses of the creature's gut, an acrid cloud of black smoke was expelled from its throat. Molly heard more gurgling and sputtering, like the frog was struggling for breath. And underneath all those soft, moist sounds, something hard and mechanical. The monster gagged and coughed, taking on a demonic air as the black smoke curled out from both corners of its gaping maw. It was a mythological beast from the underworld. Cerberus the hellhound, only in frog form. Infused with the scent of motor oil, rubber, roadkill, rot, and several dozen balloons of Leroy's Liquid Lightning, its breath burned Molly's nostrils.

She grabbed Margo's hand, bracing herself for the inevitable—getting showered with the lifeless bones of poor Nikki and her boyfriend, who'd been eaten alive. But that is not what happened.

Instead the frog breathed fire.

Molly, Margo, Arvin, Leonard, and Finn all dropped to the ground, hoping to not be incinerated. Molly realized that after their attempt to inebriate the monster, it was so soaked with flammable substance, its insides must have caught fire. And Logan's car had provided the spark.

From the center of the flames, out roared the Camaro, still fully intact, half launching itself, half being barfed up by the amphibious three-headed devil. The Green Machine blasted through the night air, a wake of glimmering frog spit and unfiltered exhaust trailing behind as the back wheels spun at top speed. Molly, Margo, Arvin, Leonard, and Finn all craned their necks, following as the hot rod emerged from the flames like a phoenix from the ashes—and revving the entire time. Coated in slime, it landed with a hard splat, then spun a full two and a half rotations before coming to a stop in front of them.

They all looked, trying to see if the occupants had survived. But the entire vehicle was coated in a thick, gooey film, making it hard to see through the windshield.

Then the wipers came to life, squeegeeing the mucus from the glass.

Nikki and Logan were both sitting there—and they were alive! In sync their terrified expressions melted into looks of joy. The Camaro, and its dirty exhaust, had saved them.

"Yes!" Margo cried.

"Woo-hoo!" Arvin shouted.

"Nine hundred degrees!" Leonard said.

But their jubilation was cut short. The frog wasn't finished expelling the contents of its stomach. Out flew a random assortment of partially digested objects. A trash can, a motorcycle, the bottom half of a door. And piles and piles of bones. Hooves. Antlers. Disassembled vertebrae. Rib cages. Femurs. Skulls large and small. The remains went clattering across the asphalt, a whole museum's worth of skeletal debris.

A few of the skulls were quite large, like they belonged to bears, but were oddly shaped. Molly recognized them as frog skulls. Oversize-frog skulls, to be precise. Molly felt her eyebrows rise in a realization. So that's what Gruncle's note meant! The frogs that had chased them hadn't just been "neutralized."... They'd been eaten. Molly gulped.

"Guys! Look! That's why we haven't seen any other frogs. This one ate them all up."

"It's a frog-eat-frog world," Arvin said.

"That's why it came into town," Margo said. "It must've eaten everything else it could find. It's just... looking for more food."

Together they identified four giant-frog skulls in total, accounting for all the ones who had chased them through the woods. There were also remains of several other smaller creatures. But their inventory was interrupted.

Amidst all the bits of bone, bleached white by the monster's digestive enzymes and acids, Molly caught a bright flash of color. Something... fuchsia? And it was headed her way. The thin band of neon looped in the air, with small flecks of silver that jingled as it flew. Time slowed down. Amid all the death and decay, this looked and sounded almost festive, conjuring memories that Molly couldn't quite place but knew were happy ones. A cheery departure from the pale heap of bones. The colorful band hit Molly in the chest with a force that nearly

Molly and the Mutants

knocked her over, and stuck to her shirt, encased in slime.

Molly reached for the object that had struck her, understanding what it was before she gave it a closer look. A circular strip of leather, with a metal ring that punched through two tags. She held Crank's collar. The clasp was still fastened. But Crank was nowhere to be seen.

Her final disappearing act.

No...

Molly's hand trembled, causing the tags to jingle again. But it wasn't a happy sound anymore. She read the familiar ID, then looked up at the monster, still spewing smoke and bones in a grotesque ritual, its cold-blooded eyes devoid of feeling. Whatever sympathy she'd felt for the creature evaporated. Rage took its place. The scene before her now blurred from tears, and was tinged with red.

She pushed down on Pink Lightning's pedal and charged.

CHAPTER 46
CHEZ DEL RAY

Stan fidgeted with the class ring in his pants pocket, rubbing the red gemstone in a small circular motion with his thumb. High school class of 1971. Just a year later he had slipped it onto a chain and given it to Caroline when they'd started going steady. And two years ago he had found it on his nightstand after she'd run off to Florida. For a while it had been hard to look at the ring and not feel a deep sadness. But those days were behind him. And now, more than anything else, he was ready to place the ring—and his heart—into the hands of a new owner.

In truth his heart had already been offered.

So why was it beating so fast? And why was he sweating?

Molly and the Mutants

This was just a class ring. They were already going steady.

"Is that another police car?" Vilomena asked.

Stanley caught the flash of lights.

"I think so."

Stanley had reserved a window table at the only restaurant in town with actual tablecloths. Chez Del Ray.

He didn't know why he felt so nervous. Or maybe he did.

Then the earth shook. Did he just imagine that?

A deep rumbling sounded in the distance. He didn't think they were expecting bad weather.

Stanley looked out the window at the downtown view, just in time to see a giant yellow excavator drive down the middle of the street, its treaded rollers spinning at full speed. The long arm extended in front of it with the bucket raised like a claw, ready to fight.

Was that Old Man Murray in the cab? And since when did he drive a...

But before Stanley could complete the thought, on the heels of the excavator, an equally large bulldozer came rumbling close behind, its blade scraping along the asphalt, showering the street in sparks. Was this some late-night construction parade he didn't know about? A precursor to next week's Fritter Fest?

In response to his silent questions, a third vehicle came into view. It was a steamroller. Things were getting weird.

Even though it was nighttime, the driver of the bulldozer was wearing sunglasses, and what looked like a dark curly wig. But something about his face looked familiar. *No,* Stan thought, *it couldn't be...*

These were the same vehicles that had been indefinitely parked out behind the school while the city awaited the funds to build more classrooms. Stan, along with everyone else, had nearly forgotten that they were there. But it looked like someone had remembered. Was this some band of thieves?

The waitress arrived with their entrees in hand.

"Glazed salmon for the lady, and meat loaf with mashed potatoes for you, sir... and what in the good gravy is that?"

The waitress stared out the window, mouth agape in amazement.

Vilomena turned and shouted. "Gunther! Wally!"

Stan watched their two boys continuing the procession, jumping impossibly high on some strange contraptions attached to their legs.

What was happening?

Vilomena jumped up from the table and ran outside, with Stan right behind her.

Molly and the Mutants

The ring was going to have to wait.

He and Vilomena hurried down the street. Soon they were joined by others, all running in the same direction to see what all the fuss was about. Just ahead of them were their bouncing boys.

Finally, Stan couldn't wait any longer.

"Vilomena?"

"Yes, darling?"

"I was wondering, uh..." He fished in his pocket. "Will you..."

"Go steady with you?" Vilomena finished for him. "Of course!"

Stan had never felt happier.

CHAPTER 47
GIDDYUP

Molly weaved her way forward through the widening pool of monster vomit, with Pink Lightning's tires slipping and sliding through the slime. Fear had left her. Dodging the bones, trash, and festival decorations that the three-headed beast had barfed all over the street, she advanced.

The colossal frog paid her no mind, preoccupied with resorbing its inside-out stomach back into its body, presumably to resume eating everything in sight. But not if Molly could help it. She could feel the heat erupting in her chest, rising up the back of her neck, blooming in her ears. It was a feeling of loss so intense that as she pedaled, she could feel herself untether just a bit from her body, and momentarily drift up above herself to witness the burning emotion that had enveloped her, propelling her forward. She had to concentrate to anchor herself back in her body, and focus on the task at hand, which was: take down that frog. Through a blur of tears she eyed her target, weaving closer still to get in perfect firing position.

"Molly! What are you doing?" Margo shouted.

"Let's go!" Finn said.

"C'mon, Molly...," Leonard pleaded.

"Turn around," Arvin said.

Molly wasn't hearing it. She plucked a shiny green crab apple from her basket, notched it into the rubber sling between her handlebars, and fired. Direct hit. Molly reloaded, pelting the frog with nut after nut, screaming the whole time.

"HOW? COULD? YOU?" Molly yelled as she fired. "WHY?" The crab apples zinged through the air and thudded into the mutant's thick amphibious hide.

"WHAT'D SHE EVER DO TO YOU? WHAT?"

The frog said nothing. But Molly knew there was no answer that would satisfy her. No reason that would make it okay. And the truth was, underneath all those questions, Molly already knew the answer. That this was how the world worked. Bigger things ate smaller things. As unnatural as a giant three-headed frog might be, it was still nature.

What could she do? Molly spied the end of a Fritter Fest banner that was still burning on the end, and an idea popped into her head. Maybe she could reignite the flame? End this nightmare once and for all?

Molly made her way to the tiny fire. She was going to blow that monster up. She made her way closer to the smoldering shred of cloth, positioning herself in the gap between the creature's center head and the one to her right. Molly looked up at the creature. It had successfully retracted its stomach, and now looked a little smaller—for a giant.

Just as the fire was almost in reach, Pink Lightning stopped. Molly looked down and saw that another one of the banners had gotten tangled in Pink Lightning's chain. She followed the line of it and saw that it was draped up and over the frog's center head. Not good.

"Oh. Shoot," Molly said.

She heard someone shouting in her direction, but the warning got cut short with a *SLAM*. The wrecking-ball tongue from the frog head around to her left swung sideways and smashed a crater in the pavement right behind her. Luckily, it had missed her. But the impact sent a wave of bones and slime cascading down all over Molly and her bike.

Molly coughed and gagged.

As the tongue began retracting into the monster's mouth, it dragged across the debris. Molly saw that it had entangled with the knot of banners strewn over the opposite side of the center head. The beast was wearing so many of banners. It had unknowingly decorated itself with them as it had pushed its way down State Street.

Molly's eyes shot back to the other side of the banner—the one stuck in her chain—as it suddenly went taut. And she realized what was happening just a moment too late to do anything about it. The ground fell away below her as she and Pink Lightning were pulled up around the side of the frog's middle head. She passed up and over one of the beast's bulging black-and-yellow eyes, and caught her reflection, her own open-mouthed surprise staring back at her from the glassy dark depths of its pupil. The wrecking-ball tongue had pulled the knot of banners as far as they would go. They went slack again, depositing Molly squarely on top of the creature. The tires of her bike found a groove that ran up along the center of its head, in the middle of a patch of nubby tendrils. The soft, bumpy surface reminded Molly of a sea anemone.

From the top of the creature, Molly looked down at her friends, who now seemed so far away. They all stared back at her, their expressions as incredulous as her own must have been.

The bike swayed under her. The great frog's head beneath turned right and left, possibly sensing her presence. But from what Molly could tell, in this exact spot, behind the twin domes that held its eyes, she was hidden from its view. She watched the backs of its two protruding eyes shift back and forth. When the frog turned to the right, Molly felt the slight pull from the banner still stuck in her chain. When it turned back to the left, she watched the banners on her right move away just a little. *They must run all the way under the creature's chin,* she thought.

Just like reins.

That gave Molly an idea.

She backed up, dislodging the banner from her chain. Instead she wrapped it around her left handlebar. Then she grabbed the other banner and wrapped it around her right until they were both good and snug. Time for a little experiment. Molly turned her handlebars to the right. In tandem the giant frog turned right. Then she turned to the left. Again, in perfect sync, the center head veered to the left.

Molly and the Mutants

"What are you doing?" Arvin called over.

"I'm gonna ride this no-good frog back to where it belongs!" Molly explained. "You guys back away, but slowly. Don't draw its attention."

"Giddyup!" called Leonard.

"Yeah, ride 'em, cowgirl," said Margo.

"Um . . . just be careful," added Finn.

In sequence all three of the monster's heads let out a series of long tired croaks, like the frog version of a yawn. It did seem to have taken a pause from wreaking havoc on the center square. Maybe it was weary. Or full. Or too drunk to keep going. But Molly had a feeling this respite wouldn't last forever.

Logan had been keeping the Camaro in idle. Now he was slowly circumnavigating the beast, as quietly as the rumbly engine allowed, in what looked like an attempt to not be the first target when the frog regained its senses. She could understand why Logan wouldn't want to take a second tour inside the belly of the beast.

Molly snapped the reins.

"Yah!" she said.

Nothing. The behemoth didn't budge.

"Psssst!" Molly called. "Hey, Logan!"

"Yeah?"

"Maybe you could back up your car to its butt and give it a nudge with your exhaust?"

"Um, and get sat on? Death by mutant frog butt?" Logan spat. "After already getting barfed up in a big stinking pile of monster barf? Lemme think about that. Nope."

The Camaro scooched past them, down the road, and around the corner until it was gone.

Looked like it was up to Molly. But if the monster wouldn't cooperate, what could she do?

CHAPTER 48
MESMERIZED

Molly kicked her heels into the frog's soft, squishy head. "Yah!" she said again. Below her, the massive mutant stood virtually still. But she knew that would change eventually. She stared at the woods ahead. Molly had to figure out a way to get this creature out of town before it got hungry again, or restless, or both. If she didn't, there might not be a town left.

"C'mon, you dumb frog-faced freak," she grumbled. "You're lucky I didn't blow you up when I had the chance . . . but I'm not through with you yet." Below her the creature's tendrils undulated around her feet, brushing her ankles.

Gwaaaaaarrrrrp, it croaked lazily.

Molly sighed. From behind, the rumble of an approaching

engine caught her ear. She turned, expecting to see Logan return. But it wasn't the Green Machine. Instead it was something bright yellow, and much, much larger. A massive excavator with treads like a tank came rolling up behind them and stopped just a few yards shy of the beast's backside. Molly immediately recognized it from the stalled-out construction site behind Trailer-Trash Academy. It was the first time she'd actually seen it moving. Old Man Murray leaned his head out from the side of the massive machine's cab and waved.

"Somebody call the cavalry?" he called.

Molly waved back from atop the monster frog.

"Well!" Murray exclaimed. "You weren't exaggeratin'. That is quite the beast. And I've seen a few.... Y'okay up 'ere?"

"No," Molly called back. "It ate Crank."

"What's that, hon?" Murray cupped a hand to his ear. "Ate *who*?"

"Crank. My cat," Molly explained, the emotion welling back up inside her body. "She was the best cat ever."

"Oh, my darlin'. I am so sorry to hear that," Murray said. "I'm sure she was."

Molly sniffed and nodded. She brushed her thumb along the ridge of Crank's collar, which now dangled from her handlebars. It was all she had left of her.

Molly and the Mutants

Then a huge steamroller pulled up to the excavator's right and stopped just short of the mutant's hind leg. And behind the wheel sat none other than...

"Mr. Gatlin!" screamed Molly. "But I thought—"

"That I was dead? Nope!" he said. "Almost, though!"

"But I saw you get... squished."

"Ah, yes, you saw *my car* get squished," Mr. Gatlin corrected. "Rolled out the door just in time."

"But why—"

"My plan had been to lure the beast away from everyone, but in the end I was barely able to escape myself," her teacher explained. "Sorry to have left you, Molly. But it appears you managed just fine! By the time I made it back around to the ol' rink, everyone was gone."

Molly explained how they'd escaped with the help of the secret stash of Leroy's Liquid Lightning. Gatlin and Murray exchanged looks.

"Well. That explains the odor," Murray said. "Smells like a distillery around here."

"Some of the balloon bombs missed," Molly said.

"So I see," Mr. Gatlin said.

They surveyed the small stretch of asphalt between them, strewn with multicolored bits of latex. The road was still slick with the payload from the burst balloons.

"Wait," Molly said. "Mr. Gatlin? How did you know about the plan?"

Molly's mind flashed to all the names she'd seen on the wall in Spider Junction.

"You're Deloss G.!" Molly said.

"The moon may wax, the moon may wane," Murray started.

"And the moon will do it all over again," Mr. Gatlin finished.

A third vehicle, a full-size bulldozer, pulled up between the two others, completing the yellow barricade. When the dozer stopped, it dropped its huge blade to the ground with a clang, revealing its driver. He wore dark glasses and a thick mop of hair but somehow looked familiar....

Before she could give it another moment's thought, two more people arrived on the scene. It was Wally and Gunther, hopping up and down on their spring feet.

"Hi, Molly!" Wally said, waving as he bounced. "We're here to help. Gunther's got a—"

"Thanks, guys," Molly said. "But don't get too close...."

"And just how did you manage to get to your current location atop the creature?" Gatlin asked.

"It's a long story," Molly said. "Kind of an accident."

Molly and the Mutants

"Accident or no, it's darn impressive," Murray said. "I can see why they call you 'McCrusher.'"

Molly smiled.

Dark Glasses chimed in, "How about you climb on down, and we'll attempt to give your ugly friend here a firm nudge back into the woods?"

"If it's all right with you, I think somebody's gotta drive this thing." Molly gripped her handlebars. "And that somebody's me."

"And me."

"And me."

"And me."

"And me," came four familiar voices.

Molly spun her head to see Arvin, Margo, Leonard, and Finn. And they were all standing right beside her.

"You didn't think we were going to miss out on the fun, did you?" Arvin said.

"Yeah, how often do you get to ride a giant three-headed mutant?" Leonard said.

"Figured you could use a little company," Finn said.

"And muscle," Margo said, flexing her biceps.

At the sight of her friends by her side, Molly's heart exploded with joy. Leonard and Finn took up position on

Molly's left, while Margo and Arvin stood to her right. Together they all took ahold of her handlebars, ready to help her steer the monster back to where it belonged ... wherever that was.

"Wait!" Molly exclaimed. "But how— " She was as confused as she was happy.

"The banners!" Finn said, pointing a thumb behind him.

"Yeah, we kinda followed your lead, stuntgirl," Margo said.

"Only, we came up the back way. Because we're not insane," Arvin said.

"Yeah, uh, less chance of getting eaten, going up the side that doesn't have three mouths," Leonard said.

Everyone laughed, even Molly. She looked back at all the festival banners trailing down the monster's sloping backside. By the number of them, the creature must have pulled down every decoration in town.

"Okay, now what?" Arvin asked.

"Nudge?" Murray called from below.

"Nudge!" Molly called back.

Simultaneously the three earthmovers pushed into the back of the frog, trying to get it to return to the woods. They pressed and pressed, but had zero effect.

"Maybe we could dynamite it?" Dark Glasses suggested from the bulldozer.

Molly and the Mutants

Molly thought his voice sounded familiar. Whoever it was, the idea definitely had appeal. Dynamite felt fair for a devourer of cats. She had just tried to blow up the monster herself not a few minutes earlier. Maybe there was still a chance. Molly was just about to voice her agreement when something cut her short. A surge of emotion passed through her body and pushed up her throat until she felt her mouth open and heard herself say something that caught everyone by surprise, especially herself....

"No dynamite," Molly said. "It's not its fault that it's so big.... It just needs to find the right home."

Molly looked down by her feet. Some of the tendrils had curled around her ankles. They were pulsing with light. Molly wasn't sure what was happening, but she no longer felt mad, just sad. And she felt connected to the creature, like she knew it. Her ankles tingled.

I'm Seven. I'm Eight. I'm Nine....

Molly didn't hear it speaking. She felt it. Felt *them*.

"I've got an idea," she said. "We need something to draw it forward."

"Like what?" Murray asked.

Something giant came crashing through the woods in their direction. And it was glowing green.

"Oh no, not another one," Margo said.

But it wasn't.

Between the trees emerged the robot head, rolling on its side like an enormous silver wheel. It stopped directly in front of Molly and the giant frog. The green glow from its two circular eyes nearly matched the bioluminescence of the mutant creature. Molly couldn't believe what she was seeing.

"N-N-Number One?" she asked.

"HELLO. MOLLY," Number One said.

"But how—?"

"PICKED. UP. YOUR. DISTRESS. SIGNAL."

"My distress—"

"MY. ANTENNAS. ARE. EQUIPPED. TO. RECEIVE. TWO. WAY. RADIO."

"That was you listening in on the CB?"

"YES. I. AM. A. GOOD. LISTENER. REMEMBER?"

"You are."

"AND. I. AM. HERE. TO. HELP," Number One said.

"How?" Molly asked.

Its eyes stared back at her. They began strobing.

So beautiful, Molly felt the creature under her say.

Of course! Number One would hypnotize Frogzilla. Just

like she had done with Pink Lightning's strobe light in the tunnel.

A small crowd of townspeople had earthmovers. Molly spotted a very anxious-looking Mrs. Tipper, the PTA president, clutching a SAFER. pin on the lapel of her jacket. And there were several other grown-ups Molly recognized . . . including her dad and Vilomena.

"Molly!" her dad shouted. "What in the heck is that? And what in the heck are you doing on it?"

"It's okay, Dad," Molly said. "I've got my friends with me. And Number One."

"Oh . . . okay, then," he said. "Uh, be careful."

"Don't worry, Dad, we will," Molly said. She watched the expression on her dad's face change from concern to something she couldn't quite read.

"Hey, Mollz?" he called out.

"Yeah, Dad?"

"I just want you to know . . . your mom would be proud of you . . . uh, *is* proud of you, I mean. . . ." Stan managed a half smile. "And so am I."

"Thanks, Dad," Molly said.

"Okay," he said. "Just don't die or anything."

"Don't worry, Mr. Stanley," Leonard said. "I'll keep an eye on her."

"Thank you, Leonard," Stan said, a deep look of concern immediately returning to his face.

The frog stirred and let out a grunt. The light show was having an effect.

"I think that's our cue, friends," Gatlin said.

The three drivers of the borrowed earthmovers revved their engines. In concert they pushed forward, giving the three-headed monster a three-way shove.

Gwaa-aaarp, the frog responded. It came out like a complaint.

"Again," Molly called. "It's working."

In sync the Moonlighters backed up their vehicles, then pressed forward.

Still in the down position, the bulldozer's blade scraped across the asphalt, kicking up a wave of hot sparks along the moonshine-soaked street.

Murray was the first to spot the danger.

"Hold up!" he shouted, but it was too late. As soon as the sparks reached the spill, the street ignited into flames. The fire spread out from the center in both directions, following the arc of the burst balloons that had missed their mark

Molly and the Mutants

earlier. In moments a semicircular wall of raging fire separated the vehicles from Molly and her friends.

Whereas the prodding had failed to move the monster, the instant conflagration proved more than enough motivation. Finally the gargantuan frog jumped.

"Whooooaaa!" yelled Molly and all her friends, holding on to Pink Lightning's handlebars and banners for dear life.

Number One rolled out of the way just in time to avoid getting crushed, retreating back into the woods, and luring the beast forward. The frog, mesmerized by the strobes, followed. Sure and steady, it chased the rolling robot head up and down the hills of Far Flung Falls and farther away from town.

"WHERE. ARE. WE. TAKING. OUR. GREEN. FRIEND?" Number One asked.

"Funny, I had the same question," Arvin said.

"Yes, please tell me there's a plan... that doesn't involve us all dying," Margo said.

"Number One!" Molly shouted back to the robot. "Do you know where Ole Stoney is?"

"HOLD. PLEASE. CONSULTING. MAPS." The robot paused the conversation a moment as it rolled ahead of them. "OKAY. GOT. IT."

"Great. Set a course. We're going to the far west side of it," Molly said. "There's a place I think it'll like."

The robot head tilted and veered left. Molly tried turning her handlebars to follow.

Leonard, to her left, flexed his skinny arms and heaved for all he was worth.

"Pull!" he shouted between gritted teeth.

"I'm pulling," Finn grunted back beside him.

"We push," Arvin said from the right.

"Pushing," Margo said.

From the middle Molly tried again to gain some leverage on her handlebars.

"Grrrrrrrrrr..."

Together the five of them dug in their heels and heaved, pushing and pulling the mutant frog's reins with all their might. Molly could feel Pink Lightning's frame tremble from the pressure. On both sides the polyurethane banners drew tight, but held.

Then below them, miraculously, the monster followed their lead and turned.

"Whew...," Molly breathed. "Thanks, guys. This might just work...."

"Might?" squeaked Leonard.

CHAPTER 49
ONE BIG HOLE

Molly's arms ached. But at long last, after what felt like a zillion twists and turns through the rolling hills and hollows of Far Flung Falls, past all the bike trails and abandoned rails, over the creeks and falls, woods and fields, Molly and her friends finally arrived at their destination: the fabled Bottomless Pit. It was the very same one that her gramps had allegedly jumped into... and never come out of.

"There it is," Molly whispered, pointing straight ahead. She had already explained the plan to her friends, but now the sight of it gave her a shiver.

Home? Safe? Molly felt the questions rise up through her

body, starting down where the frog's tendrils gently pressed on her skin.

"Whoa. That's one big hole," Margo said.

"Yeah," Arvin said. "Put that on the list of things I don't ever wanna get swallowed by . . . right behind Frogatron here." He tapped his foot on the beast they were riding.

"Something about it . . . ," Leonard said. "Doesn't it kinda look . . . I dunno, almost like it's waiting for us or something?"

"I've got a bad feeling about this," Finn said.

The cavernous sinkhole lay just past Booby-Trap Valley, where they had captured the four frogs that now seemed small by comparison. It was tucked in around the back side of Ole Stoney. And if not for the moonlight clearly outlining its edges, it would have been all but invisible. They had taken a route that would be impossible for anyone to follow, Molly figured, unless they were riding by way of giant robot head, or mutant frog back. It was up to them.

Molly was grateful to have her friends by her side for what she hoped was the last leg of this journey. Even with the five of them pushing and pulling at the handlebar reins, it had taken every last ounce of their strength to coax Frogzilla to one side or the other whenever it had tried to veer off course. More than once she'd been all but certain her handlebars would break clean off her bike from the pressure of the banners that tied them to the monster's center head. But Pink Lightning had held together—and so had they.

Number One stayed just ahead of them, its mesmerizing light show continuing unabated. With each revolution of its head, its strobing eyes popped back into view as it rolled through the countryside like an oversize wagon wheel.

"HERE. WE. ARE," the robot announced, its tinny voice echoing through the wood.

Without hesitation it rolled right up to the edge of the sinkhole, as if it intended to drop into its depths and out of sight. But at the last moment the great metal head tilted to one side, deftly skirting the edge of the hole until it arrived at the exact opposite side. Its glowing eyes faced them from across the drop, still flickering rapidly to hold the frog's attention.

Having reached its destination, Number One leaned over and fell flat onto the earth so that it no longer stood sideways.

"MOLLY. AND. FRIENDS. THANK. YOU. FOR. YOUR. HELP."

"You're welcome!" Margo shouted back across the pit.

"Yeah," Arvin said. "It was pretty rad."

The great frog had slowed its pace. It continued to follow the robot, up to the edge of the hole. Then stopped.

Gwaaaarrrp, it croaked, the sound echoing down into the endless depths of the pit.

"THIS. IS. YOUR. STOP," the robot announced to Molly and her friends. "TIME. TO. DISEMBARK."

Molly tried dismounting Pink Lightning, but discovered her feet were stuck where she'd planted them. She looked down. Those tendrils were now wrapped around her feet and tires.

Stay with us, she felt it say. *We're afraid.*

From the top of the monster's head, she looked over the edge of the pit.

"It's okay," Molly whispered. She leaned over her handlebars, cupping a hand to her mouth. "It'll be good down there. Plenty of water and creepy-crawly snacks. Plus, you glow, so it won't be dark. And no one will try to blow you up, I promise."

Do you hate us? Gently the tendrils pressed against her skin.

"Listen, I know I said some things earlier..." Molly lowered her voice even further. "I was just mad is all.... It's not your fault what happened to you... or Crank. I get that now."

"Who ya talking to?" Leonard asked.

"This might sound crazy," Molly said, "but I think it can understand me."

"Rad," Leonard said.

Molly and the Mutants

"Yeah, pretty rad," Molly agreed.

The monster was rocking back and forth. It looked unsure. On the other side of the chasm, Number One's eyes alternated the pace of their strobing, slower, then faster, trying to coax the entranced beast forward. But the frog had reached its limit and stayed at the edge of the hole. Molly realized this was a good thing—since they were still on top of it.

"MUST. DISEMBARK. NOW," the robot insisted.

"You heard it, guys. C'mon!" Arvin said.

Struggling to keep their balance, Molly's friends inched toward the back of the frog, and quickly saw what was missing from their exit plan.

"The banners!" Finn cried. "Where'd they go?"

In their passage through the woods, any of the festival banners the frog had collected that hadn't been secured to Molly's handlebars had fallen to the wayside—including the ones they'd used to climb up... which were the same ones they'd counted on to climb back down. Without them it was a steep drop.

"We're trapped!" Margo said.

"Thinking...," Molly said. "Gimme a minute...."

"We don't have a min—" Arvin started to say, turning to Molly. "Why aren't you coming?"

"I think I might be stuck," Molly said.

"Wait a sec!" Leonard said, tilting his head toward the woods. "You hear something?"

Molly did hear something, carrying over the trees.

It was the powerhouse voice of Pat Benatar, one of her songs playing full blast, which could only mean one thing:

"Number 42!" Molly shouted.

The orange bus came crashing through the brush. Ronda was at the wheel, with a megaphone to her mouth, and was shouting over the music.

"Start running, kids, and get ready to jump!" Ronda yelled.

"Run? Where?" Arvin said. "To the edge of the frog's butt? It's too steep at the end!"

"Beats a bottomless pit," Finn said.

Don't leave us . . ., Molly felt the creature say.

"Go!" Molly yelled to her friends.

"Not without you."

It was Leonard. He grabbed her by the waist, trying desperately with his lanky arms to pry her loose. Arvin, Margo, and Finn quickly joined the effort, tugging on her from all sides.

"Brace for impact!" Ronda yelled.

She made a sharp turn to the right, swinging the entire length of the old school bus sideways. It reared up on two wheels, slamming squarely with its full weight into the butt of the mutant frog. The impact sent a wavelike ripple up the creature's backside. When the wave reached Molly and her friends, it was enough to buck her free from the tendrils' grip. The five of them launched into the air.

"Double time!" Ronda called through the megaphone.

They scrambled to their feet and started running across the flat stretch of the creature's sloping back, on a collision course for the bus. Anything was better than falling into that hole.

The music blared through Ronda's speakers, urging them on:

We're running with the shadows of the night

So, baby, take my hand, you'll be all right...

Molly felt everything shift under her feet as the mammoth frog began slipping, tilting farther toward the abyss. She scrambled even harder. Just ahead, the emergency door at the back of the bus flung open. Her Gruncle was there, holding it with one hand and extending the other in their direction.

"Jump, kiddos!" he said. "We gotcha!"

For the first time ever, Margo was not the last.

In fact, to everyone's astonishment—especially Molly's—Margo was the first to jump. Without hesitation she leapt past Gruncle and tumbled into the safety of the bus. She was immediately followed by Finn, Arvin, and Leonard, who all crashed into one another in the aisle.

That left Molly. And the gap between the frog's back and the emergency door was getting wider by the second. She leapt through the air for all she was worth—just as the beast toppled over the edge, all six of its legs kicking and thrashing for a hold. The motion from one of its hindlegs propelled Molly. She went hurtling through the air like a missile and slammed into her Gruncle's arms, nearly causing him to lose his grip on the door. But he held fast. The two hung there. Molly's feet kicked at the empty space underneath her.

"You're safe now, kiddo...." Molly's Gruncle gave her a familiar grin. Then his eyes widened. "Well, maybe... Hold on!"

Number 42 hadn't stopped moving. Up front Ronda was frantically pumping the brakes, but the inertia from the twelve-ton vehicle kept pushing it closer and closer to the chasm's edge, turning the bus nearly one hundred eighty degrees until its rear tires met the lip of the drop. The back fender hung precariously over the edge—with Molly and her Gruncle dangling in the air.

Gwaaaaarrrrrrrp! An anguished croak echoed up from the walls of the pit directly below them. The mutant frog had not dropped into the abyss as planned. Instead it hung, spread eagle, its many limbs extended to secure whatever hold it could manage on the chasm's edges, which wasn't much. Then, from these depths, out shot a tongue.

C-C-CRASH. The tongue slammed into Number One's left eye, shattering the circular lens, and the control panel behind it. Shards of glass rained down into the pit.

"UH. OH," said Number One, sliding closer toward the edge as the prehensile tongue flexed its muscle, pulling it from below in a desperate attempt to avoid the confines of the pit. Sparks sputtered from the robot's eye socket like hot tears.

Arvin and Leonard pulled Molly and her Gruncle into the bus.

"Everyone secure?" Ronda called from the front of the bus.

"As secure as we can be next to a giant beastie," Gruncle called back.

"Good. Now what?"

After dangling midair, Molly liked having something solid under her feet again. But what was going to happen to the mutant frog? And to Number One? Molly looked down again. Unlike the last time she'd peered into its depths, the pit was now surprisingly well lit, thanks to the bioluminescence of its reluctant new resident. To her surprise Molly saw that the Bottomless Pit was not, in fact, bottomless. It was very, very deep, to be sure, and even appeared to widen down at the bottom, revealing a whole subterranean world.

Two heads popped up in the seat in front of her.

"What if it doesn't cooperate?" asked the first head.

"That appears to be its current attitude toward the situation," said the second head.

"Wally? Gunther?" Molly was dumbfounded. "How did you get here?"

"Families stick together," Wally said.

"We got some stowaways, huh?" Gruncle asked.

"Just needs another nudge," said Gunther. He was fiddling with some toggles on a remote control.

"Exactly," said Wally.

That's when stomps shook the earth.

CHAPTER 50
ENCORE

B*oom.... Boom.... Boom....*
Over the trees came the headless, armless corpse of the fallen robot, still dripping from every blasted joint. The waterlogged giant towered over everything—the forest, the frog, and the Bottomless Pit. It even made Ole Stoney look not quite so big. The mechanical body paused, wobbling wildly on its kneecapped legs. Through the escape hatch in the body's midsection, the golden glow from Formula X, mixed with water from the gorge, could be seen as it sloshed around.

"DO. NOT. WORRY," Number One assured them. "BODY. HERE. TO. HELP."

A second tongue shot upward—the one that worked like a

wrecking ball. It swung over the edge of the pit and came crashing down on the robot's left foot, crushing it. With the leverage from the two tongue-holds, the monster raised itself up just enough for its six bulbous eyes to peek over the lip of the pit.

The sudden impact to the robot's foot caused its damaged legs to wobble even more. The entire torso swayed uncontrollably, then bent forward at the waist, spilling the glowing mixture of radioactive ooze and pooled water directly onto the frog below.

"What is that stuff?" Finn asked.

"Formula X," Gunther said.

Police sirens were wailing, and getting closer. Molly saw flashes of red and blue lights break through the trees.

"First time I've ever been happy to see those lights," Arvin said.

"Yeah, we need all the help we can get," Leonard agreed.

Gruncle quietly put his wig and sunglasses back on.

"That was you on the steamroller. I knew it!" Molly said.

Gruncle put a finger to his lips and smiled.

Three squad cars pulled into view, lights blazing, and screeched to a halt. Officer Wasserbaum jumped out of the first. He was disheveled and out of breath. Five other officers poured out of the other two vehicles right behind him.

Molly and the Mutants

Apparently, they had a plan of their own. Every one of the men was holding a Taser gun in each hand.

"Hold it right there, you frognacious fiend!" Wasserbaum called, both his Tasers drawn and at the ready. "That's destruction of private property, disturbing the peace... and attempted grand theft robot!"

The tilting robot body continued to shower the frog below with the contaminated contents of its interior, which had slowed to a luminous trickle. Along with the glowing liquid, it rained random debris: a mishmash of small cogs and gears, nuts and bolts...

And one black-and-white checkerboard Vans slip-on.

The lone shoe went tumbling through the air. Its thick rubber sole bounced off the back of one of the frog's many bulbous eyes, before coming to rest among the robotic rubble.

Gunther eyed Finn. "Recognize anything?"

All the blood had drained from Finn's face. "My shoe," he whispered.

Molly exchanged glances with Gunther, then looked back to Finn. And in that moment she understood what had caused all the mutations in the first place. There had been a leak.

"Sorry," Finn said. "It was an accident."

"It's okay," Molly said. "You didn't mean—"

But Molly was interrupted when the mutant's third tongue shot out in the direction of the police. This was the tongue that had tongues of its own. It hovered in the air above the officers for a moment, before the smaller tongues shot toward them and plucked the hat off Wasserbaum's head and ripped the belt off another, which caused his pants to drop to his ankles, revealing underwear that looked like the American flag. Most of the other tongues shot downward, anchoring themselves to the ground.

"I pledge allegiance to the undies...," Arvin began.

"Oh brother," Molly said.

Wasserbaum was having a complete conniption.

"And...assault of an officer!" he screamed, the veins in his neck looking like they might just pop. "C'mon, guys! Time to give that frog the shock of its life!"

The police officers all stepped forward and took aim. Their faces wore hard expressions, but the one with his pants down looked especially angry—or silly, depending on your view.

"Noooooo!" Molly protested from the bus. "It's not—"

"Don't worry, Molly, it's okay," Gunther whispered into her ear. "Trust me."

"FIRE!" Wasserbaum screamed. Molly had never seen anyone so furious.

Molly and the Mutants

At his command the five officers fired their Taser guns, each wired electrode delivering a fifty-thousand-volt charge to surge through the mutant's body. The rapid click-click-clicking of a dozen discharging weapons filled the air, followed by an intense *buzzzzt*.

Gwaaaarrrrp! The creature groaned again. Each of its three tongues spasmed, but remained fully extended.

"We need more juice!" said the officer in his undies.

"That's all we got," Wasserbaum said, deflated. "It's just too much frog."

"Number One!" Gunther shouted from across the chasm.

"PERHAPS. I. CAN. BE. OF. ASSISTANCE."

The robot head started to crackle and hum with energy. From the destroyed eye socket, a cascade of sparks showered out from behind the broken glass, dancing down the length of the tongue like a tiny electrical storm. The surge enveloped the entire creature, causing it to spasm as the current of energy thrummed through its grotesque body, radiating lightning in every direction. Then the spasming stopped. The frog went slack.

Meanwhile the last of the ooze from the robot's bent torso dripped onto its head. And the frog began glowing even brighter.

"Sonuva monkey...," Wasserbaum muttered. "What have we done?"

"What's happening?" Margo asked.

"It's... pulsating," Ronda said.

Molly watched the scene unfold from a side window at the back of the bus (which was still parked a little closer to the pulsating mutant than it needed to be).

"Look!" Leonard shouted. "It's... it's..."

"I'd say it's fixin' to 'splode," Gruncle said.

Something was definitely happening. From all three of its mouths, the beast roared more loudly than ever before as twin beams of searing yellow light rippled across the length of its back, splitting the frog's massive body into three distinct parts.

Then the frog divided.

The three newly birthed frogs each used the hold from their tongues to pull themselves over the lip of the pit. Molly's plan was failing.

On the seams where the frog had split into three, the raw exposed surfaces writhed and bubbled in a gooey mess. From the glutinous mass, out sprouted more legs. In moments all three separate frogs were moving, albeit very clumsily. They released their tongue-holds on the robot's head, the robot's foot, and the ground near the officers.

Molly and the Mutants

Amid the spectacle, the frog that emerged from the original creature's center—the one who had been carrying Pink Lightning on its back—shed the remaining banners that had held the bike in place. Molly watched her prize possession slip off the transforming creature and slide down to the ground.

No sooner had the newly generated creatures begun moving than the three frogs were overtaken by what looked like a collective seizure, and another searing yellow line traveled horizontally around their midsections, dividing them in half. Again the raw parts where they'd split foamed and bubbled like pots of boiling stew, and then—

"Look, they're growing heads on their butts!"

"And butts on their heads!"

"The mutants are... mutating!"

Everyone watched in amazement as the three frogs became six, each portion from the original frog growing whatever parts had been missing, until they formed completely new, intact frogs... with each new generation only half the size of the original.

"Like cells dividing," Molly said.

"Yeah, maybe," Leonard said.

A few second later it happened again. Now the edge of the Bottomless Pit was covered in giant frogs. An even dozen.

Each one about the size of the ones that had chased them the night before.

"What are we gonna do?" Margo asked.

"We're gonna wait," Molly said. "I think I know what's happening...."

The frogs pulsed with light again, and the pulses grew more rapid. The frogs writhed on the ground, bright lines crisscrossing their bodes until they were all balls of light. This time the brightness was so intense, it was hard to look at. Molly shielded her eyes.

"It's like staring at the sun," she said.

Boing. From one of the white-hot balls of light, out sprang a single completely normal-size frog. It paused where it landed, then began hopping toward the woods.

Another one popped from the light.

Ribbit, it called as it leapt.

Before long each ball of light was exploding with frogs that were totally regular-proportioned. They tumbled in every direction, covering the ground as far as Molly could see.

"Whoa," Leonard said. "It's like the frog version of a Jiffy Pop."

The police officers retreated into their cars, with Wasserbaum yelling something about plagues of Egypt. But his veins weren't popping anymore. He looked happy, for Wasserbaum.

Molly and the Mutants

"I'm not sure I get what happened," Arvin said.

"I think when a mutant mutates...it kind of mutates back to normal?" Molly said.

"Correct," Gunther said.

"How did you know it would work?" Molly asked.

"I didn't," Gunther said. "But that was my theory."

"Whew! Glad you were right," Wally said.

The one-eyed robot head had been leaning precariously over the edge of the pit. As thousands of tiny frogs popped, many of them landed on top of it, upsetting its balance. The head wobbled.

"Number One, look out!" Molly called.

"THANK. YOU. MOLLY." Its one eye flickered. "GOODBYE."

And with that, it tilted over the edge of the Bottomless Pit, briefly reflecting the light of the moon onto everyone in the bus before dropping into the darkness and out of sight.

Moments passed, the silence broken only by hundreds of happy chorusing frogs.

Molly stood there stunned.

BOOM-M-M-M-M-M.

The impact of the crashing robot head sent tremors back up to the surface, reverberating all around them. In response the headless robot body swayed and wobbled, trying to keep its balance. But with the control center gone, it was helpless. Succumbing to the tremors, the giant's torso tipped even farther forward, folding itself in half and following the robot head into the hole. Another BOOM-M-M-M-M-M-M, even louder than the first.

This time, as the earth quaked yet again, the enormous overhanging rock that some considered the cowlick on the back of Ole Stoney's mountainous head broke free and rolled downhill, causing a not-so-small landslide right above the pit. Several tons of black sandstone boulders came tumbling down the hillside, burying the robot's head and body in the pit, beneath a literal mountain of rock.

When the dust cleared, the occupants of Number 42 were left wide eyed and silent. Molly took a seat at the back of the bus. She was utterly astonished at the day's events. And even more so when, seemingly out of nowhere, a familiar-looking bundle of dull orange fur jumped in through the window and made itself at home in her arms. The bundle was a graying tabby. Slightly rougher for the wear, but very much alive, and totally in one piece. Minus her collar.

"Meow," said the cat. *Hello there.*

Molly looked down at what she was holding.

"Crank?"

SEVERAL HOURS EARLIER

CHAPTER 51
WHAT ACTUALLY HAPPENED

In the light of the midmorning sun, Crank leapt through the air in full attack mode, ready to show this strange green intruder who was boss in these woods. She'd made a meal of many of its kind before. Granted, this one had a couple of extra heads, and was several thousand times bigger than any she had met before. Well, at least since the Pleistocene epoch. But she'd been a different cat back then.

Claws out, fangs bared, and flexing every muscle from whisker to paw, Crank prepared for impact, whereupon she would commence with the infliction of maximum damage on this disgusting, warty, frog-faced trespasser—until it was sent hopping back to whatever hole it had crawled out of.

Molly and the Mutants

"Mwwwwwrrrawww!" she roared, pushing the sound out from the bottom of her belly. But without warning her battle cry was cut short, concluding in a small hair ball.

"Ack!"

Instead of sinking her teeth into frog flesh, Crank hung there suspended in the air, still several feet away from her target. Yet, inexplicably, not moving. What had happened? She felt pressure against her windpipe, as her collar pressed up into the fluffy folds of her neck. Oh no. How utterly embarrassing.

Alas, she had miscalculated her trajectory, failing to take into account a key piece of foliage... and on her descent had somehow managed to catch herself by the collar on a spindly, leafless branch jutting out from a bramble at just the right angle—or just the wrong angle. With lightning efficiency and precision timing, the offshoot had slipped into the thinnest of gaps between the top of her neck and her collar, made possible through her faulty acrobatics.

Snagged!

She looked at her adversary and attempted a growl. All six of its eyes looked back at her. Crank became painfully aware of how vulnerable she was at that moment. And worse, how ridiculous. She cursed growing old. She cursed the vegetation. She cursed that fuchsia collar.

There truly was no justice in this world.

What would her past selves think of her now? She could feel the stares of saber tooth, of Aoife, of countless others.

Crank thrashed and scrambled with every bit of life still left in her, before it seeped entirely from her body. The indignity of it! She must have looked pathetic. This was not the way for a warrior to go!

It was getting harder to breath. Her lungs felt as if they might burst. She tried to howl, but was unable to produce even the weakest mew. Then her field of vision started to narrow, darkening around the edges. In seconds she'd be unconscious, only to awaken in the bile-filled bowels of this beast. As she squirmed and kicked, she felt the pressure point that was cutting into her larynx slip upward by a notch, almost to her jawline. Heartened, she wriggled some more. Another slip. One last jerk of her body and . . .

Crank dropped through the air like a sack of potatoes.

Which, for some reason, also caught the cat by surprise.

Now what was happening? How was she now free? And not just free, it appeared, but free-falling?

Crank had to admit, with her appetite having waned of late, she had probably lost a pound or two over the last few months. The collar had felt less snug than before. Her newly svelte frame had slipped right out of it.

SPLOOP. Into the cushion of a soft, muddy bank.

And not a moment too soon.

Above her a prehensile tongue of gargantuan proportions darkened the sky, propelling itself through the air at an unnatural speed, smashing the very same branch that had foiled her attack, and enveloping the fuchsia collar in its sticky folds. Then, as quickly as it had appeared, the tongue retracted and was gone.

Crank kept still where she'd landed (on her feet, of course). The splatter from the impact of her fall had rendered her well camouflaged. Quietly she sniffed the air. Something about this creature didn't smell right. A sharp chemical tang infused with mucus and muck.

The monster flexed, then sprang into the air, pushing itself out of Bottom Basin and into the woods. Crank felt some satisfaction at eluding the creature. It probably thought she had retreated. What a dummy.

But even with the monster gone, the not-right smell persisted. Something about it felt off—and yet, not entirely unfamiliar. It stirred a bad memory. Crank felt compelled to investigate. She circumnavigated the pond and followed the scent up the bank of a trickling creek that fed Bottom Basin . . . but from where? Still covered in mud, Crank made the climb up the rocky slope until she crested the hill and answered her own question.

Of course, the old cat thought, staring at the dead metal giant lying in the middle of its watery grave. She took a few more whiffs of the air and narrowed her eyes. *I knew you were behind this,* she thought accusingly. Satisfied that she had found the guilty party, Crank watched it for several minutes before deciding it was time for a nap. It wasn't even midday yet, but she was exhausted.

Hours later she awoke with a start. It was dark overhead. How long had she been sleeping? The metal giant was stirring, causing ripples that made their way to edge of the pond, lapping at her feet. Maybe cats weren't the only creature with multiple lives? She watched the riddled torso slowly rise from its watery grave. The holes where its arms had once been attached spilled water. One leg contracted, bending where its knee had been. Then the other.

Crank stretched, the dried, caked mud cracking all over her body. She'd forgotten about that. It was going to take hours of licking to fix this. But that would have to wait. She had a giant to keep watch on.

After several awkward attempts, the giant finally managed to get its feet under it and stood. Then took a step. Crank

Molly and the Mutants

feared she might get flattened, so she bolted across the open stretch for the cover of trees. The robot took another step and teetered forward. From the glowing circle in the center of its body, out poured gallons of water—which came crashing in buckets all over Crank, soaking her to the bone.

Crank sputtered and hissed. *The nerve of this guy*, she thought. Crank coughed and spat a few more times, the taste of murky water and stale robot still in her mouth. And something else too, maybe. How much of it had she ingested?

But the water did wash off the mud. She tried to shake herself dry, but something about this luminescent water was hard to shake. And that smell! It was the same smell she had sensed from the froggy-looking creature downstream. Only now the smell was much stronger. If this was what had happened to that hapless frog, what would happen to—

Outraged at the possibility that she'd been infected, she leapt after her attacker to exact some sort of vengeance. Between all the holes, rips, and exposed girders that made up what was left of the robot's body, there were plenty of grips and holds for an expert climber such as herself.

As she hung on to the giant's leg, she noticed that something else was happening. Her entire body was tingling. The dull ache she'd felt at the base of her skull throbbed. Crank cried out, her mewing whimper lost to the woods. For a moment the pain was so excruciating, she was sure she had met her end right then and there. Death by dousing. And then the pain was simply... gone. All of it. Not just the throb but the dull ache that had been her constant companion for weeks. The pressure had completely evaporated, leaving only a lightness in her cat skull that made her think she might float.

A million scenes from all her past lives flashed before her mind's eye in rapid succession, then faded out of memory, like dreams do just as soon as you start to awake.

Crank wasn't sure what that luminescent water had done to her, to the clump of mutated cells at the back of her brain. But the pressure was gone. And more than that, her entire body felt rejuvenated. Almost like she was a kitten again.

Meanwhile the robot she'd been clinging to had found its stride, albeit a jangly one. It's legs didn't feel very stable. Maybe that was how it was when you rose from the dead. Unless you happened to be a cat, of course. With her newfound strength she held on tight to see where this strange ride would take her. From up here it was a great view.

And oh look, who do we have here but my nemesis, the frog-faced trespasser, stretched over a pit, getting its just desserts,

Molly and the Mutants

ha! First total rejuvenation, and now this? Crank wondered: *Could this day get any better?*

Just shy of the action, the robot came to an abrupt halt, which sent her flying into the top of the nearest pine. From her perch Crank kept watch on the monster that had nearly done her in, until it received a similar shower and underwent a transformation of its own.

Something about what was happening to the monster below made sense in her feline mind. Whatever strange liquid that robot had held within its gut reeked of danger—but just as it had undoubtedly turned something good into something bad, it also had the power to do the exact opposite. From natural to unnatural, and back again.

After the show there was only one thing to do, and that was go check in on her favorite human, who proved to be much closer than she would have guessed. Crank got a running start, from branch to branch, and—with the agility and grace of a cat a fraction of her true age—jumped perfectly through the bus window and into Molly's lap.

As it turns out, the day could get even better.

TWO WEEKS LATER

CHAPTER 52
ONE MORE

Deep inside the mountain, Molly watched Leonard carefully scrawl his name into the cave wall, just below her own. He had chosen the largest of the bowie knives to do it, which looked almost like a sword in his hand. As soon as he finished, Leonard turned around to face the other Moonlighters. He was beaming from ear to ear.

"To our newest member!" Gruncle announced. "Hear, hear!"

"Hear, hear!" everyone cheered, raising tin cups filled with stalactite-filtered cave water.

"Blood, sweat, and cheers!" someone called.

At that, Leonard brandished the bowie knife in the air like a triumphant knight.

Molly and the Mutants

"Okay, let's put that away before somebody loses a finger... or worse," Old Man Murray grumbled (but with a smile).

Everyone had shown up for the occasion: Molly, Arvin, Margo, and Finn, along with Gruncle, Ronda, Old Man Murray, and Mr. G.... not to mention a few other folks from town that Molly would never have guessed were members. Together they dipped their cups in the stone basin and raised them again and again. "To old traditions and new friends! To brave souls and beloved pets! To second lives and second chances!" Gruncle kept them going for several more rounds, until anything and everything worthy of a toast had been toasted.

"To the frogs!" had been the last.

This had all been Molly's idea. Shortly after the night they'd ridden Frogzilla through the woods, she had petitioned her Gruncle to induct Leonard into their crew. Molly had made a convincing case that it would be all but impossible for her and her friends to keep it from him, since they always hung out together—and also, that he deserved it. Leonard had been there for her, for all of them, right up to the moment when they'd nearly plunged into the Bottomless Pit.

Gruncle had agreed.

After a feast of specially made fluffernutter sandwiches, beef jerky, and several more vintage Twinkies from Spider

Junction's stash, the entire group sang a rousing chorus of "The moon may wax, and the moon may wane, and the moon will do it all over again," echoing through the cavernous space. Gruncle added several new verses, which he made up on the spot. And then, with their hearts and bellies full, the Moonlighters boarded various handcars (aka velocipedes) and went their separate ways.

Well, everyone except Gruncle, who had "temporarily" taken up residence inside the mountain while he remained "officially deceased," as he put it. As Molly and her friends prepared to depart, her Gruncle slipped something into her hand.

"This came to my address, but to your attention," he said with a wink.

It was a postcard . . . from Florida. The card showed a picture of a lush citrus grove. Bright yellow lemons hung heavily on the trees, with the sun peeking behind them. Molly knew immediately who it must have been from. But when she turned it over in her hand, the card was blank.

"It doesn't say anything," Molly said.

"Hmm," Gruncle mused. "Might hafta hold it closer to the light."

Molly stepped over to the headlamp on the front of Ronda's handcar. Still nothing.

Molly and the Mutants

"Maybe a little closer," Gruncle nudged.

Molly nearly set the card on top of the hot lamp, practically burning her hand in the process. As if by magic, thin brown letters bloomed across the paper's surface, first spelling out the word *brave* in the center, then spreading outward in all directions. *Of course*, Molly thought, *the citrus grove was a clue!* The message had been written in lemon juice. It read:

> Welcome to the Crew, Molly.
> The Moonlighters are lucky to have you!
> And so am I.
> Keep being brave, and I hope to see you again someday soon.
> Sorry it's been so long.
> All my love, Mom
>
> P.S. Give Wally, your dad, and Crank my best.

"Wow, I never get cards like that from my mom," Margo said, peeking over her shoulder. "You're lucky."

And maybe she was. Molly pressed the card to her chest. She could almost feel the warmth from that picture of the Florida sun. Her dad had been right: her mom was proud of her. But how had her mom known?

"I might've spilled the beans to some of our more prominent

members abroad," Gruncle whispered, laying a hand on Molly's shoulder. "Best get going."

"C'mon, slowpoke!" Arvin called, already aboard the velocipede.

Ronda ushered Molly and her friends out of Ole Stoney's southwest pass, past Booby-Trap Valley—and all the memories that came with it. But in the absence of fog, or ravenous mutants, and under the light of a bright midday sun, the whole area appeared much cheerier. Past the field, Molly could see the remnants of the avalanche that had sealed off the Bottomless Pit. For half a second, amidst all the rock and debris, Molly thought she caught the glint of metal. But she knew it was just wishful thinking.

The tracks carried them farther into the woods, and before long they arrived at a clearing two miles away where they had all parked their bikes. As they climbed off the handcar, Ronda fished into her jacket pocket for something, then handed it to Molly.

"For you," she said.

Molly held a cassette. It was a mixtape labeled **MCCRUSHER ROCKS** in black Sharpie.

"Thank you," Molly said.

Molly and the Mutants

"Don't mention it," Ronda said, already backing away.

From there the kids rode through the woods together, past the crashed escape pod (no longer frozen), past BMX Alley (no longer crawling with giant frogs), and past the boneyard (still very creepy). Every time the trail forked, their number grew thinner, from five, to four, to three, until eventually it was just Molly and Leonard. Side by side the two young Moonlighters pedaled along under the cover of turning leaves until the trail split one final time. They were less than a mile from their houses. The riders stopped.

"Thanks again for vouching for me, Molly," Leonard said. "Means a lot."

"Thanks for always being there," Molly said.

Just then she heard a rustle in the bushes right beside them. Leonard turned to look. They had stopped in the shade of several trees, and yet the spot where they stood was growing unmistakably brighter. But not from sunlight. Instead the source of illumination was coming from below, tinging everything with a green glow. Suddenly an army of tiny bioluminescent frogs jumped out onto the path. There were hundreds of them, each one looking as if it had swallowed a mouthful of live fireflies.

"Whoa...," Leonard breathed.

"Yeah," Molly agreed.

They were still straddling their bikes, so close that their handlebars bumped. The combined effect of all the frogs moving en masse bathed both their faces in swells of green light.

"It's... so... magical," Leonard said.

That was when Molly knew this was the moment. It hadn't been by the Slew. Or on a dare. Or with Finn. The moment was here, and now, under the spell of this magical light, with Leonard. The words from her mom—*keep being brave*—burned in her pocket. Before Molly could give it another thought, she leaned over and gave him the softest peck, brushing her lips against the boy's unsuspecting cheek. His skin tasted sweet and salty, a combination of smeared cream filling from too many Twinkies and maybe a little sweat. It wasn't bad.

She pulled away, and Leonard's eyes grew wide. His face flushed.

"What was that for?" he asked.

Molly shrugged. "I dunno. Just for being you, I guess.... Was that okay?"

"Yeah," Leonard said. "Definitely okay."

"Okay," Molly said.

Leonard lifted a hand to his cheek and pressed the tips

Molly and the Mutants

of his fingers to the spot where she'd kissed him, like he was checking to see if it had left a mark.

And Molly could tell that it had.

They stared at each other for another moment. The frogs kept hopping, their traveling light show gradually growing fainter as, one by one, they disappeared into the bushes on the other side of the trail.

This continued until there were only three left in view. The stragglers faced Molly, waiting patiently for her to give them her attention.

"No . . . ," she whispered. "It can't be . . . Seven, Eight, and Nine?"

In unison the trio let out an exuberant croak. And then, as quickly as they had appeared, they were gone.

"Wait," Leonard said. "You can . . . talk to them, too?"

"Maybe?" Molly smiled.

"Ra-a-a-ad." Leonard drew out the word. Then he appeared to gather himself. "Okay, see ya!" And just like the frogs, he was gone too.

Molly cruised along the last leg of the trail alone, the old oak in her backyard coming into view. But it wouldn't be the same without Number One's giant head parked next to it. Even though it was probably safer for everyone to have it buried under several tons of rock, she already missed talking to the robot.

As she approached the empty space where her mechanical confidant had been, Molly fidgeted with the latest addition to Pink Lightning, a gift from her dad. It was a portable CB radio, which would power up with the help of a generator whenever she was pedaling. Molly adjusted the dial to channel thirty-nine.

"Breaker, breaker, three-nine." She patted the mixtape in her pocket. "McCrusher here. Anyone out there today? Over."

Since everything that had happened, Molly had grown into the nickname. She might even like it a little.

Molly left the channel open and waited. She didn't have anything especially urgent to share. It was nice not to be in the middle of an emergency for once. She tried again.

"Breaker, breaker, three-nine. This is McCrusher. I'm on the trails, just north of Far Flung Falls Drive. Any Crew members on the waves today? Over."

Molly waited for a response. Her tires crunched over leaves, which in the last week had begun carpeting the bike paths in bright yellow.

The static broke, replaced by some strange clicking

Molly and the Mutants

sounds, and a few odd beeps and boops. It was a sequence she remembered hearing before.

"Hello?" Molly called. "Anyone listening out there? Over."

After a pause a familiar voice answered.

"HELLO. MCCRUSHER."

"Number ... *One*?" Molly skidded to a stop in the dirt.

"HOW. IS. LIFE. TOPSIDE?" the mechanical voice continued.

The robot was talking to her. This was impossible.

"Number One!" Molly screamed. "No way! How are you even talking to me? You're hundreds of feet below—"

"YES. BUT. VERY. LONG. ANTENNAS."

This news made Molly laugh so hard, she nearly fell off her bike.

"I've got so much to tell you!"

Author's Note

Frogs fascinate me. They begin life as one thing, then wind up another. How wild is that?

But I suppose we all go through metamorphoses in our lives. It might look different for us humans, but the transformation of growing up is no less dramatic. As if by magic, we go from child to adolescent to adult—then one day, if we're lucky, we might turn into old-timers.

I'm inching closer to that last one, so I know from my own life that many of these changes can be hard, or scary, or embarrassing, just like they are for Molly, or like they might be for you. Some of life's changes take us by complete surprise, maybe even hurt a little.

But they're not all like that. There are other changes we don't even notice until long after we've passed through them and reemerged as newer (and better) versions of ourselves. I'm not talking about the surface changes we see in our bodies, like a first tooth or first pimple. I'm more interested in the ones working below the surface. I bet this has already happened to you. Just think about the person you were a couple of years ago. Did they even have an inkling back then of all the things you know today?

This is the most exciting part for me. Over our lifetime, through all these changes, we have the chance to become more compassionate, more grateful, and more interesting. We can get better at solving complex problems. We might even become wise.

So I wish you a life full of metamorphoses. In fact, I'm counting on it.

That's because, as you've probably noticed, our whole world is going through some big changes too. Some of these changes fill me with hope, but others make me worry a little.

When I was a kid in the eighties, I watched sci-fi movies where calamity was brought about by an accidental leak from some kind of mysterious radioactive ooze. It would immediately turn everyone into mutants or zombies, and wreak havoc on nature. (Sound familiar? It's where I got the idea in this book for Formula X.) This usually isn't how it happens in real life of course. More often, change is a slower, more incremental process. But I think all those outlandish stories about toxic goo might have been born from a truth: We were beginning to realize the unintended effects that our modern way of life was having on the earth around us. We had changed things, but in ways we hadn't planned.

The thing is: for better or worse, it took a lot of ingenuity on our part to get us this far. Together, as a species, we've gone through big changes in how we see, think, and live.

And if we want to go farther, if we hope to fix any mistakes we've made along the way, it'll take even more.

Here's to change,

—Erik

Columbus, Ohio, 2023

Acknowledgments

Before a book ever appears on the shelf, there's a long period of time when it's all soft and squishy, like a tadpole. During that stretch, when it's so delicate and vulnerable, waiting to become the truer version of itself, there are these amazing people who look at this unfinished story and can clearly see what it might one day grow up to be. Gently, they cheer it on, with nudges and pats, knowing just what to feed it to help your story on its way.

And then, there are these other amazing people, who never even see what you're working on, because they're busy putting their own amazing things out into the world—and somehow, their work makes yours better too.

I am deeply grateful to all these people:

To my dear friend and agent, Elizabeth Rudnick, who continues to be Molly's biggest champion (and mine too).

To my tip-top editor Jessica Smith, who gives the absolute best margin comments an author could ever hope for.

To the dynamite designers Laura Lyn DiSiena and Ginny Kemmerer, whose care and craftsmanship make this story not just something to hold in my heart, but a beautiful artifact I can hold in my hands.

To the gifted illustrator Oriol Vidal, who, for the second time, perfectly captured not only a scene from the story, but the entire spirit of it. *Bien hecho, compadre.*

To the many expert eyes and brilliant brains at Aladdin with whom I am lucky enough to have touched this tale, including Christina Solazzo, Lauren Forte, Sara Berko, Bara MacNeill, and Stacey Sakal.

To my fellow middle-grade authors, all treasures, namely Margaret Peterson Haddix, Jarrett Lerner, Christyne Morrell, Alysa Wishingrad, Jenn Bishop, Sam Subity, and Ben Gartner, whose kind, well-placed words along the way really helped to grease the skids.

To my fellow 22 Debuts, in particular Sylvia Liu, George Jreije, Refe Tuma, Nancy Tandon, Shawn Peters, Leigh Lewis, Kellye Crocker, Nicole D. Collier, Dannie M. Olguin, and Brieanna Wilkoff, for your enthusiastic support of this series from the get-go.

To Krissy, the spark of my heart, who once reminded me that "today is a good day to write," which I have never forgotten and continues to always be true.

To our three unstoppable shield maidens, Nina, Evelyn,

and Olivia, who make every day an adventure, whether I was planning on it or not.

To my biggies, Dalton, Landon, and Ella, for reminding me by their sheer existence that I can make extraordinary things.

To my mom, whose love and support for all my creative pursuits were such constant forces throughout the entirety of her life, that I can still hear the echoes of her cheers every day.

To my other mom, the one-and-only Lucy Smith, aka "Mama Bear," aka "Gigi," aka "Sitter Extraordinaire," aka "Loo," aka "Best M.I.L. Ever," for whisking away the girls at just the right time, multiple times, and for having a heart so big there's even room for me in there.

To my cousins Mary Jane Hansen and Polly Gage for generously sharing their memories of frogs and pollywogs in "the slew."

To my childhood friends and teachers in "the portables" tucked behind the Ross Elementary building in Memphis, Tennessee, where I attended sixth through eighth grade, for making the years between 1981 and 1983 so memorable. (And to my fellow clumsy patrons of East End Skate, for the same.)

To my middle school bus driver, who's name regrettably I

never knew, but who took the time to hook up speakers in the back of our bus, just like Ronda Seltzer, and give us an education in music every day on the way to and from school.

To school bus drivers everywhere (because you know why).

To all the legendary female rebel rockers of the eighties, especially Joan Jett, Annie Lennox, Pat Benatar, Cyndi Lauper, Stevie Nicks, and Chrissie Hynde, for providing the perfect soundtrack to that time of my life.

To my dear Auntie Beanie, Uncle Joe, and the entire Ravey Clan, for fueling my writer's engine in countless ways.

To Slangerups past and present, for infusing my veins with a love of adventure.

To Mother Nature, for Her boundless inspiration, particularly frogs.

And most of all, to the readers, who make it all worth it.

I raise a tin cup of cool, stalactite-filtered cave water to all of you—

"Blood, sweat, and cheers."